BY BUCKLIN MOON

Without Magnolias
The High Cost of Prejudice
Primer for White Folks
The Darker Brother

WITHOUT MAGNOLIAS

BUCKLIN MOON

WITHOUT MAGNOLIAS

DOUBLEDAY & COMPANY, INC., GARDEN CITY, N.Y., 1949

This one was for Kenneth Lloyd Bright

"A slow sort of country!" said the Queen. "Now, *here,* you see, it takes all the running *you* can do, to keep in the same place."

THROUGH THE LOOKING GLASS by Lewis Carroll

WITHOUT MAGNOLIAS

1. Behind him Luther heard the bus as it crossed the railroad tracks, the slight gulp of the motor as the gears were shifted, then the stuttering mutter of the tires before they bit once more into the smooth macadam road that led into the little Florida town. It was early morning and there was a nip of cold in the air; he stuck his hands deep into his pants pockets as he walked along with a cigarette in the corner of his mouth, turning his head a little every now and then when the smoke came too near his eyes. He was thinking about breakfast, and as he turned off the pavement onto a side street he could smell wood smoke in the air, sharpening his appetite.

Ahead lay Hannibal Square—a cluster of several grocery stores, a barbershop, three poolrooms, and what passed for a hotel; in the morning light all had the soft silver gray of unpainted and weather-worn wood seen not too closely, but by noon they would seem merely faded and ugly. As Luther passed the hotel a big woman was standing on the side stoop with her hands against her hips, endless and incapable of being completely confined within the wash dress of blue and white. Her head, too small for the broad shoulders which supported it, was shaped like a cannon ball and set low to the rest of her body with scarcely any neck; she wore no stockings, and the elephantine black columns of her legs ended in bedroom slippers, tattered and run over at the heels. Seeing Luther pass, she smiled and waved a heavy hand, then turned back inside.

In the distance he heard a car start, catch with a roar, then sputter and backfire into silence again. He turned right at the next corner and cut across to the opposite side of the dirt street. When he came to the house near the corner he went in at the gate, running quickly up the wooden steps onto the narrow porch.

From the moment he opened the front door he could smell the aroma of coffee from the kitchen. He sailed his hat toward the table under the window and walked on through to the back. In the doorway he stood for a moment without speaking, looking at his mother standing by the kitchen range. The faint sunlight that came through the screen door at the rear caught her in outline, and a wave of tenderness and of being part of a family came over him, almost the way it had so often happened when he was only a boy.

"Mama," he said softly, "cawfee sho smell good."

She turned then and smiled at him as he came toward her, opening her arms to him. A woman in her mid-fifties, she looked much younger; she stood straight, and where the warmth from the stove had made her face glisten she was free of wrinkles, and her skin, the color of rich brown leather, was drawn tight across her skull and up at the cheekbones. There was an almost Indian cast to her features, which were regularly drawn and too sharp to be pure African. He came to her for a moment and she kissed his cheek lightly before letting him go.

"I was thinkin bout you, son," she said. "Seemed like my clock might be fast. I was fixin to set it back a little. Now you here I kin see it ain no clock runnin fast. Hit me inside was goin too fast."

Turning back to the stove, she poured a cup of coffee and brought it over to the kitchen table. He sat down and lit a cigarette before he creamed and sugared the black mixture, then drank deeply and grunted a little in satisfaction.

"Bessie up, Mama?"

"She up but she ain doesin. Be ten minutes fo she ready to eat."

He finished the coffee, got to his feet and stretched.

"Mama, reckon I cross over an see Eulia, maybe walk her to the Boulevard she ready."

She smiled and stood aside so he could go out through the kitchen door.

He cut across the sandy back lots toward the street, which was a continuation of Hannibal Square. In the stillness of the morning he heard a quail whistle, and over in the direction of the packing house a dog was barking persistently in a high, shrill key. Chickens squawked their protest at his invasion of their privacy, too stupid to know that chicken wire set them off from him and forgetful of the times it had brought them up short. Secure within the confines of a coquina-rock-bordered back yard, a small boy stood watching him with a mixture of interest and some doubt, his black face untroubled but his gentle brown eyes insecure as those of a small wild animal.

"Hey, Clarence Junior," Luther called to him. "What you doin up in the middle of the night?"

The boy turned and ran, the trap door of his blue breeches down and his bare little buttocks shifting with each plunge of his short black legs. At the corner of the house he stopped and looked around at Luther again, as though the distance between them gave him sudden courage. That boy sho rabbity, Luther thought, and waved at him again as he cut in behind a miniature junk yard of rusted tin cans.

Ahead of him now lay the house where Eulia lived, the back yard neatly bordered with whitewashed rocks and patterned with colorful flower beds. An old rowboat, sunk partially into the earth and painted a bright blue, was planted solid with petunias, a wild splash of color against the late fall grass. Deep Stuff, the feisty little mottled cur that belonged to Eulia, saw him and started off into a hysterical eruption of barking, until, recognizing him, she came crawling up, dragging her belly across the sand. Then he heard Eulia call and, looking up, he saw her come out on the back stoop.

He felt again the sudden excitement that he had felt the first time he had seen her, fifteen years ago, when she had moved into that house and he had noticed her one day on the front porch sitting in the patched old hammock. She was in her early teens then, a ginger-colored girl with a thin face and eyes that were almost too big for the rest of her features. And seeing her for that moment, only the length of time it had taken to walk past on the street, he knew that she was going to be the only one for him. And it had been that way. He called to her and she waved her hand.

"You had coffee?" she asked.

"Sho," he answered. "You ready to go?"

"Be right out, Luther. Get my jacket and I be set to go."

"I walk you far as the corner, baby."

She nodded and disappeared into the house. In a moment she came out again wearing a bright red jacket with a plaid lining over her dark blue woolen dress. As she came down the steps they kissed lightly; his need for holding her was so great it was like an ache, but she patted his cheek and put her arm through his.

"Cmon," she said. "I belong to be late I don't hurry."

They walked along silently, and he thought, as he so often did, about the two of them, how it had been since he first met her and how it was

3

likely to be from then on. It had not taken them long to know that they wanted to be together always; he had known it at once, but they had been going together for almost three months before he had asked her to marry him, and she had accepted at once. It seemed a long time ago, longer than ten years. First they had agreed to wait until things were more settled; he was working at the packing house then and wages were low, she was cooking on her first job and earning only four dollars a week. As they walked along he wondered where the years had gone to so fast, for even after he had started out as a bellboy in the hotel in nearby Citrus City, and later in its taproom with a good pay check and almost double that in tips, their marriage had somehow gotten no closer. There was always something coming up just when they had decided that at last they could afford to marry.

It was not always on his side; almost as often it was on hers. Before her mother had died, there had been the long illness—three operations and doctor's bills that you had to run to even keep up with—and then after the bills were finally paid Eulia's mother had died anyway, which meant even more expenses. And he, whose education had never gone beyond the eighth grade, had always regretted it so much that he had vowed that both of his sisters were going to have everything which he had been denied. There was Alberta, who had gone on from high school to the local Negro college, and from there to Columbia in New York. He had not seen her in five years, for after she had graduated she had taken a job in New York City. That made him proud; to know that Alberta was doing something for her race made it worth it, no matter how hard the pull had been. Bessie had wanted to go to Columbia too, but he had been unable to swing it; after she had graduated from the small college past the outskirts of town she had gotten a job as private secretary to its president. It had not been favoritism on his part, at least not intentionally; it was only that Alberta was older and had about her a way that made it seem logical for her to have the best.

So he and Eulia were still unmarried, still living apart and having only hurried hours together to which to look forward. Was it worth it? Sometimes it was, but more often, when he was with her the way he was now, it wasn't; needing her and wanting her the way he did, nothing was. The morning whistle at the packing house alongside the railroad tracks blasted, and it brought him out of himself with a jerk. He looked at Eulia and grinned sheepishly.

"What you dreamin on, Luther?" she asked.

4

"Hunh? Aw, Eulia, I was just dreamin an that whistle like to scairt me silly."

She chuckled. "Seem like you was really dreamin. You thinkin on us, Luther?" she asked softly.

"Sho," he answered, "what else? Seem like I been doin that long as I can remember."

"I know. Things sho a mess. Here we gettin old just waitin. Sometimes I think we shoulda just gone ahead the first time we talked about it. I know people done it and got along all right. You take Estelle, and Jimmy working at the drugstore. If they done all right, I reckon we woulda too. Seems you wait too long for something, it ain never comin. Get out of the habit just waitin. Time come you never will do it."

"Yeah," he said, "I know. You right, Eulia. All you had to do was say the word. Lots of times I felt the same way."

She reached for his hand as they walked along, as naturally as she would reach out for something to steady herself had she tripped. Hand in hand, both thinking alike, they felt the uselessness of talk. Soon they came to the Boulevard, the one thin artery that joined colored town to the main section of the town at the dividing line of the railroad tracks. For perhaps a block a trickle of poor whites lived almost side by side with Negroes, but beyond was pure white Caucasian, neatly hemmed in by streets of black macadam or paving bricks, plainly marked with freshly painted signs and guarded by the little town's one traffic light. Ahead the light changed, though there were no cars to obey. In the distance, off toward Citrus City, a train whistled thinly as an echo.

"Honey, I got to hurry," she said, then, looking quickly around, she raised on her toes and kissed him full on the lips. "You be by for me, baby?"

"Sho, Eulia. I be there."

She nodded. Twice a week, she thought, as regular as the seasons, as carefully maintained as a train schedule, and all else snatched furtively and always in desperate haste. It was something, but it was not enough.

Turning, she hurried off.

When Luther came back into the kitchen his mother was still standing by the range, but the table near the window was neatly set for the morning meal. He sat down at the head of the table and turned his chair so that he could tilt it back against the window frame. It was warm in the kitchen and he unbuttoned his coat.

5

"Where Bessie?" he asked.

"She comin directly. You know how gals is. She got to have that last minute."

He nodded, letting the smoke come slowly out of his nostrils and the good smell of the kitchen come in.

"Damn, Mama," he said suddenly, "that sausage cookin?"

"Sho, son. You know Mama ain goin to starve you. That fresh country sausage. Eggs too. That gonna fill you up?"

"Ought to, Mama. Got some more of that cawfee?"

She brought over the pot to fill his cup. "I like breakfast," she said, smiling, "hit the one meal we all together. All save Alberta, that is. I sho miss that gal."

"We all misses her, Mama. Nice knowin she doin so good up there though, ain it?"

"Yeah, hit nice," she sighed.

She sat down at the table across from him, and when he looked over at her she smiled. Then her smile faded and she looked suddenly older.

"I like to see Alberta once before I die. I ain gettin no younger, son."

"You ain old, Mama."

"No, I reckon I ain old. Hit just I worries bout Alberta. I gets to thinkin bout her all alone up there. I doan know none of her friends. I doan know who she livin with, what mens she seein, how she eatin, who take care of her she get sick. Old women plumb foolish, son."

"Some of these days she come home, Mama. She catch a train an pay us a visit. You see I ain right."

She nodded and got to her feet. On her way back to the stove she laid a hand on his shoulder and, squeezing it gently, she bent to kiss him, laying her cheek alongside his for a moment.

"I got me a good boy," she said. "You been a tower of strength to me, Luther." Straightening up, she called toward the bedroom, "You, Bessie. We waitin on you. You be late you doan hurry."

"I'll be there in a minute, Mama."

Almost before her voice had died down, the bedroom door opened and Bessie came out into the kitchen. She was wearing a dark gray suit with a white chalk stripe, a red and white candy-striped blouse, and red alligator pumps. Looking at her Luther realized, with genuine surprise, that without his somehow knowing it Bessie had grown into a beautiful woman. It was hard for him to think of her as anything but a girl, the youngest, the one who would always be the baby of the family whenever he thought of her. He would know how old she was, just as he knew now that she was twenty-two, but it would never register with him somehow, for he would always remember her as a little girl with colt legs, pigtails tied neatly with freshly ironed ribbons perfectly bowed, and soft eyes that looked up to him because he was the oldest, the head of the family.

She took her place at the table, and as she helped herself to food from the platter he could not keep his eyes from her. Her hands, which he had not noticed before, were slender and graceful; her face in profile was more like his mother's than he had remembered, regular and finely chiseled, yet soft with youth. She looked at him and smiled impishly.

"What's wrong with me this morning, brother? Did I forget to put on my face, or did I get it on crooked?"

"No, Bessie," he said, suddenly helping himself to food, "I jest thinkin how nice you look."

"Why, thank you, sir," she said, giving him a mock bow.

He made a face at her and broke the yellow center of his egg with his fork so that it might run over into the grits. When he was finished he pushed back his chair, took out his cigarettes, and after giving one to Bessie he held a match cupped for her before he lit his own.

"Got another cup of cawfee, Mama?"

"Sho, son," she answered, getting up. "How bout you, Bessie?"

"No, thanks, Mama."

He looked at the alarm on the shelf to the right of the stove. There was time for the coffee, this cup to be dawdled over and enjoyed, and then he would run Bessie out to the college. On any other day she would take the car, but this was Eulia's afternoon off. He never took the car over to the hotel in Citrus City where he worked at night; it was easier and cheaper to take the bus.

"You best to hurry, you two," Mama said suddenly.

"Aw, Mama, we got plenty time."

"Bessie doan belong to be late," she answered crisply. "That one thing wrong with colored people. They ain never on time."

Luther looked across at Bessie and the two of them broke into spontaneous laughter.

"What you two laughin at?"

They knew, the old joke that went back to before they had lost their father. It was almost as though he were in the room with them now.

"You know what the old man always said," Luther answered. "He say the reason colored people always late because they learned long ago ain no use to be on time. Ain no use even bein early. No matter when they get there, they find some white man got there first an didn leave nothin anyhow."

Esther let a smile flick her face for a moment and said, "Your daddy was a good man. But he never was on time for nothin. He never even carried no watch."

For a moment he was there in the room with them and then as quickly he was gone again. Luther got to his feet and walked over to throw his cigarette butt out the kitchen door. Turning back, he stretched lazily.

"I go get the car, Bessie. Meet you out front."

"Son?"

"Yeah, Mama."

"You stop by for the mail on the way home?"

"Sho, Mama. Anythin you want over to town?"

"I reckon not, son. You pass by the big market I can use coffee and sugar."

He nodded and went out through the front to get his hat.

When Luther stepped on the starter the motor caught with a sure surge of power. The car was old but the engine idled smoothly; it was his one symbol of ownership and he knew every part of it, for it had been a far different car when he had bought it secondhand three years before. It was the first that he had ever owned all to himself, though he had been fooling around with cars for years. And everything that he had learned, plus whatever money he had been able to spare from time to time, had gone into its rejuvenation. He had done a good job.

Backing out from under the shelter he had built of four-by-four posts and a sheet of corrugated tin, he swung around and drove out to the front of the house. Bessie was waiting on the porch, wearing a little red hat with a feather and a coat which matched her suit. Her legs twinkled as she hurried down the path toward the car. When she was seated he drove off toward the Boulevard.

"How long since Mama heard from Alberta, Bessie?"

"It hasn't been too long, Luther."

"Hunh. I wish she write more often. Mama like to worry herself sick she doan hear from her."

"I know, Luther, but Alberta's probably working hard and too busy to be writing all the time."

Ahead of him the light turned red and he applied the brakes. The clock on the front of the bank chimed the hour. Up the street a Negro porter was folding back the wire doors that covered the whole front of a liquor store. The town was beginning to come to life drowsily. On the corner the day policeman leaned against the side of the supermarket twirling his night stick by the attached cord, letting it fall and somersault, then jump back into his hand like a small boy with a yo-yo. He looked up at them, his face red and raw-looking below his blond hair, then spat lazily across the sidewalk onto the grass. Neither of them looked at him, except out of the corners of their eyes.

The light changed and Luther let out the clutch slowly and turned left. They both were silent until they reached the outskirts of town and turned onto the highway toward the college.

"You reckon Alberta ever comin down to see Mama?" he said slowly.

"I don't know, Luther."

"It do Mama a world of good."

She shrugged. "I don't know. If it was me up there instead of Alberta, I still wouldn't know."

"You still want to go North, Bessie?"

"Who doesn't?"

"I doan. I doan care if I ever go North."

"Sure," she answered. "You've got Eulia. What have I got?"

"You got that good job at the college. You doin good, Bessie. And I know lots uh boys crazy bout you. What about Si?"

"What about him? Oh, don't get me wrong. Si's a nice enough boy. I like him all right. Maybe I might like him a whole lot if I let myself. But he'll always be the same. Ten years from now he'll still have the same job, the same outlook on life."

"He ain doin so bad, Bessie."

She turned her shoulders so that she was facing him, her back against the closed door of the car and her legs drawn up under her.

"Luther, why didn't you and Eulia ever get married?"

"Shucks, Bessie, we goin to get married."

"Sure, I know. You should have, Luther, a long time ago. What you did for Alberta and me, what you did for Mama, was it worth it?"

He had never talked this way before with Bessie; it was the same as at breakfast, she had grown up without his knowing it. Although it seemed a little strange and even made him self-conscious, he liked the feeling.

"You know, I thinkin that this very mornin when I walkin Eulia over to the Boulevard."

9

"It wasn't, Luther," she said gently. "We've all got so little time."

There was no need to answer. He knew what she meant, and then again he wasn't sure. They were approaching the place where they would turn off the main highway onto the side road that led to the college. Unconsciously he slowed down after he had made the turnoff.

"Bessie."

"What, Luther?"

"Why you want so bad to go North?"

"You don't know why?" She laughed and slurred her words. "Ain you a nigger, man, ain you heerd?"

He shrugged. "I leave em alone, Bessie. They doan mess with me."

"But can you really?"

"Naw," he said slowly, "I guess you cain."

"Luther, a very great man once said that we had nothing to lose but our chains." She was silent for a moment, then went on. "We were slaves once, and then Lincoln signed the Emancipation Proclamation to free us. We aren't slaves now, but we still have our chains. I want to find out how to get rid of those chains."

Ahead of them lay the college, off to the right of the road and surrounded by an unpainted rail fence. The group of buildings had once been used as a private school for boys, started during the first Florida boom by a man who had chosen his location badly and as soon as the bubble burst had fled elsewhere to put down new and deeper roots. The state inherited the buildings, badly run down by then, through a claim on unpaid back taxes, tried to sell them and, failing, had turned them into a college for Negroes, after a rather feeble effort to bring them back to their former condition.

Luther swung the car into the driveway and drew up before the administration building.

"Bessie, we got to talk more often."

"I know," she said, putting her hand over his on the steering wheel.

He sat watching her until she was swallowed up by the front door.

2. For Eulia the walk out from colored town to the new lemon-yellow stucco house on the lake where she worked was the best time of the day. It was early enough for her to have a feeling of aloneness, almost as though the rest of the world had been caught and suspended in motion while she alone had retained the will to movement. She liked walking when she was fresh and going toward something which was just beginning; it was different from the returning at the end of the day with everything behind her, tired out from working too hard and too long in a house that was not even her own. She even enjoyed the feeling of knowing the way, each turn and just what she would see after taking it; it gave her a feeling of security which she would never have been able to put into words. It was something ordered and not subject too quickly to change; it was a part in a whole picture, a piece that fell neatly into place with a faint little click that was almost audible.

Ahead of her the paving blocks lay endlessly stretched in a pattern, mostly a dull red but in places a flat pink merging into a warm brown. On either side were tall trees, planted by the town's founders in the image of the austere New England to which they had returned each summer. There was a freshness even to the houses, as though they had been newly washed, a few pinks and even an occasional pale green among the more familiar whites. As she made another turn she saw far off through the trees the intense blue of the lake. She unconsciously quickened her stride and in a moment she could see the house which was her destination. Taking a short cut across some vacant lots, she approached it from the rear. At the back of the house she fumbled for a key in her purse and, finding it, opened the door. She put down her pocketbook atop the big electric icebox and hung her coat on the hanger back of the kitchen door. Standing still for a moment, she looked around the room.

It gave her a feeling of satisfaction; if you had to have a job, it was good to have a pleasant place and the proper tools with which to work. The black-tiled floor and the same linoleum on the work counter and the drainboards of the double sink, the walls and the cupboards of pale lemon yellow—together they seemed to form a continuity which was just right. She quickly put on coffee and a pot of water to boil, then went to the icebox for the oranges, kept there because the people for whom she worked liked their juice to be ice cold.

Coming back to the work counter, she looked at the kitchen clock set flush into the wall. She had plenty of time and she felt herself inwardly relax into a rhythmic pattern. Slice the oranges and feed them into the bright chromium squeezer that worked as effortlessly as a machine when her hand supplied the power, and the juice appeared, all strained, in a trickle into the waiting glass below. Finished, she put the glasses back into the refrigerator and changed into her freshly starched white uniform. Her eyes flicked to the wall clock again.

In a moment the water was boiling and she carefully lowered the eggs in with a big spoon, then set the bread into the toaster, ready to be popped down at the proper time. She started to set the table in the cool green dining room so that all would be ready when she heard their steps upon the stairs. Then as she stood there idly fingering the pretty breakfast things an overpowering longing came over her. There was in it no feeling of coveting something which was not hers, no desire certainly to change places with these two young married white people for whom she worked. It was only that someday she wanted something that was hers by right, only what she was entitled to and no more. But it had to be the way she and Luther wanted it, that was the most important thing. Always before it had seemed very close, but now somehow it seemed very far away.

The table was set, the smoky-blue service plates atop the dull yellow linen mats and the crude blue-green Mexican glasses ready for the water which she would presently pour. She went out the front door for the paper and brought it in to prop against the sugar bowl before his place. Then, hearing steps upon the stairs, she went back to the kitchen for the orange juice.

Both greeted her and she returned their good morning in her low, rich voice. At the head of the table Jefferson Randall returned his close-cropped blond head to the morning paper and reached out absently for the glass of juice she set down before him. There was very little that she did not know about Mr. Jefferson Randall; she had worked for his mother, had gone, in fact, into the stately white house across the lake a tall, too thin, and awkward girl in her teens who had trouble learning that plates do not have handles. She knew him all right, because in those days she had lived in and not gone home each evening as she did now.

She remembered, but always in the reverse of their ages, so that he was the one in need of her protection. In this fantasy (actually he was three years older) she could recall having sent him away up North to college, packing the shiny black wardrobe trunk so neatly with tissue paper only to see it return in June with everything crammed in every which way, as though he had waited until the hour before the train was due to leave before even starting to pack. Or the time she had awakened in her room off the garage at the sound of thrashing in the bamboo which screened the back line of the lot, and gone out to find him staggering drunk, unoriented and not even sure in which direction the house lay. She had held his head as he wobbled unsteadily and was sick at her feet, then helped him, bracing herself to support him while she opened the door and led him back to his room off the parlor and away from the rest of the house.

Once there, she had settled him upright on the edge of the bed and started to leave, but he had slumped over slowly like a sack of flour settling in a corner and she had come back to him. Kneeling down, she had unloosed his shoes and removed them; then, standing, had looked down at him, knowing loud in her head that she should go. But he had seemed so helpless there, so much in need of her, that her body refused to obey her mind and she had pulled him upright and removed his jacket. Hanging it across the back of the chair, she went back to loosen his tie and open the collar of his shirt. She looked at him again, but something would not let him seem peaceful enough for her to leave him the way he was. Feeling her breath quicken, she had unbuckled his belt and, loosening his trousers, had pulled them off, then rolled him over so she could work his arms out of his shirt. Then she creased his trousers and lay them on top of his coat on the chair. She was ready to go now, but he didn't look just right and she bent over to roll him on his back, pulling him up by the armpits so that his head lay squarely on the pillow. Now there remained only the turning out of the light, and still she could not go.

He lay there breathing easily, and her eyes, drawn to the soft rise and fall of his abdomen, followed the whole of his body, clad only in a pair of gaily striped shorts. He seemed so like a little boy, and yet something within her denied the reality of this and she felt a strange compunction she was powerless to deny. Reaching out the fingers of her right hand, she ran them softly down from his breast to the slight corrugation of his ribs, almost as though she were a child and expected the white to rub off on her fingers. Then she felt a shiver run up her arm, as though she had run her fingers across silk, and she almost cried out aloud. Suddenly she was filled with an unknown terror and, turning out the light, she fled quickly from the room.

"Eulia."

With a start she heard the voice, not having heard it before, yet knowing by the inflection that her name had been spoken twice. She heard the rustle of the newspaper and saw his face looking up at hers from the end of the breakfast table.

"Yes, Mister Jeff," she answered.

"Got any more coffee hot?"

"Sho. Coffee comin right up."

She went out the swinging door to the kitchen. She knew Mr. Jefferson Randall all right, but what about this woman he had married, what did she know about her save that she was young and blond, very pretty, and came from up North? If it were a case of complete negation, she would have known at once, without any need to wait until the wall between them, if it did not dissolve, at least reached a point where it became transparent. Inwardly she shrugged. A month was too little a time to know if this was going to work out; until she knew it was only a job, something temporary that you were trying out until you were sure it was the right size.

She heard the swinging door whisper closed behind her.

The breakfast dishes scraped and stacked, she stoppered the sink and shook in soap chips, then turned on both taps full blast and watched with satisfaction as the suds formed and stood up by themselves. She took off her wrist watch and placed it on the window ledge over the sink. Behind her she heard the kitchen door open and, looking into the mirror hung between the windows, she saw that it was Mrs. Randall. Eulia watched her as she went to the left-hand drawer in the near end of the work counter, took out the menu book, and settled down on the black-leather-topped stool, the heels of her Chinese mules caught in the rungs. Lighting a cigarette, she opened the book and sat rapping the rubbered end of a pencil gently against her teeth to inspire ideas as she looked at Eulia, whose back was to her at the sink.

"Eulia," she said in desperation, "what are we going to have for supper?"

Eulia turned and they looked at each other for a moment, then both broke into laughter. With a slender, ginger-colored arm Eulia wiped her forehead in concentration and then gave way to suppressed mirth again.

"I knows what he likes," she said. "It ain that. But we had it last night. I ain wrong, we had it twicet this week and it ain but Thursday."

Joan Randall nodded. Before she had married, a kitchen was for her an alien place; now it had usurped the little office she had once ruled as the assistant to a New York department-store buyer and Eulia seemed more necessary to her than had any of the girls at the store who had crisply called her Miss Thompson.

"I know," she said, "that's the trouble with the man."

"That's the trouble with all men, Miz Randall."

Looking again at Eulia, she wondered what it was that Eulia's man liked only, what he was like, where and how they lived and what their life together was, even what Eulia herself was really like. For though she had been here in this house as long as Eulia had, all she knew about her was the way she looked. She knew merely that she was the color of ginger and that it was a wonderful color to be of; that she was tall, slender, and neat as the shiny new kitchen. Aside from that, there was a wall between them that was never seen but always felt and through which she had never been able to penetrate.

It had not bothered her at first. Before she had married and come South she had never thought much about Negroes save that they were around her—in the store and on the subways and busses in New York. She had known no Negroes even in the limited way she now knew Eulia, except once at a cocktail party when a well-known Negro actor had appeared and after being introduced to each other they had stood by the window looking out over the East River and talked for perhaps ten minutes. She had found him well-mannered and intelligent, but she had not thought about him quite as being a Negro. By his well-tailored clothes and his beautifully modulated voice he was something else again, or was he?

She ground out her cigarette in the ash tray on the work counter. In her marriage she had tried to adapt herself to Jeff's ways, but when he talked to her, as he sometimes did, about what he called niggers and how they would somehow go to hell without the helping hand of the good white folks, she always unconsciously thought of Eulia and the picture would never fit. For there was nothing childlike about Eulia when they were there in the kitchen together, and neither was there always happiness in her soft brown eyes. And as for the helping hand, it seemed to her more likely that she would always need to lean on Eulia, for there was in her a self-sufficiency and inner dignity that was lacking in herself.

The sudden sucking of the sink as the stopper was released and the water rushed down the drain brought her out of herself. She closed the menu book with a sudden snap and sailed it toward the other end of the linoleum-covered counter. She shot her legs out in front of her and her robe fell to either side; the bright red legs of her pajamas caught the sunlight and her Chinese mules made a happy little slapping sound.

"Eulia," she said softly, "what are you going to do this afternoon?" Then, noticing the worried furrow that appeared on Eulia's brow, she went on hastily, "No, I don't want you to stay. I only wanted to know what you usually do on your afternoons off."

She could feel the wall again, and she wanted to break it down but she did not know how to go about doing it.

"Reckon we goin fishin," Eulia answered. "Luther say it been cool and the speckled perch likely be bitin."

"I'll tell you what we'll do, Eulia. Make a fruit salad and leave it in the icebox, and maybe a few sandwiches. You can leave as soon as you do that and finish upstairs. We'll get our own lunch if you'll set the table. It won't help too much, but you might get off an hour earlier than usual. I'm not going to worry about getting that man any dinner. If he wants a steak badly enough he can take me over to Citrus City. We'll eat out."

"Yessum. I fix you a nice lunch and set the table."

They smiled at each other, and for a moment they were back on surer ground, yet it brought no pleasure. Joan checked over in her mind the things that she must do in town—stop for the mail, shop at the supermarket, see Jeff and Daddy Randall at the bank if she had a moment to spare. There was even no real reason why she should go to town save that it was something to do. A sudden feeling of uselessness came over her, and for the first time since her marriage to Jeff she found herself missing her job.

She looked at the kitchen clock. It was already a quarter past ten.

Just as Eulia was finishing the last-minute preparations for lunch she heard a car drive up and park by the garage. She went out the kitchen door onto the stoop and, seeing that it was Luther, called to him that she would be ready in a moment; then, going back inside, she made a final check to be certain she had forgotten nothing. Taking off her white uniform, she put it away carefully and washed her face and hands at the kitchen sink. When she put on her street dress and folded her light coat over her arm against the cool that the evening would bring she went out the back door, trying it carefully behind her to make certain that the lock had caught.

Luther was sitting in the car, and she noticed that the cane fishing poles were strapped neatly to the side of it, wrapped in soft cloth where they were tied to the door handles and the left headlight. When he saw her coming he leaned over to open the door.

"Cain get out my side," he said. "Ain no sense untyin them poles."

She nodded and got in as he started the motor and, backing around, drove slowly out the cement driveway. She settled her head so that her neck rested easily against the top of the seat and for the moment closed her eyes. A feeling of peace washed over her like a wave; she relaxed for a while, then let her head roll to the left so that she could see Luther's profile.

He was not wearing a hat, and his hair was newly cropped the way she liked it, tight to his head so that the fine line to the back of his head and the strong column of his neck merged gracefully. He was wearing a blue-and-white striped T shirt, and his outer arm, resting on the door of the car, caught the sun and shone like something polished. Sensing that she was looking at him, he turned his head for a moment and smiled. She watched the lazy change of his features, the way his eyes crinkled at the corners, and his even teeth.

"Hey, sugar," she whispered, and put her hand lightly on his arm.

They were nearing the edge of town now, passing alongside what had once been a golf course until the little town had realized that the winter people would not support it and had fled to Citrus City where the dues were not so top-heavy. Here there was a last splattering of houses, as nearly gone to seed as the golf links they had once proudly overlooked, and beyond that on the gray crushed-rock road a mile or so of neatly kept citrus groves, the dark green leaves shiny for as far as the eye could see.

"Luther," she said softly.

"Yeah, baby."

"I was readin their paper. You reckon the draft gonna get you?"

He shrugged. "Ain got me yet, honey, and now I thirty-eight I reckon hit won't. Way they talkin at the hotel, I figure I all right. Mister Bob say I got dependents in Mama. Git too bad, maybe I get a war job."

The thought that he might go away from her filled her with a sudden terror. As it was now, she hardly saw him save for brief interludes like this, still she always knew that he was near. But if he were away, anything could happen. She tried to think, to remember all that the paper had contained, but she had skimmed through it so rapidly that very little actually remained with her. Then she tried to be rational, to carefully think of a way out, to prepare for the future in any way that would make it possible for her not to lose him.

She felt the car as it turned and dipped, then shuddered as it left the paved road and settled into the two sandy ruts that twisted off through the scrub toward the lake. Luther's boss kept a rowboat there and he let them use it whenever they wanted to go fishing. The ruts veered sharply to the east, and when the car turned it was as though they had left the world behind them. A covey of quail boiled up out of the palmetto and swung across the road in front of them. Soon they came to the lake and Luther pulled up under an oak tree not far from the water's edge.

He offered Eulia a cigarette and cupped a match for her before he lit his own. She was silent and he made no motion to open the door and get out.

"Man got your tongue, baby?" he asked after a pause.

"Naw," she said softly. "I just thinking about us."

He reached behind her and brought out a folded newspaper. "Here Bessie's *Defender,* Eulia."

He slit the wrapper with his finger and, opening the paper, spread it across the steering wheel. Skimming the front page, he turned to Eulia. He closed the paper and for a moment neither spoke. His mind was confused by having something that he had always thought of in terms of happening someday in the distant future suddenly become a reality right before his eyes. He was unprepared for it and his mind refused to think ahead. He looked at Eulia and saw tears in her eyes.

"Baby," he said clumsily. "Ain nothin to cry about."

She shook her head but the tears only came faster. She put her hands on the dashboard of the car and bent forward, laying her head in the hollow between them, fighting back the grief that even then seemed nameless. It was just everything and anything—the years they had wasted between them waiting, the years they might never know, the short end of everything, the extra premium they paid for being black, and the possibility of this final blow, however remote.

"Why doan they leave us alone?" she sobbed angrily. "It their country. They got everythin. Let them defend it."

"I reckon it ours right on," he said slowly.

He remembered what Bessie had said that morning, and now in a different way Eulia was saying it too. He wasn't satisfied either, but it might be a lot worse. He had the car and the house was paid for; he had a good job, and if he got into trouble, which was not likely, he had

Mister Bob to help him out. Black was black and white was white. Live and let live. Like Mama always said, the world was big enough for everyone. Always before, that had been enough. But was it?

He was suddenly a little afraid, as though he had been walking on firm ground and somehow found himself all at once on swampy and uncertain ground.

"Baby," he said, "les get married now."

He felt her tremble a little and then she started to cry again.

"Les," she said. "We got to, cuz if they take you, least I got that. When?"

"I done tolt you. Now."

"Right now?"

"Sho. We kin go over to the coast an easy be back in time."

"You want to go fishin," she accused him.

"Could fish too," he said. "After, maybe."

She began to laugh. She didn't care if he fished, before or after. Now everything was going to be all right.

3. In the little anteroom off the large office used by the president of the college, Bessie had a desk, a chair, and a row of filing cabinets to herself. When she first came onto the job her predecessor, who had left to be married to a dentist in Jacksonville, had sat in with President Rogers, but Bessie had convinced him that this new setup would be better for them both. With a phone extension she was able to save him the bother of unimportant calls, and before long she was able to protect him as well from unwelcome visitors. At the same time it gave her a freedom that was fully as important to her as privacy was to the man for whom she worked.

She had even managed to bribe the janitor to paint the alcove a soft sea green, and with her own money she had bought two framed reproductions of modern paintings for the walls. The sun that came in through the one window across from her desk made it a pleasant place to work, so that she was always glad to get there in the morning to sort the mail, sneak a quick reading of the New York *Times,* and plan the president's day before the nine-thirty deadline which always brought the echo of his heavy steps down the corridor.

She looked at her wrist watch now and, seeing that she had time for a quick cigarette, lighted one. Behind her, through the open window, the sounds from the campus came to her faintly. Idly she turned and looked out the window. Far across the campus she saw three girls walking; they all wore bright-colored skirts and sweaters, which stood out against the dull background of the library behind them. She heard a boy's voice call and the girls stopped, then to the left of them she saw a very dark-skinned boy wearing an orange freshman cap run toward them. He was tall and gangling, but he ran with effortless grace, lifting his knees high and leaning forward slightly at the waist.

She wondered about them, trying to remember back only two short years. But it seemed to her longer ago than a mere two years, and all that her memory dredged forth was the slight resentment that she could not have gone away to a college which could have given her more. It seemed to her now that she had learned nothing until her senior year, when she had registered quite by chance in a sociology class under a new professor named Gardner. Her first look had brought disappointment, for he seemed to her alien to everything she had expected; he was too good-looking and he was too young, it seemed to her, to be a source of learning. In his late twenties, and fresh out of graduate school at the University of Chicago, Eric Gardner wore tweed jackets and gray flannel slacks on a campus whose faculty was addicted to plain blue serge and wore it like an academic uniform proclaiming their lofty standing. And his color, which was light, was matched only by the president's wife, who set herself up as the standard by which to measure.

But then, seated easily on the edge of his desk, he had begun to talk, and once her ears had become used to his slightly clipped accent she knew that here was something different in her search for knowledge, that here was someone who could show her how to forget all the nonsense she had absorbed and start over again on a firmer foundation. He was that rare thing, a great teacher in a barren area where before there had been only parrots repeating what they had learned from books. Here was someone whose first interest was in making students think for themselves and not caring how he attained that end result. It was as though he were willing to use his voice, his mind, and even his body if necessary. One moment he could be pleading and the next goading; by turn he could be sympathetic or sadistic. He could talk to them in the folk tongue of the earth or he could seem almost foreign in the inflection of his voice. Only always there was this thing they all shared: here is an idea; what is it, how can we use it, how have others used it?

She glanced at her watch again; it was a minute short of the half hour. Down the hall she heard the heavy tread of the presidential march and she poised herself to be ready to get up and walk with him into the inner sanctum, the morning mail, neatly arranged, in her left hand. She saw him now and arose.

"Good morning, Prexy," she said, and smiled.

"Morning, Bessie," he boomed as he strode past her.

She followed his broad back into the inner office and waited until he was seated at the big desk before she handed him the mail. She watched him as he leafed through it rapidly. He was seated so that the light from the row of opened windows fell across his face, a man somewhere between fifty and sixty, though she had noted no change in him in the six years that she had been at the college, four as a student and two as his secretary, and it was hard to gauge his age. There was about him that look of the Southern colored clergy, and it so happened that he had been ordained when very young, but now all that remained was the somber way he dressed, the silver spectacles, and, perhaps, the love he had for talking, even in simple conversation, as though he were addressing an audience. Heavy-set, he was more powerful than given to flesh. He was black in color.

"Nothing much here, Bessie," he boomed. "Anything on the desk calendar?"

"Nothing important, Prexy. Mostly things I can take care of myself."

"Fine, Bessie. Fine. Don't know what I'd do without you. I'll call you when I'm ready for dictation."

She nodded and started toward the door, but he called her back.

"Oh, Bessie. I forgot. The madam is going to stop in this morning. Also Professor Gardner. I'll see them both."

This time he did not look up as she went out the door.

Dictation out of the way, she took her time as she transcribed her notes on the typewriter. At first she had been terrified at taking his letters, almost sick with worry that she might miss a word of importance. Before long she learned that even the most important of men have no liking for the simple sentence, and soon she was editing his letters with as little respect as she might have had for her own.

"Mawnin, Bessie."

Hearing the burlesqued voice, she looked up; then, seeing who it was, she smiled. "Hello, Eric."

"The Kingfish in?" he asked.

"Someday he's going to hear you calling him that," she giggled. "Just a minute and I'll tell him you're here."

She picked up the phone and pressed the interoffice buzzer. "Professor Gardner is here, Prexy."

She put the phone back onto its cradle and nodded. He went through the door behind her into the inner office. When he entered, the president of the college looked up.

"Hello, Professor," he said. "Sit down."

Eric took a chair by the window and looked over at the older man, who took off his metal-rimmed glasses and, putting them on the desk for a moment, rubbed his eyes. Then, taking a large white handkerchief out of his pocket, he slowly began polishing his glasses. When he was finished he carefully put them back on and looked over at Eric. He started to say something and then, as though thinking better of it, he went over to the window and stood looking out. Presently he spoke, without looking back into the room.

"In a manner of speaking," he said slowly, "you might say I built this college." Turning around, he rested his buttocks on the window sill and went on. "The buildings were here when I came. Leastways most of them were. But I put the kids here. I put the faculty here. For twenty years I've been putting my whole soul into this place. Sometimes I've been, in a way, a beggar. Every year when the time comes for the appropriation to come up I die nine times, same as a cat."

He sighed heavily and went back to his desk. Eric watched him, and when he saw that the older man was not going to continue he leaned forward in his chair and smiled.

"What have I done now, Prexy?" he asked.

The president chuckled. He held out the hammered-bronze cigarette case that was always kept filled on his desk, and when both had cigarettes he reached for the silver lighter that was made in the form of a golf ball.

"Guilty conscience?" he asked.

"No, Prexy. I guess I'm just used to being in the doghouse," Eric answered, leaning over toward the flame.

"Eric, what I said about the college goes. This place means my whole life. I'm not going to let anything happen to it or me."

"I know that."

"Good. Just so we understand each other. There's nothing personal in what I say. You're the best man I've got, Eric. I know that. It's hard to get men like you down here."

22

"But?"

"You're right, Eric. I've been beating around the bush." He got to his feet and walked over to the window again. "Eric," he said slowly, "your job here is to teach sociology, not solve the race problem."

"I'd like to solve the race problem," Eric laughed. "How am I going about it?"

"Eric, you know what I mean. First, there's the business of this boycott of that drugstore in Citrus City. Second, there's the statement you made in class about what Negroes should do if they're drafted."

Eric shrugged. "It seems to me you're making a fuss about nothing, Prexy. There's nothing serious about boycotting a store that won't treat you like a human being. Some of my kids asked me in class what they could do and I told them."

"One of the things we have to do is teach those kids how to get along down here, not how to cause a ruckus."

"The other thing was purely a theoretical question. One of my kids asked me what position Negroes should take about the Selective Service Act. You've got to admit that it is paradoxical after several years of the war."

The president ground out his cigarette in the ash tray. He was silent for a moment, and when he finally spoke his voice was very calm.

"Eric, when I go to New York I go to a lot of parties. I sit around until all hours drinking more than is good for me and arguing about the race question. I like that as much as the next one. But when I come home I'm not one of those Sugar Hill leaders sitting around with a scotch and soda in each hand. Down here I've really got a problem. It's all around me. And these crackers down here aren't fooling. They really play for keeps."

"So that means we ought to take it sitting down, Prexy?"

"No, Eric," he laughed, "but we've got to take the long view. I'm not what you Sugar Hill Negroes call an Uncle Tom. I'm just a realist." He got to his feet. "That's all I've got to say, Eric."

"It's a warning, Prexy?"

"Now, son." He put his arm around Eric's shoulder. "Not a warning at all. I know you're doing a wonderful job, but I don't want you to get yourself into a position where I can't save you from the wolves."

They stopped at the door.

"Prexy, you're going to have to take a stand sooner or later."

"I've taken my stand." He pointed out the window across the campus. "It's right there. That's my job."

"Someday it won't be enough, Prexy."

"We'll worry about that when it comes, Eric."

After he closed the door behind him Eric walked over to Bessie's desk and sat down. Lighting a cigarette, he looked at her, seeing her through the haze of smoke he let curl slowly from his mouth. He liked Bessie: she had been one of the best of his kids, and he always knew where she stood.

"You look whole," she said in a low voice.

"Jedge say I uh good nigger, we forgit de whole thing," he answered. She giggled.

"Bessie, come on and have lunch with me."

"I'd like to, Eric. But today I've got to eat at Prexy's."

"Queen Ethel going to let you eat right there with them at the table?"

"Sho, man." She looked at him and said suddenly, "Eric, if you aren't doing anything tonight, come on home and eat with us."

When she had said it she was sorry; it might seem to him as though she were throwing herself at him.

"You mean that?" he asked, and she knew by the tone of his voice that it was all right.

"Sure, but I don't know what you'll draw."

"You've eaten at the Co-op, so you know that as long as it's home-cooked that's good enough for me. What time, Bessie?"

"I'll meet you at the Co-op at five."

"I'll be there."

She watched him until he was out of sight and then, feeling a little guilty, she turned back to her typewriter. For the next half hour she worked so hard that when the president came out he had to speak twice before she looked up.

"Ready, Bessie?"

She covered the typewriter quickly and got to her feet. Together they walked down the corridor to the main entrance and out onto the campus. The president's house lay across the road and down a way from the main entrance. It was a neat little frame cottage, painted white, to which a low wing had been added in the rear. It was surrounded by a white picket fence and neatly bordered by colorful flower beds. They turned in at the gate.

The president opened the front door and stood aside for Bessie to enter. She went in, feeling the uncomfortableness that the house always

24

brought her, as though it were a model room in a department store that had never really been lived in. As they came into the living room Ethel, the president's wife, got up from her chair. She was so light-skinned that in many places she could have passed for white, for her eyes were a blue gray and her hair, now turning gray, had once been brown with a soft and natural roll. Once she had been slight, but her figure had expanded with the years so that now she was rather on the plump side, although with the aid of a girdle she held herself rigidly in. Turning her cheek from her husband's kiss, she nodded to Bessie.

"Well, Bessie," she said, "taking good care of the doctor?"

Although the doctor had no real degree beyond that of his undergraduate days at a small Southern college, he had later been given an honorary degree by an even smaller Negro college, and ever since then his wife had used his new title on every occasion.

"Oh, I couldn't get along without Bessie, Ethel. Lunch ready?"

She nodded and led the way into the dining room in the new wing of the house, which was pleasant and flooded with sunshine from the many windows. They sat down at the imitation-antique table and Ethel tinkled the glass bell by her plate for the maid.

"Well, dear," she said, turning toward her husband, "any news from your sheltered ivy tower?"

Feeling the laughter starting deep within her, Bessie nervously drank from her water glass. She wondered how it was that such a woman could live so long in this fantasy of false importance that now it was no longer fantasy but, for her, actuality, and looking down the table at the president, she saw a look on his face that told her what Ethel meant to him. She wondered how Ethel had ever come to marry him in the first place, for that was back in the days before he had become a college president and had been only a struggling young Baptist preacher with a backwoods parish. And she, who placed such a premium now on fairness, how had she married a man who was so dark and had so little about him that seemed a qualification of her standards?

"Nothing new, Ethel," the president boomed, "but that's when I like it best. I like the old and the familiar, my dear. Old shoes are the best after all."

"You saw Professor Gardner, Doctor."

"Yes," he answered, "we had our usual talk."

He winked at Bessie and then returned a little guiltily to his lunch.

"Doctor, that man's dangerous. You mark my words."

"Nonsense, Ethel. He's the only real teacher I've got. Maybe he is a little hotheaded, but he'll get over that as he gets older. What he needs is a wife to settle him down."

"That may be, Doctor, but he's altogether too radical for us down here. It wouldn't surprise me if he were a communist. We can't afford that kind of thing here on the campus. Stirring up the students. Making them militant. You know what that can lead to, Doctor. I even feel that new man the N.A.A.C.P. sent down here to Citrus City doesn't entirely understand the situation. These Northern folks never do. Our problem here is altogether different. We have to live with the white folks and we have to have their help. That's where our real progress lies."

"Now, dear," he said gently, "you run the house, I'll run the college."

"But of course, Doctor. I'm only saying what you yourself so often say."

The president winked at Bessie, showing her his pride in his wife and yet his feeling too that she sometimes forgot who wore the pants in the family.

Bessie was glad to get back to her desk, but even more glad when the afternoon was over and she headed across the campus toward the Co-op, which was located in the basement of one of the dormitories. When she entered the low-ceilinged room she saw that she was early. She got a coke and walked over to one of the corner tables and sat down. It was cool there and pleasant. Unconsciously she tapped her foot to the tempo of the honky-tonk blaring in the corner and looked around the room. Only a few others were there, mainly a big table of students over by the jook organ.

She looked at the new mural the art students had painted on the west wall, laughing as she remembered how the president's wife had made them cover the pert young breasts of a native girl with a narrow bra. It had caused quite an uproar. Then she noticed a shadow fall across the table and, looking up, she saw Eric. He sat down beside her with his coke.

"You know me, Bessie," he said. "I never could figure out this white folks' time."

She laughed. "You're not late."

He had changed to an unbleached linen suit and his hair was damp and faintly curled at the temples from his shower. He finished his coke and they got up from the table. In the parking lot back of the men's dormitory she saw his light gray convertible. They got in and he drove off toward town.

"How was Madam Queen?" he asked. "She still love me?"

Bessie giggled. "That woman sure has it in for you. Now her line is that you are a dangerous radical, probably a communist."

"I am dangerous, Bessie. I make people want to think."

He was silent, and she lay her head back and looked up at the whole of the sky: it was almost cloudless, and overhead a tiny yellow plane from the airport at Citrus City seemed to be pushing itself to keep up with them.

"You know, I like that old bastard really," Eric said suddenly. "I call him Kingfish and he makes me pretty mad always curving the way he does. But if someone could just get through to him, I'd like him on my side."

"Best way to get through to him would be to poison Ethel."

"Yeah, I know. What's that boy of his like, Bessie?"

"George? He's a nice kid—a little too nice, I guess. He was at Boston University and doing very well in his studies before he was drafted. But Mama's got her foot on him too much."

"That's too bad. This morning Prexy pulled that old chestnut again about looking out the window and saying how he built the college. Then for the first time I saw into his eyes, and I guess he did. If anything ever happened that he lost that job, I guess he'd die."

She nodded lazily, too saturated with the contentment of being near him to even listen with her mind to what he was saying. They came to the underpass and she felt the car pick up speed under them as they went down the incline.

"It's the fourth turn on your left," she said, "the one paved with brick."

He slowed down and made the turn.

"Third dirt road to the left. The white folks ran out of paving bricks."

She pointed out the house and he pulled up and parked under a chinaberry tree. For a moment she was afraid; the house seemed even smaller and more boxlike than she had remembered from that morning, and she thought about her mother and how maybe Luther wouldn't put on a coat for dinner. Then inside she told herself angrily that if he didn't like it he just wasn't worth her time. Mama and Luther were the salt of the earth. When she got out of the car and looked at the house again it seemed bigger, and the yard, with its splashed brilliance of flowers, was neat and well cared for. She opened the gate and he followed her into the house.

"Mama," she called from the living room, "I'm home."

In a moment Esther came in from the kitchen with a little band of perspiration beaded on her forehead.

"Mama, this is Professor Gardner. I brought him home to supper."

"He right welcome. Glad to see you, Professor."

She held out her hand and he took it firmly.

"Luther gone, Mama?"

"No, you know what them rascals done? Him and Eulia done got married this afternoon. They over to Daytona for their honeymoon. Be back tomorrow, I reckon."

Bessie looked at her mother and they both laughed. Then Esther turned quickly to Eric.

"They been goin together fifteen years," she chuckled. "Bessie and me jest about give them up. But you two sit down."

"Can't I help, Mama?"

"Naw, chile, it jest before ready now."

She turned back to the kitchen, and Eric and Bessie sat down on the overstuffed couch.

"Now I know where you got so good-looking," he said.

She smiled. Then suddenly her mother was in the room again.

"Bessie," she said, "they's a couple of beers in the icebox. I figured maybe the professor might like one."

"Eric?"

"Sure," he answered.

She went out into the kitchen with her mother and got glasses and two bottles of beer from the top of the ice chest, where they had notched themselves down into the cake of ice and were good and cold. She poured them and, feeling her mother's eyes on her, she looked up. Her mother said nothing but smiled and nodded her head. Bessie went quickly to her and gave her a short hug.

4. Even now that he and Eulia had been married for several months, there was little change in Luther's life. It had merely meant that he moved his things over to her house, which was near enough so that he saw his mother and Bessie almost as often as when he had lived with them. But by now Eulia was so much a part of his life that he wondered how he had ever gotten along without her. It was hard for him to think back to the days when he had seen her for only brief interludes each day.

His draft board still had him in 3-A and he knew that this made Eulia feel easier, but his own feelings were for the most part unformed. When he saw boys whom he knew going away he felt sometimes a tinge of envy, but more often he was glad that he was being left behind. He was happy in his job, or probably as happy as he would ever be in any other kind of work. The main thing was that he was working for someone he knew, a white man he had known since he was a boy, and this brought him a feeling of security. Beyond this it did not matter a great deal to him; he was paid regularly and got enough to take care of his needs. He had what he wanted—a wife he loved, a good secondhand car, and a little money in the bank—and as long as he could maintain that status he was satisfied. There was no place else to go, so why should he get himself all worked up over nothing?

This was what he could not understand about Bessie, and even more about Alberta. He had no desire to leave his home, and it was beyond him why Alberta had wanted to go away to New York. She could have stayed here and gotten a job, maybe even a better one than Bessie had. But even Bessie was not satisfied, and he knew that, given the opportunity, she too would leave. You were what you were, he felt, and all the worrying you did, all the yearning to be something else, not only was not capable of changing anything but only made it worse.

It was even hard for him to understand the way that Eulia's father felt, although that certainly made more sense than did his own sisters. Eulia's daddy was an old man, or so it seemed to Luther, for he had been married three times and when Eulia was born she had grown brothers and sisters by another mother, who had moved on to Macon, taking them with her. He was a big man, well over six feet and grown gaunt with the years, but he retained a sense of power that came close to being majestic. His close-cropped hair was now iron gray and often he used a cane when he walked, but when he talked, even in a low voice, the words came out deep and full-toned.

"White folks doan bother me none," he would say. "They doan want me round them and I doan want them round me. I got a loaded scattergun back uh the door and they knows hit. Long time ago I drawed a line halfway from the gate to the stoop. I let it be known that any white man pass that line I shoot him dead. They ain bothered me none, then or now. That gun still back uh the door an I reckon they still knows it."

Sitting as he was now, on the stoop, Luther thought about the old man. There had been no line drawn at his house, either before or after his father had died, nor was there a loaded gun behind the door. In what way, then, did they differ from Eulia's father? He was not sure. This much he knew, however: Eulia's father had a dignity about him that was matched by none other in the community. They might call him a fool to his back, as they sometimes did, but there was hidden admiration in the way they said it, in the very word itself. He had heard also that the white folks said he was touched in the head, yet they too, in their own peculiar way, respected him.

Behind him he heard the old man now, heard the soft slap-slap of his worn carpet slippers as he came out of the porch and sat down silently in the green rocker reserved for him alone. Before them on the dirt street there was little activity in the dulled heat of midafternoon. With others Luther would have felt the need for talking, but now there seemed no such compunction. There was an understanding between them and that was enough.

Soon it would be time to leave for his job in Citrus City. It was only a short walk over to the highway where he would catch the bus, ride the four miles into the city, and then he had only to cross the street to the taproom. No need to use the car for that, even if Bessie did not want it to take her to and from her job at the college. And yet, for no reason that he could figure out, he did not want to go. It troubled him because it was a new sensation, a feeling that had come over him too rapidly for him to have caught up with it. He looked across at Jeff, as though somehow in him might lie the answer.

The older man sat serenely, straight up in his chair and with his hands folded in his lap almost at the point where the heavy chain from his old railway watch crossed his opened vest. There was on his face the look of a man seeing things far away. Turning his head, he looked over at Luther and smiled.

Luther got to his feet and stretched. "I reckon I best git on over to the job," he said slowly.

Eulia's father nodded, looked at the sun and compared it with his watch. Picking his coat up from the back of the chair, Luther walked slowly out to the gate. As he passed through and heard it swing to behind him, it seemed to him that he could feel Jeff's eyes clear through the back of his coat. He knew that this could not be so, for between them there was nothing but good feeling. He thought about his car and the money he brought home from the job every Saturday night and put into Eulia's lap. Always before this had been enough. Today it was not and he didn't know why.

Of all the times at his job, Luther liked best the interlude when the crowd thinned out to go home for dinner and Ed, the regular bartender, went home to eat his own meal. He was alone then except for his boss, Bob Giddings, and an occasional customer at the end of the long mahogany bar.

Among the white men he knew, Bob Giddings was the only one with whom he felt completely at ease. He had heard himself called Mr. Giddings' nigger, and unlike so many Negroes he knew, this neither angered him nor made him feel that an insult had been intended. If anything, it seemed to strengthen the bond that existed between him and his employer. There were Negroes who neither had white folks nor seemed to want them, he knew, and often he wondered how they managed to get along in a world controlled by white men. As a boy he had played with Bob Giddings and as a young man he had hunted and fished with him. To him this white man was his insurance against injustice, protection against violence, and the meal ticket that would keep him from going hungry. If in return he did what any Negro must do to stay alive, it seemed to him a fair enough bargain.

He looked up at the clock over the archway which led into the cocktail room. In a half hour or so people would begin to drift back, but because it was a night in the middle of the week business would probably be slow and the chances were that he would be able to get off a little early. His boss was down at the other end of the bar talking to the only two remaining customers, the butcher who worked in the supermarket across the street and a salesman from a used-car lot out at the north end of Tangerine Avenue. Luther went out to the back door for a cigarette.

The alley had a life all its own. Three houses backed up to it on the side across from the hotel, and from these he could hear voices, too far away to be distinguished and coming to him in a low hum like the sound of distant insects. Up above the back door of the bar he could hear, in a hotel room above him, the querulous voice of an old woman talking to someone she obviously expected to listen to her every word. In the room next to that a radio was turned too loud and a little off the station, so that the tired twang of hillbilly music was distorted to a point where it affected him like chalk squealing across a blackboard. Budweiser, the cat who lived in the taproom, came through his legs and, tail up and curled at the end, wandered off into the shadows made by the bushes, looking back at him sardonically and even a little lewdly.

Luther looked up at the sky. The night was clear and the stars seemed closer than they really were. The wind, moving in the leaves of the trees high above him, was from the west and a little to the south. It would be a good day tomorrow, and he thought idly of going fishing for speckled perch. Nobody could fix speckled perch the way Eulia could, and then he thought about her in another way.

It was almost but not quite sexual. Rather it was the realization that she would be waiting for him when he came home that night, that she was his. It was a warm feeling, not so much tender as of complete well-being. He thought of his need for her and how she would be in the room that opened off the parlor, asleep perhaps, but stirring when she heard him at the door. They would be alone then, almost as alone as though the house were theirs, for Eulia's father slept through anything, the one reminder of his presence the prolonged and soaring snore as regular as life itself. But Luther had grown so used to it now that he scarcely heard it, and when he did, it served only as added security, an assurance that he and Eulia were alone. He flicked his cigarette away into the night and turned back toward the corridor that led to the taproom.

There were a few people at the bar, but when he looked into the cocktail lounge it was almost deserted. He stood with his back against the arch. The jook box was merely an insistent throbbing behind him, another segment in the web of sound, along with the whisper of the two rotary fans suspended by shafts from the ceiling and the blurred conversation along the bar. He looked up at the clock over the head of the returned bartender. The larger of the two hands seemed scarcely to have moved at all.

Luther stood on the corner and let the first bus go past. Downtown the clock in the courthouse tower struck the half hour after midnight. That was the one good thing the war had done: because of the nearby military camp, an ordinance had been passed closing all bars at midnight. As he waited for the next bus to come along he remembered that he was hungry and had planned to eat a sandwich before going home. He turned down toward Oak Street.

While he was still a block away from Uncle Bud's Bar-B-Que he could hear the jook box in the stilled night air, the high soaring smear of the brass answered by the throaty rise and fall of the reed instruments. The record ended as he turned in at the door. A tall Negro soldier was standing with his back to the bar, an empty double-shot glass in his hand. He squeezed it in his huge fist like an egg and, glancing down, seemed surprised that it was not broken.

"Evening, brother," he said, bowing. He bowed so low that his overseas cap fell off his head, but he caught it before it hit the floor. Reaching backward with his arm, he rapped the shot glass sharply on the bar.

Luther came up beside him and ordered a pork barbecue and a bottle of Jax beer. The soldier turned around and picked up the drink that the bartender had poured him.

He drank the whisky down neat, then lighted a cigarette and leaned his two forearms on the ridge of the bar. Turning back to Luther, he asked, "And what do you do in this beautiful lilywhite city of the gallant South?"

Luther looked at him and took another swallow from his bottle of beer before he answered. He had never heard a Negro talk in quite that way, not even the professor whom Bessie sometimes brought to his mother's house.

"Work in the taproom up the street," he said slowly.

"With the mop or with the tray, brother?"

"I wait on tables."

"Ah," the soldier said, "the aristocracy of labor." He banged his shot glass down on the bar, and when the bartender filled it he drank it in one gulp.

"What do you do in this town, Jack, of an evening?"

Luther shrugged.

"That's all, Jack. You said it all right there."

He knocked on the bar for another drink and when it came he stood slowly turning the glass on the bar with his long black fingers. Luther finished his sandwich and turned to go, but the soldier put out his hand and stopped him.

"Have a beer on me, Jack," he said. "I want somebody to talk to. Just one beer and then I'm going back to the Elite Hotel for colored."

Luther looked at the clock and nodded. One more beer wouldn't take long, and Eulia was probably asleep anyway.

"Jack, why is it that in all colored hotels the tap marked cold always gives hot water and the one marked hot gives cold?"

Luther shrugged.

"You going to have to get into this white man's army, Jack?"

"I doan reckon so. They got me in 3-A and I thirty-eight."

"You married, then?"

"Yeah."

"Any kids?"

"Naw, not yet."

"Better get busy, Jack. Better get you a defense job too. This army is rugged, Jack. Them white folks ain't fooling. Any way you can, Jack, stay out. It's a bitch."

The soldier was silent for a moment, still spinning his shot glass atop the worn old bar. Every now and then he took a sip of the whisky and a long pull from his cigarette to chase it.

"You lived here all your life, Jack?"

Luther nodded.

"Well, it's better than Georgia, I hear, and I know it's better than Mississippi. At least here if the white folks shoot you they give you a sporting chance. They give you a running start. In Mississippi, where I was born and left a long time ago, they pot you before you even take step one."

He took another sip from his glass and went over to the jook organ. Putting in a quarter, he punched five of the chromium keys and came back to the bar. The first selection that he punched was a blues, sung by a woman with a deep and haunting contralto voice. She was backed up by a piano and two guitars.

> *"Now Uncle Sam ain no woman, but he sho kin take yo man*
> *I said, Uncle Sam ain no woman, but he sho kin take yo man*
> *Women wringing their hands and crying*
> *All over the land . . ."*

The noise of the room swallowed up the ending of the record, but in a moment the next selection came on loud and strong.

The soldier finished the last of his drink with a gulp and lit another cigarette. Suddenly in the room the sound of voices died out ike a high wind suddenly fades, then rises again in tempo, but never to its original ferocity.

"What gives, Jack?"

"Law, I reckon. They come in once a night to check up."

The door opened and two white policemen came into the room. The one in front was heavy-set and red-faced; he had a mean look and his eyes roamed around the room almost angrily.

"You Godam niggers making too much noise," he said. "We heard you raising hell clean out on the east-coast road. Just because you out of the midnight closing zone ain't no sign you belong to raise hell all night long."

He walked up to the bar, and those who were standing there moved to one side to make a large gap for him, but the soldier, who was on the other side, stayed where he was and with his back turned. The bartender put a tumbler in front of the white man and filled it half full of whisky.

"You sure that's my glass, nigger?"

"Yessuh, hit sho is. That yo glass and I give you thuh best licker in thuh joint. Yessuh."

The policeman grunted and drank the whisky. The bartender refilled the tumbler half full and, corking the bottle, put it on the back bar. The white man looked over his shoulder at the other cop.

"Come on, George, you better take you a little charge. It's a long night and we got most of it in front of us."

The other man shook his head. "Not right now, Hoke."

Hoke laughed. "You just as well to get your feet wet. These niggers won't bite you. There ain't no bad niggers in here. These is my niggers, George." His eyes roamed around the room again and he put the glass down on the bar. "Come to think of it," he went on, "maybe I better make sure of that."

Luther looked at the soldier beside him. He was staring straight ahead, but the fingers that were still spinning the shot glass were shaking a little. The fat policeman made no effort to pay for his drinks, and as he walked away from the bar he stopped and looked hard at the soldier.

"You, nigger, where you from?"

The soldier did not answer.

"You, boy, I'm talkin to you. You, the nigger in the soldier suit."

The soldier looked up and saw him in the mirror on the back bar,

35

but still he did not answer. The white policeman came over to him angrily.

"Where you from?" he asked again.

"Fort Brannin."

"Fort Brannin, what?"

"Fort Brannin, Florida."

"Godamit, nigger, don't you know how to talk to a white man? Where you come from before you went in the army?"

"New York."

"Godamit, say 'sir' when you're talking to a white man."

The soldier did not answer. There was nothing defiant in his attitude, he simply did not answer. The room was quiet save for the jook organ which played on until the end of the record, and then, because there were no more nickels inside, it too became silent. A woman at the extreme end of the bar giggled nervously, and the white policeman started to walk over to her, then stopped and came back toward the soldier. He stopped about six feet away.

"You goin to say sir to me, nigger?"

Still the soldier did not answer.

"I got a mind to run you in."

"You can't," the soldier said, evenly and in a low voice. "You have no jurisdiction over me, only the military police does."

The tension in the room was building up to a point where something had to give. The other policeman was obviously nervous, but he held his ground.

"Come on, Hoke," he said, "let's get on with it."

"I'm takin this nigger into town," Hoke said. "Maybe the army likes uppity niggers, but I sure as hell don't. It's time somebody learned him some manners."

He took a step forward and the soldier set himself. Hoke patted the revolver which he wore in a black holster in his belt.

"I'd just as soon shoot you, nigger, as look at you."

"You do and I'll take you with me. I don't want to die, but if I do, I want you along for company."

"You hear that, George?" Hoke asked. "He threatened me. Let's get him."

It was plain that George did not want any part of it, but he moved slowly up alongside.

"You apologize to Mr. Timson," he said, "and maybe we might let you go."

36

"You haven't got me yet," the soldier answered.

"Let's call the military police, Hoke. They can handle him."

"Balls," Hoke said, "I can handle him. I eat uppity niggers like him for breakfast."

Suddenly he kicked out hard at the soldier's shin, and when he bent over in pain the white policeman released his billy and sapped him hard over the side of the head.

"Get behind him, George," he yelled as the soldier groggily started to get up. He was still dazed and he kept shaking his head slowly from side to side to clear away the cobwebs. He got almost to his knees and then slid down again.

The white policeman went over and snapped the cuffs on him and then prodded him with his foot. Nobody in the room made a sound. Finally the soldier got to his feet and stood wavering as Hoke told him to move along out to the prowl car.

"Good-by, brothers in black," he said. "You sure showed racial solidarity tonight. If I had me an old man and a small boy from up North, I'd have killed me a peckerwood."

Partly supported by the white policeman, who steered him by the arm, he lurched out the door. Nobody made a noise until they heard the motor start and the car drive off, turning hard so that the whine of the tires against the pavement was clearly audible in the room. Then suddenly, as though a cork were withdrawn from a bottle, everyone started to talk.

"That mother frigger," somebody said. "He sho a mean sonofabitch. We oughta kill that cracker some dark night."

Luther turned to the person standing next to him at the bar.

"What you reckon they do to the soldier?"

"Take him down tuh the station and beat thuh crap outa him."

"That right what he said about the military police?"

The other shrugged. "I reckon so, but hit too late now. White folks ain gonna do nuthin once anythin done. The boy black, ain he?"

Luther nodded and started toward the door. Somebody put a nickel in the honky-tonk and the music blared out, seeming louder than it was by the suddenness of its opening blast. As he came by, two men were arguing near the door.

"That Hoke come near me Ida kilt him," one said. "Ida cut him every way but out. He uh mean peckerwood, but he know better than tuh mess with me. He mean, but he know how evil I is. I gonna piss in his glass and leave hit in there overnight."

"You right," the shorter one answered. "He know better than tuh git salty with me an you."

Luther went out the door and walked slowly along Oak Street toward the bus stop on the corner at Tangerine Avenue. The streets were deserted and his footsteps sounded loud in his ears. He kept hearing the dulled thud of the billy against the side of a human head and seeing the soldier standing there groggily looking at him. He knew he should have done something but there had been nothing to do. He felt tired and almost a little sick to his stomach. He no longer cared when he got home, or even that Eulia was there waiting for him. He felt, somehow, less than a man.

5. For Eric, teaching was more than a way of earning a livelihood. He had gone into it by choice and over the strong opposition of his father, a prominent doctor in Washington, who had felt that for him to do so would only be a waste of time. His mother, who worshiped him, had taken his side but had told him privately that she thought him foolish to go into a field that gave so little financial return. In thinking and in politics both of his parents were conservative. Socially they belonged to that little segment of Washington society which is as tightly knit and as strongly bulwarked against change as is any other in the United States. True, none of their forebears had come over on the *Mayflower*, but all of them put great stress on the fact that they had come from free Negro stock, and that today most of them could have passed for white if they had so desired. None of them did, save occasionally for convenience in traveling below the Mason and Dixon line, for they were far more secure in their own tight little world.

That Eric, coming from such an environment, should have turned out as he did puzzled them. They had sent him to one of the best of the little New England colleges and he had done his postgraduate work at the University of Chicago. In every outward way he seemed to be like them. He dressed as well and with the same care, was at ease in their social gatherings, and yet they knew that he was not one of them. His father had talked to him in as rational a way as he could ever achieve in discussing politics and ended by calling him a radical and/or a communist. His mother had tried, in as tactful a way as possible, to point out to him that the Negroes with whom he was associating were below him socially and much too dark in complexion. With his father he had merely argued pleasantly, but he laughed to his mother's face, and for this she found it hard to forgive him, though in the end she had.

His success in the academic world, the occasional articles or book reviews which he had published, pleased them both. When his book appeared and was well received they were ecstatic, for it gave them prestige among their friends even if, indirectly, it attacked them and everything for which they stood. But he had achieved recognition in the New York papers and thus they were proud of him and a little ashamed of him at the same time.

Their home was large enough so that they could ignore the friends he brought in, and without appearing rude. If they did not have to see them, however, it was often difficult to pretend that they were not there. One night he had brought home a pianist who was appearing in a Washington night club and had sat with him in the music room drinking and listening to records on the huge radio-phonograph. Although his father and mother were in a bedroom far removed from the scene, there was something about the insistent beat of the music, particularly in the intricate patterns of the compelling bass, that simply would not be denied.

Then, as though this were not enough, they had turned up the volume, and against the booming sound of the record the pianist had sat down at their white studio grand and played the second part, a variation so perfectly timed that the illusion was of two pianos played by different men. He had then played for an hour by himself, ranging from an earthy barrel-house piano, which had the disquieting effect of reminding them, supposedly secure in their expensively decorated bedroom, that they too were Negroes, to a boogiewoogie so finely spun and delicate in texture that it seemed to them almost like Mozart.

Too, Eric liked to play blues records, and preferably as loud as possible. This bothered his mother, for though she secretly rather enjoyed them herself, she was worried about the effect it might have on her neighbors, for this was at a time before collecting hot jazz records had become as socially acceptable as it was later to become.

Yet, in spite of all this, they had been saddened when he took the position at Bayerton College, for Florida seemed to them at the end of the world. And Eric, though he was glad to get away, also missed them in his own way.

Eric's classes always seemed to end reluctantly. In other classrooms the bell that ended the period was the signal for a general and hurried exodus toward freedom, but in his room it merely meant that a group of students would come forward and gather around his desk. Usually he was glad to have them, but on this particular Saturday morning he was in a hurry.

"Prof," one of them asked, "can we come up tonight and play records?"

Lately a group of them had been doing that about once a week, and he enjoyed having them, for it gave him a chance to really know them in a way that was never possible in the classroom. They came to hear his records, but the evening was more likely to end in a bull session. His field was sociology, and the students who came most often were from his classes, but more often they talked about books and writing. Some of them wanted to write, and those who didn't wanted something which they felt came from writing and books. Probably it was merely a rebellion against their environment and a culture which discriminated heavily against them.

Today it was hard to say no, but he was going over to the coast with Bessie to fish in the surf.

"Sorry," he said, "I can't make it tonight. Tomorrow is Sunday and that's doubtful too. Monday night all right?"

They nodded and turned away as he gathered his things together and put them in his brief case. If Bessie was ready they would get to the beach in time for him to fish the last two hours of the incoming tide and the first two or three hours after it started out to sea again. He walked quickly up to his room, changed his clothes and, gathering his tackle, walked over to the shed where he kept his car.

Bessie was already waiting for him. She was wearing tailored navy-blue slacks, a chartreuse blouse, and a bright-patterned batik handkerchief, peasant fashion, around her head.

"See," she called to him, "I'm on time."

"I was afraid the Kingfish would get an idea and start dictating about now," he said.

She laughed and made a face at him. "He's gone to Tampa, my friend."

He opened the door on her side and she got in. He closed it then and tied his long surf pole, padded with strips of soft cloth, so that it would ride easily against the side of the car. Then he stowed away the tackle box and a pail in the back and got in beside her.

"You've got everything?" he asked.

"Sure," she answered, "don't you know I'm a most efficient secretary? I got a big steak instead of ground round steak, and your mullet for bait is in that other package. I even got some ice from the kitchen. Rolls, butter, potato chips, a pie, and some beer."

He nodded. "Good," he said. "You keep this up and you might even turn out to be more than a secretary."

He turned on the motor and ground down the starter. When the motor caught he backed out and swung around toward the underpass. Soon they were through town and cutting across to the east-coast highway.

"This is good, Eric. A whole afternoon away from everything."

"I know. I've been saving the gas to go fishing for months."

She lit a cigarette, passed it over to him, and lit another for herself. He took it without taking his eyes from the road.

"How's your mother, Bessie?"

"She's fine. Still worries a lot about Alberta, and when she doesn't hear from her she imagines all kinds of things. Trouble is Alberta won't come back down here to see her and Mama won't go up there to New York."

"I like your mother," he said simply.

He came to the east-coast highway and turned left. The road stretched out far ahead of them, straight and wide.

"How's Luther?"

"He's all right. He and Eulia seem very happy."

He lapsed into silence again. The road was almost empty of traffic and he drove fast. The top was down and the sun was hot on their faces. They passed two little towns and then they were on the prairie which stretched treeless, far as the eye could see. Cattle were almost everywhere and they saw one dull gray Brahman bull, imported to develop a strain that would be immune to the cattle tic. In a little under an hour they were crossing the Indian River to the lonely road that lay across a strip of swamp and lagoons to the ocean seven miles away.

The road was narrow and winding and they passed no other cars. In the open spaces of water they saw a variety of cranes and herons —small white ones, larger ones which were blue gray and had long yellow legs, an occasional blue heron with a five-foot wing span, which rose clumsily from the water and flew awkwardly with great thrusts of its long wings.

"Ever come over here early in the morning, Bessie?"

She shook her head.

"I did," he went on, "just about dawn. The ducks had just started to come South and there must have been a million of them. The hunting season hadn't opened and they weren't wild the way they are when they've been shot at. There had been a heavy fog and it was just starting to lift, so that there were great open spots. It was really something to see."

She nodded as they crossed a wooden bridge over open water, and soon they were able to see a thin slice of ocean over the dunes a quarter of a mile away. At the end of the regular road they drove a little way onto the sand and Eric got up and sat on the back of the seat. The surf was coming in a regular pattern, breaking not too far out and rolling up onto the beach clear of sand and white as soapsuds.

"It looks good," he told her. "Looks like we might do some business."

He got down on the seat again and started the motor. Backing out, he turned left along the twin ruts that ran down the beach this side of the dunes.

"I guess we might as well go down to that old shack," he said, looking at his watch. "We've got plenty of time and no one will bother us there."

Bessie lay her head back against the seat and closed her eyes. It was good to get away from things, she thought, good to be alone with Eric.

Eric aligned his reel with the guides on his rod and tightened the ring clamps on the reel seat. Stripping off line, he threaded it through the guides and, driving the butt of the rod deep into the sand so that it would stand upright, opened his tackle box and took out a package of leader wire, a hook, swivel, and a pair of pliers. He turned around and grinned at Bessie as he cut the leader wire and began to make his rig.

"You all set?" he asked.

"Sure, Eric, don't worry about me. I'm going to take a nap and then maybe walk up the beach a ways."

He nodded and, taking the fishing knife from the tackle box, went over to where he had buried the bait so that the gulls and sandpipers couldn't steal it. He looked around for a piece of driftwood and, finding it, dug up a mullet and cut it into strips. Taking one, he worked his hook back and forth through the skin three or four times, then buried the rest, marking the spot with a mound of sand. Stripping to his trunks, he walked down to the edge of the water and cast easily, dipping the rod tip so that the line would wet easily, then reeled in again.

He stood for a moment looking out at the ocean. It lay, seemingly endless and not unlike a relief map, in colors ranging from a deep blue through blue green, gray green, and finally, in spots, pure gray. Some distance offshore two shrimp boats moved slowly to the north toward the inlet and a long stream of pelicans coming in the other direction soared low over the water. When he had located a slough he raised the rod and, running out at the break in the outgoing surf, cast beyond the first breakers. He reeled in the slack and, rod tip raised, waited for a strike. The sun felt good on his back and, looking around, he saw that Bessie was lying outstretched on a striped beach towel with her eyes closed.

He worked his bait in closer to shore. Whenever he fished like this it reminded him of the summers at Oak Bluffs on Martha's Vineyard, where his father had taught him to fish in the surf for striped bass. They used to leave Washington, usually early in June or late in May, on their cabin cruiser *Toussaint*. His father would cruise up with them as far as New Bedford, where he would take the train back to Washington, then return to their cottage for the entire month of August. It seemed to him very real at the moment, so real that he could remember clearly the way things had looked and even how they had smelled. But in a moment it was gone and seemed very far away again.

Bessie called to him that she was going to walk up the beach and he turned around to watch her for a moment. Even in slacks he noticed the beautiful lines of her, her long, lithe legs and the fine way that she was put together, the ease of her walk and the dignity with which she held her head. He had a light strike, a series of taps relayed to the tip of the rod, and he set the hook. He reeled in a little and knew that he had missed, that a whiting had stripped his hook.

Putting on a fresh bait, he cast far out and, resting the rod butt on the wet-packed sand, lit a cigarette. A lone water turkey flew past, looking a little like a wild goose but betraying its true origin by the way it flew. He had another strike, and this time he hooked the fish solidly. It felt like a blue by the savage way it took the bait, and it was—a nice three or four-pounder. Almost as quickly he caught three other smaller blues and then, strangely enough, a sea trout. The tide was now high and he began to fish nearer to shore. Looking far down the beach, he saw Bessie heading back toward where he was standing.

Presently he hooked a heavy fish, and for a moment he thought it was a channel bass, but when it did not show in the breakers and he played it for perhaps five minutes it gave up easily and he beached it—a four-foot sand shark hooked deep in the throat. He hunted until he found a heavy piece of driftwood and clubbed it to death. Cutting the wire leader, he put on a new hook, baited, and cast out again.

Before long Bessie came up.

"Any luck?" she asked.

"Four blues and a trout. Then that damn shark over there. What have you got?"

She held out her hand. In it was a round glass ball about the size of a small grapefruit and tinted a pale blue green.

"Know what it is?" he asked her.

She shook her head.

"Cork is getting scarce and the price has gone way up. Commercial fishermen use these on their nets instead of cork floats. I've got one up in my room you can have. It's a deeper blue."

Suddenly he felt a savage strike and he set the hook hard. The fish made a run out to sea; he tightened the star drag a little and turned it back toward shore. He thought it was a bass, and he was sure a moment later, when he saw it through a wave, bronze as a new penny as it turned completely over and made another short run. He played it carefully and eventually brought it into the last surf that broke onto the shore. He waited for the next wave and then beached it, pulling it high above the surf line by the wire leader.

Bessie came down and looked at it—the pure white belly, the red bronze sides, and the twin black spots just above the tail. Quickly he baited up again and cast out into the same hole.

"Here," he told Bessie, handing her the rod, "there might be another one out there. I'll get the fire started so we'll have coals for cooking the steak. It won't be any use fishing in another half hour or so, when the water goes out over the bar."

He turned up the beach toward the dunes.

They had eaten and the fish were gutted and packed in ice in the galvanized-iron washtub in the back of the car. Eric had stowed away the tackle and even tied the two poles onto the side of the car. The sun was down below the sand dunes at their backs and the two of them lay on a blanket, side by side, smoking cigarettes as they looked up into the sky. Above them a lone plane, a little red Piper Cub, cruised up the beach toward the inlet. As it passed over them at less than a thousand feet Bessie giggled.

"Reckon they can see us?" she asked.

"What if they can?"

"See us niggers on their white beach?" she said bitterly. "They might land and run us off."

He flicked his cigarette at a sandpiper moving so fast across the sand that its legs were only a blur. The bird ran faster for a moment, then stopped and came back to the burning butt. Its beady little eyes looked it over greedily, but in a moment it went on.

"Why did you come down here, Eric?" Bessie suddenly asked. "Take a job in the South, I mean. There must have been positions up North you could have had for the asking."

"There were a couple, Bessie. But I wanted to see what the South was really like. I'm glad I came."

"Now you know."

"Yeah, now I know."

Both of them were silent. There was no sound anywhere save the steady pound of the surf, spaced differently but almost as regular as their own breathing. The sun was almost gone but it was still light. Both knew that they should make a start toward going, but neither wanted to be the first to suggest it.

"What do you want out of life, Bessie?"

"I don't know," she answered softly. "I guess all I want really is to live like a human being. And I can't do that here. Probably next year I'll go to New York. I know that's not everything, but it must be better than this." She looked across at him and then asked, almost fiercely, "Is that so wrong?"

He shook his head. "No, it's not wrong, but I'm not sure that it's the answer."

"What is, then?"

He shrugged. "I wish I knew. My family thinks it's to make enough money so that you can live on a little island with other Negroes who have also made a lot of money and don't have skins darker than yours. Then you don't let anyone else on the island, neither whites nor poor Negroes with dark skins."

"Like Queen Ethel?" she asked.

"No," he said, "that's something else again. Sometimes you purposely marry a 'big nigger' who is very black, maybe the president of the college like the Kingfish, and then you become the power behind the throne. You run everything, including your husband, because you feel that he ought to be grateful to you for marrying a man so black."

He lit two cigarettes and passed one of them to Bessie. In a moment he went on. "If you happen to be black yourself, then maybe you hate everyone who isn't, white folks and fair Negroes alike. But the truth is that you hate yourself worst of all. You know Jones?"

She nodded; he was a history professor at the college.

"I heard him lecture one day and he was talking about Africa. He said that once we had black kings, and when he said it he looked proud and a little fierce. Trouble is, if he were a black king he'd be Hitler in reverse."

"And Prexy?"

"The Kingfish is all right. He means well but he's caught in the middle. He's got Queen Ethel on one side and the white folks on the other. He doesn't know which is worse. And neither one of them will let him forget about their being there."

"And Georgie is worse than Prexy. He's scared to draw a deep breath without asking Ethel. She had to go with him when he went away to college, you know. He stayed with her sister in Boston while he was in B.U. I don't know what the army is going to do with him."

"That's one thing I don't have to worry about," he said. "I'm 4-F and it looks like I'll stay that way."

"Glad?" she asked.

"I don't know," he said slowly. "I don't want to fight the white folks' war, and still maybe this one will prove something. It looks less like it all the time, yet you never know."

He went up to the car and came back presently with the last two bottles of beer and two paper cups.

"Actually," he said, handing her an opened bottle, "there isn't any one answer. This war might be a part of it, since they need Negro man power badly both in the army and in heavy industry. A strong labor movement might help a lot. But don't lie awake waiting for it, baby, because if you do, you're going to get awful damned sleepy."

He got to his feet, poured the rest of his beer into his paper cup, and threw the bottle far out into the ocean.

"I should have put a note in it," he said, grinning down at her. "Anyone solving the race problem please communicate with Miss Bessie Mathews."

She looked up at him and smiled back. It was almost dark and she could hardly see him; when he settled back onto the blanket he was only a blur. She reached back of her head for her jacket and slipped it over her shoulders. Now that the sun was gone the air was suddenly chilly.

"Cold?" he asked.

"A little, Eric."

He leaned over and kissed her at the juncture of her eyes and nose, then gently on the lips. She shuddered slightly.

"I've been hoping you would do that," she said softly. "Why didn't you do it sooner?"

He kissed her again and she put her arms around him and drew him down to her.

"Is that an answer?" she asked softly.

"I don't know," he answered. "I honestly don't know. It might be." Then he kissed her again.

6.

Ezekiel Rogers, the president of the college, often said in jest that the thing most responsible for keeping his marriage on an even keel was that Ethel knew better than to speak to him in the morning until after he had had his third cup of coffee. As is often the case with things spoken in jest, there was more than a little truth in the statement. Actually Ezekiel was a hard sleeper and a harder waker; in the early morning the world appeared to him at its lowest ebb and he was apt to lash out at all the things which frustrated him most. Lapsing into the idiom which he often affected because he felt it helped make him seem human in spite of his academic position, he would say that in the morning he was *pure evil*.

But on this particular morning he was feeling far better than was usually the case. This was mainly because he was leaving on the noon train for Georgia to attend a meeting which would not only provide a change of scenery but also a chance to get out from under the dominance of Ethel for a few days. Publicly he would never have admitted this, but privately he was well aware of how completely she ran his life and for what reasons. And yet he knew that he would be lost without her, that she was as necessary to maintaining his status as any one factor in his life. He was even fond of her, in an odd way that was perhaps habit more than anything else, and he

47

realized that he would be glad to come back to her once the convention was over. But as he started on his third cup of coffee and looked across the table at her, he felt that these few days away would be a welcome relief.

She smiled at him. "I'll have your things packed, dear," she said. "I'll have a lunch for you as well."

Finishing his coffee, he lighted a cigar and settled back in his chair. Bessie had attended to his accommodations, the usual compartment that he was given by a special arrangement with the railroad. It was better than traveling in a hot and dirty jimcrow coach, even with the humiliation of knowing the railroad's reasons for providing it so generously whenever such space was available.

He took out his heavy, old-fashioned watch and studied it carefully. "Well," he said, "I'd better get on over to the office and look through the mail with Bessie. You going to drive me to the train?"

"Of course, you know I always do. I think we ought to leave here by eleven-thirty."

It seemed to him more than double the time necessary, but he nodded absently and got to his feet. Outdoors he noted that the day was cloudless and that it would not likely be overly hot. As he crossed the campus toward the administration building he had the same feeling of elation that so often possessed him. This was somehow all his; he had taken it from nothing and with his own hands had made it blossom. It was as much his as was his own son George.

Going down the hall, he nodded curtly to those he passed. As he went by the clock on the wall in the reception room he took his own watch from his pocket for comparison. They tallied exactly. It had been a good investment, that clock, worth every penny that it had cost.

"Morning, Bessie," he boomed as he passed her desk and strode into his office. Sitting down at his desk, he looked around the room. It seemed a good room to him, one that neared perfection and would in due time attain it. He got to his feet and examined the new painting that he had recently acquired from a young Negro artist who, it was rumored, was likely to go places. It had been a gift—well, almost a gift. He had offered to buy it for a nominal sum, but the artist had offered to give it to him and he had readily acquiesced without again offering payment. It was a good painting and it fitted in the wall space provided for it as though it belonged there.

Bessie brought in the mail and laid it on his desk. He went over and thumbed through it quickly, then looked up at her.

"Nothing important here, Bessie. You answer it and explain I'm out of town and why. You've got those notes typed up?"

She nodded.

"Good girl. I don't know how I ever got along without you, Bessie. I wish I could take you along with me. You're my good right arm."

He liked to see her smile. It warmed him all over.

"When the next appropriation comes through, Bessie, I'll have to see what I can do about stretching it a little to include a raise for you."

She thanked him and started out the door.

"Oh, Bessie," he called after her, "be sure to remind me when it's ten minutes after eleven, will you?"

She nodded and closed the door gently behind her.

Through the window of the slowly moving train he saw Ethel, standing by the car, her hand raised to him in farewell. He leaned forward on the seat and waved back, turning his head so that he would see her until the last possible moment, when finally she would slip away out of sight as the train gathered speed. He settled back and looked around the compartment, then raised his hand and adjusted the air tube between the two windows so that a flow of coolness could come freely into the tiny room. He liked trains, enjoyed the feel of them moving under him and the hidden sense of power which they seemed to possess. His baggage and the box of lunch were safely stowed away under the seat. The one thing that upset him was that he was not traveling with the same porter he had grown to know and depend on and who always before had been on this run at least as far as Jacksonville. This one was obviously unaware of his identity, had in fact made the retort that the coaches were up forward when he had approached with his baggage.

He wondered idly what Ethel had put in the box of lunch for him to eat that evening. He had eaten lunch before he had come to the station. He could, of course, have gone into the dining car that evening, but of all the forms of segregation, the green curtains used to shut off Negroes from the other diners seemed to him the most odious. The few times that he had tried to eat under such surroundings he had found that he was unable to enjoy his food. In fact he had been scarcely able to force the food down his throat and had merely sat there feeling his resentment churning around inside him and finding it almost impossible to restrain it. It made him hate every white face in the dining car, and the last time that this had happened it had made him so nervous that he had quickly left enough money to cover the cost of what he had ordered, plus a tip, and gone back to his compartment, leaving his food untouched.

Now as he sat looking out of the compartment window he remembered how as a boy he used to stand in the station of the little South Carolina hamlet where he had been raised and watch the trains go by. They had seemed strange and wonderful to him, and the people who traveled on them mysterious beings almost from another planet. He came back to the present abruptly and, reaching down for his brief case, took out the folder which contained everything pertinent to the meeting, the outcome of which was scheduled to be a sort of manifesto to the white South to correct some of the racial ills of the region. He thumbed through it rapidly but put it aside for a new book by a prominent Negro writer, which had been sent him recently through one of the larger book clubs.

He read until it was almost dark, then put the book aside angrily. The man could write, of that there was little doubt, but he did not see things as they really were. His vision was clouded by his bitterness, so distorted that he ignored completely the progress many Negroes in the South had made. Besides, it was a dangerous book, a book that the white South would resent. Now was not the time for resentment; rather it was a time for even closer co-operation, to gain concessions and then nail them down solidly against the storm that was certain to come after the war. He made a note and filed it away in his brief case, a reminder to ask Cal Thornton, the liberal editor of the Citrus City *Telegram,* to let him take a shot at reviewing the book after he returned from the conference.

At six-thirty he opened his lunch box and ate the contents slowly. Ethel had done well by him; there was cold chicken, three buttered rolls, a large wedge of pie, and a thermos of coffee. After he had finished he lit a fresh cigar and settled back, his feet up on the other seat. He started to nod and almost dozed off when suddenly he was aroused by a knock at the door. Coming the way it had, so abruptly and unexpected when he was more than half asleep, it filled him with a sudden strange terror that made him for the moment want to hide, perhaps in the tiny bathroom, because he was where he did not belong. Then as quickly his momentary panic left him and he called in his normal voice, "Come in."

It was only the porter, who entered and closed the door softly behind him. He was young, a gangling person who seemed at once all arms and legs.

"White folks been runnin me raggedy-assed," he said, then giggled foolishly, almost like a young girl. "I figured us brothers in black could sit an visit."

The enormity of this invasion of his privacy left Ezekiel speechless for the moment. It also filled him with a sudden and burning rage. Damned impudent nigger, he said to himself, fresh out of somebody's cotton patch and not hardly housebroken yet.

He looked up icily. "What time are we due in?"

The porter took out his watch and studied it for a long time before he answered.

"Two-seventeen," he said slowly, "but we runnin a little late."

"You can make up my berth now," Ezekiel said coldly. "Call me a half hour before we get in."

Angrily he got to his feet and walked out of the compartment to wait, on the platform between the cars, until this intruder had done his work and left him the room again.

Last to get off the train, Ezekiel walked slowly back along the long line of cars toward the station. He had hoped to be able to catch a few hours' sleep on the train, but he had merely lain there in the darkness, caught in a web of irritation. Now it seemed to him that he was more tired from the concentrated effort to sleep than he would have been had he merely sat up or tried to do some work. From that point on everything had seemed to go wrong, and he had a premonition that it was likely to continue so. The bag he carried, and the brief case, seemed filled with rocks.

He passed quickly through the colored waiting room, as though by his haste he was not subject to any humiliation, and went out to the sidewalk beyond. Until this moment he had not thought of the possible difficulty of getting a cab, which was heightened by the lateness of the hour. This was the first time that he had ever been in this particular city, but he assumed that it was like Atlanta, where white drivers did not carry colored passengers and Negro hacks could not transport whites. But with an added surge of frustration he realized that he was not certain; racial mores differed locally and what might be the accepted etiquette for Atlanta might as easily be a near insult elsewhere. Still it was always safe to hail a Negro driver.

He stood in a well-lighted place and looked around for a cab, hoping to make sure of the driver's pigmentation before hailing him. None was passing on the lighted street to his right. He had purposely taken his time in embarking and walking through to the station; his intent had been to avoid the crowd, and now it seemed that this very action was the one which had defeated him, for all the cabs seemed to have already loaded and gone. He looked in the other direction, and far down at the end of the platform, in the shadowy darkness, he saw one lone taxi.

He looked at it tentatively and then raised his hand in a half gesture. He listened for a moment for the sound of the motor starting, but there was no sound. Uncertain what to do, for the moment he did nothing. Of course he could have asked someone, the porter in the station or even a well-dressed white person, but this was against a policy to which he rigidly adhered at all times. By asking he would admit not only to himself, but to the other person as well, the humiliation of segregation, while if he merely went along as though it were a normal part of his life it no longer seemed to exist.

At last he picked up his luggage and walked down toward the taxi. When he got nearer he could see that there was no one in it, and now he was right back where he had started. He put his bags down where he could keep an eye on them and lit a cigar. Then he walked slowly past the cab, moving aimlessly and as though he were merely passing the time while waiting for someone to pick him up.

He had hoped that there would be something printed on the doors which might give him a possible clue. In one town, he remembered, such cabs carried an advertising slogan: *Colored Cabs with Colored Drivers for Colored Riders.* But on the door of this cab there was nothing like that, not even the name of the company; only the unrevealing word TAXI. Within him he could feel his resentment rising slowly until it spread out over his whole body like a rash. It made no difference that he was an established educator, the president of a college; here he had to stand, tired and humiliated.

He looked at the taxi again angrily, almost as though it alone were responsible for his predicament. Old and battered around the fenders, it was badly in need of a coat of paint. It looked like a colored cab, he told himself angrily, not good enough for the white folks to be riding in and probably driven by some shiftless nigger (he said the word bitterly) off somewhere with a bottle of liquor and some women no better than he was.

He was tempted to get into the car and wait, but he could not be sure that the driver would turn out to be colored. What if he were not? he asked himself angrily; it would be breaking no law to make a mistake. But he could not bring himself to do it. He was in no mood to be insulted by some ignorant peckerwood with no more than a grammar-school education, and he knew by a kind of intuition that this was how it would be.

He was filled suddenly with a hatred for all things white—not only men and women, but small children as well. If there had been one near he might have struck out blindly without stopping to think. Frustrated, he went back to his bags and, picking them up, started out to the street. At the stop light he paused, and as he waited for the light to change he took his bearings. There was no need to ask anyone where the colored section was, he told himself bitterly; it would be on the other side of the tracks, in the meanest part of town.

The light turned green; he picked up his bags and crossed the street.

He locked the door of his hotel room carefully, checking it again to be sure that he was securely shut off from the dimly lit corridor. Looking around, he felt his resentment again rising within him. The town's finest, he said to himself, and made a face. Bessie had made certain that this was the best hotel, and she never made a mistake, but the room depressed him; it was dreary and into the bargain not very clean. He went over and pulled down the shade, which had a crack at one side and hung uneven at the corner. From the street three floors below him came the sounds of the city. He heard a woman's laugh, rich and throaty and ending on an elongated rise of tone, then the deepening chuckle of a man in reply.

This was once a white hotel, he said to himself, knowing that what he said was the truth without having to prove it. When they wore it out they sold it to some inept Negro for twice what it was worth, he told himself, and felt again a hatred for things white. The best room and bath, Bessie had specified, and this was what he got for as much money as it would have cost him to stay in a decent hotel in the main part of town. He laughed harshly and went into the bathroom. It was small and the plumbing was old-fashioned; the tub was on fluted feet and above it was a shower fixture, surrounded by a metal hoop from which hung a dejected and mildewed white canvas shower curtain. There was another door on the opposite side of the room, and he threw the bolt angrily, hammering it tight with the base of the heavy tumbler on the shelf over the yellow-stained basin. Then he went into the bedroom and threw himself down on the bed, but he knew he would not sleep and he could feel a throbbing at his left temple.

Suddenly he got to his feet and went to his brief case. He took out a lined yellow pad, then went to the desk by the window and began to write. The *New National* had often written him asking him for articles —well, he would give them one. His ideas came clearly, and with a rapidly mounting excitement he knew that what he was writing was good; the sentences clicked into place almost audibly and each paragraph was like a brick mortised firmly atop the preceding one. He wrote, not as he usually wrote, pulling his punches and trying to placate the white South, but calling for a dual pressure, the militancy of the Northern Negro working closely with Negroes in the South going as fast and as hard as they were able to, short only of actual danger from the violent mores of the region. In effect, what he called for was a tempered militancy as militant as any the North had ever advocated, and he marshaled his points to prove the need of such a program in perhaps the most effective answer to his own position that had ever been stated.

When he had finished he did not even bother to read it over. He did not need to, for he knew that it was as good as anything he had ever written. He folded it carefully and put it into an envelope, then enclosed a short note to Bessie.

Bessie, he wrote, *this is for Ransome at the* New National. *Will you type it up and send it on to him; he will know about it. Put a carbon in my files. It may need editing, as it was written at white heat. Any corrections you make are all for the good. . . .*

He signed his initials briskly and read over his instructions. He crossed out *white,* then *at heat,* and substituted *in haste.* Sealing the envelope, he went back to his brief case for the envelope that Bessie always kept filled with stamps. He put the stamped letter on the bureau and lay down again on the bed.

He felt no urge to sleep, but nonetheless he set the red leather traveling alarm clock that Ethel had given him the Christmas before, in case he should drop off. He felt better and at peace with himself. Light was beginning to come in at the window and the sounds of the morning had begun to replace those of the night. He heard a rooster crow far off, and the sound seemed incongruous to the city. Below he heard the rattle of garbage cans and the deep grunt of a truck as it started off in low gear. All at once he realized that he was hungry. He got up, washed his face and hands, went downstairs and out through the lobby. In front of the hotel he stood on the pavement for a moment and looked up and down the street.

Across from him and perhaps halfway down the block he saw a restaurant that seemed to be open. He crossed over and, walking down, looked in; it was clean and well lighted; he walked inside. When he sat down at a table a waitress came over immediately with a glass of water and a menu.

"Mawnin," she said, the sound of the farm not yet erased by the city. "You up early."

He nodded and smiled at her. She was only a girl, and in her clean uniform she was very attractive.

"Look," he told her, "could I have coffee right away and then order?"

"Sho," she answered, "I like that too. I got tuh have my cawfee *right* off in the mawnin."

When she returned he ordered a large orange juice and scrambled eggs.

"We got some good sausage," she told him. "Country sausage. Like some with yo eggs?"

"Wonderful," he said, "better make it a double order."

"Hot biscuits?"

"Of course hot biscuits."

She turned away and in a moment came back with his orange juice. "I knows you wants more cawfee."

He nodded and drank the orange juice. The eggs came and the sausage was just the way he liked it. After he finished the eggs and sausage he buttered another hot biscuit and had his third cup of coffee. By now he felt like a human being again. After paying his bill he left a larger tip than was necessary and went back to his room. In the light of morning it seemed somehow less dreary. He noticed the letter on the bureau and looked at the little traveling clock; there would be plenty of time to mail it now, but he decided against it. He would shave and shower first, then drop it into a mailbox downtown on his way to the meeting.

The sting of the shower made him feel even better. Being inside the round enclosure of the shower curtain suddenly tickled him and he began to laugh. He soaped all over carefully and suddenly he began to sing. After a brisk rubdown he got his things from his bag and began to shave, then doused his face with water as cold as the tap would run. He took his time about dressing, but it was still so early that he decided to walk downtown. There was nothing like walking to orient oneself in a strange town. Just as he was about to go out the door he noticed the letter propped up against the lamp on the bureau.

He took it and started to put it in his pocket, then stood tapping it gently against the index finger of his left hand. It was too late; he knew that he could not do it now. It was not so much himself—no, he had no personal fear—but there were others involved: Ethel, his son George, and, of course, the college. He tried to keep it on that plane, but inwardly he knew that this was not true. Almost hating himself, he tore the envelope and the article inside into tiny little strips and let them flutter down into the wastebasket.

7. Of all her children, Esther had always been fondest of Alberta. Bessie was the youngest, the baby, and Luther was the oldest and the only son, but somehow from the beginning it had always been Alberta who seemed dearest to her heart. Yet Alberta had been the one who had gone away. She often wondered if it would have been different if Hezekiah had lived. Perhaps then Luther would have been the one to go.

She knew that it had been hard for Luther to step aside, to become the head of the family and give up so many of the things that he might ordinarily have done, so that the two girls could do them instead. Luther meant a great deal to her; he had been like a foundation stone and he had never given her a moment's worry. He was always there for her to lean on, and even now that he was married and had moved over to live with Eulia she still retained that same feeling. Without him she would many times have found it difficult to go on in the days when it had so often seemed a question of staying afloat or sinking beneath a sea of economic troubles.

Of the three, it had been Bessie who had been the most appealing as a baby, the one who had seemed to need her most. And of them all, Bessie had been the only one to whom she had been able to give her undivided attention; for after Bessie was born she had never gone back to work in the white kitchens as she had always done before, save for those periods of final gestation, ever since she and Hezekiah had been married.

Or was it this very thing, perhaps, which made her feeling for Alberta the stronger? She was not certain. With Luther it had seemed inevitable that he would early develop a sense of independence; he was a boy and that was to be expected of boys. She had felt no qualms about leaving his care, and even much of his upbringing, to others while she was away from home at work. He had been able to take care of himself almost from the very beginning; in his body there had been a lean maleness so different from Alberta.

But with Alberta it had not been that way. There had been about her a look of defenselessness, and leaving her with others had almost torn Esther's heart from her breast. Each day was a race with time until the hour when she would be able to return to Alberta, and from the day that first she walked Esther found it impossible to leave her behind. Instead she had made it a condition of her employment—as clearly understood as hours, wages, and time off—that she could bring the child to work with her, bargaining against this one undesirable element the fact that she was one of the best cooks in town. And she had always kept her part of the agreement. Alberta had never been a deterrent to the amount of work she did. Her child had been trained to play out of doors on good days, and within a certain designated area where her mother could see her from the kitchen window. Sometimes she would play with the children of the people for whom Esther worked, but most often she played alone and thus acquired a self-reliance and even an expression of serious intentness that was mature beyond her years.

If Luther reminded her of her dead husband, it was Alberta who reminded her of herself. It was not that she had not loved Hezekiah; she had loved him wholly, completely, and without reservation, and his death had filled her with an emptiness that not even her children, including Alberta, could fill. Even now, after fourteen years, it was hard for her to realize that Hezekiah was gone. It was only the memory of the accident, and the twenty-odd hours afterward while he had clung to the thin thread of life, that seemed to bring finality to the fact that he was gone beyond recall. He had been working on a railroad gang and had been crushed while helping to right a derailed freight car. And the gesture that he had made, choosing to save others instead of himself, gave to his death a double irony.

When she had met Hezekiah she had been teaching a one-room colored school over on the Gulf. He had been an itinerant worker, a drifter seemingly without purpose, but a man tall and strong, full of a kind of inherent kindness and gentleness that had touched her deeply. She had given up the school to marry him and she had never gone back. Nor had she regretted it. In an age when school requirements were low for white teachers in the South, and almost nonexistent for Negroes, her background was hardly intellectual. And yet it had had some meaning for her, and she had passed it on to Alberta with a kind of savage intensity. Nothing must stand in the way of an education. But she had not foreseen the results.

Her day, then, both began and ended when Luther or Bessie brought the mail home from the post office. Most days it never seemed to begin, for Alberta rarely wrote more than once a week and often went for several weeks without bothering to send a letter or even a postcard. In those arid periods Esther's thoughts were a welter of calamities imagined so realistically that they seemed rooted deeply in fact. Then a letter would finally arrive and all would be well again until the next week passed without so much as a word from New York.

She wished that Alberta would come back for a visit, a vacation from the complexities she complained about in her letters, but Alberta would always suggest instead that her mother come to New York. This Esther had no desire to do; she was deeply rooted by ties she had no desire to break. Besides, the thought of the trip terrified her, and the bigness of New York, once she got there, was something too filled with strangeness for her even to anticipate. And yet she knew that there was really nothing to keep her here. Luther had Eulia, and Bessie was more than capable of looking out for herself.

As it was, she was hard put to know what to do with her days. She had earned a rest, but to be inactive was something which seemed somehow an admission that she was growing old. The house was not enough to occupy her, especially now that Luther had moved over to Eulia's. There was really only one big meal to prepare, now that Bessie ate her lunch at the college. In an hour or two in the morning she had the house spotless, and before her the whole day stretched until it was time to prepare the evening meal. Bessie had bought her a sewing machine, and she loved to make clothes for Bessie. It pleased her to see Bessie smartly dressed, for all her children had always been kept neat, even as babies. But still this left her with more time than she knew what to do with, even counting her weekly wash.

She read a little, usually the Bible, but more often she sat on the front porch in her familiar rocker. Before her spread the life of the community, and for a while it would manage to hold her attention. On the dusty street there was usually some sort of activity, if only the passing of a stray cur hurrying to get nowhere because it did not know where it belonged. Often she would watch the red Dominicker chickens across the street in their never-ending search for food. Sometimes she would see the lusty cock single out a hen and, after cornering her, tread her with a masculine gusto that made Esther breathe the faster. She always chuckled at the way the hens acted when singled out for this honor. Their feminine reticence and the silly and meaningless protesting squacks which they let forth in the stilled air amused her. They were not fooling her; she knew, she remembered all too well.

Such feelings did not bother her, for there was no false modesty about her. She was a woman yet, in spite of her three grown children, and the fact seemed as inevitable to her as that of night following day. Her life was incomplete without a man, and yet she had never married again, or assumed any relationship with a man, since Hezekiah had died. Was it only the memory of him that had kept her from it, or was it merely that the right man had never come along? There had been men, especially when she was younger, but none of them had moved her. Was it because of herself or merely a lack in them? She was not sure.

Other women bored her. It was all right occasionally to talk over the fence to a neighbor or pass the time of day while waiting in line at the colored market on Hannibal Square where she usually did her shopping. But anything beyond that seemed to her a waste of time. The sound of a room full of women filled her with an unexplained anger; a group of women on a porch as she passed by seemed to her as foolish as a flock of birds twittering away their lives in a tree.

There remained only her garden, neatly arranged in geometric precision with each bed outlined by chunks of coquina rock freshly whitewashed. She spent much of her time there, in the early morning or the late afternoon, and she would have been lost without the splash of color that her flowers gave to the yard. Without them it would not have seemed like a home to her. But it was not enough; even when the various segments were tallied together, it was still not enough.

She had not been fishing for years, then suddenly one day she had gone out to the garage and, taking down one of Hezekiah's old cane poles, had walked out to the nearest lake. When her husband had been alive they had gone often, but after he died she had suddenly lost interest. Now it brought her a feeling of peace and contentment.

Several times as she had walked home past Eulia's house she had noticed Eulia's father on the stoop and nodded to him. At first he had merely nodded back, but one day he called out to her.

"Any luck?" he asked.

She walked up on his grass and held up her string.

"Just bream," she told him. "Fishin from shore like I do, I ain likely to catch nothin bigger."

He nodded. "Leastways no trouts," he told her, "nor speckled perch neither. Anyways, with speckled perch you got to find where they beddin, an that man's work. Some say they can smell a bed and others claim to hear one. Now me, I doan rightly know how I can tell, but I sho can."

"Breams is all right," she said, "they right good in the mornin for breakfast."

"Sho," he acknowledged, "they sweet to the taste too. But they somehow doan seem to stick to a man's ribs. Now I got me a boat out on Lake Lonely where they's real fishin. Why doan I carry you along with me next time I go?"

"I'd be right proud to go," she told him.

And so they had gone out the next morning, walking together down the little-used back road while the dew was still heavy on the grass. As they walked along she was amused to realize how excited she had felt about going and with what care she had put up a lunch for the two of them. She looked at him out of the corner of her eye. He walked with his eyes straight down the road, a man tall and with stooped shoulders, yet with a walk that had nothing in it of an older man; and the cane he always carried, she realized now, was more a protective weapon than an aid to walking. She wondered how old he really was; it was hard to tell, even knowing something of his mixed marital relations.

The road they traveled was deserted, and the land through which it threaded was mainly palmetto scrub with an occasional scattered strand of pine. Off to their left she heard a cock quail whistle twice, and across the road and behind her the answering trill of the hen. In the sky, buzzards were hanging low off to the east and moving almost as though they were secured to a fixed axis by string. She heard a woodpecker and saw it ahead of her on a telephone pole, the one discordant note in a world that seemed inhabited only by herself and Eulia's father. It was strange; she realized that she did not even know his Christian name.

"You tired?" he asked curtly, turning his head a little toward her.

She shook her head and saw his face almost as though it were somehow not related to his body. It was a strong face; the hair, close-cropped to the skull and tinged with gray, seemingly bringing it into a stronger relief. He was darker than she, even darker than Hezekiah had been, but still it was a color that had little in it of real black. There was a blue, perhaps even more a purple, and a deep brown that had a tinge of red even; yet, put together, none of them seemed predominant. He carried his head high and a little to one side; his eyes seemed deeper set than most, which gave to his face an indrawn look that only added to his dignity.

"Hit ain far now," he said, "jest past that next crook in the road."

"I ain tuckered," she told him. "Most of my life I been active, and I reckon I walked more than most. My feets is good and not gone back on me the way they do on some."

He did not answer or show that he had heard by so much as a movement of his head. There was no need for it. She knew him for a man who made an economy of words and wasted none where silence would do as easily. They came to the turning of the road and around it she saw the lake in the distance. It lay in a direction from which life had grown away when the new north-south highway had been laid off to the east more than ten years ago. It had been claimed again by the wilderness from which it had momentarily been wrested, and the only sign remaining of this temporary change in status was the narrow, pitted road which curled around the west end of the water.

In a moment they left the road and cut off through the scrub.

The boat he kept hidden in the high grass that grew thick and tall around the edges of the water, the oars more carefully cached perhaps a dozen paces away. Then, as though this were not enough, a crudely painted sign lay atop the overturned bottom. *This here my boat,* it said, *it doan belong to you so doan use it, this means white well as colored.* It was signed with his name in full—Jefferson H. Bronson. Turning it over, he laid the two oars in, resting along the middle and the rear seats, and, bending low, worked the boat along through the weed grass and out into the water. It was pulled high, and to move it he had to widen his stance and bend low to get the proper leverage. The muscles in his back knotted and stood up like acorns under his faded but fresh-washed blue work shirt. Standing to one side, she was conscious suddenly of the wideness of his shoulders and the movement of his body under the shirt. There was nothing of oldness in him now, she decided; he was all man no matter the number of his years.

The boat came free and adrift, the stern swinging around to the side with the last bit of released pressure. It was homemade, short in length with a rather long snout, wider toward the middle and the stern, and painted a dark green with white trim. He pulled it into shore and, bending, swung the stern in closer to the bank so that she could get in without wetting her feet. When she was settled he shoved out hard from shore and with the same movement leaped nimbly into the bow.

The lake lay calm around them, but to the east, toward the far shore, there was a faint ripple atop the water. He swung the bow around and rowed easily for a while along the shore in shallow water until he located his bait box, sunk to the bottom and anchored fast. He filled the bait well under his seat with the bailing can and, raising the screened minny box to the surface, transferred enough bait for the day's fishing into the well under the seat. Then he rowed out to deep water, keeping on a line with a pine on the shore in back of him taller than the others around it.

Presently he feathered his oars and began to look down into the water, and in a moment he reached back for the homemade anchor. Playing the rope out through his fingers, he let it down slowly to the bottom. He baited Esther's hook with a live minnow and adjusted the cork bobber, then watched her as she swung her hook out and let it fall silently into the water. He nodded with satisfaction and turned to bait his own rig.

He fished with a hand line, but between his thumb and finger it seemed a thing alive. Hardly was his line down before he jerked it up and there was a fish flopping on the bottom of the boat. She looked down at it—a good-sized speckled perch which seemed in its markings like a piece of calico cloth. Suddenly she remembered the lean years, and in particular the leanest, when Hezekiah had been out of work and she herself had been unable to secure any but part-time employment. They had existed almost wholly on the fish they caught, and after three months of it neither of them could cram down another mouthful. The memory seemed a long ways away.

He caught three more before she had even had her first bite. They ate their lunch in the boat, and after they had finished they sat for a moment before starting to fish again. In the bottom of the boat lay at least eighteen fat speckled perch.

"We got anyhows enough for a taste," he said. "You want to try for more here or see can we catch us a trout or two?"

She laughed inwardly; it amused her to hear him call the green bass so common to the region by their rural, idiomatic name. It seemed old-timy to her and yet she liked it. She told him that she would like to try, and he set the oars in the locks again, then turned backward to lift the anchor. Before long he came to a spot he liked and dropped the anchor again.

"Fish along by them lily pads," he told her. "That's where they likely to be this late in the day."

But she had little luck. She realized that soon they must start back to town. The thought did not please her, and it seemed to her that the day had cheated her in the rapidity with which it had passed. She felt a feeling of contentment, and she realized with almost a shock that much of it was because she was with Jeff. She looked over at him; he was turned profile to her, his eyes intent on his line, but she knew by intuition that he was as conscious of her as she was of him. In a moment he drew in his line.

"They ain here," he said curtly. "Leastwise if they is they sho ain payin us no mind." He turned and lifted the anchor, then went on, "We could come again. I'd be glad to carry you along next time."

"I'd like that, Jeff," she answered.

She felt herself blush a little as she said his name; it seemed strange to her lips, and the strangest was that she could have lived so close to him for these dozen years or more and yet hardly been conscious of him at all.

She felt the jar as they beached and she followed him out onto the shore. After he hid the oars and upturned the flat-bottomed boat he tried to make her take the largest share of the catch. For a moment they fought good-naturedly like children, each urging the most for the other. Finally she laughed and gave in, but made of her defeat a condition.

"You come by an eat with us tomorrow evenin," she told him. "I reckon Luther and Eulia can get along without you. You come over and we'll have us a real bait of fried fish."

"I'd be right proud," he said. "Thankee, m'am."

Gathering their tackle together, they started back toward town.

8. Each fall, and as regular as the change of the seasons, the wife of the president of the college entertained the members of the faculty and their wives, the administration staff, and a light sprinkling of outsiders. If there happened to be a distinguished visitor or two, so much the better; failing this, she drew on the small but select group of professional men in nearby Citrus City. The younger and fairer of the two colored doctors, who was both Northern-born and Northern-trained, was apt to be there, as was the more successful of the lawyers, a man who had originally come from the West Indies. Another special pet of Ethel's was the teacher of French in the local colored high school, Haitian-born and New Orleans raised. Of the three, he alone could be called dark, and he was of a darkness which could be described only by the word black. Yet his manners charmed her, and what she was fond of calling his old-world charm, plus the fact that his features were hardly Negroid and he wrote poetry into the bargain, made up for his unfortunate pigmentation.

Actually these were the ones she gave the evenings for, or, perhaps more accurately, these were the favored few who helped to make such functions bearable. For the members of the faculty she had an odd sort of contempt—lumping them together into only a slightly higher category then the help—since they were hired by her husband. There were, of course, a few exceptions, such as Eric, but on the whole she felt herself above them and the gesture of having them in her house each term was mere largess. She felt that she was bestowing upon them a rare opportunity, and she would have been deeply hurt to know that very few faculty members shared her views. Behind her back they called her Queen Ethel, and those few who had the slightest gift for mimicry built around her whole routines that were often as elaborate as vaudeville sketches.

Ethel was fond of saying that she never mixed in things academic, that Ezekiel's word was law in the college and her policy was completely one of hands off, but this was far from true. If she were not the absolute authority, she was certainly the power behind the throne. It was common knowledge that her husband made no appointments without consulting her and that each year they went over the faculty list together, talking over the possibility of reappointments. For this reason she was both hated and feared on the campus; an invitation from her was a command appearance.

All of this she would have denied if anyone had been foolish enough to bring it to her attention. She would merely have said that her whole life had been devoted to taking part of the load off the doctor's shoulders, that it was his job to analyze the academic backgrounds, hers to pass on the social. After all, it was important that the college should

64

have a well-rounded faculty and one which had the right attitudes. If all this failed, she might, as a last resort, turn on her femininity and laughingly admit that really the doctor paid very little attention to what she advised anyway.

The parties—or evenings, as she preferred to call them—had assumed a pattern that varied little over the years. If the weather was nice they began on the lawn behind the neat white house, well kept and profuse with flower beds. On a table set under the trees and neatly spread with a freshly laundered tablecloth was a large, old-fashioned, cut-glass punch bowl, which she had discovered years ago in one of the outbuildings. Around this were cut-glass cups and three or four silver trays, plus a variety of smaller dishes. In these were salted nuts or candies, while on the trays were neatly pyramided stacks of gaily colored cupcakes and tea biscuits. The punch, of course, was strictly non-alcoholic, though she realized that her husband took more favored guests into his study in the house, where he gave them furtive drinks of whisky.

At this stage of the party people would gather in little groups and talk about whatever people in such small clusters usually talk about. If the men gathered stag-like, Ethel was upon them like a flash, and she was as firm with tight little knots of women. From the time that they first gathered until perhaps eleven, when they progressed into the next and final stage of the evening, she was in constant motion, seeing to it that everyone talked to everyone else.

For the climax all were herded into the house, where they were subjected to perhaps an hour of music, always provided by the music majors among the students, who were barred from the lawn phase of the evening but allowed to partake of the supper which followed their musical chores. Even then, however, there was a tacit understanding that their status was not unlike that of children allowed up as a special favor to eat with the grownups.

At exactly a half hour after the plate supper, the evening, mysteriously and without prearranged signal, would come to an abrupt end.

Throughout the years many had remarked that these evenings were almost pure fantasy. This was not strange, for as a child in the little South Carolina town where she had been born Ethel had lived so firmly entrenched in a world half fantasy, half real, that the two had merged into one. Through no fault of her own, her family life had been irregular and confused. The one anchor had been her mother, a bitter, ambitious, and matriarchal woman with a complexion and features which might well have lifted her out of the segregated ghetto

65

had she lived under a more tolerant culture. Of her father Ethel knew little, had in fact never even seen his picture, for he had moved on before she had been able to walk, a victim of a domineering woman who had robbed him of his manhood and made him impotent in every marital situation save the sexual. There had been other men, three in fact, who had all eventually left for the same reason, drifting on and leaving little impression on her save the fact that none of them was really her father.

Only for the last had she felt any real affection, and then not until the day that he had left, in much the same way that the others had gone before him. He had taken her aside, a girl of fifteen and a junior in the local colored high school, and pressed a crumpled ten-dollar bill into her palm, telling her why he was leaving and cautioning her never to become like her mother. Thus she felt for him a sudden closeness, not as a father but as a friend, a fellow conspirator passing in the night. And on occasion she had used him in hidden revenge against her mother, a means of temporary and safe rebellion, but never anything drastic enough to quite sever the ties that bound them as securely as an umbilical cord.

No, her real father, the only one with any meaning for her, had been created out of an actual incident. It had happened when she was only six and, passing through the white business section, she had stopped before a long black car with the top down and bearing a New York license plate. It had seemed to her the most completely wonderful thing that she had ever seen, a chariot carrying no mortal but a god-like being sitting majestically alone in the rear seat. Seeing her alone also and staring at him, he had smiled and called her over to the side of the car. He was the first white man whom she had ever remembered talking to, and the fact that he had as well a trim white beard added to his magnificence. He had chatted with her awhile and then, taking out his wallet, had given her a crisp new dollar bill with which to buy candy.

That was my daddy, she had whispered fiercely to herself as she ran up the street, that was my daddy and he knew me. In time she came to believe it in a way; if not that white man, surely another almost as magnificent, a kind of prince astride a white charger, or at the very least in an open automobile from a faraway place. She had even repeated it in school, so that eventually it got back to her mother, who whipped her for the only time in her life, her arm flailing as regularly as a piston's rise and fall. But the stinging pain that had clung to her backside and the bitter taste of salt from her tears had only served to anchor her more firmly in fantasy. She was being punished not for what she had done but merely because she had happened to stumble upon a secret.

Now dead, her mother had visited the college just once, but that visit had become a part of the college legend. Ethel had given a party at which, she told people, she thought it would be amusing to serve chitterlings, which she had never had, because in her mother's charming upper-class household such common fare was naturally never served. However, the cook she now employed could make them, and it seemed to Ethel that a party would be a delightfully quaint way to be introduced to them. But that afternoon the secret was out, let escape by her mother, who had gone to a neighboring house to borrow an implement or ingredient necessary to their preparation and laughingly said that the cook did not have the faintest notion of how to prepare them so the task had fallen onto her shoulders, which was all right because she had nearabout reared Ethel on them.

The day had been fair and had continued so into the evening. Just before the first guests were to arrive Ethel made a final examination of all the preparations for their entertainment. In the kitchen she tasted the punch, looked to the crispness of the salted nuts and the freshness of the cakes and cookies, checked the supper that would be served after the musical, when all would come into the house from the lawn gaily traversed by colored paper lanterns. At first she had thought to omit these, for patriotic reasons, but at the last moment she had changed her mind and now she was glad. Her one regret was that she was forced to serve a sea-food salad, made from shrimps and the huge Florida crayfish which are called lobsters, instead of the usual baked ham and scalloped potatoes she had featured when there was no meat shortage.

She saw to the placing of the punch bowl on the table under the trees and rearranged the silver plates around it after the boy, a college student hired for the occasion, had gone back into the kitchen. Walking across the lawn and back again, as she waited for the first guests to arrive, she looked around and was satisfied with what she saw. She glanced at her wrist watch and realized that her husband would probably be late in coming down. She thought of George, away somewhere in the South Pacific, and it seemed to her that he was only a boy, a baby snatched cruelly from her before his time had come. There remained only the realization that once he came back to her, his future would again be well regulated. He would never know the uncertainty she had known, and she would always be there to help him.

She heard the light slap of the porch screen door behind her and, turning, saw her first guests coming across the lawn toward her. Among them was Motley Crawford, whose field was modern languages, one of those on her list not to be reappointed; he was a good man, but his wife, who was with him, was quite impossible, a squat black woman who was vain and took the business of being married to a professor overseriously. She was given to using multisyllabled words, usually in their wrong context and more often than not mispronounced. Greeting them, she turned away quickly and went over to Jordon Phillips, a well-known social scientist, and his wife. His tongue was as bitter as acid and he was afraid of no one; moreover, she knew, from those faculty wives who were anxious to protect their husbands' positions, that he openly satirized her in public. Yet his position was secure, for he published widely and his wife had a social prestige in Northern Negro urban centers which was almost as useful. She greeted them more cordially.

More guests arrived, and she noted with satisfaction that Ezekiel was coming toward her with the guest of honor, a woman author whose earlier books had been considered quaint and charming but whose later ones, slightly repetitive, had for the most part been ignored. She had always written of her fellow Negroes on a patronizing level only a notch or two above the folkways patterns exploited by those white writers about whom she was most caustic. Yet she was still a name to be reckoned with.

Every year or so her well ran dry and she would return to the hinterlands to prime it; at the moment she was touring the South on the lookout for material to write one of the Menckenlike articles for which she still found a fairly steady market among certain pseudo-intellectual magazines. She was dressed bizarrely but effectively in a long pink-checked gingham frock that made her look, from a distance, like a little girl. But her hair, piled high atop her finely chiseled head and secured by an exotic jeweled comb, and the huge gold hoops she wore in her ears, gave to her a sophistication that was only a little short of breathtaking.

"Laura," Ethel trilled, "how utterly fascinating you look! Come, darling, let me introduce you to all these nice people."

Ethel left her with Jordon Phillips for the moment and moved on among her guests. She was conscious that the party had been successfully launched and that from this point on it would move so rapidly that it must be rigidly timed. She glanced at her watch and hurried on.

Later, seeing Eric and Bessie together, she came toward them with a special smile. She knew Bessie's value to her husband and approved it, and for Eric she had a reluctant respect. Although she had not read his book, she had seen the reviews.

"Bessie," she said, "you shouldn't be allowed to monopolize the best-looking man at the party!"

"I like it, Ethel," Eric said easily. "The doctor beat me to it with you, so I'm working on the next best thing."

"Bless you, Eric. And Bessie, I know, realizes that I was only joking. But, Eric, I do want you to talk with Laura Burroughs. May I steal him for a little while, Bessie?"

"Of course, Mrs. Rogers."

Taking Eric by the arm, she led him through the crowd toward the guest of honor.

"Laura, darling," she said, "of course you know Eric?"

Laura made a face at him. "Mr. Gardner," she said, holding out her hand. When he took it she pulled him toward her and lay her cheek against his face. "Baby," she whispered, then blew into his ear, "where have you been all these years?"

He had known her from her college days in Washington when his father had often brought her home, sometimes for a hurried dinner but more often for a leisurely week end. Although she was five years older than he, he had nonetheless been hopelessly in love with her at sixteen. For that reason he would always have a deep affection for her in spite of the fact that he intensely disliked everything for which she stood—her studied scatterbrainedness, her profitable career as a "professional" Negro, the fact that she made a living of singing for her supper.

He watched Ethel drift away and heard Laura say, in her biting and racy voice, "Madam Queen!"

"Leave her alone, Laura," he said. "Don't use her in an article. There are more important things to write about. What do you hear from the mob?"

"Mose is marching forward," she answered. "He's coming on like The March of Time and leaving like Gang Busters."

She affected a jive idiom that was always a little out of date; it eluded her somehow, changing so rapidly that she could never quite keep pace except by the standards of the white folks who considered her an authority whose word was as final as Webster's.

"She fits into the piece I'm doing, Eric. Why shouldn't I use her?"

"It would only hurt Ezekiel. He's a good guy, Laura, give him credit for trying."

"Him?" She laughed lightly. "He rode in here on his pulpit, although I do hear that now the white folks favor veterinarians as being safer college presidents these days. Can you imagine him the president of anything but a cow college for colored? He's a pompous little ass with a 'big nigger' complex, and you know it."

"Laura," he laughed, "you're as hell-bent for suicide as the Negro press. What are you both going to do when you solve the race problem?"

She laughed and made a face at him. "Nigger," she said, "you hit me when I wasn't looking." She bowed mockingly.

The low-cut top of her dress came away and he could see the beginnings of her breasts. He thought, with an odd kind of admiration, that they were as exciting at forty-one as he had remembered them at twenty-one.

"What big eyes you have, grandma," he said, half in laughter.

"Nigger," she said, "you ain't changed a bit."

Across the lawn they heard Ethel's voice, only slightly raised but pitched so carefully that it was audible to everyone.

"We'll go in now," she said. "We're going to have a little music by some of our better music-major students."

Laura bowed to him and offered her arm. "Come on, light, polite, and almost white, les get us some red beans and rice."

The party was over. The living room had that look of the morning after which Ethel so intensely disliked, but she was too tired to do anything about it. Now that it was over she felt let down, almost defeated. She looked around the room; all that she would do was have the maid gather and stack the dishes. The rest could go until morning. She lit a cigarette and looked at Ezekiel.

"It was a nice party, my dear," he said, "even nicer than usual."

"It was," she answered, her voice tired. "Laura Burroughs helped brighten it. The students did well, but I do wish that Simpson girl wouldn't wear that white evening dress. With her complexion, she looks exactly like a fly in a pail of buttermilk."

He chuckled. "You told me that once," he said, "that time I came back from New York with a white linen suit. But it sounds bad when you talk that way, Ethel, even if it's only to me."

"Well," she snapped, "sometimes I think the white folks are right. Some of us are apelike, dirty, and lazy. Maybe if we weren't they wouldn't talk that way." Then she sighed. "I'm sorry, Doctor. I'm tired. You go on up. I'll be along as soon as I see Mamie out and pay that boy that Bessie found for me, though I can't say he really earned it."

He nodded and, getting to his feet, went slowly up the stairs.

After Ethel was through in the kitchen and had locked the door behind Mamie and the boy from the college, she went up to the bedroom which she and her husband shared. She heard Ezekiel in the bathroom, noisily engaged in brushing his teeth. Behind the opened door of the closet she undressed quickly and put on her night things. As soon as Ezekiel reappeared she went into the bathroom and closed the door.

When she came out he was already in bed, lying on his back with his eyes closed. She got in beside him and, kissing him lightly, turned out the light. She could hear his rhythmical breathing and she wished that she too could sleep; she was tired, but her mind was running like the skittering of mice, in a thousand different directions. Far off she heard the late northbound train as it whistled for the grade crossing to the east of the college. It made her think of her son George, and the loss of him left a great empty hole within her.

Below in the living room she heard the clock strike; she had been lying there sleepless for over an hour.

She wished she had not drawn the dark shades so securely. The darkness seemed oppressive to her, as though it were slowly closing in to crush her; she could feel it on her face, her forehead, pressing even against her eyeballs. It made her want to raise her hands and push it back and away from her face. She was suddenly confused and lost, as a child feels terror at finding itself cut off from those familiar things to which it has been anchored. As sometimes happened, she saw clearly through her fantasies to the real world, and what she saw only made her want to retreat yet farther into the world of unreality. But she could not find the right door; there were many doors, but none of them opened except one, and that was locked. Where was the key? Where?

She rose hurriedly to the floor in her bare feet and went over and raised both shades high. Then she half knelt, half sat on the floor, with her elbows on the sill. The moon was bright and she could see far across the flat land, over the horseshoe of the campus and between the clearly outlined buildings to the road beyond. She felt a sudden flush of hatred, all-enveloping and yet confused. It was composed of hatred for whites and hatred for herself because she was not white, but it was more than that, just how much more she could not clearly distinguish.

She looked toward the bed and saw Ezekiel, his back to her so that his haunch was raised slightly, almost as though it had once been broken and not properly set. He was wearing the maroon silk pajamas that she had given him for Christmas the year before. He seemed so solid, so big and powerful, lying there. She remembered him as he had been, as he might be even now. He was father, mother, the brother she had never had, and suddenly now again the lover. She felt a warmness of desire fanning out over her body.

She got up and, taking off her nightdress, laid it on the chair and walked barefooted quickly to the bed. She lay down on her back and for a moment closed her eyes, feeling the intensity of her desire but holding it back until she knew that she could resist it no longer. It had not been like this for a long time, and she was happy, knowing the dissatisfaction that he had tried to shield from her but couldn't.

She reached her hand up under the coat of his pajamas and ran her finger tips up and down his bare back. Feeling his skin react, she closed her eyes. In a moment he rolled over to her and she strained herself to him, seeing in her mind the darkness of his skin against hers that was so nearly white. She was close to crying as she put her arms around him and dug her fingers into his back. She wanted to swallow him completely, to keep forever the oneness that seemed to her, at times, her only safety.

9. The taproom, in a sense, was for Luther a sensitive instrument recording the collective white temper of the county. Within its four walls he could feel at what point its residents were most likely to be at their touchiest, and also when they were most filled with the milk of human kindness and well disposed toward even those citizens whose skins happened to be black. It was something which hung suspended in the air, a current not unlike electricity, a signal, a bell of warning, an equalizer of odds and a foreteller of possible fortunes. Not to be polarized to this current could prove to be dangerous.

Standing by the arch which opened into the little cocktail room, he could tell almost without looking who might be coming in from the street outside. The white South's claim to knowing the Negro could in no sense be measured against the way in which he, Luther, knew most of the white men who were regular customers at the bar. Most of them he had known even before the bar had opened up, when he was working as a bellboy in the hotel. To them he was someone who was simply not there, before whom anything was said, for he was like a deaf-mute so far as they were concerned.

Actually it would have been a great source of embarrassment to them had they realized how much he really knew. He was well aware who among them was unfaithful to his marital vows and with whom; in fact, he likely even knew the place where it most often occurred. Yet no one could have accused him of eavesdropping. How can one listen stealthily when one does not exist and conversation goes on openly? Some of them he knew better than others, for he had known them at their worst, at that hour between midnight and dawn when the resistance of the body to evil is at its lowest ebb. He had, on occasion, driven them home in their cars when they were too far gone to be trusted behind the wheel. Sometimes they had thanked him in a human way, as though the alcohol which they had absorbed within their blood stream had somehow made them forgetful of the superiority to which they ordinarily clung with such terrifying persistence. More often, however, they were merely grateful with their money, taking it from their pockets in careless crumpled wads and looking at it owlishly in the dim light from the dashboard of the car or street light, forcing it on him in a pitiful effort to make themselves seem less like weaklings than they knew, with drunken logic, that they had become. At least one of them had drunkenly told him of the wrongs that were done him by others as white as himself, and in this confessional mood he had not only embarrassed Luther but also filled him with a rage that shook him inwardly. He was able to function thinking that white men acted as they did through self-ignorance or an unconscious baseness; that they should openly confess to their guilt made him furious but at the same time insecure. The crackers who sometimes came into the bar on Saturday afternoons in their faded overalls and black wool hats filled him with a different hatred, but they at least were predictable, and because they were he felt toward them even a strange kind of respect. At the other extreme were the big spenders and the fancy tippers, but it was their money that really talked to him. In between was a whole area of whites who did not affect him in any way so long as they did not bother him.

Luther had never been North, and all that he really knew about it had been gleaned from the two Negro papers that Bessie brought home from the college and passed along to him. And even that little seemed to him very remote, for he was apt to look at only the two or three comic strips, especially the large cartoon about a Negro named Bootsie who was always in trouble, then turn to the sports page. He had played baseball himself, and there was more meaning for him in the batting average of the first baseman for the Kansas City Monarchs than in the page of editorials and Negro columnists. Sometimes he would look at their pictures and wonder what kind of people they really were. Once in a while he might even read what they had written, but it seemed to him that they were really talking about another world. Often he carried the paper to work with him, and if the evening was slow he looked at it down at the end of the bar, which by mutual but unspoken agreement seemed to be reserved for his leisure.

One night he was reading the *Defender* but was aware that a conversation was going on at the other end of the bar. It was about baseball and was between two white men who were only casual customers of the bar. Hearing their voices raised a little, he closed himself out from their conversation, almost as a turtle withdraws into its shell.

"Hey, boy, less see that paper."

He did not realize that they were talking to him until they raised their voices. Then he looked up.

"Less see the paper, boy."

"This is my paper, suh," he said, meaning only that it was not the regular afternoon paper.

"Godamit, I don't care whose paper it is. You fetch it over here and be damn fast about it."

They were a little drunk and he didn't like the way they looked at him.

"This here a colored paper, cap'n," he said softly.

"Lissen, nigger," the taller of the two said, "I don't care if it's black an white and read all over." He laughed heartily at his own joke and when Luther silently handed him the paper he spread it out before him on the bar.

"Jesus Christ," he said, looking down at the front page, "what the hell kind of a paper is this?"

When Luther told him again, he said, "A nigger paper, huh. Well, I'll be godamed. Heh, Bob, did you know there was a nigger paper?"

"I never even knew niggers could read," the shorter of the two said, then looked over at Luther and grinned.

As Luther walked away he heard Bob Giddings, his boss, join them and he could hear the rustle of the pages as they were turned. He tried not to listen, but he could not help hearing their amused comments about Negroes trying to act like white people but still looking more like apes. He was not angry; his feeling was something different from that. It was more a feeling of futility, almost one of hopelessness. Just then the phone rang, and after the boss answered it he called Luther over.

"Bottle of whisky for room 1802, Luther. You got some change?"

Luther nodded and, taking the bottle, neatly rolled in a piece of wrapping paper, started for the door that led into the lobby. Behind him he could hear the voices of the two at the bar, drunken and slightly raised.

"Fred, lookit this one here in the bathing suit. Ain't that something?"

"Jesus, yes, how you would like to get her out in the bushes, huh?"

"Bushes, hell, I'd take her right in my bed with the light on. Hell, I was eighteen years old before I even knew a white girl would do it. One of the things I never could understand was why they put the best pussy on niggers."

He heard their ribald laughter and it hit him full force like a sudden sheet of rain turning to hail. His futility turned suddenly to a hot, hard indigestible mass deep in his belly. But his face showed no hint of his feelings as he went through into the lobby and across to the elevators beyond.

He got off the elevator at the eighteenth floor, turned right, and went down the corridor, then turned left again. Stopping at the door of 1802, he knocked and, hearing a voice in answer, opened the door.

When he came into the room he saw old man Jordon sitting on the bed in his pants and undershirt. He was a man in his middle fifties who owned a large citrus grove out on the back road to Limeola, a squat and slightly ugly man who had been drinking rather heavily since he had lost his wife a few years earlier. He had one son, already drafted and gone to war, and thus no remaining responsibilities. Most of his days were spent in the taproom, usually in the back booth where he played knock rummy with the old linotype operator who ran the poker game upstairs. Sober, Mr. Jordon was all right, but once he got into the whisky he was unpredictable.

Over in the chair by the window across from Mr. Jordon a blond woman in her late thirties was seated. She was wearing a slightly rumpled and rusty-looking black dress and had her shoes off. She looked a little the worse for wear, so that she might have been younger than she looked; but if so, not by more than a few years. Like Mr. Jordon, she was already well on her way to being drunk. Luther knew that she was a hustler from over on Oak Street and worked all the hotels.

"Well, tall, dark, and handsome," she said, then added with a hard emphasis, "and I *do* mean dark. Where the hell you been? It sure as hell took you long enough, nigger; what did you do, make the whisky?"

"Listen," Mr. Jordon said, turning to her, "you keep your trap shut, you old bag. Luther's a good nigger. He's my nigger, ain't you, Luther?"

Luther nodded. He wanted to get out of the room but he knew the chances were that he was not going to be able to, and if he tried to, it would only make matters worse. Mr. Jordon looked at him and winked.

"Hey, you," he said, turning to the blonde again. "You're so all-fired hot for a drink, why don't you pour us one, two if you want. Pour Luther one too."

He looked over at Luther and winked.

"I don't drink with no niggers," she said primly.

Mr. Jordon winked at Luther again and, putting his head back, started to roar with laughter. When he stopped Luther tried to work his way toward the door, but when the white man looked up at him this time he did not wink or even smile. Instead he looked the way a white man usually looks when he feels that a Negro is trying to take advantage of his good nature. He got up from the bed and went over to get the drink that the woman had by this time poured for him, then came back and sat down.

"Daddy," the woman said. Mr. Jordon did not answer or even look at her, so she said it again. "Look, daddy, I can't sit here on my ass all night. Get that nigger out of here, honey, and less get it over with. I coulda turned two tricks the time I been up here with you."

"Shut up," Mr. Jordon said, not even bothering to turn around. "Get yourself another drink. Go in the can there if you want, but keep your big mouth shut. You and me is like the nigger in jail—we got from now on."

She got up angrily and, taking both her drink and the bottle of whisky, went into the bathroom. There was a silence in the room as thick and enveloping as fog. Mr. Jordon acted as though Luther were no longer there. Presently the toilet flushed noisily and for a time the tap began to run in the basin and then it was shut off again. Luther shifted uncomfortably.

"Mr. Jordon, please, suh," he said softly. "I got tuh go, suh. We short-handed tonight."

The white man made no move; it was as though he had not heard—or, hearing, had decided that the words had no relationship to anything there in the room. Standing there, Luther felt the perspiration start running down his back. He was filled with humiliation, anger, and, deeper than that, with a numbing fear. In the room there was a tension of something going to happen, of a string drawn so taut that it was just about to snap.

Then suddenly the bathroom door opened and, without realizing that he was doing so, Luther looked up and over the head of Mr. Jordon at the woman coming unsteadily toward the bed. She was naked, and without her clothes she had lost the little dignity that she had managed to cling to clothed. Her breasts were heavy and made a series of creases beneath them to her somewhat puffy belly. Luther looked away quickly, knowing that the white man had seen his eyes move without knowing the reason why they had done so.

"Mister Jordon," he said softly, "I got to go now."

The woman hit against the side of the bed and cursed, and Mr. Jordon looked up as she sat down.

"Listen, you old bastard," she said. She giggled foolishly and then went on. "Look, daddy, I got my working clothes on. You better send that nigger out now, honey."

Mr. Jordon got suddenly to his feet. Then he looked at her again and turned angrily to Luther.

"Godamit, nigger," he said, "you put your damned eyes to the wall and keep them there. You know better than to be looking at a white woman that-a-way."

"That's right," she said, then giggled again. "All niggers are like that. All they ever think about is sleeping with white women."

Luther felt a sudden feeling of rage hit him like a blast of wind and for a moment he thought only of killing them both. To do so would be easy and it would release him immediately from the one thing that kept him bound there to the room. The thought of the act brought him no revulsion; to snuff out both of their lives would be nothing, no more than stepping on a roach or beating a snake to death with a stick. And yet he knew that he could not do it, for in a split second he had begun to rationalize and weigh his chances. Without a word he turned and walked from the room. Behind him he heard Mr. Jordon calling for him angrily, but he paid no attention, for nothing could have made him go back.

He went through the rest of the evening like a somnambulist, walking from the bar to the cocktail room, making change and answering questions, all with another part of himself. Later in the evening he saw Mr. Jordon come in and walk unsteadily to the bar, and when Luther saw him he looked away quickly. Trying to rationalize what had happened, he reached a point where it no longer mattered, where it was out of his hands completely and there was nothing that he could do about it.

That he had seen a nude white woman mattered little; however differently they might think, he had felt no quickening desire when he had seen her there in front of him. Had she not looked like a slightly puffy white slug, he might have felt differently, might have reacted toward her as he would toward any woman who seemed to him desirable. Nor was she the first white woman he had ever seen unclothed. When he had been a bellboy in the hotel, before the taproom had opened, prostitutes stopped there regularly, usually for a week or so before they moved on to the South or North, depending on the season. Some of them moved in late in the fall and stayed straight on through until the late spring. All of them had been careless of their attire around him, almost as though he were one of them, and a few had even offered their bodies in place of his split in their fee. What would he want of any woman so long as he had Eulia? And if a woman were white, her whiteness was only a symbol of something forbidden, to be taken as something denied, or else in revenge, a way of getting back at those who treated him as less than a man. Until tonight he had harbored no feelings of revenge, and even now it was something more than that which he felt.

He asked himself what it was; but, if anything, it seemed to him that what he really was reacting to was a great many things, and all of them at cross-purposes with each other. Only one thing was clear, and that was that he felt suddenly less than a man; it seemed to him that he had been emasculated in the hotel room above, as surely as though by a surgeon's scalpel.

He was not even glad when the evening was over and the last of the customers gone. He felt nothing save a kind of self-hatred. Counting his silver, he went up to the bar in front of the cash register and laid it out neatly in piles each totaling a dollar, waiting for Bob Giddings to convert it into bills.

"Luther," Bob said, "Mr. Jordon told me about what happened upstairs."

For a moment Luther felt a sudden surge of hope, almost of elation, that now Mr. Jordon would be punished for what he had done. Inwardly, and without his being conscious of it, this white man became for him the father symbol and he the son, chosen not by the happenchance of blood but by careful selection, who had been wronged and would be avenged.

"Godamit, Luther. You know better than to do a thing like that."

The symbol shattered and it was only a white man who was talking to him. He was the rejected, the unwanted; for him there was no logic in either rewards or punishments, the two confused so that he was unsure why he was the recipient of either.

"It wasn like he said it was," Luther said. "I wasn tryin to get a look at that woman. She big as a house anyway. How I holp not seein her?"

He spoke so rapidly that his words tumbled out. The face of the white man across the bar from him hardened; in one hand he held a salt sack into which he was spilling silver from the orderly piles on the back bar.

"Godamit, nigger, you puttin your word above a white man's?"

Luther did not answer; there was nothing that could have made him answer. He saw the white man cock his wrist so that he was holding the change sack like a club. Yet even this somehow had lost its meaning for him, and he felt no emotion as he saw the hand unclench and heard the silver spill metallically into the mouth of the sack again.

"Luther, you better watch your step. Two things in this world I won't stand for. One is an uppity nigger and the other is a nigger that looks at a white woman. You got that?"

Luther nodded but he did not speak. He could not have spoken, probably, even if he had wanted to. All at once everything seemed clear. He said to himself: He better get hisself another boy; I ain comin back

79

no more, not even to collect what he owes me for the two days I worked this week.

He turned slowly and walked out the door.

10. That evening Eric was coming for dinner. As Bessie drove along the highway from the college toward town she thought idly about what she would wear. They had no real plans about what they were going to do later, though he had mentioned something about pub-crawling in search of a woman who sometimes sang blues in and around the rural jooks. She drove skillfully and mechanically, weaving through the traffic without hardly being conscious of it. When she came into town she parked across from the post office.

There were five letters, and she noted that one of them, for her mother, was from Alberta. Three of them were circulars of one kind or another, and the last was for her, a letter from a girl she had known well in college who was now married to a dentist and living in Atlanta. Sitting in the car, she read it; the usual slightly scatterbrained account of domesticity, of her two children, of clothes, and of the parties to which she had been going. Putting it back into the envelope, Bessie felt a sudden twinge of envy. Almost savagely she started the car and, ramming it into gear, pulled away from the curb angrily.

By the time that she had driven home and parked the car under the trees at the side of the house her mood had passed. Running lightly up the steps into the house, she felt a feeling of elation. As she came into the living room her mother was sitting at the table by the window.

"Hello, Bessie, you home early."

"I know, Mama. Dr. Rogers had to run up to Jacksonville today and I left half an hour earlier than I usually do." She looked at the table. "Hmm, looks nice, Mama. Who's the fourth place for—Luther? His shift been changed at the shipyard?"

"No, honey, his shift ain changed none. I figured Eulia's daddy might like a meal he didn have to cook hisself."

"Mama."

"Hunh, baby?"

"Mama, I'm getting worried about you. Looks to me like this is getting right serious."

"Hush, chile. You talkin plumb foolish."

Bessie made a face. "Mama's got a feller," she chanted, "Mama's got a feller."

Her mother made a lunge for her and, laughing, Bessie dodged to the other side of the table. Like an imp she chanted the taunt again, always moving in the opposite direction from her mother and keeping the table between them. Finally she slipped momentarily on her high heels and the older woman caught her. For a moment they clung to each other, smothered with laughter.

"Mama, I almost forgot. There's a letter for you from Alberta. It's out on the hall table."

She lit a cigarette and plopped down on the sofa. Her mother came back into the room, reading the letter as she walked. All of a sudden she looked down at Bessie and smiled.

"Honey, Alberta comin; it say so right here in this letter. For two weeks' vacation, she say. I goin to see my baby again!"

"Oh, Mama, I'm so glad for you."

Bessie got up from the sofa and went over and kissed her mother. Holding her in her arms, she could feel her start to cry, then laugh instead, but the two were so closely mixed that there was no knowing where the one started and the other left off.

Bessie took off her clothes and slipped into her dressing gown, then went down the hall to the bathroom. She turned on the tub and, seasoning the churning water with bubblebath, went back to her room. Lighting a cigarette, she lay down on her bed, waiting for the tub to fill. From the window a breeze flowed diagonally across her and she opened up her robe so that it could play across her bare skin. As she lay there she suddenly knew that when Alberta came she was going to lose Eric.

It did not surprise her; it had always been that way. Alberta had had the best of everything, usually handed to her, but if it were not offered she would take it anyway. Alberta had always been prettier and had nicer clothes. She had always been her mother's pet. And when the chance for one of them to go away had come, it was Alberta who went without so much as an offer to let Bessie go instead.

Bessie got up from her bed and snuffed out her cigarette in the ash tray on the night table. Gathering her robe around her and knotting the belt, she went back to the bathroom. The tub was ready, hot and heaped high with fragrant white bubbles like the foam from a heavy surf. She hung her robe on the back of the door and stood for a moment, stretching on her toes and looking into the full-length mirror.

Her skin was brown. If she had been fairer it would have been golden; darker, the rich red brown of mahogany. Her legs were long and almost colt-like, her breasts pear-shaped, high, and firm, a little pointed at the tips. She came down on her heels and slowly lowered herself into the tub so that the foam came up to her neck. Above that her hair was piled high atop her head and secured with a ribbon. She lay back and closed her eyes.

Overhead, through the small opened window, she could hear the spasmodic noises from the quiet street. She heard a car go by, labored and noisy, and a voice call shrilly to whoever was driving. In the distance she heard a train and then the hysterical shriek of the five o'clock whistle at the packing house. A catbird in a nearby tree rasped several times and a dog barked. The warmth of the water soaked the tiredness out of her limbs. She felt drowsy and almost content, unable to move.

I'm not going to give him up, she told herself angrily, but it was hard for her to overcome the feeling of fatality which had spread over her earlier. It was as though she were still a child, competing for the affection of her mother and father with Alberta, and knowing that whatever she did, no matter, the results would always be the same. She tried to hate Alberta, but she could not even do that. Even if Alberta were not her sister she would have found it as difficult. It was only possible to hate her if you did not know her; once you did, you were lost. Alberta could no more help being the way she was than winter could stop following fall.

Bessie roused from her state of near coma and soaped herself well all over. In a moment she felt for the stopper chain with her foot and, working it in between her toes, pulled out the plug. She lay for a moment until the water was nearly gone, then stepped from the tub and rubbed herself briskly with a nappy blue towel.

Back in her own room, she lit a fresh cigarette and began to dress slowly. The little radio on the night table was playing Beethoven's second symphony and she wondered idly if Eric were listening to the same program. She told herself that maybe in four years Alberta might have changed, that what she herself had might be as desirable as that which belonged to someone else. Probably not, she told herself as she sat before the mirror combing her hair, but one could always hope. She fixed two clips at the square-cut neck of her black dress and snapped a bracelet on her wrist, then, turning off the radio, went out into the living room.

It looked nice, she told herself, comfortable and lived in, not like Queen Ethel's. From the kitchen the pungent aroma of frying chicken was barely evident. I'm in love and still hungry, she told herself and laughed, or maybe I'm not in love at all. She looked at her watch; Eric would be coming any minute now.

The morning had been rainy but in the afternoon it had cleared, and now in the night the air was soft as down. When they came out to the car Eric suggested they put the top down and Bessie stood aside ready to help.

"Come on," Eric laughed, "you can get in. The modern age decrees that it no longer takes three men and a small boy to put down a one-man top."

He opened the door for her, then he went around and got in on the other side. Reaching up, he unlatched the two securing locks at the top of the windshield and lifted the top free. Then he pushed a button, and with a little *hiissh* from the hydraulic motor the top slowly folded back into the well at the rear of the seats.

"Do Jesus," Bessie said.

"Thank you, Father," Eric answered. "You know, I'm surprised the white folks let us niggers have contraptions like this. Idle hands, you know."

He started the motor and swung out into the street and off toward the Dixie Highway. He drove rapidly, as usual, but with a sureness that made her feel safer than had she been traveling half as fast with another driver. She laid her head back on the seat and closed her eyes. The wind was cool to her face and she liked the feel of it clutching at her hair, secured by a handkerchief tied peasant-fashion under her chin. For no reason at all she put her palm out over the side of the car and felt the strong resistance of the wind, then, turning her fingers forward and forming them into a gooseneck, felt the wind wash around them without effort. The century of progress, she thought, everything changing except this. She wished that they could go on driving forever far into the night without stopping. She wished there were no gas rationing.

In a moment she turned her head a little and looked at Eric. His profile was strong and finely chiseled, intent on the road. She closed her eyes again.

"You're mighty silent," she said.

"I'm full," he answered. "If I didn't know your mama better I'd think she was trying to marry you off."

She giggled.

"You folks eat that way all the time?" he asked.

"Sure thing, even when we don't have you for dinner."

He lapsed into burlesque. "You mean you don't eat no side meat and greens, no red beans and rice, and no grits three times a day?"

"Only when we want to. And we don't sell all our red ration points to the white folks, either," she added bitterly. "We like roast beef and steaks."

He laughed. "There's going to be another trial blackout next week. You bought your ice picks and sharpened up your daddy's old razor? Soon as the lights go out we got to rise up and kill all the white folks."

Bessie giggled again. They turned off the Dixie Highway into a narrow road of crushed coquina rock that wound around like a snake off into the woods.

"I liked Eulia's father, Bessie. He reminds me a little of one of those Old Testament patriarchs, only he isn't old enough yet. I'd like to see him with a long beard and long white hair."

"I wish Mama were really serious about him. But Mama is so set in her ways. I know Daddy would have wanted her to marry again."

"What was your father like, Bessie?"

"A little like Luther, the way I remember him. The way he looked, I mean. Actually Luther's like Mama; he doesn't like any sort of change. I don't think he likes his new job. Daddy was a drifter. If he hadn't married Mama, I don't think anyone could ever have tied him down. He was good-looking, gay, and wonderful with us kids, especially Alberta."

She was silent for a moment, thinking of Alberta and feeling again the strange premonition that she had felt before dinner.

"Alberta's coming down next month," she went on. "Mama's all excited about it. She hasn't seen Alberta for nearly five years."

"What's she like, Bessie?"

"You'll see, Eric. She's the beauty of the family. Got most of the brains too, I reckon."

"Pretty as you are?"

"Prettier."

"Can't be, girl. It just can't be."

He put his hand out for hers and, giving it to him, she held on tight and felt the answering pressure of his fingers. She liked the shape of his hands, strong and masculine but with fingers that were long and tapering. Make it last, she said to herself, make it last a long time.

"It's up ahead there," he said, "that long wooden building."

"Shucks," she said, "I know this jook. I used to come out here when I was a kid. That is till Daddy found out and gave me a limbing."

She let go his hand as he swung off the road and parked.

Almost before the car stopped rolling, a young curbhop came running out. She was short and very dark, dressed in a red satin uniform that was like a ballet outfit crossed with a sunsuit. As she came up she smiled broadly.

"Whatchall want?" she asked. "Or is you comin in?"

"What kind of beer have you got?"

She screwed up her little child's face in an attempt at concentration. "We got Jax," she said hopefully.

"Is that all?"

"I doan rightly know. I go see what the man say."

She scurried away inside the door and in a moment was back again. "We got Jax," she said.

"Two Jax, then."

She was back almost before she had left. She locked the tray onto the door of the car and ran back for the beer and the glasses.

"Yawl needs me agin jest mash the horn, heah?"

Eric nodded and watched her scamper away and back into the long unpainted building. He poured the beer into the two glasses and handed one of them to Bessie. Inside they could hear the steady throb of a jook box, turned low, and above it the shrill voice of a man at the dice table.

"Sho cain win if yuh doan bet. Yo chance good as mine. Git yo bets up or stay way from the table. Either yuh is or yuh ain. Keep the dices on the table. Nothin on the floor counts but yo big feets."

They drank their beer slowly. In the background the beat of the jook box was steady as the pulse of a heart. Eric looked at his watch.

"If she comes, she ought to be here before too long. Imagine one woman trying to compete with that chromium, neon-lighted monster." He laughed. "They ought to call this the age of the jook box, the machine driving the folk artist out of business. Jook meaning pleasure house, maybe from the African, maybe not. Now the white folks have started calling it juke, and I read in a magazine where some fool woman says the word goes back to Chaucer and means 'house of sleep.' Only one thing she never explained was how anyone could hope to sleep in the same room with one."

He honked the horn and ordered another beer. Shortly the jook box stopped and someone began to run chords on a piano, only slightly out of tune but limber, and with a tinny quality that made it sound, with a little imagination, almost like a harpsichord. Then whoever it was began to play. The music was merely a blues, any blues, and in a way every blues. It was as changing as light on certain kinds of silk which have a heavy metallic sheen; first it was sad and haunting, then it was brash again, hard and full of a weird defiance. In the pattern it wove, the left hand was always predominant but seldom consciously heard in the intricate weaving of the right hand. In a moment the piano was joined by something that sounded a little like drums.

"Washboard?" Bessie asked.

Eric listened for a minute. "No," he said. "It sounds like it, but I think it's a man with a pair of spoons."

Then a guitar came in, followed by a kazoo. The beat became as strong as mud-black coffee and the guitar was so complex that it sounded almost as though there might have been two stringed instruments instead of one. They stopped that blues and went into another which sounded almost the same but was as subtly different as night is from day. After a few choruses a woman began to sing; her voice was deep as a well and as rich as whipped cream; she started each phrase a little off pitch, then slurred into pitch, and the device made you focus your attention on every word.

She sang:

> "Layin in my bed wid my face turned to the wall
> Lord, layin in the bed wid my face turned to the wall
> Tryin to count these blues, so I could sing them all.
>
> "Memphis, Rampart, Beale Street set them free
> Lord, Memphis, Rampart, Beale Street set them free
> Graveyard, 'Bama bound, Lord, Lord, come from stingaree.
>
> "Lord, sittin on the Southern, gonna ride, ride all night long
> Lord, sittin on the Southern, gonna ride all night long
> Downhearted, so cold, they was all good times.
>
> "Lord, 'rested at midnight, jailhouse made me lose my mind
> Lord, 'rested at midnight, jailhouse made me lose my mind
> That luckin bo-wevil made me think of old boom times.

"Lord, goin to sleep for Mama just now got bad news
Lord, goin to sleep now, just now got bad news
To try to dream away my troubles, countin these blues . . ."

She finished one chorus and the orchestra took over, weaving the simple melody into something that was a three-voice elaboration. It kept worrying you and wouldn't let you go, accented by the rhythmic pattern of the spoons, building up to something always that was never quite there. Then the vocal came in again.

"Like it?" he whispered.

"Hmmn," she answered.

"Love me?" he whispered.

"What?"

"Love me?"

"Yes," she answered. "Yes, Eric."

She fumbled in her bag for a cigarette. In the back of her mind she was thinking of Alberta. For a moment she thought she was going to cry.

11. The college of which Ezekiel was president was, in a sense, neither fish nor fowl. It had no real endowment, nor was it actually sponsored by the state; rather its support lay somewhere between the two. A small endowment fund had been willed or given by prominent white citizens of the town, usually wealthy winter visitors from New England, but it had never reached a point where its income was sufficient to furnish more than a fraction of the amount needed for annual running expenses. The rest, after the tuition money was thrown into the general hopper, was provided by the state in a rather haphazard manner. It was almost as though the college were too important to let wither away completely, yet hardly worthy of nurturing into full usefulness.

Each year, then, the president of the college had a few weeks of preliminary worry, a day of real hell, and perhaps a week afterward when, although he was reasonably certain that his budget would be officially approved, he was nonetheless on tenterhooks until it was. The day of hell was when the three-man examining board came to the school and made a survey to determine how successful was the segregated educational experiment that the college was carrying out.

Actually the college was not too different from any number of little colleges in the Middle West which are for the most part unknown beyond the borders of the state in which they are located. Physically its plant was on a par with many such institutions. Like them, too, there was a religious background which resulted in an almost mid-Victorian set of moral standards so far as the administration was concerned. Academically there was little difference save that perhaps it had a handful of better-trained and more competent teachers, frozen into such jobs because even in the North teaching positions in white colleges were, with a very few exceptions, not open to even the best-prepared colored professors.

The student body also differed little in its actual make-up. Many of the students were from rural families but many were from urban areas, and class lines were as rigidly drawn, perhaps even more so, though for less rational reasons. Most students were a little less conservative than their parents and a good deal more eager to break down at once the restrictions which held them securely chained to second-class citizenship. Yet many of them would become more conservative and more cautious as they grew older and found that individually it was possible for them to benefit from segregation. Some few, in fact, would grow up to be greater exploiters of the Negro masses than were the whites themselves.

Perhaps there were a few more campus radicals, but if so, their make-up was slightly different. Subject practically every day to racial insult and discrimination, they were highly race-conscious and their radicalism was racial rather than economic; they thought less in terms of overthrowing those who keep all the masses of the South in check than in doing away with jimcrow.

Not all of the students came from the South by any means. Many came because in the Northern urban areas where they lived the cost of living was so high that their parents were forced to take advantage of the segregated South's lower tuition fees. Others were either barred from the supposedly unrestricted colleges of their vicinity or were excluded by that aristocrat of all quasi-segregated education, the quota system.

The actual campus life was of the sort that has become almost universal. There was a fraternity and sorority system, with the same evils apparent wherever it is tolerated, and at the top was a snobbish social system which was no better or worse than that of any college community. At the bottom were the usual barbarians, so called because they either did not choose or were not chosen to become a part of the fraternity system, and they were apt to be aloof and not a little frustrated, resentful and probably with good reason.

Each year there was the big game, the annual prom and a series of smaller dances, an elaborate home-coming day, and a great many less important social functions. It must even be admitted that there was a certain amount of drinking and some fornication but the ratio differed slightly, if at all, from that found elsewhere.

For Ezekiel the administration of the college was not easy. Being the head of any institution is usually a thankless enough task, but being a Negro and the head of a segregated school, subservient for the most part to white funds, makes it doubly difficult. It might be argued that he was really a boy sent to do a man's job. Certainly it was true that his academic background was sketchy at best and that in a competitive society unrestricted by segregation he might never have attained such a post, though in answer it could have been pointed out that many a white college head is actually little more than a glorified drummer.

But within the framework wherein he had to function because of regional mores he probably did better than the dominant society realized.

Of the three-man board who came each year to see to his budget, only Cal Thornton, the editor of the Citrus City *Telegram,* realized this. Actually the two were not unalike. Each might be conservatively rather than militantly liberal, yet both wanted to do good, though often they would compromise rather than take a stand. Each was caught up in his own Southernness and shut off from any logical solution of the problems that bothered them both because of the same wall. It was not so high a wall as it seemed; it merely cast a long shadow. Yet neither had the militancy to jump over it or the good sense to ignore it completely. It was always there between them, and both of them were acutely conscious of it.

The head of the board took Ezekiel to be a fool and a tool who would do exactly as he, Wilbur Daniels, wished him to do. Born a poor cracker over on the other side of the state, Wilbur had, by a series of incidents, become a very wealthy man, if measured by local rather than national standards. How he had gained these riches varied with each telling. After he had seen the movie *Gone with the Wind* he had been known to mutter about the old plantation house, for he was a man with an intense regional pride and he was not unaware of class lines. Usually, however, and rather closer to the truth, it was a story of hard work and native shrewdness, and his luck in buying into a soft-drink company native to the South at a time when such stock was a phenomenal bargain which would pyramid to dizzy heights never hoped for by its founder, let alone Wilbur Daniels. With part of his profits he had bought, during the depression, a huge estate completely surrounded by vast citrus groves which more than repaid this investment over a period of years.

Wilbur Daniels was fond of saying that no one was a greater friend to the Negro than he was; that is, he would add, providing that the nigger knew his place. That place was clearly defined in his mind, and it resembled nothing so much as an endless assembly line of Negroes patterned after those he had seen in the movies. He yearned for bosomy mammies with handkerchiefed heads, kindly old family retainers with gray hair and gnarled black hands bearing trays of frosted juleps, and erect young chauffeurs and strong-backed yard boys who would gladly lay down their lives for Old Massa Daniels. In secret he also sometimes visioned comely young and light-skinned upstairs maids as well.

But somehow none of these ever seemed to come his way. At times Wilbur thought of Ezekiel as a sort of latter-day Booker T. Washington, who would set up what in reality would prove to be a personal training center for future Daniels employees. In his vanity he did not realize how easy he was to fool by a special brand of cajolery, and had he known it, the results would have been catastrophic. Probably if he had ever found out how cynically Ezekiel Uncle-Tommed to get around him, he would not only have joined the Klan but given his personal fortune to expedite its program.

The third member of the board was a nonentity, though his name was actually Roger Sherman. Never having had an opinion of his own, he sat back and waited for others to make up his mind for him. Facts bored him because he could not absorb them; like certain kinds of food, they gave him acute indigestion. Personally he much preferred Cal Thornton to old Wilbur, Cal's father-in-law, but he was not enough of a fool to show which way his likes and dislikes lay. He was wise enough to give the impression that he was always impartial, but actually he always sided with Wilbur on any issue of real importance. After all, Wilbur had money and he was also a power in the state political machine.

Ezekiel had formed the habit of dropping into Cal Thornton's office at the *Telegram* to talk over the budget a week or so before the day that the three-man committee was scheduled to visit the college. Of the three-man board, Thornton was the only one who realized what Ezekiel was trying to accomplish, and also he was the only one who had any real interest in race relations. He had inherited the paper from his father, and since he had become its guardian it had not only become more liberal but had also taken on a vitality which shortly made it one of the most important organs in the state.

Cal Thornton was in his late thirties, a tall man, but with a thinness which seemed almost a deformity and was released only by the intense vitality of his movements. His hair, blond and beginning to thin at the top, was worn long and always seemed tousled; in conversation he was apt to worry it with his right hand, as though by so doing he was helped in reaching for the exact word he wanted. Careless of his personal appearance, he was much given to odd jackets and slacks in cool weather and to rumpled seersucker suits when it turned humid.

He had been educated at Harvard and had gone from there to the Columbia School of Journalism. After half the term was over he had left in a huff after a long and particularly bitter argument about the South with one of the professors of that graduate school. The next week he had landed a job on the desk of one of the wire services, where he was completely content and learned more about a great many things than he had in his four years at Harvard and his short stint at Columbia.

He had shared an apartment with a boy whom he had known at Harvard, and this was perhaps the happiest period in his whole life, for it was the nearest he had ever come to the intellectual life and in that one year he had formed a wide circle of acquaintances who were in some way or another connected with the arts. It had been a year of informal evenings when anyone was liable to drop around and sit over a bottle talking brilliantly about a wide variety of subjects. And since he had a retentive mind and one which absorbed ideas like a sponge, he was able to hold his own and even gain the reputation of being a bright young man.

He had never wanted to write himself, in the creative sense, but he had a great deal of respect for and even a little awe of those who did. At one of these informal evenings he had been instantly drawn to a girl who dropped in with a group late one night. There had been a long conversation about the South and he had talked brilliantly about the thing he knew best: the history of that region up to the turn of this century. As she had left he had asked her if he might see her again and she had given him her address and phone number.

Two days later he called her and made a date for the following evening. As he sat waiting in the living room of her apartment for her to finish dressing he came across her name on the cover of one of the magazines on the coffee table; with his bad association of names, he had not until now realized that she was one of his favorite short-story writers. They had gone out that night and frequently thereafter, until they arrived at a sort of understanding that they would see each other without the bother of having to make dates. They did all the rather foolish but enjoyable things that one did in that period when budgets were none too expendable—rode the Staten Island ferry, went to Hoboken to drink beer, saw plays when he was able to secure free tickets, and rode on Sunday afternoons up Riverside Drive atop a Fifth Avenue bus after eating in the cafeteria at the zoo in Central Park.

Then one night he had ended up in her bed, exactly how he was unable to recall. It had merely happened quite naturally and with a wonderful ease and lack of embarrassment for him. The next morning he had awakened early, when it was light enough to see clearly within the room but before it was actually daylight. He had looked around the room for a moment, orienting himself, and then turned his head toward her. She lay on her back, one arm thrown up and her long dark hair, tinged slightly with red, a little tousled but not untidy against the white pillow and partially covering her right breast. He had had women before, but never in this way; always before it had been the hurried and fumbling act in the back seat of an automobile, or on the sofa in some living room, harried by the realization that parents at double-feature movies sometimes leave after the A picture. Her body was beautiful, almost mystical, the upright and firmed young breasts, the gentled curve of the abdomen, the long, clean limbs.

As he looked at her she had awakened drowsily, almost as though he had somehow willed it.

"Hello," she whispered, and, turning to him, kissed his lips gently.

He had rolled over to her with almost a sob. Afterward she had looked at him and smiled.

"You don't have to marry me," she laughed softly.

He was a little angry that his feelings should be so transparent to her.

"Darling," she taunted him, "your mother told you that nice girls don't, didn't she? That sometimes they may want to, but a gentleman must always help them to be strong, not encourage them in their weakness."

He nodded, and the image of his mother materialized in his mind, the tall woman with the stately walk, white hair, and a vacant but beautiful face.

"Well," she added, kissing him again, "now you know. Darling, the whole trouble is that you were brought up all wrong. I've got to do something about it, I guess. You don't really know very much, do you?"

He started to protest, but she broke in. "Sure, I know. You know the history of the dead and the figures made glittering by time and because they played hard and lost. Baby, I've been in the South, and almost any bartender knows as much about the War between the States as you do."

Again he started to be angry, but he knew it was true. If he had loved her less, he might have walked out. Instead he stayed, and she had done a good job of starting his re-education. She told him what books to read, she introduced him to the histrionics of left-wingers who fought the revolution, past, present, and future, in Greenwich Village apartments, and, most important, she took him to Harlem. It was not to the uptown cabarets that they went, but to parties given by intellectuals and artists, and because of her they accepted him in spite of his accent. At times this was hard for him to swallow, but he did, in great and often undigested chunks. And then his father died.

He went home and took over the paper. He was happy in his work, and yet because of what she had done for him he felt almost at times an alien; then his mother took him over and the whole overrich pull of the region got to him again. In terror he fled back to New York, supposedly on a vacation but actually to see Kay. They had one evening together in which they fought in the cold gray of morning and then, crying, made up. But she knew and she told him so.

"I've lost, Cal," she told him. "I didn't have you long enough."

Torn between two things he loved, he chose the older and, without being conscious of it, also the safer. He wrote to her upon his return and begged her to marry him, to come down at once. Her answer was that she could not compete against both the magnolias and his mother. Furious, he did not write her again for a week, and then his letter was returned unopened a few days after he read about her marriage in the paper.

That night he went out and got drunker than he had ever been in his life, and he stayed that way for three days; shortly after this he married Willie Mae Daniels. They built a large modern house on one of the lakes, and at regular intervals they had slightly antiseptic children until they reached the number of four, and there were then no more.

He thought a great deal about Kay and read her novels without writing to tell her how much he liked them. What liberality he had was due to her, but it was tempered by the doubts instilled in him by his mother, his wife's money, and most of all by his Southernness, composed of legend and myth which was in perpetual conflict with what he knew to be right.

At heart he was a human man; he wanted to do good but he had dulled the will for doing so.

In the building where the *Telegram* was located there were no problems for Ezekiel. Entering the building, he felt, as he always did, the assurance that he was known as the president of the college and that almost everyone there realized that he had free access to Cal. The elevator operator, a squat little black man, greeted him as he always did when there were no white people in the cage, with deference. He closed the grilled door with a flourish and opened it again with the same flourish when Ezekiel got off.

On this day Ezekiel was not kept waiting as long as usual. As he sat there on the bench he purposely watched the clock, and a bare six minutes later the girl at the desk told him that Mr. Thornton would see him now. It was not quite twenty minutes past eleven by the clock.

When he entered the editor's inner office he was greeted warmly and with a firm handshake.

"Well, Ezekiel," Cal Thornton said, "I've been expecting you this week. Sit down, sit down."

"You're sure you aren't too busy?"

"Never too busy for you, Ezekiel. Anything special, or did you just want to run over the budget and brief me?"

"Well, I did think I might tell you beforehand what to expect. Not that I anticipate anything in the way of difficulties."

"Nor do I, but it's a good idea to make sure."

They went over the figures together and seemed to be in complete agreement. Cal Thornton heartily backed up Ezekiel in his desire to give Bessie a raise, and the other rather cut-and-dried faculty raises were mere routine. There was little else that seemed to call for any comment. Then suddenly Cal Thornton grew serious.

"Ezekiel," he said, "did you read the editorial I wrote last week, the one about the danger of pushing too hard for racial justice?"

"Yes, Mr. Thornton, I read it."

"What did you think about it—yourself, I mean? Be honest now, tell me the truth. We know each other well enough not to mince words."

For a moment Ezekiel did not answer. It was not that he did not know what to say, but rather that he must pharse his words in a way that would not only satisfy the white man seated across from him, but himself as well.

"I agreed with it for the most part."

"How do your people feel?"

Ezekiel hedged a little. "Well, Mr. Thornton, you know how my people are. The mistake most of you white folks make is that you think of Negroes as all being pretty much alike. They just aren't. The more solid element agrees with you for the most part, as I do. The hotheads probably think you're about as bad as Mr. Bilbo, but they are in the minority. In between are a whole lot of Negroes who never read your editorial, or any editorial for that matter."

Cal Thornton got to his feet. "That's about what I figured. We're making progress, Ezekiel, but like you once said, we've got to learn how to crawl before we can walk."

Holding out his hand, he shook Ezekiel's warmly, then, taking the other's arm, steered him toward the door. Once there, he postponed the leaving momentarily.

"I'm glad you dropped in, Ezekiel," he said. "I'm always glad to see you. We've got a job to do, you and I, and I need your help. I want you to promise me one thing, agreed?"

"Of course, Mr. Thornton."

"Well, it's this. Every man makes mistakes, honest mistakes, and I sometimes think especially myself. If I ever make one in trying to help your people, you'll let me know?"

"I promise, sir. I don't expect to ever have to say anything, but if the occasion arises, you have my word."

Cal Thornton thanked him and shook hands again briefly, then turned back to his desk. Ezekiel walked out through the big newsroom and past the gate into the open space where the elevator stopped. Going down, he spoke a few words to the elevator man and then went hastily to his car and headed back toward the college. He looked at his watch; he would be in time for lunch if he hurried, and if he wasn't, Ethel would be sure to give him a lecture.

He smiled to himself as he followed the flow of traffic out the Dixie Highway. He felt better about the coming board inspection than he had ever felt before and, thanks to Cal Thornton, more secure in feeling that as usual his budget would be approved. Suddenly he began thinking about his father, who had been dead for a number of years. Now why, he asked himself, did I happen to think of him at this particular time?

What he had remembered was that one day he had come home from school insecure and afraid over a misunderstanding that he had had with a teacher. It had started over a minor thing but had widened into what seemed to him an unsurmountable breach which could only result in his failure to pass his term's work. What he had forgotten were his father's words.

"Ezekiel," his father had said, "I glad that you come to me. A boy's father can be wrong sometimes. If I is, I want you to know that you are free to come tell me so."

All that he remembered was that he had suddenly felt secure again for some reason, that his father had provided him with what he needed most.

12. It had not been an easy decision to make. Eulia and Luther had talked it over for a month without arriving at any definite decision. It was not that they could not get along on what he was making. By now his work at the shipyard was paying him, counting overtime, as much as he had made at the bar, including even tips. No, it was not the money alone; it was more than that. Always they had thought in terms of a place of their own, and Eulia had been putting part of what she made each week into the bank toward that eventuality.

Then, hearing about the new housing project which was going up for colored shipyard workers, Luther had put in an application for one of the apartments. It was not the same, perhaps, as a house of their own, but at least it was better than living the way they had been living. Perhaps if Luther had not been working way over on the other side of Citrus City, they would have waited, but it seemed to them that he spent all his free time on the bus. If they decided to take an apartment in the project, he would be able to walk to and from work.

Too, they had to take into consideration Eulia's father. Their moving would leave him alone, and he seemed too used to having Eulia to batch it, or at least Luther felt this to be true. Eulia told him, however, that her father was not that old and they should not let his being alone stand in their way. What really bothered her was how he would get his meals, for as long as she had known him he had never so much as touched a frying pan. Finally, and without telling Luther, she spoke to her father one night as the two of them were sitting on the front stoop waiting for Luther to come back from the drugstore over town where he had gone to get some ice cream.

"Daddy," she said, "Luther an me been thinkin some on movin over to the project."

It was dark on the stoop and she could not see the expression on his face, for he was back in the shadow and away from the light. She could only see the red coal of his cigar blinking in the dark.

"What did you finally figure to do?" he asked.

She could tell nothing from the sound of his voice; it was the way it always was, deep and even-toned.

"We doan rightly know," she went on. "It ain easy to move one way or the other. Then we worried some bout you—Luther specially. How would you get along, Daddy?"

"I got along for fifty-six years," he told her. "One way or another, I reckon I can always manage to git along."

"What would you do about meals?"

"I'd manage, girl."

"But, Daddy, you cain cook."

He chuckled. "I was cookin fore you was born, chile. Even your mama didn know, but once I cooked on a railroad diner. I don't reckon I forgot how."

They had left the subject there, unsettled either way, and yet they now had an understanding. When Luther came back with the ice cream she had not told him of her talk with her father, neither there on the porch nor later in their own room. It was something to be held in reserve until such time as they really had to make up their minds. Now they could afford to wait, working the thing over between them until they reached a point where they had to act. Soon the project would be complete and then it would be time for action. Giving up her job and having a home of her own was the one thing in life she wanted most.

But now that she knew that eventually she was going to have it, that in itself was enough.

And then suddenly something on which neither of them had planned made up their minds for them. She had said nothing to Luther until she was certain, and then one night in bed she had told him that she was going to have a baby. The next day he had put down the first month's rent at the project. They would be able to move within a month or six weeks.

It had not been easy to tell Mrs. Randall she was leaving. She had never worked for a white woman before who treated her as well, or who maintained as close a relationship with her. She remembered how when first she had gone on the job she had felt a hidden resentment. She had known Jefferson Randall since he was a young man going away to college, for she had gotten her first job with his mother. This handsome girl he married had seemed to her an outsider, and she had meant to keep their relationship on those terms. But it had not worked out that way. Instead there had grown up between them a very warm feeling.

However, she had to be told. Eulia had chosen a morning when the two of them were alone in the kitchen. It had taken her several false tries in her mind before she had finally been able to put it into words.

"Miz Randall," she had said, deciding that the best way was to be direct, "I goin to be leavin you fore too long."

"Oh, Eulia, no! Why?"

"Well, me and Luther been fixin to have a place of our own. We got one now in the project. I might not have done it right off like this exceptin I goin to have a baby."

Mrs. Randall had lit a cigarette. "I don't blame you," she said slowly. "I don't think I'd like working in somebody else's kitchen either, if I could stay in my own." Then she laughed suddenly. "Only, Eulia, I don't know what to do in a kitchen. Whatever in the world am I going to do?"

"I find you another girl, Miz Randall. They hard to find now, but I get one just as good as me."

"No, Eulia, no one could be as good as you are. I want you to know that. I want you to know too that I never could have gotten along without you. Jeff would have left me months ago!"

The two of them were silent, and the only sound in the kitchen was

98

the faint whir of the electric clock on the wall. In a moment Mrs. Randall ground out her cigarette in the ash tray and looked up at Eulia. She felt as always a deep regard for this ginger-colored woman whom she had grown to depend on and who had never once let her down. She was sad at the loss but she was glad for Eulia. In her own way she thought she understood, and yet she knew that she could never be sure.

"Eulia," she said slowly, "I hope you've been happy here."

"Yessum."

"I mean I hope I've made you realize that I'm on your side. I don't know quite how to say what I mean. I've never known any Negroes and I don't like what happens down here. I"—she laughed—"I seem to be making a speech," she said hastily. "I'm sorry."

She was filled with a complete feeling of frustration that bordered almost on futility. If it were not for Jeff, she would have gone home, for in a way she was almost as much an alien as Eulia. And yet, because of what others had done and because her skin too happened to be white, there was a wall between them there in the kitchen.

"Miz Randall," Eulia said, "I liked workin for you. Better than anyone I ever worked for before. The way I feel, there ain no words for neither. You been most like a friend than someone I was workin for."

She shrugged and the two of them suddenly looked at each other and started to laugh. Their mirth seemed to be catching, and suddenly there was no wall between them.

"Eulia, you come by and see me every now and then. And let me know about the baby. I do want to know, really I do."

"Sho, Miz Randall. I'll send Luther around to tell you soon as it come."

Looking at Eulia, Mrs. Randall felt a sudden hatred of everything for which the South stood. Seeing how fine Eulia looked, clean and bright and with an inner dignity that she herself felt unable to match, she wondered how anyone could deny to her human equality. Suddenly she went and put her arms around Eulia, her head against the fresh white uniform. She smelled the clean starch aroma in the material and felt the soft and regular rise and fall of Eulia's breasts. Without embarrassment she kissed Eulia lightly on the cheek.

"Bless you," she said hurriedly, and turned away.

The next month seemed to Eulia a period of newness. Within her a new life was beginning to stir; the first time that the baby kicked lightly it filled her with a feeling of wonder. She had been near enough to birth all her life so that there could be no strangeness in it for her, but to have the cycle she knew so well happening within her own body made a difference. Too, she was thinking constantly of their apartment, and in a way it seemed to her almost the beginning point of her marriage. What had come before seemed to her somehow only the preparation for what was to happen on the day that she and Luther crossed the threshold of their own apartment in the project. Buying the little furniture that they would need added to the illusion.

It was a thing not to be rushed, an experience which must be prolonged in order to be savored to its fullest extent. She and Luther devoted their Saturday nights to shopping, the month before they moved, going about it with a care which made it become for them almost a game. Each piece they purchased had an importance out of all proportion to its material value; but in their minds a bargain became as vital a triumph as the taking of a key piece in a game of chess. To find something that they had seen in one store for a few dollars less in another was more than a saving in dollars and cents, and realizing that the white men who waited on them were in a way frustrated by their deliberation, they purposely prolonged it. And then, after the stores closed, they would drive out to a colored roadhouse or wayside stand and talk over the evening while they ate a sandwich and drank a bottle of beer.

Now that Luther was on the day shift, changed over after starting his work there at night, there was a difference too. There was an intimacy to their marriage which they had missed before, when both were working at different hours of the day and night. Discovering this, they seemed to find areas of their relationship which they had not realized existed. It made their marriage seem more stable, as if overnight they had become married a long time. Certainly they were closer than they had ever been before, and in a different way.

Eulia talked to Luther about his job, which he had not liked before but had now grown used to. He told her how the shipyard looked and how although it was located inland, welded sections were trucked to the St. John's River and shipped up to Jacksonville where they were assembled. He was vague on the details, but he was clear on the part that was played by the eight-man crew of which he was a member. It was hard work and it was dirty work, but for the first time in his life he seemed to be a part of something, where before he had only thought of himself as a single entity.

But mostly they talked about the baby. Secretly Eulia hoped it would be a girl, though because she thought Luther wanted a boy, she kept her hopes to herself. It was true that Luther wanted a son, but it was also true that he would be just as happy with a little girl. They were actually a little silly about the whole thing, and every now and then they would realize it and feel a little embarrassment; it was a little foolish at their age to be worked up over something like that.

They drove a lot on the evenings they did not shop because the stores were closed. They even formed the habit of driving by certain little houses in the white residential districts of town, as though already they saw beyond the move to the project, to the time when they would have a home of their own. But mostly they just drove on those highways and byways which were most likely to be deserted. Sometimes they felt as though the day when they were going to move to the project would never come; at other times it seemed to them as though it were rushing toward them like an express train and would catch them unprepared.

The day came at last. They had gone to the apartment the night before to make certain that the furniture which they had bought had been delivered and now, early in the morning, they were packing what they were taking from Eulia's house in the car. Luther would carry in the things and then, leaving the car under the carport, walk on to work. That evening they would have their first meal together under their new roof. . . .

When Luther was gone Eulia stood in the living room looking around at the piles of clothes and things from the store which they had not yet unpacked. She knew that there was a good day's work ahead of her, but she was unable to start at once. First she must walk around the apartment again. Even if she had seen it dozens of times, no matter; the compunction within her was too strong to resist.

She walked into the kitchen, which caught the morning light and seemed almost too tiny to contain it. The linoleum floor was dirty, marked with the footprints of the workmen who had finished laying it only a few days before. She walked over to the sink, recessed into a row of cabinets which filled the smaller wall of the room. Behind her was the stove and an electric icebox; against the far wall was the new kitchen table and chairs, brave in their red newness. The windows over the sink were dirty and without curtains, and she opened them wide to let in fresh air. It was a good kitchen, she thought, small but planned for efficient working. As she stood there she thought of the kitchen at the Randalls'. It had been bigger than this, surely, but she was glad to be free of it. It was her own where she was now.

She turned back through the living room to the bedroom which was to be hers and Luther's. Here too she opened the windows and looked out. The room faced on the back, away from the street and to the west. It was dark now, but there would be sun there in the afternoon, and not early in the morning to reach in and wake them on those days that Luther could sleep late. She walked through to the little room where they would keep the baby, and then back into the living room again.

As she stood there she could still smell faintly the sickly sweet odor of the new paint. Everything seemed so new and barren that for a moment she had a feeling closely akin to fright. Would she ever be able to make it a home, or would it always remain like this, a cold little series of boxes shoved quickly too close together? She wished that Luther were here with her, but even thinking about him made it all right again.

She looked around quickly to find a point of beginning, to form in her mind a schedule of work which would put the place in some kind of order by the time Luther returned from the shipyard around eight-thirty. On the little table by the couch she noticed the radio, the one they had purchased at the same time as the furniture. She plugged it into the wall socket behind the couch and in a moment music swelled out into the room.

She noticed the picture that Bessie had given them when she had learned that they were moving to the project. It was in the corner by the door, its face turned to the wall. Bessie had suggested that they buy things for the living room of the same colors as those in the picture, so that the whole room would blend together. Eulia went over and stood the picture against a chair where she could look at it as she worked. Then she went out into the kitchen for a mop and a pail. But when she came back she was not satisfied.

She looked around until she found a can of nails that they had brought along from her house. Picking out a long thin nail that would not crack the plaster, she looked around for the hammer. She was not able to find it and, suddenly scuffing off one shoe, she used it to drive the nail down in at an angle, and hung the picture. Standing back, she studied the effect. The whole room suddenly seemed more alive.

13. Once each year, for a day, the college took on a special atmosphere. It was no holiday, though it had some of the characteristics common to such days, for there was a feeling of anticipation in the air. Fried chicken and ice cream were served in the middle of the day, and an unofficial edict was laid down by the administration that all men students should wear coats to lunch and for this one day no girl should appear on the campus in a dress with a sun back. For over a decade or more the day had taken on a pattern as formal, in its own way, as a ritual dance. To the cynical among the faculty it was the day that the white folks came to look over their black children, and if they were found happy, carefree, and as industrious as it was safe for them to be, they were assured of the leavings from the big house for yet another year. For the new students it was likely to be something of an ordeal because it had yet to be experienced, but to those who had been through it the year before the day was a source of remarks insulting to white folks in general and to the committee in particular. Only to the president of the college, and to Ethel, his wife, who entertained at the end of the day, did the tour of inspection have a seriousness that went more than skin deep.

This pattern had not been arrived at overnight; it was something that had been evoked by trial and error, and by compromise. There was, for example, the problem of segregation. One would think that it might have been handled in one of two ways—either it existed or it did not exist. But there were too many factors involved to allow so simple and direct a point of departure. Instead the attempt was made, by a series of hairline checks and balances, and more than a measure of mumbo-jumbo, to show that although it actually did exist, it must not appear to do so.

The day always began about ten-thirty in the morning, when the three-man board arrived in the long maroon Packard sedan owned by Wilbur Daniels. The chauffeur was white, for old man Daniels firmly believed in the folklore about the Negro being constitutionally unable to cope with any bit of machinery more complex than a lawn mower. When the car entered the gates and headed for a parking spot beneath a clump of trees the president of the college was there to meet it almost before the wheels stopped spinning. For the next hour and a half there was a conducted tour of the classrooms, starting with the domestic-science department, where the board was served coffee and doughnuts by the women students. It was thought by the board that these delicacies were prepared for them by the students themselves, as was the tasty repast of fried chicken and hot biscuits served in the dining room at noon. The truth of the matter was that the woman instructor always prepared the coffee and doughnuts, and the chicanery involved concerning the chicken and biscuits was even more complicated. Actually it was prepared by an old woman who lived off in the scrub and was then transported to the college in a washtub, where it was reheated. There was no one who could cook chicken so well or turn out biscuits that were so light and flaky.

Somewhere along the way the president of the college disappeared for a hasty lunch, for although he sat at table with the board on the raised dais in the commons, he partook neither of food nor drink; eating at the same table with a Negro was for Wilbur Daniels as unbreakable a taboo as that concerning incest. Usually after the store-bought ice cream had been devoured by the three white guests there was a short program by some of the musical students. It always featured work songs and a few spirituals, sung with vigor and a certain amount of well-rehearsed pathos. Then after the board had met in the president's office to thrash over the matter of the budget for the coming year, the president's wife, weather permitting, entertained at a lawn party. Since this affair was given out of doors, even with the faculty and a handful of favored students attending, none of those rules of racial etiquette so dear to the hearts of the senior board member were violated.

Once this rather self-conscious mingling of the races had run its course, the board was quickly whisked away in the long maroon sedan. It is problematical which of the two groups was more relieved.

As Ezekiel stood by the window in his office looking down the driveway toward the road he was more than conscious of all this. The big Packard was due any moment, and the realization filled him with no special pleasure. He wished the day were over, the appropriation granted, and that he were home in his study with a book. It was a nuisance, the kind of performance that he knew he must put on, and though he always was able to justify it; nevertheless it filled him with an unclean feeling closely akin to singing for his supper. In particular he resented Wilbur Daniels. The truth of the matter was that he disliked him, and most of all because he was a white, a state of affairs that often worried him. Was it because he was jealous of what Wilbur Daniels had accomplished in spite of his limited talents? Or was it that he really hated all white men?

He did not think so, but he could never be sure. There were times, he knew, when he did, yet they did not often occur, and when they did, it seemed to him that he was only striking out at something blindly in resentment. For Cal Thornton, on the other hand, he had the utmost respect and even something which bordered on close affection. But if he were honest he was forced to admit that for Wilbur Daniels he had a contempt that came as near to hatred as any emotion he had ever experienced.

He looked down the drive again and felt a subconscious wish that when the car should appear he would be able to will it to stop at a certain point and come no farther. When it should come and he started out to meet it he knew this feeling would rapidly pass, at least on the surface, and that the day would go along fairly well. Of course Wilbur Daniels would call him doctor or professor, out of no respect but merely because he would not use the customary preface of mister where any Negro was concerned, and he realized that what the white man really meant was the universal "boy" that his kind always used in addressing all Negroes regardless of their age, but this he could ignore. The basis of his uneasiness probably was that in the presence of this old cracker he felt naked, stripped of all the symbolic clothing of his position, and made no longer a figure with status, but merely another Negro.

Down the road he saw the car approaching; it was traveling at a good clip, the way old man Daniels always liked to be driven, as though by this he showed the contempt in which he held the law. It was as if he meant to show that it pertained to lower mortals but, because of his money and position, not to himself. Ezekiel carefully put out his cigar in the big onyx ash tray on his desk and went down the corridor. As he walked toward the car he felt better; the realization of the little ways in which he was fooling the committee gave him a sense of revengeful power, a little thing blown up in his mind out of all proportion to its actual importance.

He greeted them heartily, shaking hands only with Cal Thornton and only after Thornton had made the initial move. Gathering them together in his usual tactful way, he herded them toward the building where the domestic science maintained an experimental classroom. He walked almost abreast of them but actually a shade to the rear, and as he went along he pointed out what few improvements had been made under the budget of the year before. Down the steps they went and into the large room at the south end of the building.

Knowing that they had been expected, he presented the instructor to the members of the board and was pleased at the natural way in which she explained that her students had prepared coffee and doughnuts for them. Standing aside, he watched as the three white men were served at a daintily set table to the right of the door, and by the most comely of the students. He saw too 'the way that Wilbur Daniels eyed them and then sublimated his ebbing desires by biting into one of the doughnuts. A ring of powdered sugar appeared around his mouth but he made no effort to remove it, and as he drank his coffee he drooled a little from the corners of his mouth. Sitting there, wolfing his food and washing it down with coffee, looking every now and then at the women students, he had almost the appearance of a performing bear. His greedy little eyes roamed around restlessly as he belched lightly.

From the raised dais in the dining room Ezekiel could see the whole student body. As he sat at the table with the three white men he was conscious of them, not as a group of individuals but more as a presence. Having already eaten at home, he could expend his whole time in conversation and to seeing that those at the table had a plenty of everything. He looked and saw that each had a full plate.

Wilbur Daniels looked over at him, a partly gnawed chicken leg in one hand, which he used to emphasize what he was saying. "You eat this good all the time?" he asked bluntly.

Ezekiel laughed, not at the question raised but with the white man who had offered it.

"If you mean do we have fried chicken every day, Mr. Daniels, the answer is no. As a matter of fact, we don't have it often, but when we do it's as good as this."

Wilbur Daniels grunted and speared a second joint with his fork. "Damn," he said, "I don't eat chicken this good at home. Them girls who made the coffee and doughnuts, can they all make chicken this good?"

Again Ezekiel laughed with deference. "I can't promise that," he

106

said. "We do the best we can and we turn out some people who will be good cooks. But I think that a hundred per cent is aiming a little high."

Wilbur Daniels nodded and thoughtfully helped himself to rice and cream gravy. "I tell you what you do, Doctor," he said. "You tell them girls I'm willing to do this. Kind of like a prize for the best student. You tell them the one does the best I'll give a job to, that she can move right into my kitchen the day school is out!"

Ezekiel caught the fleeting wink that Cal Thornton gave him, then said, "I'll do that, Mr. Daniels. I'll do that very thing. Of course we find that our best ones in domestic science get married off right quick."

"Shucks, Doctor, that ain't no trouble. I can put the boy to work too, not in the grove but right up by the house as yard boy!"

He chuckled and looked around the table triumphantly, then pushed his plate back as the waitress came forward and cleared the table. The ice cream and coffee set before them, Wilbur belched lightly and turned back to Ezekiel.

"We going to have singing?" he asked. "I sure like a little singing any time I can hear it."

Ezekiel nodded, and when Wilbur was finished he shoved back his plate and lit a cigar, then settled back as though he had grown to the chair. Almost as though by signal, the students from the department of music gathered at the piano under the raised dais and after a few introductory chords on the piano began to sing an old spiritual.

The words moved Ezekiel deeply and he was carried along with the music. He remembered his boyhood in South Carolina, and as he closed his eyes he could see the little wooden church where his father had been pastor until his death. The old songs pleased him; he liked things that were old and settled, and though he would have enjoyed hearing them sung under different conditions, he gave himself up completely. He knew that many of the faculty made fun of spirituals and that even now some of the students were singing under their breaths a parody not complimentary to the three men sitting beside him, but even this did not bother him. The song ended and he looked across at Wilbur Daniels.

The florid face had softened and he noted that there was more than a suggestion of tears at the corners of the white man's eyes. Wilbur took out his handkerchief and blew his nose loudly, then stealthily whisked it across his eyes. He leaned over toward Ezekiel, even laying a hand almost tenderly on his arm.

107

"Them niggers," he said, then hastily corrected himself. "Them nigrahs, I mean, them nigrahs can sho sing!"

Ezekiel nodded and turned his head away. He was glad when the singing began again; even though it was suddenly spoiled for him, he knew now that there was no doubt of the budget being approved. Old man Daniels was the stumbling block, the granite obstacle, and now he had been softened. He, Ezekiel, had planned it that way; he should be relieved, even a little proud, at the way he had fooled the white folks. Instead he felt nothing but a rage he must strive to conquer.

Like a wad of matter caught in his throat, he swallowed his anger, not once, but several times.

The meeting in the president's office in the administration building was almost over. Ezekiel knew that it had gone well and that the final approval of the budget was a mere formality, yet as he sat behind his desk fooling with the bronze paperweight and listening to the talk of the others he wished it were over. He was tired, physically as well as mentally. It had been a long day, and the tensions that had kept him keyed up were beginning to tell on him. He looked out the window and across the campus. He felt suddenly old, and for the first time in the near twenty years that he had been on the campus he thought about his eventual retirement. If he could fix it so that George, his son away in the Pacific, could take charge someday soon after the war was over, he decided that he would step down. He would, of course, stay on, but unofficially and only to help his son along over the early hardship of orientation. After that he would leave the campus for good.

He heard his name called and brought himself back to the present rapidly. It was Wilbur Daniels who had spoken, seemingly to wind up the affairs which had kept them closeted together in the room.

"I reckon that about does it, Doctor," he said. "Looks like you budgeted about right. Now, there's only one thing else I got on my mind. And what I say I say friendly. It ain't no way of being a threat. But I been hearing about Reds out here. Now, mind you, these rumors maybe ain't true. But I just figured I ought to tell you that the only thing I hate worse than an uppity nigrah is a Red nigrah."

He looked around the room as though he would fight the first one who denied him the right to hate this thing he detested most. Seeing no signs of visible protest, he relaxed.

"Just what is it that you have heard, Mr. Daniels?" Ezekiel asked slowly. "I don't like communists any more than you do. Certainly I don't want any on this campus, and I am sincere in saying that."

"Well, now, there ain't nothin a man can rightly put his fingers on. Just talk mostly, but I think I did hear somethin about some teacher out here that wrote himself a book."

Cal Thornton laughed good-naturedly. "Wilbur," he said, "not everybody who writes a book is a communist, you know."

"Well, now," Wilbur answered, "I ain't had no Harvard education, so I reckon I wouldn't know."

"No, seriously, Wilbur. You mean Eric Gardner, I guess. I know his book well, and certainly he's far from a communist."

"Well, maybe so. But I just wanted a clear understandin. It ain't like Washington down here. Any doubt in my mind about a man being Red, or even pink for that matter, and he'll have to go."

"He should go," Ezekiel said. "I'm with you on that, Mr. Daniels. And as long as I am head of this college such a man will go."

"Good. Glad to hear you feel that way. Well, that seems to wind things up. Agreed that we approve the appropriation, gentlemen?"

The other two white men nodded their heads and Wilbur Daniels got to his feet. He walked over to the window and looked out.

"Why, damn if it ain't rainin," he said over his shoulder, "it sure as hell is. Comin down bad and fixin to get worse, I reckon. Now ain't that too bad. Looks like that shuts out your function, Doctor. I declare I'm right sorry. I was plumb lookin forward to some of that cake like we had last year that them girl students baked."

He leaned out the window suddenly and bellowed for his car to be driven around to the main entrance of the administration building. Then, turning back into the room, and as though in recompense for the weather, he shook hands briefly with Ezekiel. The other two men followed him out the door.

14.

Since Esther had gotten Alberta's letter the days were something to be once more counted in advance. Each morning she would cross one off the calendar with the pencil that hung by a string in the kitchen, and then it would seem to her that Alberta was that much closer. Sometimes she felt that the days would never pass; then again it seemed as though the days crowded her in a way that brought her close to panic. At such times she would do everything as though not to complete it within a day would bring down upon her head some horrible punishment lasting for her life span. She would clean the house in a morning's time, scrubbing the floors with a harsh soap heavy with lye, only to realize when she was through that Alberta's arrival was far enough away so that they would have to be done again. Then she would feel the time wasted and forever lost, which would bring her once more the familiar panic.

Sometimes she would realize that she was being a fool and she would flush with laughter. Then, more likely than not, she would walk across to see Eulia's father and they would sit together in the two rustic chairs that Jeff had placed under the big chinaberry tree in the back yard and talk. She would often try to justify this to herself by saying that she felt sorry for a man who had suddenly been forced to bach it, but she knew it was more than that. Inwardly she knew that she was as much in need of Jeff as he was of her, but she would never admit it.

A relationship had ripened between them that was hard for her to define. It was not love, at least not the kind of love that she had felt for her husband, or before that for the one or two men who had courted her. She was too old for love, she told herself, and yet she knew that she was in need of something to take its place. For she realized that in the years that she had been a widow somehow she had ceased to be a whole woman. Even her children had not been enough.

And in this too there seemed to her a conflict, for she owed a loyalty to them that had always been one of her strongest emotions. Before she had found herself more and more closely drawn to Jeff there had been no problem. Now it was not Luther who bothered her, or even Bessie; they would understand. But about Alberta she was not sure. Was it because she was afraid that Alberta would be angry with her? Sometimes she imagined that when Alberta came back it would be for good, that she would decide to stay, seduced by the special dishes that her mother would prepare and by the new curtains and bedspread that were in the process of completion. Or perhaps, once she returned, she would suddenly realize how much she had missed her mother, and in turn how much Esther actually needed her. It was a fantasy she enjoyed, yet deep within she knew that it bore no resemblance to reality.

Alberta would come, stay her two weeks out, and then depart. No, it was something more than that. More than likely it was a feeling that Alberta would somehow unconsciously belittle Jeff, as if by inference he was too crude for her newly acquired tastes. Was it this? She hardly knew, but nonetheless realized that somehow in her mind the two had in a sense become rivals, two opposite magnetized poles, herself hopelessly caught in the middle between them.

It was all the more confusing because neither by word of mouth nor by action had Jeff conveyed to her how he really felt toward her, beyond the fact that he seemed to enjoy her company. Or was it merely that he tolerated her because Luther and Eulia had married? She did not know.

The war had little or no meaning for her. So long as Luther did not have to go—and now that he was working in the shipyard and the age limit had been lowered further, it did not appear as though he would—it seemed little more than a white folks' war into which some Negroes were unjustly drawn. She knew that Hitler was a bad man and that he had spoken of people like herself as black apes; yet he was a long way off, and people nearer than Germany had often referred to her by inference in much the same terms. For the Jews she felt sorrow, but it was a sorrow once removed from her way of life. She knew no Jews, only white men and women.

Bessie would talk to her about the wartime situation, and lately even Luther had tried to make it seem important. In a way she had tried, but beyond the ordinary interest which anything seen in a newspaper aroused in her, she felt no emotional pull one way or the other. Even when she read in the Negro papers that Bessie brought home from the college about violence done to Negro servicemen by white civilians, her reaction was a mixed one. After all, she reasoned, it was a world controlled by white men. She had known good white folks and bad ones; the bad outnumbered the good, and there was little hope for Negroes until the process was reversed. It seemed to her that acting uppity was no way to speed that hoped-for change.

Also she feared the rising feelings of Negroes around her, because for her the violence of retaliation was ever-present. Nothing that anyone could tell her would have changed that feeling, but she kept her reactions to herself once she learned that Bessie, and now even Luther, thought her old-fashioned in that respect. Perhaps she was, but she knew that she would live the longer for it. Besides, it was only common sense, the kind of protective cocoon that she had spun around her children at an early age. There was a lesson to be learned, and she did not spare them. When it had been necessary she had even switched it into the backs of their bare young legs. It was better that they learn about racial etiquette, far better than to bring down upon their heads white wrath. That wrath was wrong, but it was no question merely of right and wrong; it was the necessity of survival.

It was not that she did not want a better life, but that she was not willing to gamble the little life she already had in order to attain it. All that remained was to make the best of what there was and hope that someday, if only in the hereafter, things would be better.

She had always been a deeply religious person, and each Sunday she went to church. When her husband had been alive he had gone with her, less perhaps through inner zeal than from a desire to please her. All her children had gone too, until they were old enough to follow their own ways, then she had no longer pestered them to attend. Her faith was secure enough so that she felt no need to deliver others to the benches each Sunday in order to reassure herself of salvation.

And yet she hated to go alone each Sunday. Bessie no longer bothered to attend, and now that Luther and Eulia had moved to Citrus City their attending her church was out of the question. She supposed that life was like that, that families grew apart from each other and little could be done about it. At least now that Alberta was coming back there would be an excuse for them all to be together again.

But now, on this particular Saturday afternoon, there was another lonely Sunday morning before her. Bessie had gone over to the beach with friends from the college, and Esther realized suddenly that because of this she would be even more alone. As she sat on the stoop Jeff suddenly appeared around the corner of the house. Seeing him, she was for a moment startled, as though the fact that she had been thinking about him had suddenly made him appear. It made her feel a little shy and yet at the same time a little bold, as though she possessed some strange power that she had not known about until this moment.

"Hi, Jeff," she greeted him.

"Howdy," he answered. "I was fixin to go fishin tomorrow and I was wonderin would you care to go?"

"I might," she said boldly, "was you to carry me to church in the mornin."

"I ain been to church in twenty-five years, Miss Esther."

"Time you went, then."

"You want me, I be right proud to go."

"Good," she told him, "you eat with us after, then we go by the lake."

He nodded and turned back toward his own house.

She had never seen Jeff dressed in a store suit before. Always he was neat and clean, but he usually wore work clothes, or at best odd trousers and a white shirt, collarless and worn open at the neck. Even when he had come to supper at her house, the night that Bessie and Eric had been there, he had not worn a coat, though he had put on a tie. Now he wore an old but neatly pressed blue serge suit, a stiff collar and a tie, and his shoes were newly shined. She liked the way he looked, and as they walked toward the church she wondered what people would think, seeing them together, bound for the morning worship.

She liked the feeling of Sunday and the way it differed from all other days; she enjoyed the festiveness of it and greeting people whom she largely ignored for the balance of the week. Inside the church they found a seat on a bench near the rear and sat down. Hers was a small church, bare to a point where it was almost austere. The only things that relieved this bareness and made it seem different from an ordinary hall were the two stained-glass windows on the left facing the pulpit, and a mural on either side painted by art students from the college. She looked around, nodding to people and feeling an anticipation of what was to flood over her.

When the singing began she immersed herself in it as though it were a flowing stream. The sweep of the music carried her along, lifting her and making her body seem almost weightless. She raised her voice with the others and became selfless, a part of the whole. Out of the corner of her eye she looked at Jeff. He was not singing, but it seemed to her that his face looked relaxed. Sensing that her eyes were on him, he turned toward her and smiled.

If he should ask me, she thought, I'd likely accept him. Then she remembered Alberta and felt again the imagined conflict between her and Jeff. Put to the test, she was unsure which would win out.

It was Alberta who would probably exert the stronger pull had she been there, but she was not here as yet, and the waiting only intensified that pull. With Luther gone she realized again how strange it seemed not to have a man around the house; there was something lacking, a feeling of unfulfillment, almost a sterile dryness that clung to the house the way mustiness clings to a place which has been closed and not lived in.

The congregation bent to pray and she felt guilty to have been caught with her thoughts so far away from what was going on in the big room. She closed her eyes, and as she whispered the words of the prayer she tried to give herself over completely, but she was too conscious of the man sitting there beside her. She sat up, followed the mechanics of the service, knelt again, and sat back afterward, but it was not until the sermon began that she was actually able to lose herself once more.

It was a new man who preached; he was introduced by the regular pastor as one who had given himself to the Lord's work and the spreading of it throughout the land, and in no one locale. He was short and very black, and his bald head, wreathed with gray, shone like something polished in the light which came down on him from the window above. He started his words slowly and in a deep register, almost as though he were talking to but one person. But as he progressed he began to walk nervously up and down, stopping every now and then to take out a huge pocket handkerchief and wipe his perspiring face, even the top of his head. Then he began to slowly increase his tempo until it was the same as the hushed breathing of the congregation and throbbed with their common pulse until gradually he began to anticipate even that. She felt herself carried along and becoming a part of it.

Suddenly he sprang high into the air and slashed at the air with his handkerchief, almost as though it were a whip.

"Are you with me," he shouted, "and through me with Him?"

The response came spontaneously from all over the room, and once more he quickened the tempo. She could hear the *aaaaauuuh* of his breathing at the end of each phrase, a punctuation as compelling as a drumbeat, and against it the word patterns in an irregular rhythm that made the whole building rock. It no longer mattered what he said, and she could not distinguish one word from the next, but there was no need to do so. All that was important was that she was carried along, lifted up out of herself onto the crest of a wave, a leaf in a whirlpool grown dizzy and lightheaded by the irresistible current it rode.

That was all; that and nothing more. But it was more than enough.

Coming back along the dusty road to her house, the walking was warm. The day had been cool in the early morning, but with noon had come the sudden hotness of a Florida spring, so that it lay along the street in a haze. As they turned in at the gate and started up the stoop Bessie met them at the screen door.

"You all set outside and cool off, Mama. I've got everything under control in the kitchen. When it's ready I'll call and you can help me."

"Thanks, baby," she said.

Bessie was dressed in a canary-yellow dress with a wide gray pleat down one side of the skirt. There was a radiance about her that even a kitchen apron could not hide. Her mother had almost forgotten that anyone could look that way. She thought, That's what a man does for a woman, and looked across at Jeff.

He was sitting back in the rocker, gazing out at the street.

"How did you like your return to the fold?" she asked him.

"I doan hold with it," he said softly. "With churches, I mean. Especially a church full of niggers acted the way you all acted."

"You don't hold with God?" she asked a little smugly.

"What's God got to do with niggers cuttin up like a passel of monkeys? White folks ought to been there so they coulda laughed some more. You all was so holied up that jackleg preacher coulda robbed you blind and you never even knowed it. Niggers cut the fool like that, white folks got a right to treat em like they do."

He snorted and lapsed back into silence. Then, as though he had suddenly remembered something, he went on.

"I mind the time that white man passed through sellin them Bibles with the colored pictures. They knowed what God looked like, they likely woulda had him black too. All them simple-minded niggers bought at least one; some of them got two so they have a spare did they wear the one out looking at it."

"You mad you ain white," she said.

He snorted again angrily. "I ain no such a thing. I doan have to be white not to have no man come around my house and sell me something like that. Or a watch without no works in it so he kin come back next week and when I tell him it doan run he say he send it back to the factory, then sell it to some other fool. And iffen I did, it wouldn take me no two weeks to know the white folks done took me again."

He got to his feet angrily and started to walk up and down the porch. Then suddenly he stopped before her and, reaching down, took her hand. It was the first time he had ever touched her, and she felt a sudden shiver run down her spine. She looked up at him almost shyly and saw that he was smiling down at her.

"We ain like that," he said softly, "not you an me. You go to your church, and you want me, I do too. But if they's one thing I hate worsn a white folks' nigger, it one so simple-minded he cain see his hand before his face at noon on a sunny day."

He let her hand go and it fell back limply into her lap.

"Go help Bessie," he told her. "I gettin hongry, and when I hongry I got to eat."

15. Ezekiel stood by the hotel-room window. Below him the traffic on Seventh Avenue crawled along like a snake on its belly. It was night and rain was falling hard, so that the sounds from the street seemed barely able to penetrate to him. He had not even opened his bags; the bellboy had but recently set them down at the foot of the bed. He took a fresh cigar from his pocket and carefully cut off the tip with the little golden knife attached to the end of his watch chain. Lighting a match, he methodically rolled the cigar in his fingers to get an even light.

He looked out the window again and saw Harlem stretched out below him. It seemed different in the dark, as though it were being washed clean by the rain and would not emerge in the morning in its familiar tawdriness, something that the rest of the city had worn out and passed on to less demanding tenants. He could as easily have stayed downtown; it would have cost him no more for a larger room and service that was not only better but less sullen. He wondered why it was that some Negroes so resented having to wait on other Negroes. In the past he had stayed at downtown hotels, but he could never feel quite comfortable; it always seemed to him that everyone was looking at him.

In his pocket he felt the mail that had been waiting for him in New York and the two notices of telephone calls. There was, he knew, a letter from Ethel, but he had not even bothered to open it. Knowing what it would contain, and feeling the initial release from her dominance, it gave him a sense of power not to do so. Standing there, he thought about his marriage and his relationship with her. It seemed to him an odd one, based on habit rather than on deep affection, and yet for all that, it had a stability which seemed to him, a person who believed in order, all to the good. He wondered how it would have been had he married a woman whom he really loved and who loved him deeply in return. You can't live on love, he told himself, and yet he had missed somehow the naked intimacy and the mutual sharing of such a union. For usually it seemed to him that in such moments with Ethel he was alone, that her giving herself to him was either a duty or an act of pity, he was never certain which.

And yet there had been moments when this was not so. She seemed to him then all that he could ever want in a woman, but now such moments were unpredictable and apparently without pattern or logic. He had had other women in his life, but those occasions seemed to him hollow experiences, and the dangers involved had never acted as a stimulus to his reactions. Afterward such experiments either filled him with a feeling of extreme guilt, if transient, or in those rare instances where they had threatened to assume permanence he had broken them off of his own volition.

In the past there had been times when he had thought of leaving Ethel. His justification for not doing so had always been George, his son, but when he was really honest with himself he knew that this was not the true reason. Rather it was the fact that there was so much at stake.

As he stood there he felt a sudden urge to be with a woman, any woman, but he knew that he would probably end up by going to a movie, and somehow he hated himself for this realization. Then he remembered that one of the telephone messages had been from a friend urging him to attend a party that night. He took the message out and looked at it again. *Sally Borden is having a party,* he read, *and when I told her that you were going to be in town she urged me to bring you. Meet me there about ten.* It was signed Joe Richardson.

He took out his watch and looked at it. He had eaten some hours ago on the train, and if he shaved and bathed he would just about make it at the specified time. It would be good to see Joe again, a casual acquaintance but a person he had instinctively liked the first time he met him. He turned from the window and went into the bathroom to start the tub.

Ezekiel had never been in the Borden apartment before, though he had met Sally, a well-known Harlem hostess, and her husband, who worked on one of the Harlem papers, several times in the past. Located on the Hill, that part of Harlem which winds up past and above the Polo Grounds, it was one of the nicest buildings in the area.

Ezekiel rang the bell and Sally Borden met him at the door. As he came into the smallish but pleasant apartment he wondered if he would ever get any farther, for every available space seemed already to be occupied. But Sally laughingly led him through a hall that was filled with the overflow from the kitchen, into a small extra bedroom which evidently served as a study. On the way he met a great many people, few of whose names he even managed to catch. In the smaller room it was less crowded, and after the introductions were over he managed to find a place on the double box springs, covered in monk's cloth, which served as a couch.

On one side of him was a well-known Negro poet, on the other a woman of perhaps thirty-eight who was tall and wore her hair in an upsweep which gave to her features an almost foreign appearance, heightened by the hammered-bronze costume jewelry she was wearing. In an easy chair by the window sat a white professor from a girls' college up the Hudson, and on the arm of the chair was his wife, a blond woman who looked young enough to be one of his students. At the other end of the room was a Negro who had written a recent best seller about Harlem. In front of the low bookcases which lined the wall opposite the couch stood a tall, gangling man, one of the few Negro reporters working on a white newspaper in New York. The woman beside him was one of the most beautiful women Ezekiel had ever seen. She was of that color which was almost too light to be brown and yet too warm and rich to be any variant of tan. Her eyes, large and deep brown, had the faintest suggestion of an upward slant and her features were regular and finely drawn. With her straight hair, she might have been taken for any nationality, save for her color.

Now that he had everyone straight in his mind, Ezekiel settled back and took a sip from the drink that Sally Borden had thoughtfully left at his elbow. His eyes roamed around the room, noting the books and the magazines in the bookcases and the two paintings above them. Both were abstractions, painted in what were almost, but not quite, primary colors—pinks and yellows, greens and blues that might have clashed save for their relative positions.

He was paying little attention to the conversation going on around him. What impressed him was the feeling in the room and its difference from what he felt on the campus. He tried to analyze it, but it was too subtle. If he had not known the North, he would have attributed it to a complete freedom from discrimination. Yet he knew that even these people—the cream of Harlem's best, of Du Bois' talented tenth, these artists, writers, actors, political appointees, and professional people—were really hardly less free from the sting of prejudice than he. Perhaps it was merely that though they did not have complete democracy they at least had *some* democracy, while in the South the word was meaningless for the Negro. Too, they were free from the fear that he and every Negro in the South knew—fear for one's own life, for one's own property, for one's own family. In any event it was a good feeling, in spite of the frantic tension that also seemed to be there in the room.

Ezekiel could not help wondering what would have happened if he had come North when he was young enough to try to be somebody. It was an intriguing thought and he let his fantasy run wild. In the living room which he had passed through on his way to the study there had been a judge, a well-known doctor, an actor who was nationally known . . .

He came back to the present with a start, knowing that someone had spoken to him, but unsure not only of what had been said but of which person in the room had spoken. Then the writer at the end of the room spoke to him again.

"I asked," he said, "what are we going to do about the South?"

Ezekiel shrugged. "Why ask me?"

"Well, you happen to live there and I don't. I was born in the North and I've never been south of Washington in my life. When they sing 'Carry Me Back to Old Virginny' I always say they got to *drag* me."

Ezekiel took a sip of his drink. "Seems to me," he said, "that you had something to say about that in your book. Let me see now, if I remember correctly, you said that if people like myself, who speak softly, would get a little backbone . . ."

Those in the room laughed and Ralph Freeman grinned. "That's it. And I think I was right, don't you?"

"I don't know that you were," Ezekiel answered. "After all, we have to live down there. It's another thing to sit up here on Sugar Hill and fight the good fight over scotch and sodas. Remember the poem Sterling Brown wrote, about Old Lem?

> "They got the judges
> They got the lawyers
> They got the jury rolls
> They got the law
> They don't come by ones
> They got the sheriffs
> They got the deputies
> They don't come by twos
> They got the shotguns
> They got the rope
> We git the justice
> In the end
> And they come by tens."

"That's all very true," Ralph Freeman answered, "but it seems to me that there is a point beyond which it is not necessary to go. It seems to me you have to take a stand somewhere. Lem knew that."

Ezekiel thought for a moment before he answered. "What was there in the manifesto we issued that was any different from what you Northern Negroes have been calling for?"

"It wasn't so much what you said, but how you said it. Of course I don't mean you personally, but I think you boys curved around the issue of segregation, for one thing. From all I hear, you were far from unanimous about going even as far as you did. You pretty much avoided a lot of other things too. I don't think, for instance, that you have to beg the white folks to listen any longer. It seems to me that we have reached a point where we can tell them a few things for a change. The South has been forced to make some concessions, and unless she voluntarily makes more, she is going to be made to make them just the same. We have made some gains in this war, and I think we ought to be damn well sure that we keep them. Booker T. Washington tried co-operation and look what happened to him."

"I agree with you on that, Mr. Freeman, but what techniques are we to use? I know this may sound too simple, but what would you do? Put yourself in my position. I have to depend on the county for a good bit of my money, on the state for a little more of it. If that were to be withheld, my college would go under. Now I know we aren't doing all we can, probably, but the point is that we are doing something. Is something better than nothing?"

"Sometimes it is, Doctor, but not always."

Ezekiel shrugged. The argument had gone far enough for him, and he started to get to his feet to go out to the kitchen for another drink. The white professor from the girls' college looked up at him and grinned. When he spoke his accent was so Southern it almost hit Ezekiel in the face like a blow.

"I know how you feel," he said. "It's not easy for a white man to speak out in the South, even when he knows he's right. Some don't speak out because they feel it will hurt the Negro, but most of them use that as an excuse. Yet the point is that some white men do. Some of them get run out and some of them don't, but they keep on speaking out just the same. I don't know what makes the difference."

"And yourself?".

"I don't fit into either category. I happen to be an economic refugee lured up here by Yankee gold."

"I can understand that," Ezekiel laughed. He looked around the room. "Anyone else want me to bring them a drink?"

Nobody answered except the white professor, who got up from his chair and went out with him. They managed to work their way through to the kitchen.

"How's Cal Thornton?" the professor asked.

"Oh, fine. I saw him just before I left. He's a great help to me down there."

"Yeah, Cal's a nice guy and he means well. His trouble is he wants to please everybody, and someday he's going to end up pleasing nobody. I know just what's going to happen to Cal.

"He'll get a Pulitzer prize for those editorials he writes, and next he'll start writing for the popular national magazines. He'll become a professional Southerner—something, by the way, that he isn't far off from right now. He'll write articles just like that one editorial he wrote a while back telling Negroes to take it easy because they'll get their pie in the sky by and by. Only this time he'll be saying that if the Yankees would just leave the South alone she could solve all her problems, including the race problem. The whole fallacy there is that the South can't afford to have the North leave her alone. The

North doesn't need the South, but the South sure as hell needs the North. If the South isn't careful, the next civil war is going to be fought not because the South secedes from the Union but because it refuses to get out." He took Ezekiel's arm and led him to the bar at the end of the kitchen.

It was a good party. Ezekiel neither stayed in the kitchen nor went back to the study. Instead he went into the living room and bumped into Joe Richardson, and they got to talking together. As he looked around the room he thought of Ethel's parties; they were command performances and no one really enjoyed them but Ethel. In a moment he saw someone coming toward him who looked vaguely familiar.

"How's Bessie?" the young woman said as she came up beside him.

He looked at her more closely. She was prettier than Bessie, a little taller, and had a great deal more self-assurance. But there was something about her which disturbed him; he prided himself on never forgetting people, but he could not place her. Then suddenly it came to him; of course, this was Bessie's sister and she had been a student at the college, that was how he had seemed to know her.

"You're Alberta," he said. "I thought you looked familiar, but you've changed since you left the campus. All for the better, I might add. Bessie's fine. She's my right arm, that girl."

They talked for a few moments and then she drifted off into the crowd. Joe had also gone, so Ezekiel went back into the kitchen for another, and final, drink. When he got it he sat down at the table with a group made up almost equally of Negroes and whites. After the initial conversation he found it difficult to tell who was on whose side. One of the Negroes was married to a white woman, and as he looked at her he remembered, without realizing the connection, the only time that he had ever been intimate with a white woman.

He had been young, barely eighteen, and had gone with a friend of his to visit the middle-aged white prostitute who made her living off Negroes, whom she charged three times what the white traffic would bear. He tried to remember his emotions. He knew that first of all there had been the lure of the unfamiliar, but subconsciously he knew that basically he had gone out of revenge, that by taking this woman he wanted to humiliate all the white women who had ever humiliated him, and, through them, all the white men who had ever mistreated him. And yet when he had gone into her he himself had been the one humiliated, for a mixture of fear and hopeless rage had made him impotent, and the woman had taken his money and then openly taunted him for his inadequacy.

He got up from the table and, leaving his drink, went out of the kitchen. In the corridor he saw the woman whom he had admired in the study; she had on her coat and was headed for the front door.

"Going so soon?" he asked.

She smiled. "I'm a working girl, Doctor. The rest of these people can sleep all morning, but I've got to pop out of that bed at seven-thirty."

"Going all alone?"

"I only live around the corner."

"Then let me at least walk you home. Maybe I'm old-fashioned, but I always feel a woman ought not to be alone on the streets this late at night."

"Always a gentleman," she said.

He was not certain whether she was kidding him or not. "No," he said, "not that I'm a gentleman, merely because I would like to."

"Come on, then," she said. "I'd like you to."

He got his coat and said good-by to Joe and Sally, then came back and picked her up at the front door. They went down in the elevator and out onto Edgecombe Avenue. It was early spring but there was an unnatural touch of summer in the air now that the rain had stopped. They walked down the hill and crossed 155th Street, and as they went down St. Nicholas Place, Ezekiel heard a sudden high whoop of laughter, then a too-loud voice, from in front of a bar across the street. It's like back home, he told himself angrily; a nigger's a nigger in New York, the same as he is in Atlanta, and Harlem's really no different than Hannibal Square or Citrus City.

"You're mighty quiet," she said.

"I reckon I'm quiet by nature," he answered honestly.

"I like quiet people. Most of the people I know talk too much."

In the middle of the block she stopped and, mounting a flight of stone steps, turned at the front door of her apartment house.

"Would you like to come in and have a nightcap?" she asked.

He wanted to, but something made him say instead, "I'd like to, but I guess you'd better give me a rain check. I've got a busy day in the morning."

She held out her hand to him and he took it in his, feeling the coolness of her long fingers. She smiled at him and started to withdraw her hand, but he could not let it go.

"Look," he said, "I'm only in town for a few days and I have a kind of tight schedule. But if I can work it so I can get shut of things, would you have dinner with me one night before I go back?"

"Of course," she said sincerely, "I'd like to. I'm in the book, why don't you call me?"

"I will," he told her, finally letting go of her hand.

She let it drop naturally to her side and he heard the faint clank of her heavy metal bracelets. She smiled again and went through the door. He could see her through the frosted pane only as a dark shadow growing smaller and smaller. He turned away and walked rapidly to the corner, where he hailed a passing taxi. Giving his destination, he settled back in the seat.

He suddenly knew that he hated Ethel and had probably always hated her, and now that George was grown there was nothing really to keep them together. He would leave her and come to New York, get into something here. It was not only the experience of seeing and feeling the difference of life here; after all, he had been in New York enough times to find that no real novelty. But he thought of the woman he had just left and built a sudden fantasy of being married to her instead of to Ethel. He could do it; he knew as much as Ralph Freeman and could write a book; he was, or could be, as good a reporter as the man who worked on the *Evening Herald* and had the room in hysterics over his stories about his early life in Hopkinsville, Kentucky. Then as suddenly the balloon collapsed.

He was over fifty, secure in a job that meant too much for him to leave it, and he was chained to Ethel by something too strong for him ever to have the courage to break. He was, he thought, just what Ralph Freeman felt him to be but was too polite to say aloud: he was an Uncle Tom bowing and scraping to the white folks for favors. He had lived too long by patronage to risk a new life without it. Even the woman he had just left, he knew that he would never call her on the phone, and probably she had merely been humoring him because he reminded her of her father.

With his clenched fist Ezekiel beat once hard on the leather seat and looked angrily at the neck of the Negro driver in front of him. The driver's hair needed cutting; he wore no cap and the hair stood up on top every which way, like so many little spikes; it was like the hair on the comic black figures that used to appear on humorous calendars, usually frightened by ghosts or graveyards. He probably could use a bath too. Damned burrheaded nigger, Ezekiel said savagely under his breath, he's probably taking me the long way home.

16. It was a new experience for Luther to work in a shipyard, to feel himself a part of something that was bigger than himself. At first he had not liked it, because it had seemed to swallow him up. In the morning when he went through the gate marked Colored he felt as though he were passing through a great mouth, sucked into the craw of some great beast. He knew almost no one, and because of this he was unsure of himself. Everyone seemed a threat to him, even the Negroes in his own crew. But the feeling had passed and been replaced by another, that of belonging, of a common goal toward which all were moving. Now he knew those with whom he worked and he no longer felt an alien in a strange land.

His work was hard but simple. Like all Negroes in the yard, he was graded as unskilled labor and given the jobs which were hot, heavy, and hard, while few white men had a similiar rating no matter how inexperienced they might be. If this seemed wrong to him, it also seemed inevitable; it was the way things had always been and probably the way that they would continue to be. There was no sense in beating your head against a stone wall.

Yet he found that this feeling of fatality was not shared by all the Negroes in the yard. He had heard talk against the white folks all his life, though perhaps less than others who had been ground under economically more than he had been. But never before had he heard hatred of whites so openly expressed and with such bitterness. To some of those who worked around him it seemed to be a tonic, the one thing that kept them going, the inner conditioning that they had taken in with their mother's milk and would retain even at the moment of dying. At first this had frightened him a little, so that he had functioned only with a part of himself; that which was not fully utilized seemed to be always looking over his shoulder for the inevitable white man who, hearing, would come to mete out punishment. But that man never came, and in time he came to accept such talk as merely another of the conditions of his employment. Eventually he lost all consciousness of it, and the mumbled cursing, the bitching and the griping, the sly and obscene fantasies of getting even on some dark night became as familiar to him as the observations about the weather. Yet even though he would have denied sincerely that all this had in any way changed him, it had, although perhaps he was not aware of the fact.

For the whites the Negroes seemed hardly to exist. In the morning they came in by a separate gate and at night left by the same exit through which they had come that morning. At the lunch hour they were segregated as effectively as though by a wall. If they were needed they were there, not unlike a machine to be set in motion by methods as mechanical as pushing a button or throwing a switch. Yet by this very device of separation no Negro could be unconscious of a white worker. He would still have been there, even if shut off by a curtain or by a wall of one-way glass, for every time a Negro went into a separate washroom, drank from a jimcrow fountain or water cooler, saw a sign marked FOR COLORED, he knew that a white worker was responsible for its being there. Consciously he might ignore this, or even, as in the case of Luther, accept it, but below the surface it registered as acutely as a bell is rung or a bumper is lit up by a careening steel ball working its way down the side of a pinball machine. It was always there, and the white workers, on a subconscious level, were as conscious of it as the Negroes; it lay dormant like an ungrounded electric current, ever a potential threat which might erupt into violence if some spark were to jump the gap.

Little was done to avert this danger by management, save for some vague and ambiguous posters which could as easily have been applied to curbing the tempers which might explode in an argument over who would win the World Series. If there was any better instrument for racial understanding, it was one of the two unions which operated within the shipyard.

Luther had joined the union. This was mainly because he had been under a misapprehension that failing to do so would be a violation of the conditions under which he had been hired, heightened by the fact that he had been approached by a white union member who urged him to join. If the union man had been another Negro it is doubtful whether Luther would have joined so readily, at least without going more thoroughly into just what membership in a union entailed. In any event, he had signed up, paid his first dues, and promptly forgotten all about it. After all, it was white folks' business.

Actually he might as easily have joined the other union, had he been approached, or no union at all, if he had been left alone. The benefits of union membership had never been explained to him; nor, for that matter, had anyone tried to point out to him any reasons for not joining. The fact that there were two unions in the yard was a rather common phenomenon and one to which management certainly had no objections. The position of the state politicians was clear enough; they played ball with the AFL, in preference to the CIO, and fought within the legislature for an open shop, expensive license fees for each union organizer, and a number of other amendments aimed at seriously crippling labor.

Although neither union had a clear majority of the whole plant, the union which Luther had happened to join was in the better strategic position. One reason for this was that it was organized on an industrial rather than on a crafts pattern, which meant that its membership was made up of all the workers in the yard rather than only those with special skills. Another reason was that it included Negroes within the parent organization, rather than drifting them into auxiliary or jimcrow locals with no real authority in the affairs of the union even though they paid the same dues. Perhaps it could be said that in the end the results were the same, but those Negroes who had been around were conscious of the difference and were vocal about it.

For one thing, Negro membership was represented on the administrative board of the local, and if there was segregation at meetings it was a different kind of segregation, a sop to local laws rather than to regional mores. It was not an arrangement that placed Negroes in a less desirable position, in the balcony or at the extreme rear of the union hall. It was simply this: whites sat on one side and Negroes on the other, and the mixed administrative board sat together on the platform.

To say that there was no racial tension in such an arrangement, or that it lessened prejudice, was of course pure nonsense. Some of the whites resented it bitterly, and there had been instances where the union had lost membership because of it. But on the whole whites accepted it, if not with enthusiasm at least with a realization that little could be done about it, though some of them never gave up trying.

The union's position in this was at once visible. This was no phony crusade for the fellowship of man, or even for better racial understanding; it was a realistic approach to industrial power. What the union constantly stressed was the fact that what hurts a colored worker eventually hurts a white one too, that when a Negro is helped by a union and learns worker solidarity white workers will also benefit from this in the long run. The past history of the trades-union movement was full of examples of how industry pitted white workers against black to keep wages down and unions impotent while management stayed firmly in the saddle.

It could have been done better, perhaps, but the wonder was that in the South it was being done at all. Certainly the community was against it, and those put into office by the community conscientiously put every possible obstacle in the way of its successful utilization. Sometimes locals went against the wishes of the national headquarters, but though occasionally they got away with it, they were conscious that they were always bucking a strong pressure.

If at first Luther had not been aware of what unions meant, he was fast learning. For him it was a totally new experience.

There was to be a union meeting that Wednesday night, and a rumor was making the rounds that it was important, that something big was in the air. On Luther's gang they talked about it all that day. None of them was certain what was up, but most of them had their own ideas.

"Them pecks is up to no good," said one of them, a tall black worker they called Blue. "Any time they git to decidin somethin big they ain up to no good. They fixin to do somethin to Mose. I can feel it burnin, man."

"Shucks, Blue, you know them pecks loves us."

"Sho, Seaboard, loves us so much they jest befo doin to us what the bull done to the cow!"

"Trouble with yuu niggers is yuu just ignorant," said the oldest of them, a man whose hair was turning gray and who had worked all over the South. His name was Roger but everybody called him Bull Snake. "Ain but one thing it could be, man. They fixin to call us out on strike. Sho, thas all it could be."

"Who gonna call us out, Bull Snake?"

"Who yuu think?"

"Shucks, man, I doan know. What the hell you think I askin for? Some niggers do think they knows it all."

"Gwan, Seaboard, keep talkin. We can use a little breeze round here. Like I tolt yuh, the union gonna call us out on strike."

"Hucome? What the hell all this talk about a strike? Who want tuh strike?"

"Just what I say, man. They call us out and we doan work till they pays us more money."

"Who they, nigger?"

"Man owns the damn shipyard."

"You mean we ain gonna work no more? Well, hell, man, les go. I doan like workin anyway."

"Quit cuttin the fool, Blue. You know yuu doan work yuu doan git paid."

"What? Godam, I done tolt you them pecks was out to frig us. Hell, man, I ain goin out on no damn strike."

Bull Snake shrugged. "Yuu ain gonna be popular with them pecks in the union yuh doan."

Blue shook his head. "I cain hep that. I got to have stuff. Cain git no place I got no money. What the hell them fools in the union want to strike for? Gawdam, what I join this mother-friggin union for anyway? Ain this a bitch?"

Bull Snake took out a plug of tobacco and bit off a corner. "Look," he said, "yuu jest stand round here shootin the breeze the man gonna come by an fire yo black ass anyway. Keep workin while yuu talk. Comes a time you gotta strike."

"Hell, man, hucome? It doan do no good. How in the hell I gonna eat I ain got no pay check?"

"How far that check goin now, Blue? Yo check lastin the way it did, Seaboard?"

"Hell, no. Man, everythin gone up so high I gots to quit eatin fust thing I know. Cain buy nothin no more way I could uh while back."

"Thas why we gotta strike. Doan get nothin yuu doan ask fer it, and strikin the only way we got uh askin. Only thing worse than a peckerwood is a peck got somebody workin for him. Only thing a boss man understands is a pisselm club."

"What bout the war effort, Bull Snake?"

"Hell, Blue," Seaboard broke in, "only lass week you sayin yuu hopes them Japs kills off *all* the peckerwoods."

Blue laughed, high and clear as a bell. "Thas right," he agreed, "kill off all the mens and leaves the womens fer ole Blue!"

Bull Snake had been a jackleg preacher, working all the week and spreading the gospel on Sundays. He had been around and he knew more than all the rest of them, Luther thought, even if Blue and Seaboard didn't want to give him credit for it.

"What we ought to do, Bull Snake?" Luther asked.

Bull Snake turned to him. "Now see, here's a nigger got some sense. Look, all them pecks is gonna think we ain goin out. But we is, all of us. I wants to talk to every cullud in this yard. Les meet in the vacant lot back of the hall fore the meetin. Ain many of us, but we stick together we can throw some weight round, hear?"

Just then the whistle blew and, nodding, the crew moved off toward the lockers to check out.

The hall was not filled but there was a good turnout. On the platform under the American flag flanked by CIO posters sat the local officials, four white men and one Negro. They sat impassively under the eyes of the members who had elected them, every now and then putting their heads together to whisper until no one else seemed to be coming and they called the meeting to order.

First came old business, and a white man called for and got the floor. He was dressed in a white shirt, the collar open and so heavily starched that it stood out from the base of his neck like wings. Obviously he was unused to speaking, and as the words came out the effort made him red in the face.

"I'm an American," he said. "I got two boys over there fightin. Now the point is, I been hearin a lot of things. Seems we got communists in this here local. I ain't for that. I be dogged if I ain't goin to get out if I got to belong to no outfit full of godam reds. I vote we run em out."

He sat down heavily to scattered applause, mostly from the men sitting around him. The chairman of the meeting started to answer and then, seeing a raised hand on the other side of the hall, shrugged. Bull Snake got to his feet slowly. He was wearing his Sunday suit and a black tie.

"I like tuh say a few words, please, suh," he said softly.

When the chairman nodded he began to talk, and as he went on his voice gradually grew louder.

"Most you white gentlemen doan know me," he said. "I what they calls a jackleg preacher; I gives one day a week to the Lord and the rest of the time I works with my hands." He held them out before him for all to see. "I worked all my life, worked hard doin all kinds of things. I knows what it means to be a worker. I done what the Book says; six days' work for me an one for the Lord. I got a reason for tellin you this. Lemme tell you why."

He took out his handkerchief and mopped his brow.

"I is cullud," he went on. "I been cullud all my life an expects to be right on. I been called black an I doan mind that. But every time I tries to hep myself thuh white folks say I tryin to be white. Now I done joined the CIO." He paused for a moment, and when he resumed there was almost a bantering tone to his voice. "What happens?" he asked. "Seems the boss man doan like that. Doan like it fer cullud, doan like it fer white. What he say?" Again he paused for effect and raised his voice. "Boss man say I must be red. Now ain that a mess? How can a black man be white and red all at thuh same time?"

He waited for his applause and got it.

"I doan reckon," he said slowly, "a man preaches the gospel Sundays likely be the kind uh red the boss man means thuh rest of thuh week. I doan know. I got red blood and yawl on thuh other side thuh hall got red blood too. I sees red stripes of that flag on thuh wall. Now if the boss man means I red cuz I want better pay, enough so I can feed my own an save a little for my ole age, and that I willin tuh hep the CIO git me more better pay, then I is that kind uh red, I reckon. I figures we all maybe red, excusin the white folks spoke fore I did."

He sat down, and this time the applause came from all sides of the hall. The chairman then introduced a speaker from the state headquarters at Jacksonville who read them statistics on the rise in the cost of living and how because of this the money they took home in their pay envelopes had also shrunk. He told them that this was happening all over the country and that the union had only one recourse. That was to get pay boosts, by collective bargaining on peaceful terms wherever possible, but if not, by labor's only effective weapon against the autonomy of management—the strike.

When he sat down another speaker went over for them the numerical strength of the union and the difficulties involved in a show of strength where an open shop was not concerned. He pointed out that with the present membership, calling a vote for plant representation might well end in defeat. The only way out of this dilemma was for increased membership, and to do that the union needed the help of every member.

Bull Snake called for the floor again and got it.

"I jest wants tuh say one thin more," he said. "I is cullud an thuh rest of this side thuh hall is too. They's been some talk bout us cullud not goin along with the union. That ain right. Whut heps yawl heps us. We knows that. Boss man know it too and he doan like it, but we all in this together. We gonna git more cullud members. If we gots tuh go out on strike, us cullud goin out too."

The meeting broke up slowly. From a sound truck outside a record played and was followed by a short plea for new members. As Luther walked toward home he felt the presence of someone by his side; he looked up and saw that it was a white man.

"That preacher talked sense," the white man said. "He sho stood up there and talked plenty sense. I liked that."

Luther nodded. In a moment they came to where he had to turn off toward the project. He stopped and said, "Well, here where I turn off."

"Yeah," the white man said, "I keep straight on here over to town. Well, so long."

"So long," Luther answered, and walked slowly away.

Half a block later he realized that he had spoken to a white man for the first time in his life without using a courtesy title.

17.

So she was going home: outside the grimy windows of the jimcrow coach she could sense the morning soon to come, though it was still dark and difficult to see through the dirt-streaked windows. She was uncertain whether or not she had slept; it seemed to her as though she had been sitting like this forever, her chin cupped in her hand, the back of her head against the seat, and her right temple pressed tight against the cooled glass of the window. Stirring uneasily, she changed her position and thought of the luxury of a tub full of steaming water, of fresh clothes or a newly made bed.

Where was home? She fumbled in her bag for a cigarette and lit it from the silver lighter that was beginning to run short of fluid. As she let the smoke come out of her nose she thought about everything that was wrapped up for her in that one word. She remembered her childhood as something far away but happy; then, more realistically, the way it had really been, confused, and as she came into adolescence the relentless drive to get away. To get away from what? She was not sure; it could have been any number of things.

Was it her mother, or had it merely been the South? She loved her mother, loved her still, but there was in their relationship something which was so intense that it was overpowering. It wanted to smother her, to possess her, even to keep her jealously away from others. At the time when she had yearned to make the transference to her father, she remembered, her mother had unconsciously given to her a sense of guilt, of being disloyal, and this had left her even more confused. And then she thought of the time when her father had taken her, freshly scrubbed and starched of dress, to the Exposition in Citrus City, and how he had allowed her to throw baseballs at fake milk bottles on a pedestal to try to win a kewpie doll. She had failed miserably, and that night in bed she had cried herself to sleep thinking: He does not want me, he wishes that I were a boy.

She ground out her cigarette angrily with her shoe and looked around the dimly lit railroad coach. It was in need of ventilation and the aisle was unsightly with litter. Down at the far end someone was snoring loud as a buzz saw, and across the aisle from her a very black woman sat slumped with a handkerchief over her face. There was the sour-sweet smell of cheap whisky and perfume in the car. My people, she thought bitterly, and lit another cigarette.

Why had she come? She knew only that she had been filled with a sudden nostalgia and, making up her mind all at once, had gone ahead with plans so definite that it would be impossible to back out of them. She had wanted to see her mother again, to find out how Bessie was, to get to know Eulia, Luther's wife, whom she remembered only vaguely. But it had been foolish to give in to this sudden urge to know again what it really felt like to be a Negro in the South; she could as easily have gone by plane, or even taken a compartment by herself. Rob had urged her to, had even offered to pay the difference, or, if she insisted, merely lend her the money. But no, she had had to let something that one of the girls at the office had said get under her skin and, simplemindedly, ruin the trip.

The girl was a nobody and black as ink but, overhearing Alberta say that she was going home, the girl had made a remark which had infuriated her.

"You better ride the jimcrow and find out how to act, honey," the girl had said. "Down there you going to be just as black as I am. Those pecks won't care a bit because you live on the Hill and run around with the white folks. You better learn what it means to be black or they'll teach you the hard way."

The girl was ignorant, a little fool; she, Alberta, knew what it was to be a Negro. She looked around the jimcrow coach with disgust and experienced a sudden wave of self-hatred.

She went into the diner early, the moment that the waiter stuck his head in the car and announced first call for breakfast. It would be a change from the dingy coach, and, by doing so, she hoped that she would be able to eat by herself. She might even finish before it was necessary to pull the green curtains shutting off the two end tables, which were reserved for Negroes, from the rest of the car.

She was the first one in the dining car, but as she sat down at the smaller of the two tables the curtain was already drawn, though there were no white people there. Annoyed, she looked down toward the opposite end of the diner, but the steward carefully ignored her, pretending to be busy with his stack of menus. She stared out of the window angrily; it was not quite light and she could see plainly through the huge pane of glass the flat and uninteresting Georgia landscape. Turning back to the menu, she took the pencil from the silver stand at her elbow and hurriedly wrote:

> 1 Special Breakfast ✻1
> orange juice
> toast and marmalade
> boiled eggs
> coffee

She was hungry. The evening before, she had eaten in the Washington station rather than undergo the bother and possible humiliation of the dining car. But it had been an unsuccessful meal, for although she knew that the train stopped there for forty minutes while it took on additional southbound cars, she was all too conscious of the big clock over the entrance. She was glad that she had not allowed her friends in Washington to come down to the train to see her; it would only have added to the confusion and made her still more conscious of the fact that here was the starting point of legal segregation. Consequently she had hurried through her meal so quickly that nothing had had a taste of its own; it all was merely something thrown hastily into her stomach to fight off the pangs of hunger. Luckily, returning to the train, she had found a redcap on his way back to the station who had efficiently transferred her baggage from the regular to the jimcrow coach.

She reached into her bag for a cigarette. It seemed to her dry and tasteless, its only function to give her something to do. A waiter neatly tore off the underpart of her check and was gone again before she had a chance to speak to him. But she had liked his looks. Probably, she imagined, he was only a waiter in his spare time, a nice boy who was earning the money necessary to put himself through college. She felt automatically that he was on her side, not only a defender against the white steward but also a bulwark against the black peasants she had left behind in the coach.

In a moment he came back and neatly slid her orange juice into place in front of her, as well as a cup, saucer, and square little pot of coffee. She looked up at him and smiled. The drawn green curtain was at her back, but she was as conscious of it as though she were facing the other way.

"Couldn't you draw back the curtain?" she asked politely.

He bent forward and looked out the window.

"This is Georgia, baby," he said, "or didn you know?"

"I know that," she answered, "but there's no one in here except me."

"Look," he said, "I don't make the rules."

"Then couldn't you ask the steward?"

"That peck back there don't make the rules either. Anyway, that man's really Simon Legree and he ain mellowed none in the years. Honest, lady, that man is pure evil and there ain a thing I can do."

"Not even ask him?"

"Unh-unh, baby, not even for you. I ask him anything this early in the morning he bite my arm off. I always stay short of him, but until noon I avoid him completely."

She shrugged and drank her orange juice, then poured a cup of coffee. It was good, strong the way she liked it. She was conscious of the steward passing and she called out to him.

"Could you draw back the curtain behind me?" she asked. "It cuts off the light and it's really most unpleasant."

He turned around and looked at her.

"The laws of this state are that colored patrons must eat behind that curtain," he said. "I don't make those rules, I merely carry them out."

"I know that," she said. "I'm not blaming you, but since I am the one person in here——"

"I'm not interested in what you think," he broke in.

"I merely——" she protested.

But he gave her no time to finish. "I don't care what you merely," he said. "If you don't like it, you can leave now. I won't charge you for the orange juice and coffee."

She wished now that she had kept her mouth shut. At the other end of the car she saw some white people entering and she hated scenes, but she was in so far now that she could not possibly withdraw without making her position clear.

"All I ask is a little courtesy," she said slowly. "I've done nothing to deserve abuse."

"You want me to call the conductor? He'll put you off at the next whistle stop, if that's what you want. Or would you rather talk to a policeman in Jacksonville? I don't have the time nor the patience to argue with you. If you don't like the way we do things down here, why didn't you stay up North?"

He turned abruptly and walked past her down the aisle to where the white people were waiting. She felt the tears rise to her eyes and the sting of his words across her face like a lash. In a moment she knew that she was going to cry and, like a wound-up mechanical toy, once started, she would stop only when she had run down. Blindly she got up from her chair and hurried out of the car.

The train lay idly in the Jacksonville station, as though exhausted from the jerky backings into the yard to drop the cars slated for Miami and to pick up others in their place for the run diagonally across the state to Tampa. It was still early enough in the morning for a little coolness to remain in the air, but soon it would be warm, and then by noonday actually hot. Alberta walked up and down the crushed-stone pathway smoking a cigarette. The front end of the train stretched out past the covered platform and she could feel the soft air and the sun warm on her face.

For the first time she had the feeling of being almost there. She was impatient at the slowness of the train in starting and looked at her watch as if by so doing she could hurry it along. Then as she turned to retrace her steps she was conscious of someone coming toward her. Looking up, she saw a man who she remembered having been in the same coach.

Partly she knew this by his clothes, because he wore the kind of suit of which she was most contemptuous. It was the sort of thing, she told herself bitterly, that could have belonged only to a Negro, and to the sort of person, moreover, whom she particularly detested. In New York, riding to work on the subway, she used to see Negro men wearing zoot suits and would want to get off at the next station and change trains. This was not only a zoot suit but it was also green; above it was a wide-brimmed pork-pie hat and below it tan shoes that were too narrow and pointed at the toes. She turned back the way she had been going, feeling a disgust at the too handsome brown face which wore the slightly cynical look she had grown to associate with a certain type of man who was always on the prowl.

136

Dropping into step beside her, he said, "How far you goin, baby?"

She did not answer, or even act as though she was conscious that he was walking along beside her.

"My, my," he laughed, turning up his coat collar, "sho is gotten cold around here."

He looked at her and she kept her eyes straight ahead, as though she were alone or there were a wall between them.

"Lissen, baby," he said softly, "you don't have to give me no jive. Back in my bag I got a bottle of good whisky. Couple of drinks, you liable to thaw out bout the time we get to Tampa. I could show you a good time in Tampa."

Turning her head, she said, "Why don't you drop dead?"

He shrugged. "Your loss, baby," he said, and walked away.

When he left she was in a rage, and she kicked out angrily at the crushed stones, sending a shower of pebbles before her. The conceit of Negro men infuriated her, and the whole mythology of their sexual desirability seemed to her distorted beyond all belief. They were arrogant, ignorant, and above all incapable of giving to any woman the security which was hers by right. Even her father, she thought bitterly, had never been able to provide. It was the money that her mother earned as a domestic fully as much as his pay check from the railroad that had kept them going, and in hard times it was her mother alone who had managed to hold the family together. She remembered the mornings when her mother used to take her along when she went to work, leaving her outdoors to play by herself or with the white children of the woman for whom she was at that moment cooking. None of the white children's mothers had to work; the fathers were the ones who carried the whole load.

Even now, trained as she was in social work and knowing something of the cause and effect in relation to Negro employment, she could think of her father only as a failure. It seemed to her unconsciously that he had rejected her because she was not a boy, and through the years this had added to her feeling of hidden resentment against him, so that she had been thrown back into her mother's orbit completely.

Restlessly she looked at her watch; it was almost time for the train to be on its way again. She was conscious that two white men on a baggage cart across the tracks were looking over at her, and she gave them an aloof stare. One of them leaned toward the other and said something, then the two of them threw back their heads and laughed. She knew what had been said as surely as though she could read their lips, but it did not bother her; their sexual interest seemed almost a compliment.

Leisurely she walked toward the open door at the rear of the standing jimcrow coach and got onto the train.

Under her the wheels seemed to be reminding Alberta that she was almost home. With each mile that fell away behind her, the feeling became stronger and stronger. It seemed to her now as though she had never really been very far from home in spite of all her efforts to forget and the many times she had sworn that she would never return, not even if she were starving to death. She looked out the window at the high-bonneted native pine, the sandy loam, and the palmetto scrub. Soon there would be orderly and cool green citrus groves, and then she would know that they were almost there.

Then suddenly she remembered the incident in the dining car, and she steeled herself against the feeling that had been slowly taking possession of her, the sentimentality that she had hung behind her on a peg tagged childhood and which she had outgrown forever. That was what home was—the South. Not the gallant South of the magnolia and the julep, of the handsome white man and his beautiful wife, the lost cause that the movies were so fond of portraying, but the real South in back of the stage-set big house—niggertown across the tracks, circled by a harsh and frightened ring of poor whites whose only justification for being alive was that those above them had decreed that they would always, no matter how low they might sink, be better than a Negro. Home, sweet home, she thought, and it tasted bitter to her mouth.

Then why was she returning? She told herself that it was because she wanted to see her mother again, because in spite of all her pleas and her offer to pay her mother's way, she knew that she would never be able to persuade Esther to come North to New York. It was only that, she told herself, that and nothing more. The train slowed and, looking out, she saw that they were bridging a river; after the muddy red water of Georgia it seemed almost black, deep and moody, choked at the sides and out to the middle of the channel by delicate lavender water hyacinth.

Or was it merely that she had wanted to get out of New York and its tensions, to be free for a while of Rob, of too many frantic parties and the dark brown taste in her mouth the morning after? She liked her job, and yet inwardly she knew that she was afraid that she had gotten from it all the possible prestige and promotion. Often there seemed an aimlessness to her life that distressed her; she was too ambitious, and once she got what she wanted, she no longer seemed to want it.

She reached for one of the magazines she had bought in Penn Station in New York and, hardly looking at it, thumbed through the pages, stopping at a picture here and there, reading an occasional line, glancing idly at the advertisements. The new clothes seemed to her ugly, not suited to her at all; the new hats were impossible, but at least hemlines were not going to change. Carelessly she threw the magazine down; it spanked the seat and fell on the floor, but she did not bother to pick it up. She looked at her watch again.

Glancing out the window, she saw the little station at Avalon Springs where now not even the milk trains bothered to stop. She began gathering her things together. Who would meet her? Not Luther; he would probably be at work. Maybe Bessie would be able to get off. Bessie, then, and her mother. For a moment she tried to picture Mama, but all she could see was the woman she remembered from the framed picture she kept in her apartment on the bedroom bureau. But that was at least ten years old. How old was Mama? She realized that she did not know. Luther was thirty-eight and she herself had passed thirty, although no one would really think it, and she had stopped counting the years.

The train whistled again and suddenly she was filled with an unknown terror. Why had she come? She thought of the security and comfort of her little apartment and it filled her with a longing that was almost painful. The whole thing had been a mistake, as Rob had told her it would be, and now it was too late to do anything about it. Nervously she lit a cigarette and almost as suddenly her near panic left her.

She was coming home and it was going to be all right.

18. After Bessie left for work in the morning Esther would prepare Alberta's breakfast. It made her feel a little like a conspirator as she prepared the tray neatly, usually with a fresh-cut flower in a glass or a newly opened camellia floating in a shallow bowl of water. Then she would go into the room that had been Luther's, softly walk across the floor to the window, and quietly raise the shade so that the sun could come streaming into the room. Often before she awakened her sleeping daughter she would stand at the foot of the bed and look down at her, the face softened in repose and one arm thrown up in almost the gesture of a defenseless child. It seemed to her then that Alberta had grown more beautiful in the years that she had been away from home, especially now that she had lost the tired, drawn look which she had had when first she stepped off the train.

Presently Alberta would awaken, opening her eyes slowly and stretching a little.

"Hello, Mama," she would whisper, her voice still dulled by sleep.

"Mornin, baby, want yo breakfast? It all ready and on the tray."

Then she would bend down and kiss her, and as Alberta held her cheek close to hers Esther would smell the delicate aroma of leftover scent.

"Thank you, Mama. I'll be ready by the time you come back."

Back in the kitchen she would always have a slight feeling of guilt, for she knew that it irked Bessie a little that Alberta never got up for breakfast. Then she would tell herself that the way Alberta looked when she got off the train, so tired and drawn, she had earned the rest, and besides, it was her right to spoil her for a little if she had a mind to.

This morning she put a large glass of cold orange juice on the tray, along with chilled half grapefruit, and from the freshly brewed coffee on the back of the wood stove she poured enough for two or three cups into a teapot. Opening the oven, she took out the thin, crisp toast that Alberta liked and put it under an inverted soup dish on the tray. Now she was ready.

When she went back to the bedroom Alberta was propped up with pillows, her hair neatly combed and her face freshly made up. Her mother put the tray on the night table by the bed and sat down in the chair by the window.

"Everythin there, baby?"

"Mmm, Mama. Just the way I like it, too."

Alberta finished the orange juice and began leisurely to spoon the grapefruit.

"You don't get grapefruit like this in New York, Mama. You know you're spoiling me, don't you? I'll have to make a lot of money so I can have a maid. I want a *lot* of money, Mama."

"Tell me bout your day, baby. I always wondered, but your letters never told me."

"Well, Mama," Alberta said, pouring more coffee, "there's not much to tell. I get up and have breakfast and then go down to the office. I get off at five, come home and eat, and then maybe in the evening I go to a party."

"What kind of a party, honey?"

"Oh, usually a big party, Mama. It's crowded and it's gay, and usually people never want to go home and sometimes some of them don't. They just sit up and talk and have fun."

"Who's there, baby? Tell Mama about it."

"Everybody's there, Mama. There'll be professors and writers, musicians, actors, dancers, and then a lot of people like me. Mama, why wouldn't you ever come to New York?"

"Reckon I too old, baby, old and sot in my ways."

"Pooh, you aren't old. How old are you, Mama?"

"Old enough to know I cain change my ways. This is where I belong, baby. I wouldn't fit in New York. I just rattle round and shame you fore your friends."

"No, Mama, never that. Say you'll come next year."

"No, baby," she said, getting up, "my roots is too deep." She looked at the traveling clock on the bureau in its bright red leather case. "I got to go to the market, Alberta. You like to come?"

Alberta lit a cigarette and stretched lazily. "I don't guess so, Mama. You go, and by the time you get back I'll be up and dressed. This time I promise."

Her mother laughed. It was good to see her baby getting her rest. She looked around the room. Alberta had such lovely things, even to sleep in or to loll around the house the whole morning long. In the closet her dresses looked so new, almost as though they had never been worn. She went over and kissed Alberta.

"You smell good enough to eat," she said. "You git your rest, chile. Don't git up till you feels like it. Woan be gone long, baby."

She turned away and went out the door.

Even with the ration book that Alberta had brought, it was hard to market. Everything was costly, and then you were never sure of what you were getting. Shopping, it seemed to Esther, used to be like a game, a good-natured give-and-take between merchant and customer, but now it was more like an ill-tempered exchange of insults; if you would not take what they had to offer, someone else would. By the time that she was done and on her way home it seemed to her as though she had already done a good day's work.

As she was gathering her packages together she saw Jeff coming toward her.

"Better let me hep you tote them," he said. "Looks to me like you got more bundles than they is of you. I just been down to the Square to get me a can of tobacco."

Taking most of her packages, he walked along beside her. Since Alberta had come home she had not been seeing much of Jeff. He had come over once when they were sitting out in the back the way they usually did in the afternoon. She had introduced him to Alberta almost shyly, feeling as she always did the conflict that the two of them seemed to set up within her. He had not stayed long, and when he had gone Alberta had said nothing that would give Esther any possible clue as to how she had liked him. Now that she was with him Esther realized she had missed seeing him; when he was with her she always seemed to feel more complete.

"How you been, Jeff?" she asked.

"I been good," he answered. "I was out to the lake yestiday, but I didn do no good. Speckled perch done stopped bitin and them trouts wouldn even take live bait. I figure to go again in the mornin, now that the wind's shifted. You like to go?"

"I'd like to, Jeff," she said, "I sho would. But I reckon I better not."

"Sho, I know how hit is. You ain seen yo gal in a long time. I know you wants to be with her. Be right funny if you didn."

She nodded. "You take me soon as Alberta gone back to New York?"

"Any time you wants to go. All you got to do is say the word."

They turned into their street and walked along on the shady side. When they reached her house he brought the packages into the kitchen and, after she thanked him, he said his good-by, then went out the back and across the yard toward his house. His going left her with an emptiness, so that she busied herself putting things away. When she was done she looked at the alarm clock by the stove.

"Baby," she called over her shoulder.

"Almost, Mama. I'm up but I'm not dressed."

"What you want for lunch, baby?"

"I don't care, Mama. Not much, though. Can I have iced tea?"

"Sho, baby. I have it ready directly."

She put the kettle on the stove to boil.

In the afternoons, after she had eaten lunch, Alberta liked to go out in the back yard under a shade tree and read. There were two old deck chairs there that Luther had found in a secondhand store and had recovered himself with some bright-colored canvas. Often Esther would come out and sit with her after the dishes were done, for she felt that Alberta was going to be there for so short a time that she hated to let her out of her sight.

She would be in the kitchen and, looking out, would be torn between wanting to be with Alberta and feeling that she should respect her privacy, but in the end the magnet was too strong and she would leave what she was doing and go out into the back yard. Alberta would not hear her, so that her head would still be bent over the book she was reading. Esther would note the graceful curve of her neck and the one hand and arm hanging loosely over the arm of the deck chair. Alberta's hands were to her as beautiful as flowers.

Today as she came closer Alberta looked up. "Hey, Mama. Come sit in the shade."

Esther sat down and watched Alberta as she laid the book face down on the grass and lit a cigarette.

"I ain bustin in on you, chile? You was readin, I know. You go ahead an read and I'll just sit here a spell to catch my breath."

Alberta shrugged. "I was getting a little bored anyway, Mama. If I'd read two or three minutes more, I think I would have fallen asleep."

Just to be there was enough for Esther. Under the tree it was cool and there was a suggestion of a breeze in the air. The sky was almost cloudless.

"It's certainly peaceful here, Mama."

"It sho is, baby. I set here a lot in the afternoon."

"New York seems far away. I needed this, Mama. You get so tense up there and everyone hurries so. Another week of this and I'll be so healthy you won't know me."

"You doan want to shut yoself off completely, chile. Do you good to go out. You got to socialize some. Maybe one night you go with Bessie and Eric?"

"Maybe, Mama," Alberta shrugged. "What's Eric like?"

"He right nice, Alberta. I reckon Bessie is kind of gone on him. But what about you, chile? I figured you to be married by now. Lawd, I'd near about had all of you by the time I was your age."

Alberta laughed. "I know, Mama, but you married Daddy so young you hardly knew what you were doing. I want to be sure before I marry."

"I was sure," Esther answered simply. "I knowed the minute I seen him."

Alberta sighed. "Well, I'm not. I like it the way it is. I have all the fun I want and a nice place to live. I really don't need a husband."

"Every woman needs a man, chile."

"I see you were with your gentleman friend, Mama," Alberta said, laughing.

"Now doan you start ridin me like Bessie does. To hear her talk, you think me and Jeff was courtin. He just a friend, a good friend who carries me fishin sometimes."

Alberta laughed again. "Methinks the lady doth protest too much," she said mockingly.

"What you mean, chile?"

"Nothing, Mama, just something a man named Shakespeare once said in a play."

"Oh. Baby, you got a man? A special man, I mean."

"Mama, I've got lots of men."

"No special man?"

"Yes, Mama, one special one."

"I wants to see you married, Alberta. Luther he gone and done it, and Bessie actin like she might. I hope fore I die to see all my children happily married, happy as I was."

Alberta got to her feet and looked at her watch. It was a little after four.

"Mama, I think I'll get my bath in before Bessie comes home."

"You better. She goin out tonight."

"I'll hurry, Mama, and then I'll help you with dinner."

Esther watched Alberta as she picked up her things and walked across the yard to the kitchen door. That she had not gone out at night, or even during the day, seemed strange; she was too pretty a girl to be closed off that way. She wished she knew more about Alberta. It made her feel shut out by a door to know that she didn't.

Dinner was over and the dishes washed. Bessie was in her room putting on the finishing touches for Eric, who would be coming for her any minute. It was the first time that he had been by since Alberta had arrived, and Esther was wondering why. It seemed to her a little strange. Had she been Bessie, it seemed to her that the first thing she would want would be to show off Eric to Alberta. He was an attractive and charming man; she had grown as fond of him as if he were her own.

She looked across at Alberta, sitting in the big chair by the radio. She kept twirling the dial, trying to find a program that she liked, but in a moment she turned the radio off and got up.

"What's the matter, chile? You plumb feisty tonight."

"I don't know, Mama, just restless."

In a moment they both heard a car drive up in front of the house. Esther went over and opened the door.

"Come in, Eric," she called. "Bessie be ready directly."

He was wearing a white linen suit; it looked good on him, and in it he looked so nearly like a white man tanned by the sun that for a moment it gave her a shock.

"Eric," she said slowly, "I doan think you met Alberta yet."

"No," he said casually, "I haven't, but I've heard a lot about her."

Alberta looked at him and smiled. "I've heard about you too, Eric. And of course I read your book when it first came out."

"A woman after my own heart," he told her.

"I know people you know in Washington," she went on. "Sterling and Daisy, the Fraziers, and a lot more, I guess."

"Fine," he said, and grinned, "but let's not play 'Who do you know?' now. Sometime we'll devote a whole evening to it." He turned back to Alberta's mother. "How are you, Mrs. Mathews?"

"I is fine, Eric. I reckon you best to sit down. Bessie may be a minute or so."

"Yes," he said, sitting down beside her on the couch, "I know that from past experience. The only thing good is that Bessie is usually worth waiting for."

There was a slight lull in the conversation then, and Esther looked over at Alberta. Her eyes were on Eric, and the nervous listlessness of a moment ago had vanished. In its place was a vivaciousness that was almost contagious. Just then Bessie came into the room. She was wearing a black linen suit and black-and-white shoes; atop her head was a tiny white hat and the only bit of color was a canary-yellow artificial flower on her left shoulder.

"I told you she'd be worth waiting for, Mrs. Mathews," Eric said.

"Flatterer," Bessie laughed. "I know why you're making up to Mama, too. You like her cooking." She went over and kissed her mother. "I won't be late, Mama. Good night, Alberta. Come on, Eric."

He stood up, and just as they were about to go out he stopped.

"Come on along, Alberta," he said. "We aren't going to do anything special. If you hadn't been born around here we might even show you the sights."

"Oh, I wouldn't do that. I'd just be in the way, wouldn't I, Bessie?"

Bessie paused for a moment before she answered. "No," she said slowly. "No, you wouldn't be in the way. Come along if you'd like to."

"Maybe I will, then. I'll go get a hat and put on my face. I won't be a minute."

Esther watched Bessie's face as Alberta went back to her room. Then Bessie turned toward Eric and her expression was natural again.

"How do you like my big sister?" she asked.

"All right," Eric answered, "but then I like all you Mathewses."

"Listen to him, Mama. He wants to come to dinner again and have some more of that strawberry shortcake."

"Of course I do," he laughed, "and soon, too."

Alberta entered the room; she had not only put on a hat but had changed her dress and shoes as well.

"See," she said, "I wasn't long."

Laughing, the three of them went out the door. Esther heard the motor start and the changing gears as the car pulled away and down the street.

19.

Eulia awakened and lay listening to Luther's regular breathing; she couldn't seem able to get back to sleep and yet she knew it was too early to get up. Within she could feel the baby stirring, and its movements made her content, knowing that all was well. The end of gestation seemed a long way off, though she knew that it really wasn't. Three months was not so very long. Finally, in desperation, she got out of bed and went into the kitchen to brew a pot of coffee.

As she stood by the electric range she remembered the day, a few months ago, when they had moved into the project. It had seemed so barren and unfamiliar to her then that she had been filled with terror that she would never be able to make it a real home. You would never know it now, she thought as she looked around the room.

The sunlight was beginning to come in the window; it lay now in a pool at the edge of the black linoleum, and by midmorning it would flood the room. The curtains were as fresh and crisp as though she had laundered them only yesterday. She set two places at the bright red kitchen table and put in the center one of the blossoming plants growing in pots along the sill over the kitchen sink. Then she squeezed orange juice and put it into the refrigerator to chill.

It was still too early to call Luther. Turning, she went into the room that was to be the baby's, feeling a little foolish and yet desperately wanting to do so. Sitting down in a chair by the window, she planned the way the room would be once the baby came. She wondered how Luther really felt about it, if he wanted a child as much as she. It seemed to her that she should know, that she should be able to sense his every mood, but she knew that she could not. It was a man's world, and often she felt shut out of it; tricked by a biological quirk of nature, she could never know it as he did. And, loving him as much as she did, there were still times when she resented it. It seemed to close her in, shut her off from things. It seemed almost as though everyone expected that a woman should always, figuratively, walk two steps behind a man.

She resented the union, and this talk of a strike seemed to her the greatest folly in the world. What was the good of it when even if they won they would never earn enough to make up for what they had lost while they were not working? Luther had tried to explain it to her, but every time she tried to question what he was saying it seemed to her that he would grow angry and withdraw into his shell. She knew that the cost of living had gone up, knew it better than he, and yet the possibility of losing all of his pay check for a period that might extend into weeks seemed to her no answer. Far better to tighten his belt and eat less.

She looked at the electric clock on the wall. It was almost time to call Luther, and yet she hated to do so. She loved Luther; even though it often seemed to her that he would never listen to her, she could never love anyone else. She looked at the clock again. If she put off calling him any longer, he would be late for work.

Luther had finished his breakfast but was having one last cup of coffee before starting off for the shipyard. This was the time Eulia liked best, the moment during the day when they seemed closest to each other. It was, in fact, the time when she usually asked for things to which she felt he might normally object.

"I'm glad Bessie and Eric brought Alberta over the other night," she said. "Alberta sho has changed."

"Changed?" he asked.

Eulia shrugged. "Aw, I doan know. Course I never knew her well as I knew Bessie. If I was Bessie, I'd look out."

"What you mean, Eulia?"

"Luther, you an awful good man but sometimes you plumb blind. You mean you couldn see Alberta was tryin to snatch Eric away from Bessie?"

"Woman, sometimes I think you teched. I didn see no such thing. Looked to me like the three of them was having a ball."

Eulia got up from the table and went behind his chair. Bending down, she put her arms around his neck and kissed him lightly on the side of the cheek.

"Suppose you doan see what happenin between yo mama and my daddy neither."

"Trouble with you women is you think you know everythin. Mama knowed yo daddy most all her life."

"Trouble with you women," she mocked, then blew down the back of his shirt.

He laughed good-naturedly and got up from his chair. "Yeah," he said, "an you keep messin round me like that an I ain gonna git to no job."

"Why not?" she asked innocently.

He grinned at her. "You keep it up you find out why not."

"I reckon I better not."

Taking the coat that lay on the chair by the door, he came over to her. Kissing her, he said, "If I was you I quit this nonsense bout Alberta and Mama. You got enough to keep you busy round here."

Eulia made a face at him and turned away. As she did so he hit her a glancing smack across the buttocks and, wheeling around, she went for him. For a moment they tussled by the door in mock fury and then he left.

"I woan be home for lunch," he called to her. "I like to forgot to tell you."

"Where you goin?" she asked.

"I got me another woman. One got some fat on her bones."

"She woan be good as me."

"Hunh, how you know?"

She made another face at him. "Ain no woman have you."

"Thas right, belittle me. Ain that jest like a woman?" He stopped to light a cigarette, exploding a kitchen match into flame against his thumbnail. "Naw, Eulia, I eatin with some uh the boys. We got business to talk over. I be home this evenin the reglar time."

He waved to her and started across the back lot toward the road that led to the shipyard. She watched him for a moment before turning back into the kitchen. Sprinkling soap chips into the kitchen sink, she turned the spigots on hard, then put in the few breakfast dishes. Today was the day that she did her washing in the electric washing machine over in the community laundry. Probably if she hurried she would be one of the first there, but she could never seem to leave an untidy house, even to avoid standing in line. She decided to do the house first and then, after the washing, she would walk a ways out into the country since Luther was not coming home for lunch. The project was on the edge of town, and in ten minutes she could be away from everything.

She left the dishes to soak in the sink and went into the room that she and Luther shared to make up the bed.

When Eulia arrived at the laundry with her wash there was only one person ahead of her, a huge and very black woman who lived in the block of apartments across from her and whom she knew slightly.

"Hey, Eulia," the woman called. "I be done directly. How you doin?"

"Purty good, Mabel. How you?"

"I doin good. That machine sho beat all that fuss we used to do. Heatin that ole iron washtub in the back yard with a fire, an I hopes I never sees another washboard. Umm-munh."

"We had a machine where I worked."

"Yeah? Well, you was lucky tuh work out. All I did was wash for the white folks, and top of that I had all them younguns."

In a few minutes two other women came and got into line behind them. Shortly after, they began talking.

"I heerd they got three machines over to the white project. Less of them than they is of us, too."

"Sho? Ain it so. The white folks got everythin."

"That ain all, gal. They doan have to put but a nickel in the machine, not a dime like we does."

"Do tell! Now ain that awful?"

"Gits free soap, too, the way I heerd it. Machines better, too. Doan have to mess with all them levers a-tall. You jest puts in yo nickel and mashes a button."

"White folks wussn uh hawg in a goober patch," the other one said.

Then their laughter came, sudden and acrid, full of the inevitability of being born the wrong color.

At last it was Eulia's turn and she quickly prepared the machine. She lit a cigarette as she waited for it to run its cycle. She did not join in the talk with the others around her, and she was hardly conscious of what they were saying. Later, when the machine turned itself off and delivered her clothes, washed, rinsed, and damp-dried, she took her basket and went quickly back to her apartment. She hurried as she hung the clothes on the line that worked on a pulley from the kitchen window. When she was through she went into the bedroom for her bag, making sure that there was a package of cigarettes in it.

Outdoors again, she walked off slowly toward the east. The day was beautiful, clear and hot but with enough of a breeze so that it was not uncomfortable on the road. She knew where she was going. Perhaps half a mile away there was a tiny lake where she liked to go. It lay off the road several hundred yards and she had stumbled across it quite by chance one day. Evidently it had once, during the boom, been intended for a subdivision, for there was a crumbled stucco arch at the entrance and a tired-looking dock jutted out into the water. Actually it was less a lake than a large pond.

Once there, she walked out onto the dock and sat down at the end. She knew from past experience where the planking was safe and where it was rotten. Reaching into her pocketbook, she took out a paper napkin full of bread crusts and, crumbling them, fed the panfish that hung around under the dock. She watched them eat greedily, mostly bream and a few catfish. When the bread was all gone she took off her shoes and dangled her bare feet in the water.

She seemed far away from where she was, and she liked the feeling. Across the pond she saw a little Ward's heron standing in the water like something carved out of wood. She wriggled her toes and watched the bubbles that resulted from the movement. Within she felt the movement of her baby as it kicked hard against the lower wall of her abdomen.

"Thas right," she laughed, "kick me, you rascal. You knows I cain kick back."

Mentally she counted the time left of her pregnancy, and though she tried to cheat a little, it still seemed a very long time. It was not that she was tired of pregnancy, for she had never felt better in her life, but merely that she was anxious to see what was within her, to hold it in her arms, to realize that it had a life of its own independent of herself. Was it a boy or a girl? She did not know, and her doctor refused to say either way. Others guessed by the way she carried the baby, but she put little faith in that, even though the older women all seemed so sure that it was to be a boy.

Suddenly she hoped it would be a girl, and an almost fierce feeling came over her. If it was, she was not going to end up the way Eulia had, a prisoner in a man's world. Nor, she told herself, were the white folks going to crush her spirit the way they tried to crush everyone whose skin did not happen to be white. No, her child was going to have the things that she herself had so badly wanted.

When Eulia got back from her walk she rested, as the doctor had told her to do, for the better part of an hour. Each day she would not mean to nap, but often, as today, she would feel herself slipping off and she seemed powerless to resist the sensation. She awakened later, not dulled from sleep, but refreshed and feeling even better than she had felt before she lay down. Getting up, she guiltily smoothed out the bed, went into the bathroom and hastily washed her face with cold water. Then, coming back into the bedroom, she began to comb her hair.

Outside she heard a car drive up and stop. Idly she wondered who it could be, and as she came out of the bedroom and crossed the living room she looked through the latched screen door. She could see a car, but the light was so much in her eyes that it was hard to see who was in it.

Then her eyes grew more accustomed to the light and she saw that it was Mrs. Randall in her little green convertible. Eulia went down the lawn to where the car was parked.

"Hello, Miz Randall," she called, and, coming up to the car, put one foot on the running board.

"You were going to come see me, Eulia, but you never did. So when I happened to be coming over this way I thought I'd stop by."

"I glad you did, Miz Randall. How Mister Jeff?"

"Same as ever, Eulia. Essie Mae is a lamb, but we both wish we had you back."

Eulia felt resentment swell up within her like a balloon. "I ain comin back," she said slowly. "I ain never comin back."

"I know that, Eulia. That's not why I came."

But how could she be sure? She did not quite know how she should treat this woman for whom she had once worked; now it was different and she knew that the white woman was trying to break down the wall between them, but she, Eulia, was not even sure that she wanted it down. Maybe things were better the way they were, the way they had always been.

"How's Luther, Eulia?"

"He fine, Miz Randall."

"It doesn't seem the same without him at the taproom. Jeff and I stopped by there the other night."

"He like it where he at," Eulia said defensively. "I don't reckon he ever go back."

The two of them were silent. Eulia wished that the white woman would go, but she made no move toward starting the car.

Mrs. Randall offered Eulia a cigarette and took one for herself.

"How's the baby coming along?" she asked. "When are you going to have it?"

"Not for three months now, Miz Randall. The doctor say everythin all right, though."

"Well, I've got to run along. I'm glad I stopped by. Let me know how you are."

"I will, Miz Randall, I sho will. I send word bout the baby by Luther."

"Which hospital will you be in, Eulia?"

Eulia laughed bitterly. "I ain goin to no hospital. I got a cullud doctuh an they woan let him work in the hospital here. I reckon I could stay there and be delivered by a white intern, but I doan want no boy experimentin on me. I wants my own doctor. I know he good."

"I'm sorry, Eulia."

"Ain yo fault, Miz Randall."

"No, I know," she said slowly, "but sometimes I feel as though I were responsible. I want to do what's right. I find I don't know how down here. Sometimes I feel, I think, as much an outsider as you do, Eulia. Only I'm white."

She started the car, then, reaching over, patted Eulia on the hand and drove off. Eulia stood watching until the car was out of sight.

20. Ethel was not unaware of the relationship which had sprung up between Bessie and Eric. She had learned of it via the campus grapevine, composed mainly of those faculty wives who saw in rumormongering a chance to strengthen the status of their husbands, many of which were at best at a low ebb. Ethel's initial reaction had been one of slight annoyance, and for several reasons. For one thing, since Bessie worked for the president of the college, Ethel felt that a certain loyalty was only her due, and it irked her that Bessie had not brought her the news before it sifted down secondhand. Besides, she was not at all certain that it was a good match.

Bessie, after all, had a background that was far from imposing, and in addition to this she was dark. But this initial response was soon replaced by another far more realistic; the fact that Bessie was not so fair as she at once eliminated her as a possible threat to Ethel's social position in the community. And even more important was the possibility that if the two married, Bessie would act as an anchor to keep Eric on the campus. Ethel was no fool, and she realized far more than Ezekiel the importance of having a man like Eric on the faculty. Also, unlike her husband, she was well aware that other Negro colleges would be quite willing to pay through the nose in order to get him.

She knew what he meant to the college in the way of publicity. Whenever an article of his appeared in a magazine there was likely to be mention of where he taught in the notes about the contributors. His book had appeared before he had come to the campus, but recently a reprint edition had been issued, and on the back of the jacket, under his picture, the fact that he was teaching at the college was prominently mentioned. Even had she disliked him, which she didn't, she would have done everything within her power to keep him on campus.

So once her initial response had been changed by a realistic revaluation, she became at once partisan. Having no daughters of her own, she entered into the thing with a spirit that was dynamic. Almost overnight the affair became as much hers as theirs and she assumed the position, at least in her own mind, of official matchmaker. Not knowing how far the relationship had advanced was a serious handicap, but one that she was certain could be overcome. Her hope was that she would be able to maneuver them into a position where marriage would naturally appear as the next step.

What had first appealed to her was an intimate little dinner party, preferably herself and the doctor, Bessie and Eric. At heart she was an incurable romantic, in spite of the fact that what little romance had ever been a part of her own marriage had long ago evaporated with the years. But she had envisioned the two of them being set an example by herself and Ezekiel, a backdrop of perfect connubial bliss, plus a dinner carefully planned and cooked to perfection, then served by candlelight. There would be the soft gleam of her perfectly polished mahogany table, the snowy whiteness of her best table linen, and naturally she would use only her best china and silver.

She felt that in this way Eric would be reminded of Washington and his own family. As for Bessie, even a brown-skinned woman would seem alluring, more soft and increasingly feminine, in such a setting. But above all, Ethel felt, such a gesture would firmly establish the fact that she and the doctor bestowed upon them their complete approval. For all she knew, this in itself might be the final tipping of the balance.

And then, just when she had her campaign so well planned, Alberta had arrived. There were no eligible bachelors among the faculty save Eric, at least none to match the sophistication that she was certain Alberta, after five years in New York, had acquired. So it seemed to her that a dinner party was hardly the answer.

The next morning at the breakfast table she told her husband something of her dilemma. She knew better than to approach him until after he had had his third cup of coffee and lighted his morning cigar, and then she approached him only obliquely. In the years of their marriage, if she had learned no other thing it was the exact moment at which his almost psychopathic early-morning grouch began to give way to his normal attitude of rather good-natured banter.

"Doctor," she said.

He looked up from his paper.

"We really should do something about Bessie and Eric."

"What do you mean?" he said patiently. "What about Bessie and Eric?"

"Well, surely you must have noticed that they are going around together."

"I hadn't," he said, and chuckled. "After all, my dear, I have more important things to do than checking up on the love life of my secretary. But what if they are? I can't see any great harm in that."

"It's not that at all, Doctor. I've thought the whole thing over carefully, and I think it would be a worth-while match."

"Match," he snorted. "Honestly, Ethel, you women do beat all. A man takes a girl out twice and the next thing he knows you've got him slated for the altar."

"You're a man, Doctor. You don't understand about such things."

He shrugged. "I guess I don't, Ethel."

"Anyway," she went on, "I thought it would be nice if we had them here at the house. I had planned on dinner, then Bessie's sister arrived from New York, so I guess that's out. There's no man here on the campus that would be right for her."

"I guess not," he chuckled, "not for Alberta."

"You know her?" she asked.

"Well, I wouldn't say I know her exactly. I remember her slightly from the time she was here on campus, and I did happen to bump into her in New York at a party."

"You never told me," she said, and her tone was slightly irritated.

"I thought I had, my dear, but I guess it just slipped my mind. I assure you it was of no importance. After all, at least two thirds of Harlem was there."

"What's she like?"

"Pretty much like all New Yorkers, I reckon. She probably talks the Negro problem all the time and thinks I'm an old Uncle Tom and a traitor to the race merely because I don't stick my neck out so the white folks can chop it off."

"Oh, I don't mean that. What does she look like?"

"Pretty enough, maybe a little prettier than Bessie. A little fairer, too, I reckon. Dresses well, but looks a little hard, the way so many New York women do. I'm surprised that she came back down South."

Ethel was silent for a moment, still a little resentful that he had not told her about meeting Alberta but more convinced than ever that a dinner party was out of the question. Anyway, she told herself angrily, most of the men on the faculty were as liable as not to use their knives at the dinner table.

"How would it be if we had the three of them over one afternoon for tea?"

He chuckled. "Must it be tea, Ethel?"

155

"We've discussed that before, Doctor. I'm convinced it's wrong to serve drinks to the faculty or to the students. You know I have no objections on moral grounds. It's just that it makes for too informal a relationship."

He shrugged. "Maybe you're right, Ethel. But it's awfully hard on me. Well, I best get on over to the office."

"You'll bear up under it," she said, holding her cheek up to be kissed. "I'll call Bessie a little later in the morning and arrange a day."

"All right, but you'd better have Bessie jot it down on my calendar. Otherwise I might schedule something that would conflict."

"All right, dear. And if there's a letter from George, call me. It's been so long since we heard from him. It seems months, but I know it can't really be that long."

"Well, out there in the Pacific I reckon a boy doesn't get too much time for letter writing."

After he had gone she sat for a moment at the dining-room table. She thought of George, out there somewhere alone and away from her, with no one to take care of him. She fought the image out of her mind. Surely today there would be a letter, or tomorrow at the latest.

It had started harmlessly enough, as a tea party should, but somehow it had gotten out of hand somewhere along the line. For one thing, Ethel had taken an immediate dislike to Alberta, had in some way known the moment that she came into the room that here was someone with whom to reckon. She recognized a sophistication that was more than skin deep, and this had managed to unnerve her. Knowing that she would have done the same thing herself if the tables had been turned, she sensed that any slip on her part, any putting on of airs, would be pantomimed all over Harlem. She merely should have acted natural, but it had been so long since she had done so in company other than her husband's that she had forgotten how. The result was that she was self-conscious and gave what amounted to almost a parody of herself at her worst.

When Ethel had first sat down to pour, Alberta had looked the situation over and found it not to her liking.

"Why, Mrs. Rogers," she said gaily, "you aren't going to give these poor men tea! It always seems to me sadistic to make a man try to balance a tiny cup on his knee."

"I agree with that," Ezekiel said. "I'd like to see a law passed barring tea. Somehow, drinking it never seemed quite manly to me. How about you, Eric?"

Eric shrugged. "Well, if I were forced to make a stand, I imagine I'd have to line up on your side, sir."

Feeling that this was the first test of her strength, Ethel was ready to take a firm stand, but suddenly she realized that to do so would merely add more ammunition for the caricature that Alberta was bound to spread about her.

"All right," she said, "we can as easily have cocktails." She turned to Eric. "But you make them, Eric. I declare, the doctor could never learn how to make even an old-fashioned."

"Well, Eric," Ezekiel said, "it looks like it's up to us."

Eric followed him out into the kitchen and the three women were left alone. The momentary lull in the conversation seemed endless to Ethel, and she said the first thing that popped into her head.

"I suppose that you find us very provincial after New York, Alberta?"

Alberta, who was lighting a cigarette, finished the process leisurely before she answered. When she flicked shut the lid of her silver cigarette lighter the sound seemed loud as a pistol shot in the stilled room.

"I really hadn't noticed," she said matter-of-factly. "I came down for a rest."

"But you find us changed?"

"No, not really, but then I haven't been off Mama's place. I usually find, however, that people who live the simplest endure the longest."

To Ethel it seemed as though Alberta looked around the room insolently, but the gesture was neither one thing nor the other, and it might easily have been her imagination. Yet she was certain that a slur had been intended, and she was not one to let such things go unanswered. But just as she was framing a lethal retort Eric and Ezekiel came in from the kitchen with a cocktail shaker and a tray of glasses, and Alberta went over to help them. You might imagine, Ethel thought, that Alberta was giving the party instead of myself. And looking at Alberta, dressed simply but stunningly in a black dress with a wide red belt, she felt suddenly overdressed and because of this conspicuous.

It was this, perhaps, which led to her downfall. Ordinarily she never took more than one cocktail, and then only to be polite, for she had never learned to enjoy any form of alcohol. But whatever it was that Eric had mixed seemed to her as harmless as lemonade, and being also a little nervous, she kept up with the rest of them. Almost before she knew it, and with complete surprise, she suddenly realized that for the first time in her life she was well on her way to being completely under the influence of alcohol. She found it a not unpleasant experience. In fact it seemed to her suddenly that the roles were reversed and that it was now Alberta who was at a disadvantage.

Looking across the room, she saw that Alberta was devoting her whole attention to Ezekiel. Rather than annoying her, this seemed suddenly very funny. She remembered a line she had once heard in a movie: "If she gets any closer to him," one of the characters had said, "she'll be behind him." From that point on she remembered very little and had no recollection of anything she might have said.

Somehow, in a manner which seemed to her most mysterious, they were suddenly all gone and she was by herself in the living room. Even Ezekiel was not there, but in a moment she heard him moving around upstairs. What had happened was still very vague in her mind, yet she sensed that it was not as she had imagined it. She felt it probable that her husband would reprimand her, and for a moment she tried to think of a defense. Then she remembered how Alberta had monopolized him and she decided to accuse him of paying too much attention to Alberta. After all, a strong offense is often the best defense.

By now the effects of her indulgence had somewhat worn off; there was no longer that odd feeling that the room was full of revolving pinwheels. Yet she did not feel herself, and in spite of her strategy of attacking Ezekiel first for his own misconduct, she had grave feelings of guilt. Looking at her wrist watch, she saw that it was well after their normal hour for dinner and she knew that the maid was going to be sulky. As she started toward the kitchen the door opened and the maid came in with a letter.

"Boy just brung this over, Miz Rogers. Hit come special delivery."

Ethel took it mechanically, waiting until the maid left the room before she looked at it. The room had settled down but she was still unsteady from what she had drunk; through a slight blur she glanced down at the letter and saw that it was addressed in her son's handwriting and postmarked Washington. With one finger she opened it clumsily.

She read:

DEAR MOTHER,

I am back in the States for good. I was wounded, but I am all right now, so don't worry. The chances are that I will be here for a month at least and then I'll come home. I'll be out of the service for good. Don't try to come up here, as they won't let you see me. Anyway, I don't want to see anyone right now, even you. I can't write more now, but it will be good to get home. To you all my love and to Dad my very best.

Always,
GEORGE

When she finished she was trembling, but she was no longer woozy from the cocktails she had had. Her first thought was to go to George at once, by plane if possible; if not, by the late train that very night. She remembered how when he had been at college in Boston and had hurt himself playing football she had flown up. He had pretended that he had not wanted her to come, but she had known otherwise. This letter, however, seemed so definite. She glanced at it again and noticed that there was a postscript.

"Ordinarily," she read, "the army would have notified you. But there seems to have been considerable confusion about me, and by the time it was cleared up it was too late. I'll tell you about it when I see you. G."

All at once she started to cry, a strange mixture of grief and joy, released tension, and the aftereffects of the alcohol which she had consumed. She looked up and saw that Ezekiel had come in; without a word she handed him the letter. He looked up when he had finished reading it.

"I'm glad, my dear," he said simply. "At least now we know that the boy will be safe forever."

She nodded but could not stop her sobbing. Gently he laid his hand on her shoulder and she looked up at him.

"I don't want any dinner," she said dully.

"I know, my dear, I'll explain to Bertha. Maybe later I'll bring you up a little something."

She nodded again and got to her feet. She was steady enough now but felt as though everything had been drained out of her. Ezekiel helped her up the stairs and into their room, then turned to go. She wanted to stop him, to tell him that she was sorry she had made such a fool of herself, but somehow she found she could not yet do so. She wanted to be alone.

She lay down on the bed, but in a moment she knew she was going to be sick and, getting up, she found that the feeling left her. She undressed slowly and cold-creamed her face, then put on her nightdress, went into the bathroom, and carefully brushed her teeth. This time, when she lay down again, the nausea had passed, but it had left her with a throbbing headache.

It was no matter. George was safe; he was coming home. Nothing else mattered, not even the way she had acted at the party. Tomorrow and the day after perhaps it would bother her, but now it was something far away which somehow had very little connection with herself.

21. Waiting on the porch for Luther to come by and pick her up, Alberta took stock of the six days that she had been home and the six days that were still remaining. She didn't especially want to go to Citrus City, but she felt that if she stayed around the house another day she would completely lose her mind. It wasn't that she didn't love her mother. Mama's sweet, she thought, but after just so many days you feel as though you're being completely smothered. In Citrus City she could at least walk around and window-shop, and she really had seen almost nothing of Luther. Next to Mama, of all of them she guessed she liked Luther best. She was fond of Bessie, she supposed, but not in the same way. And after all, she had really only seen Luther the one night that she and Bessie and Eric had stopped by his apartment. She knew that Mama was having them all for Sunday dinner, but that would give her no real time for a visit. She was glad that Luther and Eulia were married, and she felt that they were wise to have moved off by themselves.

From the one night she had spent with them, she was well aware of the fact that Eulia did not like her, but this fact neither surprised nor especially bothered her. She knew that few women did, and she giggled to herself as she remembered the afternoon she had spent at the college. I guess Queen Ethel doesn't like me very much either, she thought, but I'll fix her little red wagon good after I get back to New York. In her mind she spun out the amusing tale she would make of the party and just how she would embroider it in the telling.

Down the street she saw Luther coming, and when the car stopped in front of the gate she noted how clean it looked, almost as though it had been freshly polished especially for her. She waved and hurried down the steps.

"Hey, Alberta," Luther called, opening the door for her.

"Hi, Luther, it's sweet of you to run me over to town."

He started the motor and let out the clutch; the car moved smoothly out into the road.

"It nothin, Alberta. I had this time off today an I didn hardly know what to do with it. Anyway, I hardly seen you."

They came up to the highway and cut smoothly into the traffic. As they drove along she looked idly at all the new buildings that had been erected since she had left home. Very little seemed familiar to her, even the road on which they were driving. Luther looked over at her and grinned.

"Looks different, doan it?"

She nodded, then laughed. "This doesn't even seem the same way we used to go to Citrus City."

"It ain the way we used to go, Alberta. When they put in the new highway they cut out the old one. Ain hardly nobody uses it no more. The city grown too. It the best all-year-round city in Florida now, I reckon, barrin Jacksonville."

She nodded. It seemed to her almost pathetic, the pride he seemed to take in something to which he hardly belonged. Well, she wouldn't have it on a silver platter—either this hick town or any part of the South. She was well out of it and lucky to be so. She remembered how once a party of her friends had gone to a night club in the Village which featured Negro entertainers. When the band had played "Carry Me Back to Old Virginny" a well-known Negro writer had convulsed them all by saying: "They want me, they're going to have to drag me!" That was the way she felt; never again would she travel below Washington.

Thinking of that incident for some reason reminded her of Eric. He was the only one here who even remotely interested her, and she didn't really want him. But she decided that she would try to get him away from Bessie, just to see if she could.

Your own sister, she thought; Alberta, you certainly are a bitch. But this realization in no way upset her; it was not a new discovery, and she reaffirmed it almost with admiration.

As Alberta walked down Tangerine Avenue most of the stores seemed to her shoddy and filled with things that she had seen six months ago in New York along Fourteenth Street. It gave her a great deal of personal satisfaction to realize that she was better dressed than nine tenths of the women she passed. Even the two large department stores which she had remembered somehow as being almost like Macy's or Lord and Taylor seemed to have shrunk since she had been away. She looked in the windows and saw nothing in which she would be seen dead.

Then suddenly she remembered one other store, a rather exclusive one with branches in New York, Palm Beach, and San Francisco. Once there had been a hat in the window that she had wanted so badly it had haunted her dreams, yet she had never done more than walk by each day to see if it was still there. The morning that she had arrived to find it gone still stuck in her mind. She walked across the street, and down two blocks she saw the familiar store front.

In the window was a dress that she knew she must have the moment she saw it. It didn't matter how much it was or how unpleasant the salespeople might be when they sold it to her, or even if they did not want to sell it to her at all. It almost seemed to her that if they refused to do so she would come back that night, throw a brick through the window, and take it anyway. Quickly, before she could change her mind, she walked into the store and up to the nearest clerk.

"Do you have that green dress in the window in a fourteen?" she asked.

The saleswoman looked at her scornfully. "No," she said, "we surely don't. That one in the window is the last one we have, and it's a ten."

Alberta looked around angrily, and immediately she spied three of the same dresses hanging on a rack almost at the woman's elbow. She walked over to them, and the first one she looked at was a fourteen.

"You may wrap this up," she said. "I'd like it in a box."

"Do you know how much it is?" the saleswoman asked insolently.

"Never mind that, I'll pay for it."

"I really don't think——"

Alberta opened her purse angrily. "I have the money. How much is it?"

"Fifty-nine ninety-five."

"Here's sixty dollars. And if you don't mind, I'm in rather a hurry. I'll have my dressmaker alter it after I get back to New York."

The saleswoman took the dress and the money without looking at her and started toward the rear of the store.

"Just a moment, please," Alberta called after her. "I'd like a sales slip too, made out to Miss Alberta Mathews." She stressed the Miss and gave her New York address.

As she waited for the woman's return she made no effort to stand unobtrusively to one side but walked around the store looking at other merchandise. She knew that people were giving her dirty looks, but it did not matter to her in the slightest. After a rather prolonged wait the saleswoman came back with her package.

"The sales slip is inside and here is your change, Alberta."

The intended slur made her angry, but she kept her voice level. "I hardly think you know me well enough to call me by my first name," she said. "I suppose I should make allowances for the caliber of help available these days, but I do want you to know that I don't like it. Probably I shall say something to the manager of the New York shop. I'm rather a good customer there."

Alberta watched the saleswoman's face and saw the blush start slowly and spread down even onto her neck. The woman started to say something and then found that she couldn't. Into her eyes came a look of almost fear, then it changed to rage as she turned on her heel and walked away. Alberta watched her and saw that she went on into the back of the store. Then with complete unconcern Alberta walked leisurely toward the door. When she was almost there she stopped before a table of alligator handbags and, putting her parcel down, looked them over carefully. She had no intention of buying one; it was merely a gesture to show that she would leave the store only when she was good and ready to do so. That, she thought, for the South.

She got back to the car before Luther did. Getting in, she put the brown-and-yellow box in the well back of the front seat and looked at her watch. It was ten minutes before noon, about the time Luther had said he would meet her. She laid her head back against the seat. The rancor of her treatment in the store had worn away and she decided that she had carried it off rather well. But sitting there with her eyes closed, she suddenly decided that she would get the first possible reservation for New York.

Suddenly she was conscious of someone standing beside the car and, looking up, she expected to see Luther. But it was a white man standing there, and she did not recognize him until he spoke.

"Alberta?"

"Why, Clay Burton, of all people!"

"Yeah, it's me. I thought I recognized you. You back here for good?"

"No, just a visit."

"You sure have changed. I hardly knew you."

They had played together as children, when her mother had been working for his. Between them there had been a close tie which had lessened the summer he went away to North Carolina to the mountains, and somehow when he returned it had seemed spent. Then her mother had gone on to another job and she had seen him only spasmodically.

"You've changed too, Clay," she told him. "Or I suppose I should say Mr. Clay?"

He grinned down at her lazily, unconscious of the people passing on the sidewalk. He had changed. Already he was beginning to lose his good looks, and in a few years they would probably be gone completely, but now enough of them remained for him to be quite attractive.

"No, I don't reckon so, Alberta," he said. "I guess I'd feel sort of funny if you did. How's it feel to be back?"

She shrugged. "I'm going North in a day or two. I don't guess I'll ever come back again."

"I don't blame you," he said seriously. "I reckon if I was a nigger I'd leave too." Then suddenly he said, "I'm sorry. I shouldn't use that word, should I?"

"No," she said, "you shouldn't, but I've heard you say worse."

"I know. I reckon when I was a kid I taught you a lot of bad words. But I just said it out of habit."

"It's a bad habit."

"Yeah, I know. How do you like New York?"

"Love it, Clay."

"I can see that all right. I been up there. The way I heard it before I went, Negroes were going to push me off the sidewalk and try to make dates with my wife on the subway." He laughed. "After the first day or two, when nothing happened, I kind of forgot all about it."

"You married, Clay?"

"Sure, have been for four years now. I got two kids."

"I'm not married. I'm having too much fun the way I am."

"You got something there. Well, here comes Luther. I saw you sitting there and I just wanted to come by and say hello."

"Glad you did, Clay. Look me up if you ever come to New York. I'll make a real reconstructed cracker out of you."

Luther came up alongside and he and Clay spoke briefly to each other, then Luther got into the car.

"How's your mother, Luther?"

"She fine, Mistah Clay."

"Tell her I said hello. Well, good-by, Alberta."

"By, Clay."

Luther let in the clutch and drove off. Alberta laid her head back against the seat again and closed her eyes. She wondered why Clay Burton had come up and spoken to her that way. What would happen if she repaid his call, if she dropped around late some afternoon to meet his wife and his two children? Well, she knew the answer to that one all right. And yet if he came to New York without his wife she knew he would call her up.

It all came back to the same thing: the South was just no place for her. She had to get out, right away, without even waiting for her two weeks to be up. She might even call Rob up that very night and tell him she was coming home.

"Alberta?"

She was conscious that Luther had spoken and she turned her head toward him.

"You git what you wanted all right?" he asked.

She shrugged. "I bought a dress."

She looked at him and remembered how when she had been a youngster he had seemed to her the most wonderful person in the world. Well, he still was, in a way. But she realized how far apart they had grown. There was nothing really for them to talk about.

Her thoughts returned to Clay Burton. She wondered what would have happened if Luther had not come back to the car so soon. Maybe Clay would have asked her to meet him someplace that night; that was all white men ever seemed to think a Negro woman good for, she thought bitterly. What would she have done? Possibly she might have done it out of pure boredom, for it was not as though he were a stranger to her. She remembered how nearly they had come to it when they were kids. She smiled to herself.

She closed her eyes again. Jesus, she thought, this is worse than being in jail.

That evening Alberta and her mother were left alone. Bessie was working late at the college and eating dinner at the president's house. So the two of them sat together in the living room until Alberta felt she could stand it no longer.

"Mama, I'm going to walk over to town."

"Why, baby?"

"I've got to get some things at the drugstore. I won't be long, Mama."

"All right, baby. It jest I doan want you to be out alone late at night."

She nodded absently and went to her room to get a light coat. When she came back she kissed her mother quickly and went out the door. As she walked along the dirt street she felt the dust spray up in little whirls and she knew that she was getting her brown-and-white shoes completely soiled. Jesus, she thought, you'd think the least the white folks could do for their niggers would be to give them paved streets, even if it was only every other block. The only decent thing that she had gotten out of this trip was that dress. It fitted her almost perfectly and her mother was making the few alterations that were necessary.

She decided to cut over to the Boulevard, the only paved street that ran through colored town. As she passed a dimly lit pool hall the group of men lounging in front whistled and one of them called a pleasantly suggestive remark to her. She realized again how much she hated that kind of man; it seemed to her that she would feel soiled if some uncouth jig were to come up and touch her in the dark. She was glad when she reached the Boulevard where the lights were better. At the juncture where the white part of town merged with the colored the real sidewalks began and she hurried across the tracks into town.

She was going to call Rob. There was just a chance that she might be able to catch him. He often worked late at the office, especially Thursday nights when the maid had her night out. There was a pay phone booth in front of the telephone office, she remembered, and it was the only place in town where she knew that she would have complete privacy. Fortunately there was no one in it.

Putting a nickel in the slot, she waited for the operator's voice and then asked for long distance. She heard the metallic ping as her nickel was returned to her.

She gave Rob's number and paid the charges, then waited hopefully. This seemed to be her lucky night; it sounded as though she was getting right through. She heard the ringing plainly and then his lazy voice.

"Rob, darling," she said, "it's me, Alberta."

"Hello, Bert. How are you?"

"Not so good, lambie. You were right, I never should have come down here."

"I know, Berta, but you were the one who insisted on it."

"Umm, but don't rub it in. Baby, I'm miserable. I can't stay here another day. Look, send me a night letter and sign it as though you were my boss and something unexpected had come up. Will you, Rob?"

"Sure, baby. I've missed you."

"And, Rob, I can't go back on that awful coach. Call the airlines in the morning and see if you can't get me on a plane. I can't do a thing at this end."

"I'll try, Berta, but tickets are pretty tough. Even if I do manage to get you on, you may get bumped at Jacksonville. If you do, stick tight, because I can get you through from there. Thank God it's a little after the season, though that doesn't mean much these days."

"Oh, darling, thanks. And I do so want to see you."

"All right, baby, I'll do all I can."

"Love me?"

"You know I do."

"By, then."

"By, Bert."

She heard the connection go dead, but she hung onto the receiver for a moment before she put it back on the hook. It seemed to her as though something had been severed, the last link between her and the outside world. Get me back to him, she said, get me back to New York, back to civilization.

22. From behind the wire fence at the airport Bessie watched Alberta board the plane. At the last minute Alberta turned and waved and Bessie mechanically waved back. Two ground men wheeled the boarding steps away and almost clumsily the big plane lurched down toward the end of the runway, then turned into the wind as the pilot gunned the motors hard and held them that way for several minutes. The twin motors completely warmed up, the plane started its swoop down the runway, picking up speed and losing its oafishness as it took cleanly to the air. Once air-borne and gaining a little altitude, it banked leisurely to the left and disappeared into the twilight.

"Well," Eric said, "that's that. She'll be in Jacksonville in less than half an hour. If she's not bumped there she'll be in bed in New York almost as early as you are."

Bessie nodded as the two of them walked slowly across the sandy grass toward Eric's car. Getting in, he turned on the radio, twisting the dial slowly until he got a program of dance music. Then he lit a cigarette.

"Where do you want to go, Bessie?"

"Go?" she asked. "Where is there to go?"

He laughed good-naturedly. "Well," he said, "we could go to see a movie I saw eight months ago in New York. The second half of the feature is bound to be one of those extra-supercolossal-billion-dollar productions, featuring an all-Negro cast and filmed in somebody's back yard in Brooklyn on a ten-thousand-dollar budget."

He started the motor and backed out, cutting the wheels sharply to the left. Then he headed back toward town slowly. The night was clear and the stars seemed so low, with the top down, that it was hard to believe that you could not reach up and touch them. The wind that came in to wash across their faces was cool.

"Any ideas yet?" he asked.

"No," she said dully. "Maybe could we just drive?"

"Sure, any special direction?"

"I know it's silly, but could we go to the beach? I just feel like driving very fast and then seeing the ocean. But can you spare the gas?"

He shrugged. "The tide's all wrong for fishing," he said, looking at her out of the corner of his eye. "There's a moon, but I don't think we'd catch a thing. It's even the wrong time of the year."

"I'm sorry, Eric," she laughed.

"Not your fault," he answered, turning onto the east-coast highway. "Anyway, it was a joke. I can borrow some coupons from Luther. He doesn't use his car much and he offered me some."

"I know," she said softly, "only I seem to have left my sense of humor at home."

He reached over, without taking his eyes from the road, for her hand. For a moment he held it in his, then, letting it drop into her lap, he ran his fingers along the inside of her wrist. He started to take his hand away, but she took it back and held it close to her for a moment before she gave it up.

They were well away from town now, and the black macadam road stretched out in front of the headlights and beyond that there was nothing. She listened to the clean whistle of the tires against the crushed rock and closed her eyes. It seemed to her as though she wanted this very moment never to stop, that to prolong it into infinity was more than enough for her to ask. She heard, almost without being conscious of it, the music from the radio just above her knees. There was nothing else she wanted, only this.

Where were they going, really; only to the ocean or to some place beyond where the night ended? They seemed to be hurtling through to something hidden and mysterious, always piercing the night and yet somehow never really penetrating it. It closed in behind them and lay always ahead, just out of reach. When they came out of the scrub area into the prairie there was not a tree to be seen anywhere, and the moon, which had been caught behind the trees, became now so bright that they could easily have driven without lights.

She thought about Alberta, on her way to New York. The fact that she was in a plane seemed to Bessie symbolic, as though it were additional proof that no matter what happened Alberta would always get a little the better of it. She, Bessie, had always wanted to go to New York, yet she had never gotten there even for a vacation. The one or two times she had planned on going it seemed that something always came up to thwart her.

Was it she herself who was to blame for this feeling of bitterness she felt toward Alberta? Perhaps she was only jealous; covet not, the Bible said, and it might be that subconsciously she merely wanted to reverse their roles, so that she might have the material things which Alberta had acquired. Yet she knew that she was not a materialistic person. It must be, then, that the fault lay within Alberta. It had not seemed so once when they were younger and she had worshiped her sister, but in the short time that Alberta had been back she seemed almost another person.

Bessie knew that the wire had been a frame-up so that Alberta could leave earlier than she had planned. She did not know how she knew, yet she had never been surer of anything in all her life. And it seemed to her that Alberta had taken advantage of her mother, allowing Mama to bring her breakfast in bed after she had slept late, which was fair neither to Bessie, who had to get up, nor to her mother, who had to prepare another meal. Bessie held no brief for Ethel, but what Alberta had done to her the time she asked them to tea seemed to her merciless and unfair.

But most of all she resented the way Alberta had made such an obvious play for Eric, not only the one night that the three of them had gone out together and stopped to see Luther and Eulia, but every time he had come to the house. If Bessie were not out of her room and into the living room the moment Eric came, she would usually find them together in the dark intimacy of the yard. And when Alberta had said good-by to them before boarding the plane she had kissed Eric and told him to be sure and look her up that summer when he came to New York.

Bessie was not even sure that Eric had not been seeing Alberta after he brought her home at night. Several times it had seemed to her that her sister had gone out after she herself was in bed. But she had been too proud to make certain; perhaps Alberta could not sleep and had only gone out in the yard to smoke a cigarette.

But, worst of all, she could never see herself in her own mind as being able to equal Alberta. It seemed to her, in spite of her bitterness, that Alberta was better looking, that she was more intelligent and had somehow acquired a sophisticated veneer that was impervious to anything. Bessie could never be like that. Mentally she totaled her assets —a body that she knew to be good (two breasts, right and left, in perfect condition; a rounding of hip and, less defined, of abdomen; and legs that curved long and true), and a mind that was good, if far from spectacular, not to forget a longing and a desire which she wanted to share with someone, preferably Eric.

Bessie looked over at him, his profile clearly defined by the moonlight. He was all that she wanted and he seemed worth fighting for, but she was no fighter, and even as she seemed, in her mind, to be inferior to Alberta, so did Eric somehow seem just out of her reach.

"Moody tonight?"

"Yes," she said, "I'm sorry."

"Why sorry?" he asked, reaching again for her hand.

She took his between her own and held it as though it were something to keep her from falling. For a moment she thought she was going to cry.

The car slowed for a curve, and as it came around and straightened out again the headlights caught a group of cattle near the road. In the foreground was a Brahman bull, like the one they had seen the last time they had come over to fish in the surf. Eric slowed the car to a stop and the huge animal stood there, at most twenty yards away, and his eyes, where the light reflected against them, shone red as live coals.

Then the bull turned his head a few degrees and the eyes seemed merely brown, and soft and gentle as those of a deer.

Gray as a mouse he stood, sturdy and yet a little lethargic, but as he shifted his position a little the great muscles knotted and unwound under his smooth coat. The hump between his shoulders seemed, rather than a deformity, a mark of distinction, giving to him a strange dignity. Bessie's eyes unconsciously wandered to his hanging masculinity, and he merely swished his tail out of the way as though to give her a better view, then turned and walked slowly away. She felt a slight flush of guilt, and then the absurdity of it struck her and inwardly she laughed.

Eric started the car again and they moved off slowly toward the east. She started to speak and, thinking better of it, lit two cigarettes, passing one of them over to Eric. He took it and grinned at her, then turned his face back to the road. At the corner where he usually turned he went straight ahead for several blocks and then turned north instead of continuing east. They were on the main north-south highway now and he let the motor out.

"It's not much farther this way," he said, "and at the next town we can drive right out onto the edge of the beach."

She nodded and raised her head so that the wind was against her face. What was happening seemed to her to contain the essence of a dream, and nothing that could have happened would have surprised her. Soon, ahead of them and far down the straight ribbon of the road, she saw the lights of the next town. In a few minutes they slowed for the outskirts.

The main street was almost deserted, though it was only a little after ten, and the little town seemed drowsy. It had the look of all the little towns that were always the place just before the place you were going, the town before the city where you were going to stop for the night. In front of the drugstore a few men stood looking at the cars as they passed. There was about them a certain sadness, as though they thought that one of the passing vehicles might stop, yet inwardly were aware that the odds were too much against it.

At the stop light they turned to the left and took a narrow road that wound off into the darkness. Soon Bessie could smell the river and then they were running alongside it. Dimly she could see the white shapes of anchored boats, almost like ghosts in the stilled night. They slowed for a bridge, and the few people who were fishing there ignored them completely, in the way peculiar to fishermen, save for one old man with a whitened fringe around his sunburned bald spot, who turned and glared at them fiercely over his shoulder, as though he would like to punish them for this invasion of his privacy. The smell of salt air was strong now in Bessie's nostrils and she sat up straighter in the seat. The car went up and over the drawbridge slowly and the tires made thunder against the planking beneath them.

"Good old Bessie," she said. "Let me smell an ocean and I perk right up."

"I bow to the ocean, a better man than I am."

She leaned over quickly and kissed him on the cheek. "You're a better man than the ocean, darling. You're even a better man than that Brahman bull the color elephants ought to be and never are."

Suddenly she laughed.

"Private joke?" he asked.

"Umm," she giggled, "between me and the bull."

The road they drove down was lined with trees, Australian pines which had probably been planted to mark the glories of some boom subdivision and now merely sighed in the wind. Ahead of them was what might once have been a gaily painted casino but was now merely a half-gutted old building made a gray as soft as silver under the flick of the headlights. Then they dipped down the ramp onto the beach.

They had driven far down the beach. It was almost low tide, so that when they backed up toward the dunes to park there was room enough between them and the ocean so that no passing car would likely bother them. There was a strong onshore wind and there were hardly any mosquitoes. Before them the surf was coming in steadily, and the incessant but well-spaced boom of the waves was as restful and calm as Bessie's own breathing.

Lighting two cigarettes, Eric passed one to her. "Now," he said, "what's all the gloom about?"

"Gloom?" she asked. "No, Eric, there's no gloom now. I'm very content being here."

"What was it all about, then?"

"Oh, I don't know. I was just thinking about Alberta."

"What about her?"

She sighed. "I guess one is supposed to love one's sister, or at least like her. I used to, but I'm afraid I don't any more. I think Alberta acted like a first-class bitch all the time she was down here."

"Probably she did," he said.

"That wire was a fake. I don't know how I know, but I do. I only hope that Mama didn't see through her too. Eric, what's the matter with Alberta? Has she changed, or is it merely that I've grown up?"

"There's lots wrong the matter, baby," he said, "but it's not all her fault."

"You mean all New York people are like that?"

"No, not just that, but that's a part of it. New York gets to be a state of mind. Alberta came down here thinking she could escape it, and when she found she couldn't she fled back."

"I can see that, I guess. But did she have to act the way she did?"

"No," he said slowly, "she didn't. There are other complications. She's ambitious, and I have a feeling she's gone about as far as she can in her present job and knows it. She's always wanted the thing just beyond the thing she has now. She's a woman, and that's not too easy. If she were white she would still find herself only a little bit better off than a Negro male. But she's a Negro woman, and so she thinks she has two strikes on her, which she probably has. Add to that the fact that she looks upon herself as an intellectual and you've got a really screwed-up gal."

"I don't guess I'm ambitious," she said softly, "but I'm a Negro and a woman."

"You," he laughed. "The trouble with you is that you're too well adjusted. All that's bothering you is that right now you're full of guilt because you realize that you hate your sister."

"And you?"

"Me? I'll get along all right, I guess. I don't like being what being a Negro means in America. But I don't consciously hate myself the way Alberta does, and neither do I subconsciously hate all Negroes."

She was silent for a moment and then asked, "What's going to happen to Alberta, Eric?"

"Nothing. She'll go on the way she's going, jumping from one thing to another, from one man to the next man. She'll get more and more frustrated, hating herself. After a while she'll get too old to keep it up. Then she'll marry someone who can help her be a success. She'll have parties, collect white folks and Negro artists. She'll get along all right. Frantic, maybe, but outwardly gay."

Bessie remained silent, conscious only of the beat of the surf in her ears. There was one thing she wanted to ask Eric but she didn't know quite how to go about it. She listened to the music on the radio and then looked out over the water again. Far out a shrimper was moving along slowly to the south, and idly she wondered what it was like out there. Down-beach to her right she caught the flick of the white beam from the lighthouse at Mosquito Inlet, as it started and completed its cycle.

"Eric."

"What, Bessie?"

"Will you see Alberta when you're in New York this summer?"

She was sorry when she had said it, yet glad when she realized that it was out between them.

"Why?" he asked.

"Why?" she said angrily. "You know why, but you want to make me say it. All right, I'm jealous of her, and the thought of your seeing her this summer haunts me. I know I have no claims on you, no chains, and still that's the way I feel. I can't help it. God knows I don't like it, but that's the way it is."

She closed her eyes and waited, feeling almost as though his answer would be like a lash.

"It's all right to hate your sister," he said slowly. "I don't mind that. But what's wrong in my seeing my sister-in-law?"

"What?"

"Sure, didn't you know that we were going to get married? I've known it for months, haven't you?"

"No," she said softly, "I didn't know. Tell me again."

Instead he kissed her, and she clung to him, afraid that she was going to cry.

"Will your parents like me, Eric?" she whispered.

"Of course not," he said cheerfully. "You're much too dark, your hair isn't good, and you haven't any money. I doubt that they'll even let you in the house."

"I want them to like me," she said. "I want to be a good wife. Sounds dull, doesn't it?"

"Very," he said, and kissed her again.

23. The two signs over the door at the front of the passenger compartment flashed: *Fasten Your Safety Belts. No Smoking.* Alberta heard the motor on the left wing turn over and catch, then, shortly after, the one on the opposite wing. Turning in her seat, she looked back toward the door. The stewardess was talking to the last of the ground crew, effecting the exchange of initialed reports that would make it possible for them to become air-borne. Don't let anything happen now, she said to herself, let the plane take off quickly. To be bumped now would be almost more than a human being could bear.

She remembered her terror in the Jacksonville terminal behind them. Sitting there quietly by herself, she had heard the loud-speaker monotonously intone: "Passenger Mathews, report to the Eastern passenger counter, please—Passenger Mathews, report to the Eastern passenger counter, please." She had gone forward fully convinced that she was going to be put off, only to find that there had been a mistake in names and that what she had thought was hers was really another sounding very much like it.

Behind her she heard the stewardess noisily secure the door and the throb of the motor increase as the plane wheeled and started up the runway. She knew now that she was safe and she relaxed in her seat, even carelessly thumbed through the magazine on her lap. When the stewardess came up the aisle to check on safety belts she smiled at Alberta almost as though she were a fellow conspirator. Then down the runway they swooped and, looking out of her window, Alberta saw the air terminal, outlined in neon lights, as the plane took to the air and swung away to the north.

The *No Smoking* sign flashed off and she lit a cigarette, then when the other half of the sign vanished she unfastened her safety belt and adjusted her seat. She liked the sensation of being air-borne, of hurtling through the air and knowing that below them the South was falling away behind. After she put out her cigarette she lay back in her seat and closed her eyes. She did not mean to sleep, but somehow the release from the tension of the past few hours seemed to act as a drug on her whole being.

She awoke an hour later and, after consulting her watch, fell back into slumber again. This time when she awakened they were over Washington. Now she was slept out, and she read her magazine until they were over La Guardia and at last came to earth. As she got out of the plane and hurried to find a porter she felt her excitement quicken. The wait for a cab frustrated her, as though somehow until she found herself within the four walls of her apartment she was not wholly free from what she had left behind her. She was glad that Rob had not come to meet her; this was one home-coming she wanted to have completely for her own.

At last she secured a taxi and they were on their way to Manhattan, cutting over and through the Bronx, crossing the river at the 155th Street bridge. Then they came up the hill and turned left and soon they were in front of the building where she lived. Hurriedly she paid the driver and went inside. Once in her apartment, she closed the door and for a moment stood there in the middle of the tiny living room. Why had she ever left it? Within these four walls was everything she could ever want; this was where she belonged. All this was hers—the simple but good furniture, the books in the bookcases that lined the wall opposite the windows which opened onto the street, the leather-bound portable radio-phonograph on the long table with the row of albums stacked neatly underneath.

She decided to have a drink, one now and another later while she was soaking in a hot tub before going to bed. Going out to the kitchen, she took down one of her best highball glasses from the cabinet over the sink. This was an occasion. She mixed herself a drink and raised it in a mock toast.

She was home, like some mythical character who had wandered over a strange and alien land only to find that what he had been seeking lay all the time at his very fingertips. She put her drink down on the kitchen table and went back to turn on her tub.

She awakened in the morning, not leisurely and late, as she had planned, but to the almost hysterically shrill clatter of the telephone. Still half asleep, she took the receiver from its cradle and mumbled into the speaking end. She noted by the clock on her night table that it was a little after ten o'clock.

"You might let a guy know you got in."

"Rob," she said, "darling. I'm sorry; I meant to, but it was so late. I thought I'd wake up early and call you then, but I guess I was so dead tired I slept like I'd been slugged. How are you, darling?"

"I'm all right. How was your trip?"

"Good," she laughed. "I slept from Jacksonville all the way to Washington. You were a lamb to get me on that plane. When am I going to see you?"

"How about lunch?"

She looked at the clock and shook her head. "I don't think so, Rob.

I couldn't possibly make it before two, and then only if I broke my neck. Let's make it dinner instead, if you can."

"Fine. We might as well meet at Tony's. What's good for you, a little before seven?"

"Wonderful, darling. I can't wait to see you. It seems ages."

"I know. Just before seven, then?"

"Yes, Rob. By."

She hung up and kicked the covers back. The mere energy required for getting up seemed too distant to be summoned. Finally she got to her feet and went to pull the blinds so that the sun would not fall across the bed. She took off her nightgown and lit a cigarette; in the mirror she saw herself reflected and what she saw pleased her. Raising herself on her toes, she admired herself in the glass. The whole day lay before her and the thought was too much; she went back to the bed and lay down again. Lying on her back, she looked up at the ceiling.

Today, tomorrow, and the next day, she thought, no job to go to and I'm back in the land of the free. She raised one leg and, holding it aloft, admired its symmetry. Not unlike a buddha, she looked down at her belly and found it flat. I wouldn't even need to wear a girdle if I didn't want to, she thought. She glanced at the clock and ground out her cigarette.

She thought of the whole day again and the thought was delicious as a special dessert. Reaching for the phone, she dialed the beauty parlor and asked for Ada, the girl who always did her hair. She made an appointment for later in the day, after some special pleading, and hung up, to return to a further perusal of the ceiling.

She wondered if the landlord would paint for her again in the fall. He probably wouldn't, since she had been forced to wheedle him into it the last time, but at least it was worth trying. Lying there, she thought up a whole series of special colors for every room in the apartment, even the bathroom and kitchen. She was lucky to have found a place like this; it was cheap and yet it was a good location.

Maybe she ought to go downtown. She weighed the possibility but decided against it. It was too much trouble and she really had nothing important to do. Tonight she could wear the new dress she had bought in Citrus City and had not even had on her back yet. She looked at the clock and saw that it was after one. She stretched lazily and thought again about getting up.

She decided she would wait awhile, then go up to that new place that had opened on upper Broadway just before she had gone South.

She could get a good martini there, ice cold and with only a very little vermouth and a twist of lemon peel. She would sit at the bar and drink two martinis very slowly, then have shrimp salad and iced coffee. By that time it would be almost late enough to go to the beauty parlor.

Of all the restaurants in New York, Alberta liked Tony's best. This was partially because it seemed to be their special place, the spot where she and Rob felt most at home. The food was good and the cocktails better, yet it was the atmosphere that she liked most. They always seemed glad to see her, whether she was with Rob or not, and not once in their attitude toward her was she ever conscious that she was a Negro. They were neither coldly distant nor patronizing.

Tonight when she came in at a quarter of seven Rob had not yet arrived. She went to the bar and ordered her usual martini, then, drinking it very slowly, talked with Nicky, who was tending bar. Presently Tony came in from the kitchen and, seeing her, smiled and came over.

"Good evening," he said. "Waiting for Mr. Wharton?"

"Yes, Tony, and having a drink in the meantime."

"Good, good. I save you nice table. How you been?"

"Fine, Tony, and you?"

"Me? Ha. I'm always fine."

He hurried away again and she turned back to Nicky. He was telling her why he had stopped playing the races, and just then Rob came up behind her; she felt his hands on her shoulders and, looking into the back bar mirror, she grinned at him.

"Hi," she said.

He sat down beside her and ordered a scotch old-fashioned. She turned to him, and as always, she was excited by him. She liked the way his clothes usually seemed to fit him, the bow ties he wore, his blond hair and his blue eyes, his smile and the whiteness of his skin. There was behind the smoothness of his face a delicate rosy tinge, almost like a baby's, and yet the shape of his chin and his strong mouth gave to his whole being a rampant virility.

"Have another martini," he said. "Sorry I'm a little late."

"No," she smiled, "I'll wait for you."

"Go ahead," he said. "I had two on my way over here. Nicky, give the young lady another martini."

They watched him make it, and then Tony came over and told them that their table was ready. Seated across from each other, they finished their drinks. In a moment the waiter who always took care of them came over with a menu. She put hers down without even looking at it.

"You order for me, darling."

The waiter said, "Roast beef special tonight. Delicious. Also lobster cooked in white wine, specialty of the house."

"Shrimps, I guess, and two vichyssoise. Roast beef rare. And two more drinks."

Deftly the waiter removed their empty glasses and they were alone again. She liked being with Rob because people always looked at them. What they thought didn't matter to her, so long as they noticed. He smiled.

"I missed you, Bert. Tell me about it."

Their drinks came and she waited until the waiter had gone away again.

"There's not much to tell," she said slowly. "You were right, of course. It was awful."

"I thought it would be, baby. I know it was when I tried it, when I last went home, I mean."

Inwardly she blessed him for putting it that way, for including himself so that there could be no possible racial connotation. The waiter brought their shrimps and they were silent until they had finished and their plates were cleared away.

"What do you want to do tonight?" he asked.

She shrugged. "I don't care. As long as I'm with you, that's enough."

"You don't mind not going out, then?"

"No," she said. "Let's go up to my place."

He reached over and caressed her hand. Suddenly, sitting there, she felt a physical need for him that was almost painful. She looked at him and smiled.

"Well?" he said.

"Nothing, Rob. I was just realizing how absolutely miserable I've been without you."

"Pure habit, Bert."

"No," she said slowly, "not that at all."

She awakened once during the night, in a panic that he was no longer beside her. Then she reached out, without opening her eyes, and touched his bare flank. Opening her eyes, she turned her head toward him in the faint light made by the street lamp coming through the slats of the venetian blinds. He lay on his side, facing her on the huge double box spring, and she watched the steady rise and fall of his chest as he breathed. It seemed to her then that he looked young, hardly more than a boy in spite of the mat of golden hair across his breast. She was glad that he was asleep, for she had a need now to be alone yet still to have him there beside her.

They had been going together for over a year now, seeing each other whenever they could without arousing the suspicion of his wife too much. Thinking of his wife, Alberta felt nothing, neither compassion because she was being betrayed nor hatred toward her because, like Rob, she was white and had the security of marriage vows. Alberta had never seen her and she had not the slightest desire to do so. It seemed almost as though she did not exist.

When she and Rob were together, as they had been only a short time ago, it seemed to her that no one else could ever really share him with her. Let him have his wife; it could not matter, as long as they remained so perfect together. And yet at times like this, when she knew that he would before long leave her and go back to his wife, it left her with an emptiness. She knew there was no future in their relationship, but even that was of no importance. What was between them, if only that part which was physical, was enough for her. During those times she seemed lifted up and carried away, and afterward she was complete, as she had not been after being with any other man. His body had wrung the bitterness from hers, and the peak which they had reached together seemed to make the ambition which ordinarily ruled her life unimportant. But then there was always the afterward.

For now she no longer had him. Somehow he had eluded her, even in sleep, and she was conscious now of their difference in color. I'm no better than a whore, she told herself without bitterness, accepting it somehow as being as inevitable as their racial differences. She wondered if he had ever called her that, not so much in fact but in inflection. Had he ever, she wondered, in a sort of masculine camaraderie, told another man that he was sleeping with a nigger wench up in Harlem; or in a moment of drunkenness bragged of the sexual efficiency of his black mistress? She castigated herself with the image, but it seemed, like a dull knife, unable to cut. It was the way things were, and she lay there whispering to herself words that no longer stung. *Nigger,* she whispered, *darky, jig, spade, dinge, shine, coon, black bitch.*

She told herself that she should get a man who was black and who would marry her, give her the things that she could never expect to get from a married white man. But the thought repulsed her, not so much the idea of the darkness of his body against her lighter one as the realization that she would always feel superior to him, that because of his blackness and what it meant in American mores he would always, somehow, be less than a man.

She thought of her mother and, forgetting Rob for a moment, she felt a wave of guilt. In the morning, she thought, I'll go downtown and get something nice for Mama. She envisioned it, neatly gift-wrapped and speeding toward Florida on the mail train, doing what she could not do and would never try to do again. Bessie too, she thought rashly, and something for Luther and Eulia as well. Something for each, a present with love from Alberta by proxy and courtesy of the U. S. Mails. And yet, even ridden by this guilt, she knew that she was not fooling herself. In a way she hated them all, almost as much as at this moment she hated herself, and for the same reason.

She looked at Rob again and saw him stir uneasily. She wanted to waken him so that he could hold her once more and rock her free from her own special demons, give her back to herself so that she would be whole again. There was so little an expanse of whiteness be-tween them, and yet it might as well have been a chasm. She reached over to the night table for a cigarette and flicked on the silver lighter he had given her. Holding the flame to her cigarette, she let the lighter click shut. Then, blowing smoke out in a thin streamer, she settled back again.

She felt his fingers, at her side, smoothly run up and across her ribs toward the cones of her breasts. Save me, she thought, wash me white as snow. And, sobbing, she went into his arms.

24. He swung off the front coach easily, almost before the train had stopped moving. There was a dignity about the way he carried himself, and it was not until you looked closely that you noticed he had only one arm. The empty sleeve was tucked neatly into the side pocket of his officer's uniform, which bore the in-signia of a second lieutenant. The heavy overseas bag he carried easily with his other hand, and under that same arm were tucked several magazines and a book. It was almost three in the morning, and the platform, save for several employees of the railroad, was deserted.

He went into the waiting room marked COLORED and looked around for a phone. There was none there, so he came out again and, setting the bag down against one of the pillars that supported the platform roof, he took out a pipe. Holding it for a moment by hunching it up under his chin, he took out a tobacco pouch. Now, he thought, comes the hard part. Maybe he should have let them give him a hook the way they had wanted to, but if it had to come, it could come later. Right now he wanted to forget about the whole damned thing.

In the end he gave up and, clumsily putting the pipe and tobacco away, he lighted a cigarette. He wolfed in the smoke hungrily and looked around. Perhaps he should have let them know that he was coming in on the night train instead of wiring them that he would be in at noon tomorrow, but the thought of meeting them in the middle of the night this way was just too much. He kicked out angrily at an empty candy wrapper. Probably if I were truthful, he thought, I'd admit that I didn't want her treating me like a cripple in front of the white folks. It was going to be bad enough when it happened; without making it just that much worse. He realized that he should have written them about his arm, but he could never seem to put it down on paper so that it didn't sound as though he were trying to make himself out a hero. Anyway, it was too late now.

Across from him he saw a parked taxi and he walked over to it slowly. Suddenly he wondered what he was going to do if the peckerwood inside didn't feel like riding a Negro, even though there were no other passengers in sight. It was a long walk and he was tired. Well, he thought, here goes nothing.

"Any chance you might drive me out to the college?" he asked civilly.

Damn, he thought, I let myself open on that one. I might just as well have gone into the Palmer House Shuffle, taken off my cap, and bowed three times.

"Sho, soldier, why not? Get in."

"Look, I've got to make a phone call. Can I leave my bag in the car while I walk over to the booth by the telephone office? I won't be long."

"I'll drive you over. I'm in no hurry this time of night."

"Thanks."

He walked back to get his bag, but when he reached for it the cabdriver was there first.

"Let me take it, soldier. Looks like you'd be tired of lugging it far as it's come."

Following the driver back to the cab, he thought: The millennium must have come, something's happened to the white folks. He got into the back, slumped into the corner, and closed his eyes. Feeling the cab move as it swung out toward the street, he opened his eyes again and looked out. It hadn't changed any; it was still the same sleepy little town, clean to a point that was almost sterile. In a moment the cab stopped in front of the telephone recessed into the phone-company building. The driver reached back and opened the door.

"Take your time, soldier," he said. "This hour of the night I got from now on."

He got the nickel out of his pocket all right and, holding the receiver with his hunched shoulder, he started to drop the coin into the slot. But somehow he fumbled at the last moment and the nickel went clattering down to the floor. As he bent to retrieve it he bumped his stump and felt the pain shoot all the way down the arm that was no longer there. He cursed fluently and stood there with his forehead pressed against the pebbled metal sheeting with which the booth was lined, waiting for the pain to go away. Finally it did and he successfully dropped the coin into the right slot and dialed his mother's number from memory.

Then suddenly, almost in panic, he flicked down the hook with his finger to break the connection and, hearing the nickel return, replaced the receiver. Fumbling for the coin, he found it, crammed it back into his pocket and, turning, started out the door; then he made himself turn back to the phone again. All the way down he had been in complete control of himself, and this was going to be no exception.

All right, he thought, I just won't phone. He got an image of how it would have been, the ringing phone and then his mother's voice trying to smother him, the wire that stretched between them chaining him as surely as an umbilical cord. He thought of the way it had been before he went into the army, and he knew that he would rather go back to the South Pacific again than to have things the way they had been. He had felt differently then, but what he had been through in the meantime had changed everything. Jesus, he thought, if she'll just leave me alone until I can get back to normal.

He remembered the waiting cab and walked quickly out. The driver had opened the car door in front.

"Sit up here with me, soldier," he said.

Without answering, he got in and sat down. The cab pulled out from the curb and, making a U turn, headed out toward the underpass. He slumped down in the seat and looked out at the deserted road.

"I got a boy in the army," the driver said slowly. "I sho miss him."

Well, here it comes, he thought, and said, "E.T.O. or out where I was?"

"South Pacific, same as you. Pretty tough out there, I reckon."

He nodded. "Yeah," he said, "it's pretty rugged."

He thought of the way it had really been and felt the pain in the arm that was gone clear down to the fingers. He thought too that maybe this peck's son was one of the white boys who had made his life miserable. The whole memory of the racial tension of the army made him suddenly want to hit out at the man beside him. He thought that maybe if he pulled the wheel hard suddenly and they went into the ditch he could beat him to death with a jack handle and the whole thing would look like an accident.

He remembered when the train was in the Jacksonville station and he had gotten out of the jimcrow coach to walk up and down. There had been a lot of white boys in the coach behind who had gotten on at the last stop in Georgia before they crossed the Florida line. They had been drinking, and he knew by the look of them that they had only been in some camp on this side and had never seen action. He saw them as they first became conscious that he was that strange and unlikely combination, an officer and a Negro, and they slowed to a bare walk. Then he heard one of them talking and the others trying to shut him up, but not before the words had stung him like a whip.

"Look," the voice had said, "I don't care if the black son of a bitch is a general. I know they got one nigger general, I seen it in some paper. But me, I ain't gonna salute no friggin nigger. Let's walk across them tracks yonder to that other platform, and that way we won't have to go past him."

Angrily he had turned on his heel and pretended that he had not heard, but he had, and there was no undoing that. He came back to the present with a start and shifted uncomfortably.

"Been traveling far?" the driver asked.

"Washington," he said curtly.

"Them seats get hard, I reckon. Just sitting in this cab sometimes I get butt sores. You back for good?"

"I don't know. For a while at least."

He almost said, For as long as you pecks will let me act like a man. He had a bitter vision of what would happen the first time one of them crossed him; his soldier suit would not save him then, he thought wryly. But it was not this that worried him. His fear was not so much that he might get into trouble as that somehow he might, in order to avoid it, lose his manhood. He knew that it was easy to lose, just as it had been hard to regain, to be caught up in the coils of self-preservation, to give in to the old habit patterns of those around him, to have his manliness taken from him slowly, day by day, so gradually that on the day he awoke to the fact of his emasculation he might never know how it was that he had ceased to be a man.

The whine of the tires on the pavement made him want to close his eyes and shut out the world around him.

Had he slept? He must have, for he was conscious of someone having spoken to him and then of a hand upon his shoulder. He blinked his eyes a little and shook his head to the side to clear it, then, getting out of the car, opened the rear door and took out his overseas bag.

"How much?" he asked.

"Half a buck, soldier. Help you with that baggage?"

"No, thanks," he said, shaking his head and thinking to himself that the peckerwood didn't have to feel sorry for him. He wasn't a cripple, he still had one arm.

He paid the man and closed the door, but the driver didn't drive off immediately, the way most of them did.

"Look, soldier," he said, "any time you want a cab you call me. Just tell em you want Fred. I know how most cabs are bout hauling colored. I ain't that way. Way I figure is we all got to live and I'm glad to have your business."

"Thanks," he said. He could see that the driver was still looking at him. What does he want, he thought bitterly, for me to kiss him? Now he's gone out of his way to show me how goodhearted he is, maybe he wants a dollar tip.

There was this thing between them, and neither of them knew quite what to do about it. Both were conscious of it; it was there plain to see. The soldier knew that the cabdriver, out of human decency, had made a gesture of good will, and that out of decency he should acknowledge it. Yet he could not do so; he could not even bring himself to trust the gesture entirely.

"Good night," he said, and, turning on his heel, shouldered his overseas bag and started off across the campus toward the president's house. But halfway there he stopped. He was tired, but that was not why he had stopped. Rather it was that everything seemed wrong now; he could not go busting into the house, even though it was his own and he knew where his mother always hid the key for the maid in the morning. He should have told them when he was coming, and yet that might have been even worse. He took out a cigarette and lit it, trying to think what to do. Then for a moment he was flooded again with near panic, so that he lost momentarily the will to do anything except turn around and run away from the thing he was afraid to face.

Presently the mood passed and he was in control of himself again. He looked around at what up to a year ago had been the only thing which he could think of as home, or as a base of operation. In the moonlight it seemed different from the way he had remembered it. It had a beauty and dignity, but he was realistic enough to know that it would appear different again in the harsh sunlight. Would even the moonlight, he wondered, make his mother seem again the way she had once seemed to him? He ground the cigarette into the ground with his foot.

Then suddenly he made up his mind. He would go over to the men's dormitory. Even if no one was up, he could at least have a sleep of sorts in the wicker chairs downstairs in the lounge that opened off the entrance hall. He shouldered his bag again and walked quickly toward Douglas Hall. Once inside, he leaned his bag up against the fireplace and started down the hall.

The lights were dimmed and he could hear no sound that anyone was awake, nor could he see from under any door a crack of light showing that anyone was astir. He came back and started up the stairs to the second floor. The building was old, and from its buff-colored walls came the smell peculiar to all institutions, half sterile and half a kind of mustiness that could never somehow be dispersed by any method of renovating. He got to the head of the stairs and turned left.

At the end of the hall he saw a door with a sliver of light under it. As he came very close he could hear music, probably from a radio, and as he started to knock he became conscious that it was the kind of jazz music that you almost never heard. He decided, as he knocked lightly, that it was probably a phonograph record.

He had expected a student to open the door, and for a moment he looked at the man standing in the opened doorway without saying anything. Then he realized that the other was waiting for him to explain himself and he held out his hand.

"I'm George Rogers," he said simply.

"Come in. I'm Eric Gardner."

"Oh, sure, I've heard of you. As a matter of fact, I read your book out in the South Pacific."

He took the chair that Eric motioned to and lit a cigarette.

"I guess I owe you a little explanation," he said. "The family expects me in the morning, but I came in on the late train. I came over here thinking I might find somebody up and maybe even a bed for what little there is left of the night."

"You're welcome to my couch."

"I might take you up on that."

He saw Eric's eyes rest for a moment on his empty sleeve, then pass on to his face. He liked that; it as much as said that here was someone who has lost an arm but was still a man. There was in it neither pity nor sympathy, merely the acknowledgment of an accomplished fact.

Suddenly the music stopped and the scratch of the needle across the edge of the release groove made them both start. Eric got leisurely to his feet and went over to the table; he lifted the tone arm and shut off the turntable.

"Do you by any chance like this stuff?" he asked.

George laughed. "I've acquired a taste for it. It wears well."

"I think so. I've got some students who come up here once a week and listen. Most of the others go for be-bop." He lit a cigarette and tossed the pack onto the table by George's arm. "Anything you'd especially like to hear?"

"Nothing special. From what I heard as I came in, your taste is better than mine anyway."

Eric put a stack of records on the automatic changer of the phonograph and, turning it on, closed the lid. Then he went over to the closet and took down a bottle and two glasses.

"You use this?"

"When I can get it."

Eric poured two stiff drinks and put the bottle on the floor by the table.

"If you want water for a chaser, I'll run down the hall and get some."

"Not for me. Where I came from water was strictly to wash in."

Eric sat down in the other chair. "How was it?" he asked.

George shrugged. "I don't know yet. I think I know and then suddenly I find out I don't."

"Like being back?"

"A little, I guess. I figure I got to try that on for size."

"Don't answer this if you don't want to. Learn anything? I mean not like how to use a gun or build a fire with one match."

George shrugged. "I guess I don't know that yet either."

"You know I'm not just trying to act interested, don't you? This isn't Be Kind to the Boys Week as far as I'm concerned. If you don't feel like talking, don't talk. But I want to find out things."

"I know. I read your book. That isn't what's bothering me."

Eric got up and poured another drink, then took the pack of cigarettes from the table at George's elbow. After he lit up he held out the match in his cupped hand and waited until George took out a cigarette and bent his head toward the flame. Then he tossed the matches down on the table and sat down again.

"Look," George said slowly, "I've got to have time to think things out. I've been away for nearly two years, and when I got off that train tonight I—I don't know quite how to say it, but I don't feel I belong here. Maybe it's just that I don't belong anywhere any more. I'm not the same guy I was when I went away."

"From all I hear, maybe that isn't such a bad thing."

It was like a slap in the face, bringing him up short, stopping him from the downhill rush he had felt himself suddenly taking, the descent into the pit that wanted to close in around him. It was a good thing. He sat back in his chair again and he felt the sudden terror that had started to surround him, but now it was really gone. He let the air slowly out of his lungs and then laughed softly; it was good to laugh, he had not laughed in quite that way for a very long time.

"You heard about me, then?"

"No, but I had a pretty good idea. I had to grow up too, you know."

"Not as fast, though, Eric. Jesus, it was really rugged."

"Who taught you the most?"

"Things, I guess, more than people. Sometime I'll tell you about it. But I can't now. I'm too close to it."

Eric got to his feet lazily.

"Another libation?"

"Not for me. You pour good ones, you know."

"One more question?"

"Sure, Eric."

"Any idea what you want to do now?"

"None, only that I don't want to get into education."

"Why not, George?"

He laughed. "The Negro is like a baby; he's got to learn to crawl before he can walk." He got up from his chair and walked toward the window, then turned around. "Well," he said bitterly, "I learned how to crawl, and it took me longer than it would have taken me to learn how to walk like a man. I'm not interested in crawling. I want to see others stand up and walk too."

"You know who said that about learning to crawl before you could walk?"

"Sure, my old man. I thought he was a pretty smart man." He closed his eyes and said bitterly, "Is that a part of growing up too? I remember the day he made that speech, and how good he felt when Cal Thornton ran it in his column on the front page of the *Telegram*. I was proud of him too, so damned proud."

"Don't be too hard on him, George."

He opened his eyes again. "I'm not really, Eric. Not on him, anyway. He means well and I know he's honest. But somehow that no longer seems to be enough."

He reached for a cigarette and managed to light a match without bungling it. It was a little thing, but it made him feel good.

"Eric," he said in a moment, "I want a shiny new world. I'm not going to get it, am I?"

Eric shrugged. "Maybe not, George. Sometimes I think so and then I get to thinking about it. I honestly don't know. But if we can keep enough pressure toward it, maybe that's enough, all we ought to hope for right now."

"Sure, I know. But that isn't enough for me, not now, anyway, not the way I feel."

He got up and went back to the window. Looking out, he saw that it was no longer night, that the morning had come without his having been aware of it. It was yet too early for the sun, but there was enough light to see plainly and he sensed that it was going to be a good day. What he saw was familiar; perhaps he would or would not stay, but at least now it was home, a place without terror.

He turned back to the room.

"I've kept you up all night," he said. "I'm sorry. You should have told me."

Eric laughed. "I was worse than you were. Why didn't you tell me to shut up so you could go to bed? If we turn in now, though, we can still get a couple of hours' sleep."

George shook his head. "I couldn't sleep now. Anyway, I want to walk around a little. Mind if I leave my junk here?"

"Delighted. The place is yours. Make it your home away from home."

"I may have to," George laughed. He held out his hand. "You were a help, Eric. I was a little screwed up when I came in here. I'm all right now, at least for the time being. I can thank you for that."

They shook hands and, turning, George walked out the door softly.

25. For Esther, Alberta's going had left a big old hole in everything. She knew that the going was final and beyond recall, yet even had it been possible to change things, the chances were that she would have done nothing about it. What at first seemed heresy to her had become established fact, and this had taken place even before Alberta had cut short her visit and flown back to New York. In the beginning it had merely been the realization that Alberta no longer needed her. This had been hard to take, and yet it could be easily rationalized: Alberta had grown up. There was nothing so strange about that once she got used to it.

But it was more than that, and she could not fool herself into believing otherwise, save on the outer surface. Not only did Alberta no longer have any need of her, but actually she had taken advantage of her. Esther had first become aware of it through Bessie, not by anything she had said but merely by the way Bessie had acted. For a while she had even misconstrued this, feeling that Bessie was jealous the way an only child is of a baby when its position of importance within the family has suddenly been challenged. This had made her disappointed in Bessie, and even after inwardly she knew the truth she had still refused to believe it.

Having Alberta home had meant so much to her that now she almost wished that she had never come home. Had she not done so, it would have been impossible for her to keep alive forever the illusion that her oldest daughter needed her, that she loved and cherished her. Instead she knew, without ever actually having proof, that the excuse which

Alberta had offered for leaving early was not based on truth. Alberta had left merely because she had wanted to go, and for no other reason; she had grown tired of them and perhaps even ashamed of them, especially of her mother. Once Esther had made up her mind to this, and it had not been too hard, she had been filled with a feeling closely akin to guilt. Was it because the fault lay within herself?

She had stood off from herself then and taken stock, and before long made up her mind that this was not so. Perhaps she was not what Alberta wanted her to be, but surely she was not to blame for that, and furthermore she was not sure that she would ever want to be. Alberta was different; she had changed into something that seemed to bear little relationship either to her home or to anyone in it. Well, that was all right, if that was the way Alberta wanted it to be. And if it was, perhaps it was better that Alberta had gone. Esther did not blame her, nor did she bear her any animosity. It was simply the way things were, regrettable but nonetheless established.

True, for a time she felt an emptiness and even a bitter disappointment, but after a while even that passed. She did not feel quite the same about Alberta after that, but she still loved her. It was only that she turned to others to fill the hole Alberta had left, but it was not easy. For one thing, who was there to turn to?

There was Bessie, and naturally she was the logical one, but Bessie was away all day at her job, and when she wasn't she was usually with Eric. Bessie, it seemed, had no need of her either, and no time to spare even if she had. Besides, Bessie's life was taken care of. Esther liked Eric and had respect for him; it seemed to her sometimes that he was what Alberta was trying to be but could never quite attain.

Of course there was Jeff, but lately she found her relationship with him something that was hard to define. It was not that he was not polite, or that he did not seem to want to see her. In that respect he was the same. If anything, he was too polite, but even so it seemed to her that he had withdrawn into a shell, the way a turtle does, that there was a barrier between them that she was at a loss to know how to do away with.

And so she turned toward Eulia. It was true that Eulia had Luther, but he was away for most of the day, and anyway Eulia was expecting and would be glad of her help.

To go to Citrus City seemed to Esther at first a major undertaking, and besides, Eulia's and Luther's apartment was way over on the other side of town. This meant she had to change to another bus, and the first few times she went she felt confused and even a little frightened. It would not have been so bad if she could have walked. She was not used to busses, for in the past whenever she had gone to the city for any reason Luther had always taken her in the car.

In a way it was almost like coming out into another world, and it seemed to her that she had never seen so many people. She wondered where they had all come from. The bus was always overcrowded, even when she would let two or three go past in the hope of finding one where there were plenty of seats. Usually she stood, save for those times when some polite youngster in the segregated rear section would rise and offer her his seat.

At times like that she felt as though the world was familiar, that folks had not forgotten their manners and still remembered the old ways. But most of the time it seemed to her that everything she had known as proper had been thrown into the discard. In the crowded bus she could feel the tension that existed, for tempers were short when everyone was jammed up into so small a space. It even seemed to her as though people themselves had changed.

In all her lifetime she had had no trouble with white folks. She had gone her way and they had gone theirs, and in the process there had been little friction. She was well aware that she was being discriminated against, and yet that seemed to her no reason for taking it out in surliness. It was only the way things were. But now when she got onto a bus it seemed to her that every white person resented her, as though she somehow personally were responsible for his or her uncomfortableness. She felt it in their eyes as she worked her way toward the rear of the crowded busses to the jimcrow section, and sometimes she felt it in their elbows too.

Nor, she admitted, did it stop there. Once she was in the rear of the bus among her own, she felt hate and bitterness all around her. Usually it was unspoken, remaining a kind of inner muttering and mumbling, but at times she saw Negroes who were almost as overt about it as whites. She began to get so she could spot them, usually before they even got onto the bus. They were most often young, both men and women, and they carried themselves as though they were as good as anyone else and out to prove it.

They frightened her almost as much as did the mean white men who sometimes rode the bus, or the women with hard eyes and sharp elbows who seemed to be in league with them. She was used to them, for they had been with her all her life, but this resistance in Negroes, save for isolated instances, she was not used to. Sometimes as she rode along she wondered what she would do if there was an incident, for this seemed to her as inevitable as the fact that day follows night. She would map out with her eyes the easiest and most direct route to the door. It reached a point where she even took to carrying an umbrella with her each trip she made; it seemed to her a kind of protection in case of need, for it could be utilized as a weapon of sorts if ever the need arose.

Of this she said nothing either to Luther or to Bessie, for she was afraid they might tell her she could no longer make the trip. By now she was going two or three times a week, and she found in Eulia a companionship which she did not want to lose. In time her earlier fears gave way to a sort of fatalistic acceptance, a danger which was more than compensated for by what lay at the other end of the ordeal. There was no trouble, though often everyone in the bus had seemed on the verge of it. All that was needed, it seemed to her, was a spark. When that happened there was bound to be an explosion.

Each time she got off the second bus and started toward the housing project she felt her tension melt away, so that by the time she had walked a block or two she felt all right again. She was not by nature a timid person and she knew it, so that whatever she felt on the bus made her ashamed once she had left it behind her. Each time she would tell herself that when she went back it would be different, but somehow it never was.

After her first few visits she and Eulia slipped into an easy relationship quite different from that which they had had before. She had always been fond of Eulia but she had never really known her. It seemed strange that you could live so near a person and see her every day, yet never really get to know her. But it was true.

It was not that Eulia became like another daughter to her, or that she in any way took the place that Alberta had once held. Rather, it seemed to her, they became friends in the way that only two equals can become friends. There was a casualness about their relationship, and each seemed to trust the other to keep it that way. Too, she enjoyed being in Eulia's home, because it seemed to her as neat and clean as her own and it was a place that made anyone who came in feel comfortable.

They would sit down and talk, then later they would have lunch, or if Esther came too late for that, they would sit in the middle of the afternoon over coffee and cake. There was no telling what they would talk of, and sometimes they would merely sit together without the need of conversation. The baby was not far off, but Eulia was carrying it well and she had never looked better. It seemed to Esther by its position that it would be a boy, but Eulia only laughed when she mentioned it. Once she asked Eulia if she would be disappointed if it were a girl.

"Why should I be, Mama?" Eulia asked. "All Luther wants is for it to be healthy and do better than we done."

Esther nodded. She could understand that, for it was the same way that she and Hezekiah had felt. Well, had he lived, he would not have been disappointed. He would have been proud of Bessie and he would have liked Eric too; they were so different, and yet each would have had a respect for the differentness of the other. He would have taken pride in Luther too, for Luther, working with his hands, was like his father. And Alberta? She did not know and she did not want to think about it. Sitting there, she felt again the need for a man, someone to give her a wholeness that even a relationship as satisfying as that which she had with Eulia was incapable of bringing.

"Baby do as well as you and Luther done, it be all right," she said. "You got a right nice place here and Luther got him a good job. What more you want?"

Eulia smiled. "It is nice, Mama, and Luther like his job. But I reckon since he do he wants to hang on to it—after the war, I mean. He afraid that soon as the war over cullud be the first ones to lose they jobs."

Esther shrugged. "I doan know, Eulia. I reckon maybe he right. Every time I gets on a bus I feel them white folks hatin me. Seems like the way things always was ain gonna be no more. I see white folks hatin us and a lot of us hatin white folks. How it gonna end?"

Eulia laughed easily. "Mama, things doan stay the same. I doan know whose way right. Most of the young folks I knows think the old ways is wrong. Thing is we had our day, especially you, but me too, now the baby comin, and we got to make way."

"I reckon so, Eulia. But I doan like it."

Eulia shrugged and got to her feet. "You want mo coffee, Mama?"

"Thanks, Eulia. One mo cup and I gots to go." She sat watching Eulia's back as she went out to the kitchen. In a minute she called, "You see much of yo daddy, Eulia? He been over?"

Eulia laughed. "You know how Daddy is," she said. "He came over one time an stayed maybe ten minutes. Then he went on back. He say long as he seen we all right they ain no sense in stayin. He say he hear otherwise he come back."

"That sho sound like him, Eulia. I never seen a man was so sot in his ways."

It was true, she thought, and there was nothing she could do about it. If she had not known before, she knew it at that very moment; if he should ask her to marry him, she would accept. But would he ask her? She thought of her dead husband but felt no feeling of disloyalty toward him. This was not the same. Jeff would not be taking his place. No one could do that. It was just that she needed a male relationship, and though she might even grow to love Jeff, it would not be the same. The only thing she did not know was whether or not he would ever ask her. He was a man who did things in his own time and there was no use to try to make him do otherwise.

Eulia set the coffee cup before her. Esther smiled up at her.

"I got to drink this fast," she said. "It past time I was goin now."

On the way back she was lucky enough to get a seat. She sat back and let her body move freely with the motion of the bus, her eyes on the side of the road slipping away behind them. Almost before she realized it they came to her stop and she got off, hearing the low groan of the bus as it labored away behind her. It was perhaps five o'clock of a warm afternoon and in the air was the strange feeling of spring that comes even to Florida. As she cut across toward the square it seemed to her that this was the way life should be.

There was a quiet and peace everywhere, and it seemed to her as though there had never been anything else. A young cur dog ran down the middle of the road looking as though he were running only for the sheer joy of it. As she turned into the square she saw people gathered together in groups, the men before the pool hall and the women by the market. She stopped in and bought the few things she needed for dinner, then started home. In a moment she sensed someone walking by her side and, looking up, she saw Jeff.

"Lemme tote them vittles fo you, Miss Esther," he told her, reaching over and taking the bundle from her arm.

She thanked him but said nothing more. Suddenly she felt a little shy before him, almost as though she were a girl again and not quite sure of herself. It was foolish and she knew it, but somehow she could not help herself. There was something about him that seemed to bring out all that was feminine in her, as though the positive elements of his maleness drew her toward him as a loadstone attracts metal.

"I been over to see Eulia," she said presently.

"How Eulia?" he asked politely. "I reckon she good or I hear."

"She right fine," she answered.

They lapsed into silence again, and as they walked along she stole a look at him out of the corner of her eye. His profile was turned toward her, and she thought, as she often did, of the differences between him and Hezekiah. Their tallness was the one thing they had in common besides their color, for both of them were darker than she. Where Hezekiah had been handsome and always seemed younger than his years, Jeff was almost ugly, save that the strength in his features gave him a striking look, and he seemed as old as you had a mind to make him.

They turned the corner and before long they were at her house. For the last hundred yards she had been running over in her mind whether or not she should ask him in, but at the gate he settled things for her.

"I jest best hep you into the kitchen with them bundles," he told her, and as he swung the gate open he stood aside for her to pass him.

Inside he laid the packages down on the kitchen table and, straightening up, had the look about him of a man about to be on his way. Suddenly she was filled with a strange terror that he might go, and she fumbled for some excuse to make him stay.

"I got beer in the icebox," she told him. "We could set out on the stoop while you drunk a bottle."

"I be proud to," he said. "Reckon it'd sort of wash down the dust I got in my throat walkin back from the store. We sho could use some rain to settle them streets."

She nodded and went to the ice chest. For one awful moment she was afraid that there might not be beer there, but there was. She walked across to the sink and, taking an opener, uncapped the bottle, then poured the beer slantwise into a tall glass. When she handed it to him she felt his fingers against hers and she thought: Make him ask me, God.

He took the glass and raised it to his lips, drinking deeply, and when he put it down a thin line of foam, almost like a mustache, showed above his upper lip.

"That goes right good," he told her.

"You been fishin?" she asked.

196

"Not much," he answered. "Seems they ain been bitin good. Wind been wrong, I reckon, but one of these days when everythin look right I fixin to go again. You like I should carry you along?"

"I'd like that," she nodded. "It been a long time since we been, and I tolt Bessie just the other night how good a little bait of fish would taste."

She watched him as he finished the rest of his beer and turned to go.

26. Now that George was safely home, life should have been easier for Ethel, but somehow it wasn't. Where before there had been the worry of having him far away, and always in danger into the bargain, there was now the uncertainty of his future. Being a woman who believed that there was only one right way of doing things, her own, she began to plan out a sort of campaign for his life. That this was really more George's concern than hers never occurred to her, and had it been brought to her attention she would have denied that she was running the show. It was only, she would have insisted, that if one hoped to get anyplace one must make plans.

She had had too much experience with Ezekiel to be upset by the fact that George seemed to ignore most of the advice that she gave him, that he treated her with a sort of vague kindness, as though she were something to be tolerated yet not to be taken too seriously. Such an attitude annoyed her but it in no way discouraged her, for she had been putting up with it during all of her married life and knew that eventually she always got her way, if only by her carefully calculated persistence. There was only one thing for which she would never forgive George: that he had not forewarned her about the loss of his arm.

It was this that had made the scene of first seeing him remain so vividly in her mind, so much so, in fact, that often it returned to her in dreams. She had been up early that morning, awakening shortly after dawn and, lying there hearing the incessant chattering of the birds outside her bedroom window, finding it impossible to fall back into slumber again. Later she attributed her awakening to her son's return, for she liked to think of herself as somewhat clairvoyant, but the truth of the matter was that she had been roused by the backfire of a passing truck. In any event she lay there quietly for as long as she could stand it and then got up, slipped into her dressing gown, and went down to make herself a cup of coffee.

Bertha, the maid, had not yet arrived, but came in just as the coffee was beginning to bubble itself to the proper strength. Pouring herself a cup, Ethel took it into the living room and placed it on the end table by the more comfortable of the two upholstered chairs that flanked the big window which looked out onto the front walk. She drank the coffee, feeling it warm her and drive the sleep from her eyes, then put the cup down and leisurely lighted a cigarette. In the kitchen she could hear Bertha making her usual clatter, and she thought idly, and without too much rancor, that what could you expect from a field hand.

Then suddenly, out of the corner of her eye, she saw a soldier coming up the walk toward the front door. She turned her head away, thinking that whoever it was, returning student or not, he had a nerve coming so early, then she looked again and saw that it was George. For a moment she felt her emotions well up within her to the point where she felt weak in the knees, then relief flooded over her and she got up to hurry to the front door.

She met him part way down the walk, seeing him through a mist of tears, and, putting her arms around him, she held him there until her eyes cleared. Putting a hand on each shoulder, she gently pushed him back from her a little so that she could really see him. He looked well, she thought, peaked in the face but handsome in his uniform. Her eyes traveled down from his face until they came to the half-empty sleeve. For a moment she thought she was going to faint, and then she was flooded with a wave of physical revulsion, seeing through the material of the sleeve an imagined ugly and seared stump, the skin drawn and sewed like a badly trussed fowl.

But as quickly this passed and, taking him into her arms again, she felt only pity. She did not know that she was sobbing, for all that she could think of was that his life, his brilliant future, was ruined, and that although he would never, like a professional cripple, have to make his living selling pencils on a street corner, the wonderful things that she had planned for him could never be realized under such a handicap.

"It's not as bad as all that," he told her, patting her shoulder with his good hand.

"No," she said. "No, my dear. It's only that I didn't know, that I had no warning."

Slowly her pity molded itself into something more than pity, and she thought that if she struck now, if she maneuvered him into a position of importance, his disability might even be an advantage. It gave to him almost an aura of romance, the final proof that he had been a hero who had given a part of himself for them all, for the race. Tilting her head back a little, she looked up at him and smiled.

"I'm sorry, my dear," she said. "I'm afraid that I've acted badly. It's nothing, of course, and the fact that you are home with us is the only thing that really matters." She raised her face and kissed him quickly on the cheek. "The doctor is still asleep." Then, almost with the voice of a child suggesting a conspiracy: "Shall we go up and surprise him?"

Leading the way into the house, she thought: My son, why did it have to happen to him and not to some worthless uppity young nigger whom the crackers would eventually have killed anyway?

During the next month she thought back to that scene many times. She felt no guilt for the way she had acted, only a vague sort of irritation that George should not have written her instead of turning up unannounced like a ghost. It seemed to her that it showed a weakness in him, a streak of carelessness inherited from his father. Or were all men like that, children who never seemed to grow up to adult responsibility?

Nor could she even get from him any satisfaction of what his plans were for the future. When she would ask him he would smile at her and say that for the time being he had no plans, that he wanted to loaf for a month or two until he got used to being a civilian again. This too seemed to her a possible hint of further weakness, but George was disarming in the way he put her off. For when he was like that, charming and boyish, she could not resist him.

"George," she would say.

"Hmm?" he would answer, hardly bothering to look up from the book he was reading.

"George, we've got to have a talk."

"I know about the facts of life," he would tell her, then look up and smile, his even teeth white against the face that looked more tanned than colored.

"What are you going to do?"

"Read this book. Why?"

"I don't mean now, George," she would finally say, a hint of near panic in her voice. "You're not as young as you were, George. Do you want to go back to Boston to finish school?"

"We don't have to worry about that yet, Mother. I wouldn't go before next fall anyway, you know."

So he would return to his book again and she would have to admit defeat temporarily. But not for long, she would tell herself; tomorrow she would bring it up again, and the day after, if necessary, until she reached some sort of an understanding with him. But always it would be the same.

"Have you thought any more about what we were talking about, George?" she would ask.

"That's a pretty dress you're wearing," he would tell her, "it brings out the gray in your eyes."

Then she would have to give in to him, not wanting to but finding herself completely overcome by his charm and good looks. He was handsome, even better looking than when he had gone away; he had been a boy then and there had been a softness in his face that was almost effeminate, and he had moved too gracefully. Now his face had matured and grown more rugged; his whole body had hardened and taken on a strength that had been lacking before. If he makes me react like this, Ethel thought helplessly, how must he affect a girl his own age?

It would probably not be too long before he would think of marrying, and this realization was almost more than she could bear. The thought of losing him was bad enough, but she could steel herself to that if only she could be certain that he would marry the right girl. This had never worried her before he went away to war, for then he had seemed completely hers and naturally would consult her before he became serious about anyone. But now she was not too sure. This was no boy but a grown man, and often it seemed to her that in the time that he had been away he had grown away from her completely. If she had not already lost him she could feel him gradually slipping away from her, through her fingers, like something too slippery to grasp securely.

What if he should marry a girl darker than he was, someone as black as Bertha, out in the kitchen, and his children, and children's children, steadily regressing, it seemed to her, back into the jungles of the past. She refused to think of it; better that he find himself some foolish country wench and lust with her until such a time as he could pick a wife with a clear and open mind, one who would help him to get ahead rather than merely satisfy his desire.

And so, more persistently than ever, she would try to find out what it was that he was going to do for his lifework. The other could wait, but this could not. Yet always she would end up finding herself no farther along than the last attempt. Finally one night she talked to Ezekiel about it.

She had been reading in bed, a rather stupid novel by a young Negro girl which had created rather a stir in the North. Otherwise she would not have bothered with it, for it not only bored her but disgusted her as well. If that was the way niggers were, she told herself, they ought to be treated like niggers. Then her husband had come in to get ready for bed and she had put the book aside.

"Ezekiel," she called to him as he was finishing brushing his teeth in the bathroom.

She waited until he came out and then told him of the difficulty that she had been having with George.

He laughed lightly. "I wouldn't worry, my dear. He's earned a good rest. The boy's had a tough time."

"I know," she went on, "but everyone must have a plan of action. He's got a wonderful chance to get into something good, and ahead of the others."

He shrugged and, turning out the light, crawled into bed beside her. She wanted to talk more, but she could tell by his gentled and regular breathing that he had gone to sleep the minute his head had touched the pillow. That was like him, she thought, and she remembered how sometimes after he had made love to her and she needed him most he was asleep in an instant. And yet he was always there, comforting and solid, and, she felt, probably no different from any other man. Before long she too was asleep.

If the war in Europe was not over, at least its ending was in sight. It was something for which Ethel was not prepared, and it caught her unawares. Now that George was back it seemed to have little meaning for her, aside from the fact that she found the excitement invading the campus a little contagious. There was still the war in the Pacific, but that too had little importance for her now that there was no possibility that George would have to go back to it.

If anything, however, it made her more conscious that he should choose his lifework. The urgency of it seemed to her greater now than before, and that night she again tried to talk with him, and for the first time he actually turned on her.

"Godamit," he said angrily, "what are you trying to do, drive me out? Is that what you want? If it is, I'll go and you can save yourself the effort."

He had gotten to his feet and she could see the flush in his cheeks under his tanned face. He walked toward her and for a moment she was actually afraid that he was going to strike her. Standing over her, he seemed to her taller than he was, and the look on his face frightened her. At the corner of his mouth a nerve pulsed nervously, and suddenly he took the magazine he was holding in his hand and hurled it to the floor. It spanked the flooring loudly and skidded to rest up against her chair.

"Godamit," he said, "leave me alone. You don't and I will go. I'll get out."

Turning, he walked to the window and stood looking out into the dusk. He was bent forward a little, and though she could not see his face she sensed somehow that he was sobbing inwardly. She was confused, unsure of herself, and at a loss to know what to do for perhaps the first time in her life. She wanted to go to him and comfort him, yet she was afraid to do so. She was not even sure what it was that she had done, or even if she had really been at fault. She thought, perhaps, that he needed a doctor, that he was not well, and she wondered if because of Ezekiel's standing in the community she could get one of the good white doctors from Citrus City to give a thorough checkup. Although she knew that Dr. Garvin was one of the best men in the South, somehow in a crisis like this she could not trust him, much as she liked him, for he was a Negro.

Then suddenly she had a brilliant idea. She had been wanting to go to New York, and here was the perfect excuse for going, for she could take George along and have the best doctor in town see him. At the same time she could do some shopping, get some things for the house, and see the people she never saw enough of. She started to tell him then, but some instinct within made her hold off. She looked up and saw him turn back into the room.

"I'm sorry," he said slowly. "I didn't mean to blow my top."

He smiled, but it seemed to her that it was an effort.

"It's just that this means so much," he said slowly. "You wouldn't know or feel it the way I do."

She nodded as he came over and bent to kiss her lightly on the cheek, then walked out of the room and climbed the stairs to his room. Ezekiel was in his study, and as she sat alone in the living room she knew with finality that she had lost her son, that he had come over to kiss her only because he was ashamed of himself for having lost his temper. Now, instead of wanting him to make plans for his future, her only desire was to keep him there with her. If he went away, even if only to return to Boston for the rest of his college work, some intuition told her that he would never return.

Well, wasn't that what she had wanted? Yes, she told herself, but only as an extension of herself, as a part of her that longed to think of New York or some other metropolitan area as her real home. She had no desire to cut this postnatal cord which had once bound them so securely together. So long as it had been elastic enough to stretch out to wherever he might be, it was all right, but now she realized that it was severed forever. To keep him near was her only chance.

She knew too that she should go up to bed, yet she could not bring herself to do so. Instead she merely sat there, bitterly shaken by her own defeat.

Like a wise general who even in the face of defeat regroups his forces and maps out a new strategy, Ethel changed her whole plan of action. She had no hope of victory, but she would gladly have settled for a stalemate, had even that possibility existed. But it was too late. All that remained was for her to keep him at home and she would have gone to any ends to attain it, even to the point of a marriage of which she did not approve.

It was a concession that only desperation could have forced her to make. Having made it, however, she looked around for the most likely candidate close at hand and settled upon Bessie. That only a short while before she had waged a campaign to keep Eric at the college and used Bessie as her secret weapon either never occurred to her or else she conveniently pushed it from her mind.

Her first offensive was to ask Bessie for dinner. Bessie, of course, accepted; but, hearing of it, George at once asked Eric, without so much as telling her until it was an accomplished fact. So far as Ethel was concerned the evening ended in a complete fiasco, for she found out that the three of them had been running around together ever since George had come back to the campus. Ordinarily this would have brought her at least some consolation, because it would seem as though the two of them would help to keep George there, but unfortunately she knew Eric too well not to realize that he would be against whatever she might be for.

As she lay in bed that night she racked her brain. Ezekiel lay beside her asleep, but she was as wide awake as though she had just gotten up from a deep slumber. Finally it came to her and she fell gently into sleep.

She did nothing about it the next day or even the day following. Instead she waited until an evening when they were going to have a particularly good dinner and Ezekiel was likely to be in a receptive mood. George had left early, evidently to meet Eric and Bessie, but she waited until she was certain that there was no chance of his returning. Then she turned to Ezekiel.

"Doctor," she said casually, "have you ever thought of retiring?"

He put back his head and roared with laughter. "I know I'm getting a little too much bay window, my dear, but I'm not that old, am I?"

"Of course not, and age has nothing to do with it. Lots of people even younger than yourself have retired. It's just that you've worked so hard that you've earned it. I think it's time you had a little fun."

"What would I do with myself, Ethel?"

He looked across at her, and the way that the lamplight reflected against his glasses irritated her almost as much as the look upon his face. Sometimes it seemed to her that certain of his expressions were as stupid as the look of a sheep. Besides, he was looking at her in that slightly amused way which made her certain that he was relegating her to a position as unimportant and inferior as a child's. She fought back her irritation.

"Well, for one thing, we might travel, or we could go live in New York. Probably you could write a column for one of the Harlem papers. I'm sure you could find enough to do."

"It sounds good, my dear, but you seem to have overlooked one rather important fact. For example, who would take my place?"

"George," she said matter-of-factly. "This is your college. You've made it yourself and you know it. What more natural thing than having your son take over when you step down?"

He got to his feet and, standing by the fireplace, lit a cigar.

"You're going too fast," he said. "I'll admit that nothing would please me more someday. But the boy is too young. He's had neither the training nor the experience. God knows I have trouble enough myself with the board and the white folks."

She shrugged. "Give him the experience, then. Can't you put him to work?"

He came over to her and, bending down, kissed her.

"You go too fast," he said. "You're ambitious for the boy, and I can understand that. I suppose I am too. But you can't make him an educator overnight."

Without another word he turned and went into his study. She knew it was useless to try to push him further at the moment, but she also knew that she had made a start. Her self-confidence had been at low ebb; now it began to rise.

27.

Luther had not wanted to give the party. The mere fact that he had been nominated to the executive board of the local did not seem to him sufficient grounds for celebration, but Eulia had insisted. It was not really his election that was the reason for the party, she told him, it was merely an excuse for doing something that she had wanted to do for a long time. Once Luther got used to the idea he went forward with the plans enthusiastically. He was proud of his home and proud of Eulia for making it attractive, and now others could see for themselves. Most of them had been there singly, but now they would come together, not a big party but those people for whom he cared most.

There would be the handful of workers in the plant who had been most influential in getting him placed on the executive board, and their wives or girl friends. Bessie, of course, would come with Eric, and his mother was coming with Eulia's father. Then there were a few people in the project whom Eulia had wanted to invite. There would be beer and whisky, and later in the evening Eulia would give them something to eat.

And then on the afternoon of the party something happened which had almost caused Luther to call it off. He had come home after quitting time at four o'clock and happened to turn on the radio. There was some music, to which he paid little attention, and then all at once an announcer broke in. His voice was almost hushed as he said, "Warm Springs, Georgia: The President of the United States, Franklin Delano Roosevelt, died late this morning. He had come to this sleepy little Georgia town, for which he has done so much, for a much-needed rest. He had been overtired after his return, by plane, from Yalta, but his personal physician had, after a thorough checkup, found nothing serious the matter with him. Last night he complained of a headache, and early this morning he had awakened to find it worse. After his breakfast he went to pose, as usual, for his portrait. Shortly afterward he put his hand to his eyes and complained of intense pain, and a moment later he collapsed, sinking into a coma from which he never recovered. His physician, Dr. Ross McIntire, flew down from Washington, but Mr. Roosevelt had passed away before he could get to his bedside."

Reaching over slowly, Luther turned off the radio. He looked up and saw Eulia standing in the doorway leading into the kitchen. There were tears in her eyes and she was sobbing softly. Deep within him he felt his own emotions catch, and behind his eyes he felt the sour pain that one feels before he is going to cry. He fought back the pain and, taking his handkerchief from his pocket, blew his nose loudly. Neither of them spoke, and the room was so stilled that tension rapidly built up within it. Then Eulia began to cry again.

"I cain believe it," Luther said softly.

"It true all right. Wasn it wouldn come over the radio that way."

He nodded dumbly. He tried to remember how he had felt when he lost his own father, but this, it seemed to him, was something even more shattering, however different it might be. It seemed to him as though something personal had gone out of his life.

"You reckon we ought to have the party?" he asked Eulia.

"Yeah, Luther, we goin to have the party. We cain call it off now. Anyway, I think we ought to."

He nodded and got to his feet slowly. "I still cain believe he dead. I doan reckon I ever will. Seemed like he the one thing we could always count on. What we goin to do now?"

She shrugged. "Go on the best we can, I reckon."

He nodded again. "Well," he said, "I reckon I best walk over and get the whisky. We got beer enough, ain we?"

"Sho, they's plenty beer, Luther."

"Anythin I can get you at the store?"

"Naw, I was over there this mornin."

He went over to the table and picked up his hat. He held it in his hand, looking down at it for a moment, before he put it on his head and walked out the door.

Bessie and Eric were the first to come, and with them they brought Esther, Eulia's father, and also George. Luther met them at the door, for

206

Eulia was still busy in the kitchen. He had never met George before, but he liked the way he carried himself. Greeting his mother warmly, he turned to Eulia's father to shake hands. Jeff was dressed in a black suit, and it was the only time that Luther could remember having seen him with a collar and tie.

"You kind of a stranger," Luther told him. "Eulia been tryin to git you over here again."

Jeff grinned. "Like I tolt her, I seen you two was all right. Time you ain I come, excusin a get-together like this."

Luther led them into the living room, and as they sat down he looked carefully at Jeff. It was funny, but he felt completely at ease with the older man now, almost as though they had become equals and were thus more nearly of an age. He remembered when this had not been so, when he had been uneasy in the presence of Jeff and had almost a feeling of guilt that Eulia's father was measuring him and somehow finding him lacking. What had changed things, he wondered, merely that he had changed jobs? He was not sure, but he supposed so; that, and because for the first time in his life he was doing something that seemed bigger than himself.

"What you like, Mama, beer?"

"Naw, son. Reckon maybe Eulia got some coffee out yonder. I fixin to go see directly. I want to see kin I help out."

"Bessie?"

"Whisky and soda, if you've got it, Luther."

"Eric?"

"The same. Can I help get it?"

"Doan need you, but come along anyhow."

"Jeff?"

"Whisky, I reckon, but doan go to puttin nothin in it. I always figured God made whisky strong enough it could stand by itself. I ain fixin to go agin His word."

Forgetting the name of the boy who had come with them, Luther turned to him without calling his name.

"Whisky and soda is fine by me," George told Luther quietly.

Eric got up and went into the kitchen with Luther. Mama was already there, over in the corner by the stove, talking with Eulia. Luther got ice from the refrigerator, opened a bottle of whisky, and began to prepare the drinks. To one side he placed a tumbler half filled with whisky for Jeff. From past experience he knew that the old man would work on it all evening, then, just as they were leaving, ask for a short one which he would drink quickly in one swallow and then say his good night.

"How are things out at the plant, Luther?"

"Pretty good, Eric. Figured for a while there we might have to strike, but the union ironed things out."

"You know they elected him to the executive board, Eric?" Eulia called.

"No; say, that's all right, Luther. How do you like sitting with those peckerwoods?"

Luther laughed. "White folks always gonna be white folks, I reckon," he said. "But seem like the union make em a little more human."

"Having any friction out there, Luther? I'm interested especially in the whole question of segregation and what the CIO is doing about it."

Luther opened up the soda and started filling the glasses.

"I never used to think much bout jimcrow," he said soberly. "I knowed I was colored all right, but if I had my white folks I figured I git along. I got over that awright, but I still ain worryin too much bout segregation. Seems to me it more important we got good jobs. We do, maybe the other thing take care of itself. That the way I figure it anyway."

"How does CIO national feel about it?"

"Hell, Eric," Luther laughed, "you knows more bout that than I does. We ain no different than any other local. We sits one side and they sits on the other. That ain heaven, but it better than it was."

"And you?"

"Me, I sit up on the platform with the white folks. I ain yet, but I reckon I do at the next meeting. I doan figure they gonna bite me, and they knows I ain gonna bite them. We get along."

Eric laughed. "All right, but you know me, Luther. I've got to know everything, or try to find out about it anyway. Look, Luther, that boy that came with us is just back from the Pacific. He's learned a lot out there and you've learned a lot here. If you talk to him, the two of you might learn a lot more."

Luther put the drinks on a tray. "He seem like a good boy."

"He is a good boy, Luther. Right now he finds it a little tough getting used to being back here again. What happened today doesn't help much either."

"No, it sho doan."

Luther picked up the tray and started into the living room.

When Bull Snake showed up, he was the life of the party. He didn't bring a girl, but both Shorty and Seaboard did. He was wearing a dark suit but he had on a salmon-colored sports shirt that more than made up for it. The minute he came in the door he started sniffing.

"I smell juice," he said.

"A jackleg preacher like you oughtn tuh drink no whisky," Seaboard told him.

"Man," Bull Snake said, "you ain my wife. Anyway, I ain a preacher no more. I uh good union man, thas what I is."

"The Bible say strong drink is uh mocker."

Bull Snake laughed and went out into the kitchen where Luther was and poured himself a good stiff drink. When he came back he looked over at Seaboard.

"Lord heps them that heps themselves," he said, then went over and sat down by Mama.

"You must be a good woman," he told her.

"Hucome?" she asked.

"You sho had you uh good boy," he said. "I mean uh good boy. That Luther, him and me we gonna end up runnin the whole CIO. Wait an see ain I right."

He drank the whisky and went out into the kitchen for another one. When he came back they all were talking about the death of the President.

"He was uh good man," Bull Snake said. "Even if he was uh white man he was uh good man."

"What that got to do with it?" Luther asked. "He was for you an me an the CIO. What more you want?"

Bull Snake finished his drink before he answered. "I tried tuh like white folks," he said, "I sho did. Ever did I tell you bout the time I loss my cah?"

"Naw, man, tell us bout it," Shorty said.

"That what I fixin tuh do, only I got a glass with uh hole in the bottom. Luther, you got one doan all run out the bottom?" He waited until Luther brought him another drink, then went on. "Well," he said, "eight, nine years ago I had me uh big ole cah. Them days I was preachin back in the woods an I use tuh come in Satiday night tuh frolic some an one night somebody done stole my cah. So next day I missed muh preachin cuz I gots to report it to the law."

"Why didn you do it that same night, Bull Snake?"

"Is you crazy? Nigger git even near that jail Satiday night they

209

gonna snatch him. Like I say, I tolt the man next day, give him the number of the plates and what the cah look like. Three days later he call up say he gots the cah."

"Thas good."

"Good, what the hell good bout it? Cah clean over tuh Daytona Beach. I ast the man why he doan drive me over but he say he too busy. He say just go on over an tell them other laws to gimme muh cah."

"You go, Bull Snake?"

"Unh-unh, leastways not right off. Gimme uh paper, I tolt the man, ain gonna give me no cah I ain got no paper. So the man wrote me a letter an I went on over like he say. Took off muh cap an give the man the paper nice an polite. I tells him: 'Please, suh, now can I have muh cah, suh?'"

"You git it, Bull Snake?"

"Hunh! Man read the letter an tolt me I done wrote it. I acted like he loss his mind. I tolt him he know good an well niggers cain write. How he think I kin write no letter?"

"What he do then?"

"Put my black ass in jail. Say he think I pay some white man tuh write the letter fo me."

"How you git out, Black Snake?"

"Man write the man over here. Man git a letter back in three days an lemme go."

"You git the cah then?"

"Yeah, I git the cah. Didn cost me but fo dollars fo hauling it in when they found it an three dollars an seventy cents storage time they had me jail."

When they got through laughing he looked around the room.

"I didn mean the President no disrespect," he said, and then grinned. "I been wantin tuh tell that ole lie on the white folks fo two months now and wouldn no one gimme no openin. Way it come up, I didn belong not tuh hep myself."

He got up and, taking his drink, started for the kitchen again. Halfway to the door he stopped and faced back into the room.

"He was uh good man," he said in a low voice. "Ain no one knows that bettern me. Today I done loss muh best frien. When I was raggedy an muh backsides peekin out muh britches, when I was hongry an like tuh starve, WPA done seen me through. He was muh frien an my enemies was his enemies. Seem like they always takes the good ones an leaves the bad ones be. All I got left is his missus, and she gonna say a good word for me when she can. In the meantime me and Luther gonna run the CIO."

He turned again and walked into the kitchen in search of another drink.

It seemed to Luther that things were just starting to go good when everyone went home. After they left he stood in the deserted living room talking to Eulia, who was washing up the few dishes and glasses in the kitchen. When she was through she would call him and he would come out to dry them while she got ready for bed.

It had been a good party, he thought. People had seemed to enjoy themselves and there was enough to drink, yet nobody had had too much. After a while Bull Snake had gone out to his car and gotten his guitar. All the evening, it seemed to Luther, Bull Snake had been near Mama. He wondered how Jeff felt about that, or had Eulia been wrong when she claimed that it would be only a matter of time before the two of them got married? Woman usually knew about things like that.

Later in the evening people began to go into the kitchen for their own drinks, and then he had a chance to talk with George, the boy who had come with Eric and Bessie. They had sat on the floor in the corner, with their drinks between them, and fallen easily into conversation. They had talked about the war, about the trades-union movement, the death of Roosevelt and how it might affect the peace, and lastly about the postwar world. He had enjoyed talking with the boy and he had learned something too.

Standing there, he wished that he had gone further in school, had gotten a real education so that he could talk the way Eric and George could. Eric would probably lend him some books to read if he were to ask him. For a moment he felt a slight bitterness at the opportunity he had lost, and then he thought of Bessie. It was all right then; he was glad that he had stepped aside and given her the chance instead of taking it himself. When he thought about Alberta he wasn't sure just what he thought.

"You mighty quiet," Eulia called. "What you thinkin bout?"

He walked out into the kitchen. Standing with his backside propped against the base cabinets, he looked at Eulia standing, her back to him, at the kitchen sink. He was glad that she was coming to the end of her pregnancy. Sometimes it seemed to him that her face was prettier than it had ever been, but he wanted her body to be the way it had been before. It was not that her bloated stomach in any way seemed to him unpleasant, but only that it seemed to him as though she were another person, somehow different, and because of that withdrawn from him in a way that he could not quite understand.

"Well," she said, "what was you thinkin bout?"

"Nothin much, Eulia. It was a good party, wasn it?"

"Yeah, Luther, it really was. Bull Snake sho had Daddy goin."

"What you mean?"

"I declare mens doan have no eyes, or they do they doan see. Black Snake was paying yo mama all that mind and Daddy didn like it one little bit."

Luther chuckled. "I seen him. It do yo daddy good."

"What you and that boy come with Eric an Bessie talkin about?"

"We talk bout a lot of things, honey. I like that boy. He git himself straightened out an he gonna be all right."

Going over to the sink, he took a dish towel and began to dry the dishes. Shortly Eulia took off her apron and went back into the bedroom. This was the time of day he liked, after the dishes were done and he was alone in the kitchen, knowing that Eulia was not far away. It seemed to him that this was proof of the rightness of his life. Perhaps to many it was not much, but to him it was enough. He could hold his head high, something he had not always been able to do.

He remembered how it had been when he was working in the taproom and he had felt as though he had everything he wanted. Now, as he looked back, he realized that he had had nothing, not even his self-respect. Then he had always to depend on others; now he was dependent on himself and, in a sense, others depended on him. It was a good feeling.

Standing there with a half-dried dish in his hand, he thought about the baby. It was still hard for him to realize that it belonged partly to him, either now or even after it would be born. Even when Eulia had held his hand to her swollen abdomen and he had felt the sharp, strong kick it was not easy to think of it except as something apart from him and, even in a way, from Eulia as well.

Would it be a boy or a girl? He did not, of course, know, and in a way he did not care. All that he really wanted was for it to become an entity for him, to be concrete instead of abstract, the way it was now. There would be time enough then to think about the future. Yet even as this came to his mind he also thought fiercely: It will have a better chance than I had, a better world than the one I was born into. And thinking this, he realized that the work he was doing might insure a better life for his baby. It was a good feeling to have.

He heard Eulia calling him from the bedroom and he answered that he would be along in a moment. He dried the last of the dishes and put them away carefully in the cupboard. Then he reached up and pulled the light cord over the kitchen sink.

28. For some time Jeff had known that he was going to marry Esther. This realization dated from the first time that he had taken her fishing and she had easily passed that acid test, but he had always thought her an attractive woman. He liked her spareness and the way she walked, for although she was very feminine, at the same time she had a strength of fiber that he did not usually associate with women. If he had been a younger man he might have courted her with a furious assault; he would have been eager to possess her, to sweep her off her feet, to put his mark upon her. But though he was still a man in the late prime of his life and he wanted her, he was content to proceed on his own terms. If this meant waiting, he could afford to wait.

Why, and for what? This was a question that he never bothered to ask himself, for the answer seemed readily apparent. He was getting along all right the way things were and he was a man who had lived long enough not to be stampeded into anything new. He had had women before. The last he had buried and the first had left him; the second had been no good, so he had left her. For all of them he had still a certain affection, but especially was this true for Eulia's mother, the one who had died. Yet he knew that for Esther he could care as deeply, perhaps even more so. Was it this of which he was afraid?

No, it was hardly that. On the outside he seemed a man with a shell that discouraged close relationships, but actually this was not so. He was self-sufficient to a degree alien to most men, but he enjoyed human companionship so long as it was on his own terms, and he knew that these would apply if he were to marry Esther.

If he held back, it was for one reason alone. Although he had a deep affection for Eulia, the two of them were to a large degree independent of each other. Until now he had not been sure that this was true of Esther's relationship with her children. She had lost her husband,

and this, if anything, had strengthened the ties with them, and to a point that seemed to him unnatural. It was something against which he had no desire to compete, for to do so seemed to him foolhardy, with the odds arrayed against him. Besides, it was Esther whom he wished to marry, not the whole kit and kaboodle of her children.

Even when Luther and Eulia had married he had not been sure that the break was final. He liked Luther and had no objection to him as a son-in-law so long as he kept out from underfoot. But actually he had thought that Luther was weak and not only tied to his mother's apron strings but, worse, to the white man for whom he worked. Yet he realized now that he had been wrong or else Luther had certainly changed.

Of Bessie he had few doubts, even from the beginning, and the first time that he had seen her with Eric he knew that her breakaway would be complete. For Eric he had respect, something that was not given easily, and especially to a man who at first appearance might well have turned out to be a dude.

But more than anything he had been afraid of Alberta, who before her appearance seemed to have all the elusiveness of a phantom lover. How could you be a rival of someone who was not even there, he had snorted, yet was always with the two of them wherever they might go? It was like shadowboxing or running a foot race against the wind. Then Alberta had come home and he had felt better. His native intelligence had sized her up at once; if she were any lighter she'd have passed for white. Being the way she was, he had known it could not last; when it didn't, he was neither surprised nor elated. All that remained was for Esther to get over the shock. Yet now that she had, he still held off from asking her.

Perhaps it had only been that, like a stalled mechanical toy, he needed a nudge to once more set him into motion. Without that, he might have put off asking her indefinitely, always knowing that eventually he would do something about it but never quite getting around to it. If it was this, he had received the necessary impetus at Luther's apartment the night of the party.

At first when he had seen Bull Snake make up to Esther it had, if anything, flattered him. He was not by nature a vain man, but anyone is pleased to see that that which attracts him is also pleasing to others. He even had been gratified to see the way in which Esther reacted to such attention; it brought out the warm and womanly side of her nature, which always excited him a little. Looking at her, he realized how attractive she was; no longer pretty, perhaps, but striking, alive, and vibrant. As she turned her head in a certain way he saw her almost as though for the first time. Beneath the almost reddish skin of her forehead life pulsed, and her eyes, even though she was not looking at him, were suddenly as exciting to him as though they had been in the room alone. His eyes dropped to her shoulders and then to her breasts; he felt within him an almost painful desire.

He knew then that he not only wanted this woman but that he could no longer wait, that he wanted more than her body or her companionship. It was simply that he wanted the whole of her, everything about her, so that she would be his so completely that he would never again feel the emotion he felt now. He was not a jealous man by nature, and what he felt now, perhaps, was not jealousy at all, but only the sudden realization that if he waited longer he might lose her.

Regardless of what it was, it disturbed him, and he knew that now he would ask her at his first opportunity.

Coming home in the car, there was no chance. The place was wrong and he felt crowded huddled into the back seat of the little convertible. Even though George was in front with Eric and Bessie, he had no feeling of being alone with Esther. Instead it seemed to him as though in reality the three of them in front were sitting on his and Esther's lap.

The night was warm and the top was down, so that the soft wind was on their faces. It made him squint his eyes a little. He could smell the almost sickeningly sweet aroma of citrus blossoms, and it annoyed him to find himself thinking that orange blossoms were for brides. Inwardly he snorted and called himself a fool; or was it merely that he had run past the middle of his cycle and was returning back along the way he had come? The thought made him uncomfortable, and he felt like raising his head and bawling obscenities at the moon so that all might hear and know him for what he was. He sneaked a look out of the corner of his eye and saw that Esther was relaxed and looking straight ahead. She ain goin to hep me a bit, he thought, then: godam her an me in the bargain. His frustration made him suddenly angry, so that he all but shouted for Eric to stop the car so that he could get out and walk. At least in walking he could gather his scattered wits together.

Then at last they drew up before her house and he was as anxious to get out as a man suffering from claustrophobia. He thought of saying a curt good night and walking quickly up the street, but decided against it as Esther hooked her arm through his. She drew away from the car and up to the gate.

"They want to say good night," she whispered.

She opened the gate and he followed her inside onto the walk. There was a place where they could not be seen from the car, and when they came to it she was walking a little ahead. He wanted to reach out his hand and, placing it on her shoulder, turn her gently back toward him. Feeling her against him, he thought, I could tell her and not make myself out to be a fool. But his hand seemed paralyzed at his side.

Then it was too late and he thought angrily of throwing her to the grass and having his way with her, not motivated by lust but only that in his frustration it seemed the one way of showing her the way it was between them. Or did she know? At the steps she paused, and it seemed to him that for a moment she swayed toward him but he was not sure.

He looked up at the sky; anything to keep from doing what he knew he must do. It had come on him too suddenly, he told himself, otherwise he would not be such a fool. Would he never escape? Say your piece and go, he told himself, but the words would not form within his mouth.

"I reckon I go in now, Jeff," she told him softly. "They said good night by now."

He nodded dumbly.

"Thank you for carryin me over there. I had uh right nice time."

"We could go fishin tomorrow," he blurted out suddenly. "The wind laid and we might do some good."

"I be right proud to, Jeff."

"I come by early, then," he said, and, feeling his fool's role complete, turned and walked angrily toward the gate.

All the morning they had fished, but with no great success. Yet Jeff had not really expected any. His whole idea had been to get out on the lake with Esther in his boat; if there was good fishing, so much the better; if not, at least it would be good to be alone with her. Some of his indecision of the night before had left him, but he still had not yet spoken his mind.

It had been a clear, cool morning with a little breeze ruffling the water when they first set out, but by the middle of the day the lake had become as smooth as glass and the sun baked down on them until in desperation he had gone to the west end where there was some protection close up under the trees. They had fished for speckled perch on his favorite bed but had caught only two. Now they sat fishing with live bait, yet his mind was not on his work.

It annoyed him, but he was thinking about the future and wondering whether, when he and Esther were married, he should go back to work. He was by trade a handy man, but he had done little in the years since Eulia had started working. With her wages and his small pension from the first World War, they had more than enough to get by on. But now the price of everything had gone up so much that while he was able to get along on his pension alone, he was not certain that it was elastic enough to stretch to cover the two of them.

It was not that he minded working. For nearly all of his life he had been a hard worker. But when Eulia started to bring in wages and he found that there was more than enough coming in, he had simply made up his mind that he had worked long enough, that unless economic need arose he would, from that day forward, work only for himself.

Working at his own pace around the house, he had set out to improve that which belonged to him. In this he found pleasure, doing what was needed when he felt like it, taking his pleasure when he felt he had earned the rest. When he had done all the obvious things which needed doing, he thought up others. He had even added a bathroom, picking up the fixtures from junk yards and making them look almost as good as new.

But now it looked as though he would have to hunt around for outside jobs to do. The thought did not please him, not because he was lazy but because he had been his own boss for so long. He thought that maybe the two of them should move to the country; he was tired of living in the city, he wanted a change. He looked at Esther and wondered how she would feel about it.

She was sitting sideways in the back of the boat so that her profile was turned toward him. He thought again of how much he wanted to be with her, the way they were now. She looked up and caught his eyes full upon her, but she merely smiled. He looked back toward the shore, where the water was shallow, and suddenly noticed a big bass slowly working his way along the bank.

Calling softly to Esther, he pointed with his finger.

"Reel in," he told her, "and lemme put on a fresh shiner. Then cast maybe twelve, fifteen feet front of his nose. That way he come up to see what made the splash stead of it scarin him off."

He lifted the seat and reached into the bait well for a minnow, then carefully worked the hook up under the dorsal fin. He watched her prepare to cast.

She was using a rod and reel that had belonged to Luther. He remembered how he had taught her to use it, for she had wanted to cling to the more familiar cane pole. The minnow arched out across the water and dropped a little short of its mark. He saw the bass turn leisurely and he warned her that it was headed for the bait.

"Let him swaller it," he told her. "If he want to run with it, let him take it a ways. Then, when I tell you, set the hook good."

She nodded and his eyes returned to the fish. For a moment he thought the bass was going to pass the bait by, then suddenly it rushed in on the oblique and, taking the minnow in its mouth, started off away from the boat.

"Let him take line," he cautioned. He watched carefully until he saw the tail of the shiner disappear and the mouth of the fish close tight. "Now, give him a good jerk."

She set the hook hard and he saw the bass turn and head fast for the deep water. In a moment he saw her try to turn him, but the fish had other ideas. He dropped the oars into the water and headed the boat slowly out into the lake after it.

For a while they were busy until finally the fish tired and she managed to bring him up to the side of the boat. He thought it would make one more rush and it did, but soon he had hooked his fingers into the gills and lifted it neatly into the boat.

"That a right good trout," he told her. "You done real good."

She looked up at him and smiled.

Shortly after that they went in to shore to eat their lunch. As she sat down on the grass he went back to the edge of the water and, taking the bass from the boat, reached into his pocket for his knife. Kneeling down, he neatly gutted the fish and cut out the gills, then, after washing it in the water, held it up for her to see.

"That a pretty enough trout to serve at a weddin," he said without thinking.

"Whose?" she asked.

He looked at her and he knew that at last it was out between them.

"Why, ourn, I reckon," he told her, and laid the bass down on the grass.

"I was wonderin when you was goin to ask me. I declare I was just before givin up. Ain you goin to kiss me?"

"You godam right," he said.

Sitting down on the grass, he took her in his arms. He looked down at her face, resting in the crook of his arm. Her eyes were closed and her lips parted a little; he kissed her gently and felt her come up to him, her arms go around his neck. She opened her eyes and smiled at him, then pulled his head down to hers again. Her lips were against his and he could feel the softness of her breasts against his chest.

"I still got my nature," he told her softly, and he felt her breath against his neck as she giggled.

"I reckon you have," she answered, then giggled again. "You probably rutty as a ole stud boar."

He threw back his head and roared with laughter, laughed until it hurt.

"Hucome it took so long to thaw you out? I wanted you to kiss me last night."

"I guess I gettin old," he answered. "I reckon I done forgot how to court."

"You done all right just now."

He got to his feet and stood looking down at her. It seemed to him as though he were as content as he had ever been in his life, and he could see that she felt the same. Off in the distance he heard a train whistle and on the road in back of them the whine of a passing truck. She smiled up at him and it was all he could do to keep from kissing her again.

"When you want tuh get married?" he asked her.

"Not right this minute. Right now I wants to eat some lunch. I reckon you waited this long you kin wait a little longer."

She reached over for the lunch she had brought and, opening it, spread it out on the grass between them.

"You reckon there enough there to fill you up?"

"I reckon," he said, and sat down.

He took a sandwich and the cup of coffee she poured him from the thermos jug that Bessie used to take to the beach when she and Eric went fishing. A feeling of peace came over him, and he knew that even when they were married it would be no better than this moment they shared now.

"Where we goin to live?" he asked her.

"What you mean?"

"Well, look to me like we got one house too many. I figure we might live in mine. Then, we want to, you can sell yours." He took another sandwich and bit into it. "Fact is, for all uh me, we sell em both. We belong to get us a good price now."

"What we do then?"

"I figure to move out of town. Git us a little place in the country and put us in a garden. Maybe we might raise us a few ducks and chickens, even a shoat or two."

"I wouldn mind, leastways not after Eulia's baby come. I'd want to be near a bus line so I could see the baby every now and then."

He nodded and reached for a banana. Peeling it, he ate it slowly, then took out his pipe and filled it. After he lighted it he leaned back on his elbow.

"How you want that trout fixed?" she asked him.

"Could be fried in corn meal, only this late it might be a little muddy. Might could be it taste good baked."

"With Spanish sauce?"

"Be good, I reckon. Listen, woman, can you make a lime pie?"

"Sho, why?"

"I been hankerin for some for a long time. The only I ever et I had one time down to Key West. I never found none since."

She laughed.

"Jeff."

"Hunh?"

"I doan reckon you is got yo nature. All you gonna do in this marriage is eat?"

He made a grab for her but she rolled away from him.

29. In spite of the fact that Ezekiel had apparently shown little interest when Ethel spoke to him about retiring, the idea was not new to him. He had a horror of men who stayed in important positions beyond the period of their usefulness, for he had his share of experiences in dealing with them. Nor was the idea that George might someday become head of the college something which had not occurred to him. But he had not considered either in the light of the immediate present, nor had he any intentions, as Ethel suggested, of moving to New York.

No, when he stepped down he would remain as a sort of senior statesman, a consultant behind the scenes, a kind of honorary chairman of all things pertaining to the college. This did not mean, he told himself, that he wished to remain the power behind the throne. He had no desire to retain authority. It was only that he felt he knew more than anyone else about the college and he wished to use that knowledge to make certain that his son became as much of a success at the job as he himself had been. Such a position was difficult, just how difficult no one realized until he had been caught in that no man's land and raked by the cross fire of both whites and Negroes.

Yet it would not be easy for him to step down. All his life he had been an active man, and he had no desire to be put out to pasture like a faithful horse who had served his master well. Actually he was looking forward to such a period in his life, whenever it might come, as a period of increased rather than decreased activity. True, it would be of a different kind, but merely because of this no less important.

There was some writing that he had wanted to get down to for a number of years, not only odds and ends of articles, but a whole book. It seemed to him that his had been an exciting life and one in which he had come a long way. Not that it could be compared to Booker T. Washington's or even Carver's; but after all, the Negro had passed into a new phase and no one had really told of that transition. What had been said recently was too radical; it did not take into consideration the question of the white South, or the author was so frustrated by personal bitterness as to present a distorted picture.

What he hoped to do was to show that the Negro in the South was making progress and was also working things out within an area in which the white South was quite willing to help. He felt that he could give this insight by relating it to his own personal life and how he had been able to get ahead in spite of the handicap of race. After the death of Booker T., and particularly under the New Deal, Negro leadership had moved North. This did not seem to him a good thing, for even though it had perhaps resulted in showy legislation and a few federal appointments, it seemed to him to lack realism.

For years now he had been carefully making notes, clipping items from the Negro press, tearing out articles from magazines. All these Bessie had neatly filed away for him in a separate cabinet. He had bought a number of books which he had placed in a special section on the bookshelves which were built into his study walls. He had a feeling that he was about ready to begin.

No, he would not be idle. There would be enough to do to keep him occupied, and if the book were successful it might even open up to him a whole new life. For if eventually the white South, through pressures from without, decided to allow the Negro a modified political existence, he was well aware of the kind of Negro leadership to which it would turn. It would have to be men whom the white South considered safe, men who were willing to co-operate without upsetting the status quo, leaders who were realistic enough to understand that the progress of their race rested securely in the hands of the more enlightened white people of the South.

Perhaps such a time would never come to the South. The chances were that it never would, but if it did, he would be ready.

Once Ezekiel had come this far in his thinking, he was prepared to take action. The most obvious difficulty was that George had so little academic background and training for such a position, yet even this did not bother Ezekiel too much. First, of course, he would have to finish his undergraduate work at Boston. Once this was accomplished, he, Ezekiel, would arrange for the next step, had in fact already done so.

On one of his more or less regular trips to the office of Cal Thornton, the editor of the daily paper in Citrus City, he had skillfully led the conversation around to a discussion of the future of the college. In the end he had received what he had gone for: the assurance that when George graduated from college Cal Thornton would suggest to the board that he be taken on as an assistant to the administration.

If asked how he had managed this, Ezekiel would probably have chuckled and said that you could catch more flies with sugar than you could with vinegar. In certain and select company he might even have cynically referred to "foolin the white folks" as a more truthful explanation. Actually he worked by an intricate system of checks and balances that had come to be as natural to him as speech, a combination of begging one moment and crying wolf the next. Any allusion to the possibility that this might be beneath his dignity as a college president would have been met with the answer that the ends more than justified the means.

In truth, his whole campaign had been based on the assumption that it would be better to perpetuate a man like himself in office, through his son, than to get some stranger less easy to control and quite probably contaminated by outside influences, though Ezekiel would not have admitted to using it. In this there would have been no real dishonesty; it was merely that he had done such things so often that he was no longer consciously aware of utilizing them.

This out of the way, there remained only the need of getting George to return to Boston, either for the coming summer undergraduate sessions or for the regular fall term. Ordinarily he would have thought no more about it, but though he would not have admitted it, he had been influenced by what Ethel had said. As he had watched George in the days that followed, it did seem to him that the boy lacked purpose. It was nothing you could put your finger on, but it went beyond the ordinary boundaries of a man getting used to his return to civilian life.

There was no doubt that the boy had earned a rest, even a period of downright loafing. This he would have been able to understand better than Ethel, for he was more aware of the real facts than she. A period of drunkenness he could have put up with, even a well-planned lecherous campaign to get every girl in the college into a compromising position. But this listlessness bothered him more than he would admit.

Another thing was that he was too much with Eric, a fact that Ezekiel found disturbing. He liked Eric and he had a great deal of respect for his mind and his ability as a teacher. Yet he was afraid that he was a troublemaker; if not this, at least a rebel; and to be under such an influence was bad for anyone with a future like George's. The only thing that eased his mind was that by being with Eric he was also with Bessie, and Ezekiel had a great deal of faith in her influence as a leveling agent. She had a good head on her, that girl, and she was one person on whom he knew he could depend.

He would have to have a talk with the boy, he decided, and at that time he would mention the promise of action from the board. Ordinarily he would not have done so, because he was a firm believer in the idea of the self-made man. To tell anyone what had been planned for him might well tend to destroy his initiative, and once anyone began to take his future for granted, too often he would lower his sights and stop aiming for the top. That was fatal, but this seemed to him a special case.

Perhaps it was only that George felt insecure and this would be the very thing to rid him of his lethargy. It would certainly give him an incentive for returning to college now instead of waiting until fall. And if it were handled right it need not seem as though he were being pushed by his father at all. After all, the boy was young when he had gone away and the growing-up process had been speeded up to a point where anyone might feel lost.

He decided that he would have a talk with George, but he did not mention the fact to Ethel. This was something between two men.

One night after dinner Ethel had gone to some kind of a meeting of faculty wives, leaving Ezekiel and George together in the house. After he was certain that she was gone Ezekiel had looked across at his son, who was reading in the big chair by the fireplace. He was wearing a sport shirt, open at the neck, and an old pair of flannel slacks, so Ezekiel assumed that he was not going out.

"Staying in, I see, George," he said casually.

His son looked up and grinned. "Well, almost," he said. "A little later I'm going over to Eric's to play records."

"Couldn't you stay home, son?"

"Well, it's a sort of meeting. Some of the kids are interested in jazz and we meet up in Eric's room and play records. He's got a wonderful collection, all of the old blues singers and a lot of the early New Orleans bands."

"Seems to me the Negro would do better to forget all that," Ezekiel said dryly.

"Why?"

"Oh, it's a part of our past I don't think we can be too proud of. Things like that grew up in pretty rough places, brothels and the like. White folks are always saying we are latently criminal. It seems to me that such things out of our past give them added ammunition for that argument."

He got up and went over to the table to his cigar humidor. When he offered it to George he refused but loaded and lit his pipe.

"I don't look at it that way," George said slowly. "That same music happens to be the only original American art form. I think it's important to keep it alive. It's something in which Negroes should take pride."

"Art form," Ezekiel snorted. "Some old black trollop yelling and moaning about some no-account man who stole her money and left town." He carefully knocked the ash from the end of his cigar. "Well, I'm not going to argue with you," he said tolerantly. "You listen to it if you want to. But don't tell your mother about it."

224

"I won't," George laughed. "Mother is more anti-Negro than a Florida cracker."

"Well, I guess when you come down to it, your mother does see the worse side of the race, all right." Ezekiel chuckled, then suddenly he grew more serious. "I've been thinking, George. Maybe it would be better if you went back to Boston for the summer session. That way you'd graduate ahead of a lot of the boys getting out of the army. The earlier you get a job the better off you'll be."

George blew several smoke rings and watched them drift slowly toward the ceiling until they broke up and became mere smoke.

"I'm not going back," he said slowly.

"Not until fall, eh?" Ezekiel said. "Well, maybe that's wise. I guess you know what's best."

George threw his book aside, which had been resting open across his lap, and got up from his chair. Walking over to the fireplace, he stood with his back leaning against the mantel. For a moment he stood there pulling on his pipe without speaking.

"No," he said in a low voice, "you misunderstood me. I said I wasn't going back to school at all."

The silence in the room was unbroken for several minutes. It was almost as though Ezekiel had not heard what was said, as though he were waiting for George to go on and answer him. The antique clock at George's shoulder whirred loudly and then struck the hour. It was as though the sound had suddenly released them.

"Son," Ezekiel said in a low voice, "I don't think that's a wise move. You're old enough to know your own mind and I certainly won't force you to change it, though I imagine your mother will try."

George shrugged. "I imagine she will."

"You're sure you're doing the right thing?"

George nodded.

"Well, as I say, I won't force you to change your mind, won't even try. I wasn't going to tell you this, but I think you ought to know all the facts, even if they don't change you mind. I had a talk with Cal Thornton the other day. He suggested that after graduation I might like to have you help out in administration here. I think it would be a good opening for you. I might retire before too long, and Cal knows that. He even intimated that it would be a good thing if I broke you in with that in mind. How does that sound?"

"I'm not interested in education, Dad. Anyway, I've got a job, starting the middle of June."

"Where, son?"

"In Washington, with the anti-discrimination division of CIO. I had a letter from them today."

For perhaps a minute Ezekiel was unable to say anything, then when he spoke his voice was so low it was hardly audible in the stilled room.

"You applied for the job?" he asked slowly.

"Yes."

"But why, son?"

It was hard for him to ask. It seemed to him that everything in his life for which he had worked was negated, that it had been wiped clean the way a blackboard can be cleared with one sweep of the eraser. He also felt betrayed in some way, yet not knowing how or in what way he had failed.

"Because I wanted to do something in which I believed. If you want to be corny, because I want to do something for my people."

"How can the CIO help Negroes?" his father asked angrily.

"It has helped them. It's integrated them into industries where they have never been before and got them upgrading when they got there."

Ezekiel ground out his cigar angrily into the ash tray. "Man does not live by bread alone," he said, then went on: "Education is what the Negro needs. When he has that, he can get better jobs, but not without it. I'm not anti-labor, mind you, but I don't hold with radicals and communists." He looked up angrily. "You don't deny that there are communists in the CIO, do you?"

His son shrugged. "No, probably there are."

"You want to work with communists, then?"

"No, not particularly. I want to work with people who will help the Negro and also help all the people. If some of them are communists, I can't help that."

"They'll call you a communist."

"I hope they won't, because I'm not. Some people may, but I very much doubt that most people will. But even if they do, should I give up what I believe in most?"

Ezekiel said slowly, "I think that you are wrong, that you are being misled."

"What can education, especially segregated education on the college level in the South, do for Negroes?" George asked suddenly.

"I've already told you. Prepare them for jobs."

226

"What jobs?"

"What we need most—a strong professional class. Doctors, teachers, lawyers, and businessmen."

"To perpetuate segregation?"

"How do you mean?"

"Because they have a vested interest in it, of course. Because if there was no segregation many of them could not successfully compete for those same jobs."

"Son, you can't change the world. You can't even change the South."

"Can I ask you a question, one that may hurt?"

"Of course, son."

"Have you ever tried?"

The impact hit Ezekiel like a blow, rocking him onto his heels, but as quickly he recovered.

"In my own way, and I think it is the only way possible, by mutual co-operation. Is there another way, short of revolution?" He felt himself on sure ground now, and he pressed the advantage. "Who has all the weapons, the offensive techniques, and the numerical advantage?"

George shrugged. "Can I tell you something that happened in the army?"

"Of course, but this isn't the army."

"I know that. When I was in officers' training there was no segregation. Yet we got along all right without it. We had one instructor, a white captain from Mississippi, and I suspect that he was given the job either as a practical joke or as a punishment. There happened to be only one other Negro in my class, and he usually brought the Chicago *Defender* to class each week. If he did not know it, all the rest of us did; the sight of that paper hit the captain like a blow in the face. He knew that it was a Negro paper and he knew what paper.

"The first day he asked the boy not to bring it to class again. With just as much politeness the boy refused, saying quite rightly that there was nothing in the regulations which forbade his doing so.

"Each week the fight continued, but though the white captain came close to losing his control the Negro never did. He never lost his politeness, but his firmness if anything increased. In the end he won out."

Ezekiel laughed lightly. "This is different," he said. "Do you mean I should carry the *Defender* with me to board meetings?"

George matched his politeness by laughing as well. Then he looked at the clock beside him on the mantel.

"Well," he said, "I've got to get over to Eric's. If you're up when I come back, I'll look in on you."

Ezekiel nodded and stood watching his son move toward the door, then when he was nearly there he called to him. He had meant to ask jokingly if George considered him an Uncle Tom, but he found the words stuck in his throat and he could not say them even in jest.

"Nothing," he said. "Have a nice time and remember me to Eric."

George nodded and went out the door. After he was gone his father stood immobile, then walked slowly toward his study. He knew he should work, but he could not bring himself to do so. All that he could do was sit and look at the blank wall over his desk. He had not needed to ask the question, for he had seen it answered in his son's eyes. Suddenly he was very tired and he felt old and defeated, trapped by something that he wanted to change but knew he couldn't. At that moment he wanted to give it all up, to write out his resignation and drop it in the mailbox at the front gate.

But he knew he wouldn't. It meant too much to him and to Ethel. He would keep it now, keep it until the white folks were through with him and rewarded him with a simple gesture. Then, and only then, would he be a free man. He was filled with a bitterness as acid as bile.

30. If sometimes Eric felt that because of the isolation of the college he did not know the Southern Negro, he had only to go to Willie Johnson's barbershop in Citrus City to reassure himself. Willie not only owned the shop and was the head barber but he was also the local colored politician, had a hand in much of the gambling and prostitution of the area, and was in his way an expert in the folkways of the region. Unlettered, he had more than his share of native wit well seasoned with a cynicism that was sharp and double-edged. Among educated Negroes he maintained a peculiar status that had made of him almost a colored Paul Bunyan, with perhaps the wit of the fox thrown in.

Stories about Willie had become a part of the folklore and had been carried as far north as New York, as far west as Chicago. A certain Negro prominent in governmental circles in Washington had made for himself an enviable reputation as a raconteur by simply repeating his endless series of yarns about Willie. At no time was Willie ever stumped for the comeback, the snapper that always turned the tide against anyone foolish enough to attempt to best him.

There was, for example, the time that one of the students from the college had been in the shop awaiting his turn for a haircut. Willie had been busy expounding on his favorite subject, his amorous exploits and seemingly inexhaustible virility. The student had listened for long enough to orient himself to the direction of this one-sided monologue and then had looked up at Willie.

"Willie," he said, "in the books on psychiatry I study out at the college I learned one interesting fact. It says that people who are not very potent sexually are the ones who brag most about their sexual powers."

For the moment Willie professed to ignore this heresy, as though its source was far beneath him. There was a sudden and expectant silence in the shop, so that the snip of the scissors powered by Willie's broad and spatulate fingers was amplified in the stilled room. Finally he stopped what he was doing and looked at the boy over his gold-rimmed spectacles.

"Hunh," he said. "In the psyciartry books I reads hit say could you poke yours through anthin biggern uh small knothole you wouldn be jealous cuz I can."

With a flourish of his scissors he returned to the waiting, partially sheared head. If he heard the loud and approving laughter he made no sign, acting merely as though it had not been quite fair to send a boy to do a man's job.

Nor was his tongue limited merely to the retort; rather it ranged the whole panorama of Negro life and the foibles of the white folks as well. He was afraid of no one, regardless of race, creed, or color, partially due to his excellent connections with those local white politicians who were not above taking graft, no matter its source, but also because he was a fearless man hardened in a school where it took a certain amount of desperation merely to stay alive. And Willie had been alive for a long time. He was fond of saying that Negroes didn't fool with him because they knew that he would as soon kill them as look at them, and that the white folks left him alone because they knew if they killed him he was going to take at least one of them along with him for company.

Toward the college he was particularly scornful. An apt mimic, he had a whole repertoire of almost classic imitations, and no one, from the president on down, was immune from his sharp and acid tongue. He had, in fact, a complete contempt for the whole middle class of color and always took issue with it, whatever the circumstances. He had a strong color bias, extending to anyone whose skin did not happen to be as dark as his own, which was matched only by his dislike of whites.

For the present-day Negro leadership he had little respect and was fond of saying that if the race's three best-known leaders marched down 125th Street in Harlem no one would recognize them without a brass band and banners. Only for the long-dead Frederick Douglas did he have any real respect. Though he would never have followed Marcus Garvey back to Africa, or even given him money to fulfill that dream, he grudgingly admired him for his identification with the black Negro masses and his rejection of those whose skins were light. In referring to Booker T. Washington, he would usually say that he was an Uncle Tom nigger who done all right for himself by foolin the white folks.

He was a good man to have on your side.

When Eric came in that Tuesday, Willie was alone in the shop. As he sat down Willie arranged the white sheet around his neck with a flourish and started talking almost before Eric was settled in the chair.

"Fess," Willie said, "I's glad tuh see one man out at that college ain too cheap tuh git his hair cut. Them niggers comes in here with they hair down to they shoulders. Thas the cheapest lot uh mens I ever seen."

He put his cigar down on the marble-topped cabinet in back of him, but first he took a pencil from behind his ear and carefully knocked the coal off the end.

"Last I heerd," he said, "Queen Ethel givin all them niggers out there hell, excusin you. That either or tryin to paint em all white. Thas the most hicty woman ever I seen and I doan see why Pres give her house space. Hucome she doan go up North an pass fo white? Too cheap, I reckon, thas a cheap bunch of peoples out there."

Eric laughed. "What's new, Willie? Quit giving the college hell and tell me what's going on. I haven't even had time to read my *Defender* this week."

"Ain nothin new, Fess. White folks still givin us hell, by what I reads. Hear the new President's gonna run all them niggers out uh the White House, but from what I knows, he gonna have him uh time findin any. Ain none uh em done nothin. I'd like tuh get me uh couple niggers up there tuh really raise uh little hell. Hear some them boys talk yuh think they ran the government, but they ain fooled me none. All they is is office boys."

Willie sighed and, taking a razor from the back bar, he began to strop it listlessly.

"Local news ain no better. They finally had em uh ruckus on the Tangerine bus. Damn cracker drivin tried tuh run uh couple our boys up on the roof. Boys in here talkin big bout how they tolt off that cracker, but that ain the way I heerd it. I know that cracker an he meaner than hell."

"Anyone hurt, Willie?"

"Naw. Them sojers is the ones. I on a bus onct an it took that driver and three laws to git one uh them boys off."

Willie was silent for a moment but presently he asked, "Fess, ever I tell you bout my frien on the bus comin from Atlanta?"

Eric shook his head.

"At Valdosta uh couple pecks got on with uh bottle. They jest sitting there juicin and pickin on him, cussin him out and callin him nigger. Time that bus hit Jax them titty pinks had him hot as a firecracker and he went into the station and complained. Please sah, he tell the man, cain yuh, please suh, stop them white gentlemens from callin me nigger? Man went right on the bus all swoll up to tell them crackers off. Know what he said, Fess?"

Eric shrugged.

"Lissen," he told em, "yawl gotta stop callin this nigger nigger."

Willie waited for his laugh and when he got it walked over to the front window. He looked up and down the street and then came over to Eric again.

"Yuh cain win fer losin," he said slowly. "Sometimes I think the race got it comin. Most of us lets the white folks walk all over us. White folks got niggers so they not only hate white folks but themselves too. Then yuh take uh nigger got uh little guts and stand up fo hisself an they shoot him cuz they say he uppity. Few more uh us git shot the white folks fine out they cain kill us all."

Willie took out his handkerchief and blew his nose loudly.

"Ought's an ought and uh figur's uh figur, all fer the white folks and none for the nigger. Fess, alongside you I simple-minded. What we got tuh do?"

"If I knew that!" Eric said.

When Willie was almost finished with Eric the shop began to fill up and his other barber came on duty. Some of the men came for haircuts, but most of them, workers off the afternoon shift at the plant, merely came in to pass the time of day. If this loss of revenue disturbed Willie he did not show it, for he genially greeted each new arrival by name.

After the chairs along the wall were all filled up, Willie looked over at his audience and winked.

"What I got in this chair," he told them, "is the only man out tuh the college ain too cheap tuh git his hair cut. Most uh them mens either lets they hair grow or they womans cuts it for em."

"Who de cheapest, Willie?" someone asked.

"They all cheap," he told them. "Ain none of them spent they fust dollar in here. Queen Ethel cuts Pres' hair, wears the pants too."

"Willie," someone else said, "I seen you las night."

"Whey?"

"With that big-legged woman, that ole one."

"Warn me, papa. I doan even mess with no ole women. I likes chicks."

"This one ready fo de stewpot, Willie."

"Oh, yuh mussa seen me wid yo mama."

Willie's audience gave him appreciative laughter as he finished Eric with a flourish and, taking his money, went to the old brass cash register. He hit the keys and turned the crank; there was a loud whirring noise, and as the drawer came open he jumped aside and got another laugh. As he turned to hand Eric his change there was a sudden flash announcement on the radio in the corner. The announcer's voice was a strange combination of elation and doom.

"Flash: Aboard the U.S.S. *Missouri*: Harry S. Truman, President of the United States, announced a short time ago that for the first time in this war our air force has utilized a secret weapon, long in preparation and perfection, against the Japanese. By using nuclear power, in other words, by harnessing the energy released when atoms are split, a bomb has been perfected of such destructive power as to be almost unimaginable. Returning flyers, from the target at Hiroshima where it was first dropped, report results that seem almost more applicable to a Buck Rogers or Orson Welles broadcast. When the bomb hit, observers reported a blinding flash that could be seen for miles, then columns of smoke were reported which reached from five miles to ten miles into the air.

"The best-kept secret of the war, the atom bomb was first tested in minute form in the New Mexico desert. Scientists, uncertain of the results thus far, know only that the bomb is practical. Actually it is not the detonation of the bomb itself which is devastating, but the fact that the explosion releases radioactive energy which has the power of destroying human life for a long period of time and over a wide area. It is estimated that the loss of human life at Hiroshima may be upward of a hundred thousand, either killed outright or doomed to eventual extinction.

"The President said the bomb was dropped on Hiroshima with his complete approval. It was a hard choice to make, he added, but if it will speed the end of the war with Japan, and thus save the lives of countless American boys, posterity will approve that action.

"It is too early to foretell the effects of the bomb on the outcome of the war, but experts feel that Japan cannot long stand the effects of this, or of possible future bombing. For further news of the atom bombings read your local newspapers."

For several moments there was complete silence, then a long sibilant hiss as some of the people in the room let out their breaths.

"Do Jesus," somebody said.

Afterward Eric would never be able to remember his exact reaction. All that he would be able to remember was a numbed feeling, as though the enormity of the thing was too great to be grasped all at one time. Only two things were to remain fixed in his mind. One was that a soldier, evidently home on furlough from overseas, started to cry, then stood up and brandished his overseas cap in his raised fist.

"Godamit," he yelled, "I ain gonna have to go back to no friggin white man's army. They got me this time, but next time they gonna have to fine me and then drag me."

The other was that Willie, who had been standing near him, called over to him and then came closer.

"Fess," he said, "hucome they didn drop no bomb on Germany?"

As Eric went out to his car and got in he knew the reason and he knew that Willie did too. Even if the bomb had not been ready, it was still the same answer, for if it had been they would not have dropped it on German civilians. Instead they would have waited until they could find an enemy that was not white.

As he drove back to the college he tried not to think. This thing was too new; he was too close to it for any clear perspective. It had

233

come upon him so suddenly that he was not prepared for it, and he doubted that anyone else was either, possibly not even those who had known all along that something big was in the air without knowing how big or what it was.

He thought again of Roosevelt and how much better he would have felt if the President had been alive. Certainly he had not been ignorant of the bomb, had probably been responsible for the go-ahead signal which produced it. Would he have dropped the bomb, or, having okayed its release, picked a crowded civilian center as an objective? He did not know, but it was hard for him to think so.

He pulled the car into the college shed which served him as a garage and went into the administration building for his mail. There were no letters, but there was a note from Bessie saying that a Mr. Nelson of the Citrus City *Telegram* had called and that it was urgent that Eric get in touch with him at once. He slipped the note into his pocket and went down the corridor toward the president's office.

When he came into the outer room Bessie looked up at him and smiled. He pointed toward the door to the inner office, but she shook her head.

"Where's the Kingfish?" he asked. "Gone to the lodge hall?"

"He's at a meeting in Daytona," she answered. "Get my note?"

He nodded and reached for her phone. As he was putting the call through he made a motion as though smoking a cigarette, and she lighted one and handed it to him.

"Mr. Nelson, please," he said, then, in a moment: "Mr. Nelson? Gardner calling. I got your message."

He listened for a moment.

"Well, the thing came so fast I haven't had time to know what I really think. Could I call you back? No, only half an hour, say. Yes, I'll do that. Good-by."

He slipped the phone back onto its cradle.

"Thornton wants quotes about the bomb for a box on the front page. Says he wanted me in particular, probably to keep the proper balance of genteel white liberalism."

"You're going to do it, Eric?"

"I guess, baby. Let me use that typewriter a minute."

"I wouldn't," she said slowly.

"Look, baby," he said, "don't be like the Kingfish. I'll say something and they probably won't even print it. But it's important that I at least say it. Go powder your nose or something."

234

After she left he sat before the typewriter deep in thought. Finally he began to type.

"Now that the atom bomb has been dropped, there is no sense in wishing that it had not been. But our children and our children's children may wish that we had not launched upon the world perhaps the most barbaric means of wholesale slaughter ever let loose by human hands. It is up to us now to so redeem ourselves by the thoughtful utilization of the peacetime uses of atomic energy as to cause future generations to forgive us for what we have done this day. If this is done, perhaps the ends may have justified the means.

"If the bombing of a civilian town shortens the war, as an American I can be thankful for the saving of American lives. As a human being I cannot in this way ease my feeling of personal guilt for this un-civilized outrage. As a Negro, but also as a loyal American, I cannot help but note that the bomb was first used against men and women whose skins were dark rather than against those whose skins were white. As a Negro, the facts seem to me to be clear that this was a case of an evaluation of targets, conscious or unconscious, based on those fallacies of race which we fought so hard to overthrow in the Europe we so recently liberated."

He read over what he had written quickly, then cut it to a more usable length. Calling the reporter back, he read what he had written, then waited while it was read back to him. He hung up and crumpled the typed page into a tight little ball which he carelessly put in the pocket of his tweed jacket.

When Bessie came back he had his feet on her desk.

"Done, Shakespeare?" she asked. When he nodded she said, "Let Mama see. Then I'll phone it in for you."

"You aren't Mama yet," he grinned. "If you don't stop being so bossy, maybe you won't ever be. I've already phoned it in."

"Oh, Eric, I wanted to see it."

"Kingfish II," he said. "I knew you shouldn't have worked for that man so long. You can read it in the paper in the morning."

"I only wanted to help."

"You're cute when you get mad," he said. "Jazz club tonight, baby, but tomorrow night?"

She nodded and he blew her a kiss as he went out the door.

31. All the day long Bessie had had a funny feeling. Yesterday she had tried to believe, as Eric did, that the chances were indeed slim that the *Telegram* would print what he had said about the atomic bomb. Yet when she came into her office this morning there it was on the front page. She tried to take some comfort in the fact that Eric's was not the only quote, nor was it the one leading off the column, but as she read on she realized how hopeless such a realization was. Actually his was the only one really critical of the bomb's use, and on top of this there was his playing up of the race angle.

At least Ezekiel was still away, so any trouble from that direction was at least temporarily avoided. But this was not her real concern. After all, Eric had been in hot water with the administration before and usually gotten away with nothing more serious than a mild reprimand. No, it was the white ire which concerned her most, for she had lived a lifetime in the South and knew how little it took to stir it up. And if there were trouble, even short of violence, she knew that his appointment on the faculty might not be renewed for the coming year.

Sitting at her desk, with the mail sorted and those letters answered which demanded a prompt reply, she had little of importance to do until Ezekiel returned. She was a good secretary and she had her routine organized to a point where it almost took care of itself. Yet even had there been something which demanded her full attention she would have had trouble giving it.

The possibility that he might lose his job was certainly nothing new. Yet once she had fallen in love with Eric and they had decided to marry, she had ceased thinking about it. Somehow she had begun to place their life together as limitied to the college, save for the summers when they might go North, but only to return to the campus again in the fall.

If anything happened now, Eric could always get another job, but even this realization did not ease her worry. She had been too close to the border line of poverty, too uncertain of security in the past, to forget. It was not only fear that kept Negroes docile, she realized, it was also that they clung to the small measure of security which the old racial mores gave them. It was so deeply ingrained that even she, at times, found herself unconsciously thinking in the old pattern.

All at once she knew that she could sit there no longer. She had to get out, if only for a short time. Picking up the phone, she asked the girl at the switchboard to take her calls while she went over to the Co-op for a coke.

Outdoors she somehow felt better. The day was hot and the sun felt good on her bare arms and face as she walked across the campus and down the stairs into the Co-op. She got a coke from the machine, put a couple of nickels in the honky-tonk, and sat down at a table in the corner. As she sipped her coke slowly she decided that she was really being foolish.

Eric was to stop by early for her that evening because they were going to a movie in Citrus City. She had dressed right after supper, in order to be ready when he came, and now she was sitting in the living room with her mother. Her mood of the morning had nearly passed, though deep within her there was still a hidden feeling of slight disturbance.

Looking at her mother, she thought suddenly of the possibility of her leaving home.

She wished that she were not a person who was looking constantly ahead. Her life had been a stable one, and yet here she was jumping to all kinds of conclusions. She got to her feet and walked to the front window to look out. When she turned back into the room she saw her mother look up.

"He gonna come," Esther said. "Lookin out the widow woan hurry him none."

She walked over to her mother and, bending down, kissed her lightly on the cheek. Esther looked up, and Bessie would have known, even had she not been aware of Jeff, that something had been happening to her mother. She had never seen her look better; it was almost as though some inner light under her skin were trying to work outward. You could see it in her face in the way that light shows through something which is almost but not quite transparent.

"Having a fellow agrees with you, Mama," she said. She laid her hand on her mother's cheek. "Mama, I'll dance at your wedding. I'll do the jitterbug, Mama, wait and see if I don't."

"Chile, whatever you talkin bout?"

But Bessie saw the look of near guilt and then the faint blush of pleasure that spread slowly up and over her mother's high cheekbones.

At that moment Esther seemed more like her sister than her mother.

"What are you blushing about, Mama? You haven't already snuck off and done it, have you?"

"Now, chile," Esther said slowly, "I doan know what you talkin bout. If it Jeff you talkin bout, it pure nonsense an you knows it. He old enough to be my father."

"Pooh, he is not and you know it. If I'd said that, you would have jumped all over me. Mama, who are you trying to fool? We all know about it."

"Who we and what you all know?"

"Well, Eulia knows there's something between you and her father. I know it and so does Eric. Even Luther, who has no sense about things like that and is so mixed up with the union he can't see anything else, is finally convinced of it. I expect by now it's all over town."

"Chile, I doan know it. Jeff doan know it neither, I reckon."

"Mama," Bessie asked in a conspiratorial whisper, "has he asked you yet?"

Her mother sighed and drew her lips to a thinner line.

"I told you, Mama. The minute Eric asked me, I came right away and told you."

"I declare, chile, you ain changed a bit. Time you was a youngun, you was always pesterin folks. I wish Eric would come so I could have some peace."

"What are you sewing on, Mama? Looks to me like you were getting ready for something."

Esther put her sewing on the table and got up from her chair. Bessie knew the look and started to back toward the door.

"Mama," she warned, "don't you dare muss me up. Don't you go tickling me, hear?"

But Esther kept right on coming. Bessie started to giggle and felt in back of her for the front door. With her other hand she reached for her red patent-leather pocketbook on the table by the window. Esther made a rush for her, but Bessie was too quick. She slammed the screen door and stood with her body pressed tight against it. She looked at her mother and made a face. Then behind her she heard Eric drive up and stop.

Eric always drove fast, but with a deftness that took all the fear out of it. Usually he went by the back roads because he could make better time that way, but also because it avoided any possibility of racial friction when he was with Bessie. He had started doing this after a white man had pulled up alongside him at a stop light and, not liking what he had seen, had tried to run him up over the curb when the light turned. Fortunately he had been alone and he had never told Bessie about what had happened.

Tonight Bessie wished that they were just going to drive instead of going to a movie. True, she had wanted to see the picture, had even been looking forward to it. She looked up at the sky; the stars seemed very close and she made a wish. It was only that she was somehow uneasy.

"You're certainly quiet," Eric said. "If you're like this now, what's it going to be like after I marry you?"

She turned her head so that her cheek lay against the leather top of the seat.

"You're no ball of fire yourself, my friend."

"Did you see the paper?"

"Sure, I saw it. I agree with you, but I wish you hadn't said it."

"They haven't lynched me yet," he kidded.

"No, and the Kingfish hasn't read it either. Where are you figuring on teaching next year?"

He laughed. "I thought I'd let you support me. If we don't come back here, will you mind so very much?"

She shrugged. "No. I'd hate leaving Mama all alone, but I don't guess I would be. She won't admit it even now. I wonder if Jeff has asked her yet?"

"Who knows? I don't think she'd say anything if he had, at least not until she's good and ready."

She looked up at the sky again and closed her eyes.

"Eric, if you aren't reappointed, where would we be likely to go?"

She felt the car take a curve and she knew that they were on the outskirts of town.

"I don't know," he said. "I don't think I'll have much trouble getting another job. But I haven't lost the one I have yet."

"When are you going to write another book?" she asked. "You've never said anything about it. I'm just curious."

"I don't know, Bessie. One of these days, when I can take a sabbatical."

He took a sharp left turn and turned down Oak Street. In a moment he drew up in front of the drugstore.

"I've got to get a carton of cigarettes, baby. I won't be long."

She heard the car door slam beside her and she opened her bag to light a cigarette while she waited. Idly she wondered how Eric's family was going to accept her, or even if they would. She knew that he had not told them yet. She wondered what it would be like to live in the North, if she would be self-conscious the first time that she broke one of the taboos which she had been forced to observe for all of her life.

It was a silly way to be thinking, she told herself, and closed her eyes again. In a moment Eric came back and got in beside her.

"I played the pinball machine," he told her. "I played two games and I couldn't win for losing."

"I knew you would," she answered. "I knew you'd lose, too. You always do."

"I can beat you," he said.

"You can't. I could beat you with my left hand."

She heard the car door open on her side.

"Come on," he said, "prove it."

"Eric, we don't have time."

He looked over at her and grinned. Glancing down at his watch, he said, "We've got time for three games. If we went in now, we'd only have to sit through the horse opera. I'm getting awfully tired of seeing that same cowboy."

"All right, Eric, but only three games, and this time I mean it."

"You're bossy already. You better be careful or I might change my mind."

She laughed as she followed him into the drugstore. She really didn't care if they played the pinball machine all night and never went near the movie. Just to be alone with him was more than enough.

They were lucky enough to find a place to park just around the corner from the theater, and, locking the car, Eric took her arm as they walked the short distance back to Oak Street. Of the two movie houses for Negroes, the one they were going to was the better, for it had been put up only shortly before the war started. It was owned by white men, however, and showed only out-of-date pictures with a horse opera thrown in for good measure, and the program changed only once a week.

When they got inside Roy Rogers was riding off into the sunset, and as they sat down he nudged her. She made a face and nodded.

There was no newsreel or short subjects, only a printed slide flashed on the screen urging patrons to buy war bonds, which could be purchased at the ticket window on their way out. Then the main feature started and Bessie settled back into her seat.

It was a picture that she had looked forward to seeing, but as it unrolled she found her attention wandering. A play which had had a successful Broadway run three or four years before it was made into a movie, it told the story of a woman forced to make her choice between a man with money and one with ideals. Although it was beautifully acted, it seemed to have no real meaning for her, and she wondered how it affected the others in the darkened theater around her. Probably it was as remote to their daily existence as a fairy tale. At the end she got up and followed Eric down the lighted aisle.

Outside on Oak Street she stood by Eric as he paused to light a cigarette.

"We might better have stayed at the pinball machine," she said.

He nodded as they walked on toward the corner. The contrast of the people around them hit her in a way that it had never done before.

"Eric," she suddenly asked, "did you ever sleep with a white woman?"

He threw back his head and roared with laughter.

"No," she said quickly, "I don't mean it that way. I've known white people, oh, at conferences and things, but I've never known one that wasn't always white while I was always black. They were polite and many times they broke jimcrow restrictions, easily and without obvious embarrassment. They had me in their homes, even broke the taboo about eating together, and yet all the time it was as though we hadn't really changed anything. It wasn't my fault and it wasn't theirs, it was just the way things were. I thought that maybe when you were with a person that way . . . well, it might be different."

"It can be, even without that, Bessie. But you've got to give too."

She nodded. "I can see that. I just wondered," she added lamely.

As they turned the corner he started to say something, then suddenly he saw his car.

"Jesus," he said.

The four tires were cut to ribbons, the windshield was smashed, and there were dents in the fenders and in the rear. Eric hurried forward and stood looking at the car. Bessie came up behind him and stood silently, knowing without being told what had happened and why.

Looking up, Eric saw a Negro sitting on a box at the opening of the alley.

"You see what happened to my car?" he called.

"Sho, some pecks come by an smashed hit. Yo cah?"

"Yeah, it's my car. What the hell happened?"

"Done tolt yuh what happened, them pecks done smashed yo cah."

"Why?"

"Hell, man, how I know why? Whut yuh think I gonna do, ask em why? Maybe they doan like niggers drivin new cahs. You know them bastards good as me."

"Didn't you even try to stop them? Didn't they see you sitting there?"

"Sho they seen me. I right chere all the time. Even wuz hit my own cah, how I gonna stop em? They was fo mean-lookin bastards and they wuz white, I done tolt yuh that. Whatsa matter, man, ain you got good sense?"

"Someone else must have seen them. The least you could have done was call for help."

"Hell, man, you mus be crazy. How I gonna tell nobody? I yell, them pecks gonna beat *me*. Neither is I gonna walk off, cuz them was mean mens and they might not like it. Anyways, how I know who cah hit is? Might be they cah. White folks is crazy enuf tuh wreck they own cahs, ain they? Warn none uh my business."

He got up off the box and came over to them.

"Lissen," he said, "I got old as I is mindin my own business. Why didn you tell them hit yo cah? Stand there yellin at me. I didn wreck yo friggin cah."

He spat in the gutter and turned and walked away, then he stopped and turned around.

"Go tell de law whut happened," he said, "doan ask me bout yo friggin cah. Them white laws sho gonna hep yo, hep yo black ass right under that jail."

He spat again and walked on down the street. Eric watched him until he was out of sight, then shrugged.

"Racial solidarity," he said sarcastically. "In these critical times the Negro is united as never before."

"De man done tolt you," Bessie mimicked, "hit wasn his friggin car."

He started laughing and, joining him, she thought: It's better that it was his car and not him. Then she stopped laughing.

"I'm sorry, Eric," she said slowly.

"I don't mind about the car. I think my insurance will cover it. Come

242

on, I better call a garage." He lit a cigarette. "I guess you were right, baby," he said. "I guess they didn't like what I said in the paper."

Let him leave it there, she thought, let him forget. But she knew he wouldn't.

32. The first thing that Ethel showed Ezekiel on his return from the East Coast was Eric's statement in the *Telegram*. He had come in about eleven o'clock, having driven home right after the closing evening session of the conference, tired and really wanting a hot bath, a drink, and then to go to bed. But by the look on his wife's face he knew that this would have to be postponed. He took the paper and, going over to the lamp by the sofa, read it through twice, then put the paper down.

"Well?" he said slowly.

"It's bad for the college, Doctor, you know that as well as I do. It's a dangerous statement and they aren't going to like it. And, not liking it, they are going to take it out on the college as much as they are on him. That's the unfortunate thing."

"I know," he said, "and unfortunately what he said happens to be true."

"That has very little to do with it, Doctor. You know that as well as I do."

He did not answer but instead went to the mahogany cigar box on the table and took out a fresh cigar. It was a handsome box which had been given to him by one of the graduating classes; there was a silver plate on the top engraved with his name and the occasion for its presentation. It was this, and only this, he knew that influenced Ethel to the extent of allowing him to keep it in the living room instead of at his office. Carefully he clipped off the end of the cigar and slowly lit it, knowing well how much his slowness annoyed Ethel, who was obviously waiting for him to go on.

"Well," he said slowly, "let's wait and see what the public reaction is. There's no use in rushing this thing."

"We know what the public reaction will be, Doctor."

"Well, not quite, my dear. The war has modified public opinion even in the South. I'll grant you, though, that we do have a pretty good idea. Well, what do you suggest?"

This, he knew, was what she had been waiting for, and all that had gone before was merely to justify her claim that she never intruded into the academic affairs of the college. Inwardly he sighed, wishing that it was over with and that he had had his bath and was just now sitting down with a good stiff highball.

"Of course, Doctor, I realize that this is none of my business."

"Yes, my dear," he nodded. "I asked for your opinion."

"Well, if I were doing it, I'd anticipate any trouble. I'd tell Eric tomorrow that he has not acted in the best interests of the college. After all, you have warned him before. I'd tell him that his contract for next year will not be renewed. Then I'd get word to Mr. Thornton of your action, maybe ask him to run a little item in the paper about it. That way the college would be protected."

"That seems a little drastic, my dear. Perhaps eventually it may be necessary, but I doubt that it is right now. I'll sleep on it. How's that?"

He yawned and stretched lazily.

"I'm going up, Ethel. I'm near tuckered out."

On his way out of the room he bent to kiss her, feeling in her reaction to his caress both her slight annoyance at his wanting to move slowly and also the fact that she would not want him that night. He sighed. He had been away from her for two nights; he had hoped it might be otherwise, but he was not surprised. Slowly he went upstairs and drew his bath.

As he sank slowly into the hot water he felt his tension ease and his tiredness start to slip away. He knew that Ethel was right, and yet he was fond of Eric and even admired him, in a way, for the action he had taken. He was right, damn it; dropping the atom bomb on Japan was a clear extension of the unconscious American domestic racial policy into foreign affairs. If the Nips had not been colored, the chances are that the bomb would never have been dropped, or if it were, so clearly an unmilitary target would not have been chosen.

He lumbered up out of the bath and stood rubbing himself with one of the heavy bath towels that Ethel always ordered from a New York department store. Suddenly, remembering his own infrequent anger and the bitter articles he had written but never sent off, he envied Eric.

All at once he made up his mind that he was going to do nothing about Eric save deliver a slight reprimand. He was going to stand back of him, in defiance of Ethel or of anyone else, including the board. The thought made him feel better, even that perhaps now he could somehow recapture the relationship which he once had with his son.

Now George would see that whenever a situation came up that really required courage his father could stand up like a man.

He brushed his teeth vigorously and walked into the bedroom a little like a soldier about to give battle, knowing that God was on his side.

In the morning, as soon as Ezekiel got to the office he told Bessie that he wanted to see Eric as soon as possible. He sat at his desk but found it hard somehow to get down to work. It was as though Eric were on his mind and until he had seen him he would be able to do nothing.

By now he was reconciled to the fact that George was going to work for the CIO. Perhaps it was for the best; it might even be that the boy would gain a reputation there more quickly than by the method he, Ezekiel, had planned for him. Yet the association bothered him. It was not that he was against unions; within certain limits he was all for them, but it seemed to him that they were moving too rapidly. Well, it was done now and nothing could be done about it. Even Ethel seemed to have given up after one unsuccessful siege of taking to her bed and claiming an illness that fooled no one.

He heard the buzzer on his desk and he threw open the switch on the interoffice system.

"Mr. Gardner is here, Dr. Rogers."

"Good, Bessie, send him in."

He got up from behind his desk and met Eric with a hearty handshake.

"Sit down," he boomed. "I've been meaning to have a talk with you for weeks."

He shoved the big bronze ash tray halfway between them and waited until Eric had lighted a cigarette.

"I see that you've stuck your foot in it," he said not unpleasantly. "Seems every time I leave town you go to cutting the fool. What's the answer, Eric, no more trips for me?"

"I wouldn't go quite that far," Eric laughed. "But you must at least admit that my facts were right and something like the atom bomb doesn't happen every day."

"No, I'm not disputing you on your facts, Eric. I'd even go so far, off the record, as to say that probably what you said should have been said. I don't feel, however, that the place you picked for saying it was a very wise one. Bound to hurt the college."

He looked up at Eric, as though waiting for him to agree. When he did not, he went on.

"Eric, I like you. You're the best teacher I've got here on the campus and I know I'm lucky to have you. But don't push me too far."

"I don't mean to," Eric said. "It's just that sometimes I feel that the limits you have imposed on yourself are too rigid to be effective."

Ezekiel shrugged. "I've lived a little longer than you, Eric, and I've lived my whole life in the South. I don't say that experience is the only teacher, but it's a pretty good one."

"True, but not always infallible."

"No, Eric, not always infallible. But, living so long here, I've gained a perspective that you can't have. I know how far we've come because I've come along with it. I can remember when there wasn't a Negro high school in this whole state. That's not true now, is it? Look at the colleges we have now, not only the privately endowed ones but state-supported institutions. We've made strides in education, Eric, big strides."

"So has the white South. It seems to me that the white folks' rate of progress has been as rapid as ours, and therefore the gap between us is actually just as wide."

Ezekiel shrugged. "That's a point, Eric, but it still does not take away our progress. A child's got to learn to crawl before he can learn to walk."

"I can walk, sir."

"So can I, Eric, therefore it's our job to teach others how to walk. But they've got to learn how to crawl first. Anyway, I didn't call you in here just to listen to my philosophy of race relations in the South. I just wanted you to know that I had seen the paper and how I felt about it. Now, all I want is your word that you'll take it easier in the future. If something like this comes up again, Eric, talk to me first. I don't hold with censorship; I don't mean that, only that I have a right to know about anything that might affect the college. You'll help me?"

"I won't promise," Eric said, "but at least I'll try. Now, I've got a problem and I need your help."

"Shoot, Eric. I'm always ready to help my people when I can."

Ezekiel settled back in his chair, wondering what was coming.

He listened carefully as Eric told him what had happened to his car. What he heard did not surprise him, though it did upset him. It was the same old story changed only a little, and the result was exactly the same. It was always the Negro who got it in the end. Always it had been that way, and sometimes, he thought, it always would be, no matter what was done.

When Eric had finished he hardly knew what to say, but he knew that he must say something, for he could sense that Eric was waiting.

"What can I do, Eric?" he asked in a low voice.

"That's what I want to know. It's not so much what you can do as what you will do."

Ezekiel sighed. "What is it that you feel I should do?"

"We seem to be getting nowhere," Eric laughed. "I guess I never should have mentioned it."

"Now, Eric, it's merely that I want to get your ideas. You should know me well enough by now to realize that I want all the facts before I go into something. Of course you should have mentioned it. It concerns me and it concerns the college."

"Well, it seems to me that the facts are fairly obvious. A man's car is smashed up by hoodlums. True, we don't know who the hoodlums are, but at least we know why they acted as they did. What redress has the man who owned the car, being a Negro?"

"None, I reckon. What redress would he have being white?"

"At least he would know that he would receive courteous co-operation from the officers of the law. He would know that if the men were identified he would have equality before the law."

"Eric," Ezekiel said softly, "we know all that and we can't change it. Look, have the car fixed and the college will foot the bill."

Eric got up from his chair and walked over to the window, then in a moment came back.

"The insurance company will pay for the car. Even if they didn't, I wouldn't mind. The car is not the important thing. What is important is that an incident has occurred that should not happen again. Certainly there must be some white people around here who don't approve of this sort of thing. They should know about it. I don't want it to happen again. Next time it might be me instead of the car."

Ezekiel sighed. "I know, but what can I do? I've warned you, Eric, the South is a complex thing to understand. I'll tell Cal Thornton. I'll write a letter to the mayor of Citrus City. Is that enough?"

Eric sat down on the arm of his chair.

"No," he said, "that is not enough."

"Eric, you make me feel like an old man. You make me feel ineffectual. What is it that you want, a crusade? Do you want another of those affairs where we have a committee in New York and are sponsored by white liberals, and then the communists take over? Or do you want an armed rebellion, barricades, and shooting in the streets?"

He took off his glasses and laid them on the desk. Propping his elbows on the arms of his chair, he rubbed his eyes gently with his fingers.

"You do it to me," he said. "My own son does it to me. All my life I have thought of myself as a liberal. Yet now I feel somehow as though the two of you have gotten me into the camp of the opposition, and the whole trouble is that I don't know how I got there."

Slowly he put his glasses back on and opened his eyes. He took out his handkerchief and blew his nose loudly.

"They say," he went on, "that it was Plato's wife who made him a philosopher. She goaded him so much that he found the life he had been leading unbearable. Therefore he put his intellect to work and tried to make a better world, if only on paper."

"Socrates was the one, sir, and he tried to make a better world on earth."

"I know, and ended up probably as you will end up. Is it worth it, Eric?" Then before Eric had a chance to answer he got up. Putting his arm around him, he led him to the door.

"Let me see what I can do, Eric."

He stopped at the door.

"Give me a little time," he said. "There is an irresistible force rushing toward an unmovable object, Eric. I am in the middle. Sometimes I wish I were back in South Carolina chopping cotton."

After Ezekiel came back to his desk he sat for a long time without doing anything. He tried to put himself in the place of Eric, but he always came back to the same position, the same that he had always held. Even when he backtracked his own life to the time when he had been even younger than Eric and living in South Carolina, he had felt the same. He had had nothing then. He had merely been the son of a backwoods preacher who had put his faith in God. As he thought back he supposed that by a stretch of the imagination it had been God who had put him in touch with the white man who had made it possible for him to get ahead.

Was that bad? he asked himself. The man had been good to him, had sent him first to high school and then to the nearby divinity college for Negroes. He had even seen to it that he got ahead. In a way, he supposed that thereby he had made a kind of transference, that this white man had become more of a father to him than ever his own father had been. Had this tended to lessen his father in his eyes? Could it be that this had even in a way emasculated his father, made him not only less of a father but also, because he could not do the same things for his own son that a white man could, become less of a man as well? He was not sure. At this moment he was sure of nothing save his own unsureness.

It seemed to him that now, at this moment, he was more conscious of race than he had ever been. It seemed ready to trap him. He looked back and he realized that even in those moments of his most bitter hatred against whites, the time in Atlanta, for example, when he had been in such a rage against the vacant taxicab at the station, his anger was only directed against a certain kind of white man. It was always a peckerwood or a cracker, a redneck or poor white trash, never what his father had always called a "quality white gentleman" and he himself thought of as an enlightened white Southerner.

How had his father really felt; had he hated whites but since he was a man of God denied it because it was a lie against the brotherhood of man? Had he, perhaps, hated this one qualitywhitefolksman because he had taken away his son? Ezekiel felt a sudden wave of guilt because even now he could not unravel this masquerade, which he had been forced to assume in order to become a big frog in a little pond, and remember if there was anything he had done to help neuter his father by denying him the role of father. But it was so long ago and so much had happened.

Angrily he got up and, walking to the window, looked out across the campus. Without him this might have been a nothingness, a wilderness. And his father? He remembered going back to South Carolina when the old man lay dying with a lingering illness. He had told his father that he must get well, that he wanted him to go back with him to the college and see how well he had done with his life. But his father had only smiled and shook his head, as though he had seen inside his son's heart and realized that this was only a lie born of guilt. He had not wanted his father to visit the college, for the old man was as unlettered as a field hand and his coming would have brought him and Ethel only embarrassment.

Was this true, had this been himself or was he only imagining it out of guilt? Hadn't it really been only Ethel who had felt that way? No matter, it was nonetheless himself for allowing her to feel so.

Should he call Cal Thornton now and go to see him that afternoon, even though there was little point in it, for what could Cal do? Or maybe Eric had been right; it was not a question of what he could do but what at heart he wanted to do. He knew that he did not want to go, but he made himself act.

He pushed the buzzer on his desk and spoke through the interoffice.

"Get me Mr. Thornton, Bessie, at the *Telegram.*"

He picked up his phone and waited until he heard Bessie tell Cal Thornton's secretary that Dr. Rogers was calling.

"Hello," he said, hearing Cal's voice at the end of the wire, "how are you?"

He avoided any salutation, as he so often did, because by so doing he avoided the courtesy titles that he knew would not be returned.

"Yes," he went on, "Rogers calling. I was wondering if I might see you this afternoon. No, nothing important. It's just that one of the teachers out here had a little unpleasantness in town last night and I thought you'd want to know about it. What? Yes, it was Eric Gardner. Oh, he called you and he's coming to your house tonight to tell you about it? Good. No, no sense in my coming. You've met him out here, and as a matter of fact, I wasn't even here when it happened. No, over in Daytona at a conference. Fine, I won't bother you then, Mr. Thornton. Thank you, good-by."

He put his phone down on the cradle and looked at the clock on his desk. Suddenly he realized that he was hungry, and that seemed to him a good omen. He decided to go home now, to cheat the time clock a little. He reached for his hat and went out to Bessie's desk.

"I'm going to lunch," he boomed. "Your watch is slow, Bessie."

She looked down at her wrist and then smiled up at him.

"I do believe you're right, Prexy. It's way slow."

He laughed good-naturedly. "Well, I'll be back early, in case there are any calls. Oh yes, Bessie, there's one thing on my mind. Slip a memo in Eric's box. Say I only got the chance to call Thornton a minute ago. Tell him I hope he makes out all right tonight. You edit that, Bessie, but you get the idea."

She nodded and he passed on down the hall. It was a good day after all.

33. Eric found Cal Thornton's house easily, but if he had not once driven Bessie there to deliver something for Ezekiel he would have had difficulty, for there was no light at the entrance as he parked the partially repaired car and walked toward the front door. There was a light out over the detached garage in the rear, however, and he wondered if perhaps Thornton had expected him at the back door. If so, he was wrong, Eric thought; I go in the front door or not at all. He climbed the three steps to the front door and rang the bell.

In a moment the door opened and Cal Thornton stood looking out. "Gardner?" he asked. "Good, come in."

He stood aside as Eric walked in, then led the way to the living room, where he held out his hand.

"Glad to see you," he said. "Seems like I never see enough of you people out at the college. Sit down; that big chair by the fireplace looks about right for you. Let me run out and get some ice and soda so we'll have everything right at hand."

After he left Eric looked around casually. It was a room that reflected the taste of its owner, or perhaps of its owner's wife. There was to it a lived-in look. The bookcases on either side of the fireplace were built to the ceiling and filled to overflowing with books, and across the long, low coffee table in front of the couch were a number of current magazines. Over the fireplace was a reproduction of a Cézanne painting.

In a few moments Thornton came back with a huge tray which he put down on the coffee table. On it were glasses, a tub of ice, and two or three bottles of whisky.

"Well," he said, "I guess we could use a drink. What would you like?"

Eric laughed. "You mean I have a choice, that I don't have to drink rum?"

"Yes, that's what comes of being in the newspaper business and having a rich wife. When it looked as though we might get into the war, I bought all I could get."

"I'd prefer scotch if you're sure you can spare it."

Cal nodded. "I know how you feel. I'm a bourbon man myself, always have been. When I have to drink something else I just don't feel right."

He poured the drinks and, handing one to Eric, settled down in a chair.

"I'm sorry Mrs. Thornton isn't here," he said easily. "She had something or other she had to go to—woman's club, I reckon. Now, tell me about what happened last night."

Eric took a sip of his drink and got out his pipe and packed it. After he lit up he told the salient facts briefly and without emotion. When he had finished Cal sat silently for a moment.

"How do you know it was done by whites?" he asked briefly. "Not that I doubt it," he went on hurriedly, "but I'm just naturally curious."

"A Negro who was there saw it happen."

"And did nothing about it?"

"No, I was a little curious about that too," Eric said. "He told me why in no uncertain words. It wasn't his car, he said, the men were white, and he knew better than to stick his nose into something that seemed to be the white folks' business."

Cal nodded. "Pretty familiar pattern, and an understandable one. Actually I suppose I'm at fault. Shouldn't have run what you said, I reckon, but Negroes should have a chance to state their views on things like that. It's important. I didn't happen to go all the way with you on what you said, but I liked the way you said it. For that reason I'm glad I ran it, but because of what happened to your car I wish I hadn't. Well, the thing's done now," he said. "What can we do about it? But here, let me get you another drink. I'm about ready too."

He bent over the coffee table, replenishing their glasses.

Cal put a drink before Eric and sat down with his own. Eric could sense that he was waiting for him to go ahead.

"As you say, it's done," Eric said. "The car doesn't worry me so much. Probably my insurance will cover the damages. But next time it might not be the car, it might be me. Even that doesn't bother me as much as the fact that I don't want it to happen again because it's too much like what we fought to stamp out in Germany."

"You mean that the South is fascist or on the way to becoming fascist?" Cal asked dryly.

"No, I won't say that, though you can build up a pretty convincing argument in proof of that thesis. Let's say merely that I'd like to see the South become a part of the United States."

Cal laughed. "Yes, I see what you mean. I don't go all the way with you, but there's truth in some of what you say. I'd like to see the South free of racial violence, just as much as you would. But how?"

"Aren't we getting away from why I came here, Thornton? I appreciate your letting me come, by the way. This is the first white home I've been in down here, and you're the first white man I've really had a chance to talk with. Now that that's out of the way, what can we do? Perhaps more realistically, what will you do? You're still the boss, even if you treat me like a guest."

"Gardner," Cal said slowly, "you ask me what I can do, rather what will I do. I'll be realistic too. It's not what am I willing to do, but how much the white community down here will absorb. Look, some time ago I started to capitalize the N in Negro in my paper. It seems like a little thing, but I damned near didn't get away with it. That one little thing stirred up a hornets' nest."

"You ran an editorial about it first?"

"Sure, of course."

"What if you hadn't? What if you had just gone ahead and done it? How many of your subscribers would have noticed?"

Cal got up from his chair and came over to the fireplace. He took off his coat and threw it carelessly across the back of a chair.

"I haven't had an argument like this since I used to go up to Harlem with a gal named Kay Jones," he said. "I was working on the UP in New York then. All right, go on."

"Why not? Would you come out in your paper for the abolishment of legal segregation?"

"Why, of course not."

"Why not? You obviously don't believe in jimcrow yourself. You've broken every taboo here with me tonight. You've done so in the past in New York. How can you publicly support something you privately disavow?"

"You know the answer to that one, Gardner. You found out the other night. I'd get my press wrecked the same way your car was. And probably by the very same people."

"So we both can do nothing, although we both very much want to?"

"I wouldn't say that. I'm doing something and so are you. We may employ different techniques, but they are both aimed at the same goal."

"What are we doing? What specifically are you doing?"

"You know what I'm doing. You read the *Telegram*. There are other liberal papers in the South, and we're doing all we can without being put out of business. You fellows in the North forget what we're up against."

"No, I know what you're up against. But do you know what we're up against?"

"I think so, Gardner; my heart is full of compassion for the Negro."

"Can I tell you two stories? Both of them were told to me by a white friend of mine. One concerns a white liberal, a woman of both charm and intelligence. Yet she told him in all seriousness that if the Negro would only stop this senseless agitation the problem would be completely solved in four or five hundred years."

Cal chuckled. "I know the woman."

"The second is something that another liberal in the South told him, a man with a college education, by the way. He said that he believed in complete equality for the Negro, then also said, in all seriousness, that the whole trouble was that the Negro thought he was as good as a white man."

Cal chuckled again. "Both of those stories hit the mark. But what have they got to do with me?"

"I've read your column and you're doing the same thing, Thornton. Maybe you don't realize it, but you are. You say that you want to help the Negro, with one hand, then with the other you warn him to be a 'good nigger' and take it easy."

"That's easy enough to answer, Gardner. Straws in the wind. Call it whatever you want. Racial tempers getting nasty, tensions rising, all the things that point to race violence, possibly even riots. I don't want that on my head, do you?"

Eric sighed. "No, but I'm not convinced that your backing down won't seem like a green light to the people who start race riots. Perhaps if you stuck to your guns, if you and all the people like you were firm, there would be no riots. Maybe your opinion, your combined public reaction, plus the national moral indignation could start to break this thing up. I hate race riots fully as much as you do. But I hate even worse being treated the way I am treated now."

"I don't blame you. I'm trying to change that treatment, but I've got to have time. It's got to come from the white Southerner. Every time a Northerner comes down here and tells us what to do it sets us back just that much further, makes our job that much harder. This is a Southern problem and Southerners have to solve it. We're trying to, and I think eventually we will."

"Trouble there is that a lot of Northerners think the race problem is fully as much a national problem as a Southern one."

"I'm afraid I'm a little like Mark Etheridge when he said that he didn't believe that there were armed forces enough in the world to force upon the Southern white the abolition of segregation."

"Will you really fight or are you just rattling the old Civil War saber in the family attic? Maybe the next War between the States will be fought because the South won't get out of the Union."

Cal smiled but he did not say anything. In a moment Eric looked over at him and asked, "Look, Thornton, can I be blunt?"

"Sure, why not?"

"You believe in human equality for the Negro, don't you? I don't mean social equality, whatever that is, or even intermarriage. I mean just plain old human equality."

"I do, completely and with all my heart."

"I don't think you really do. I think you're more interested in getting a better reputation for the so-called enlightened white Southerner than in getting human equality for the Negro."

For a moment the room was silent. Slowly Cal Thornton untied the bow tie he was wearing and took it off. Then he unbuttoned the collar of his blue button-down oxford shirt.

"Are you sure you wouldn't rather that I left?" Eric asked.

"Of course not. I reckon if I were a Negro I'd be a lot more bitter."

"You might not be. Some Negroes are and others aren't."

"What else am I doing that's wrong according to your way of thinking?" Cal asked.

Eric waited until Cal fixed another drink and sat down again.

"Well, you support a college which educates Negroes rather badly for jobs that just don't exist. I should think that you'd try to get your money's worth."

"CIO and the war seem to have done a better job on that than ever I could."

"What about after the war, when they try to run CIO out of the South? What about the open-shop bills and the other anti-labor legislation? When they've made the unions impotent who's going to see that the Negro keeps his foot in the employment picture?"

"I've fought the boys in Tallahassie."

"The South says the Negro is inferior, then does everything it can to keep him inferior. Slums, lack of job opportunities, lower wages, poor police protection, and no equality before the law."

"But I agree, Gardner. It seems to me that actually we aren't very far apart basically at all. Is that all?"

"No, unfortunately that is not all. There is the question of legal segregation, and note that I say legal."

"Why?"

"Well, let's be fair about it. Segregation is practiced in the North, not as widely as some Negroes claim, but the important thing is that it is practiced in spite of law, not by it."

"Here's where the trouble starts, I guess. I think that even you will admit that it can't be done overnight. The whites in the South are not ready for it, and sometimes I think they never will be."

"Well, that's your problem. It seems to me that there is no other way out, and the sooner you face it the better. Either you solve the Negro problem or others are going to solve it for you, and that time may be nearer than you think. I'll give you a clean slate on the vote, by the way. You are doing a good job."

Eric took up his drink and slowly drained the dregs.

"Well," Cal said, "I'm glad to find that I'm not all villain. Another drink?"

"Thanks, no. I've got to run along now; probably I've stayed too long as it is."

"Not at all. It's early yet."

They both got to their feet and stood for a moment facing each other. Eric smiled.

"I wish we could do this more often. Maybe we can, now that you know I'm not one of those dangerous Northern agitators with a cloven hoof and a spiked tail."

Cal Thornton laughed. "And I'm not too much like my father-in-law?"

"No, the way I see it is that we are both human."

He held out his hand and Eric took it in his.

"I'll come out to the college some night and see you. I always mean to, but somehow I never seem to find the time. Maybe you could get together some of the faculty and the students—not many, but a few."

"I'd like to. I'm afraid I can't offer you bourbon, though. A good blend is about the best I can manage these days."

"I can drink that, I reckon."

Putting his arm around Eric's shoulder, Cal walked with him to the door, but he did not turn on the outside light which illuminated the way down to the sidewalk.

"See you soon," he said. "Call me up when you want me to come out to the college. Sorry my wife was out."

Eric nodded and walked down the steps.

Cal Thornton stood in the doorway until he saw the lights go on and heard the sound of Eric's motor as it started. As he turned back into the house he was conscious of the whine of the tires as the car swung out from the curb and turned the corner. At the foot of the stairs he stopped.

"You can come down now, Willie Mae," he called sarcastically. "It's quite safe."

He went into the living room and poured himself another drink, a light one which was almost all soda. Then he sat down in the chair by the fire and took out his pipe and tobacco pouch.

"So your nigger friend's gone?"

He looked up at his wife and went on loading his pipe. She was a tall blonde who had once been very attractive but now, in her thirties, was beginning to look a little washed out. His eyes left her as he tamped in the last of the tobacco and lit a kitchen match, carefully rolling it across the bowl.

"I asked if your nigger friend had gone," she said again.

"He's gone," he answered. "It's a shame you missed him. You'd have found him attractive and intelligent, quite charming, in fact. Really much more so than Don Rivers."

"Oh, don't be cheap and vulgar."

He rose and picked up his drink. "You were a little bit cheap at the country club yourself Friday night," he said, then walked slowly into his study and closed the door. He put the drink on the leather-topped desk and sat down.

He did not want to think of Kay, but she had taken complete possession of him. In the other room Willie Mae had turned up the radio to a point where she knew it was certain to annoy him, but Kay drove both her and the South out of the room. He saw her as he would always remember her—black-haired, long-legged, and firm-breasted—and he knew that she was still that way. He shook his head slowly and rubbed his fingers over his eyes. Then he picked up the phone on his desk. When the operator answered he gave her a number and sat waiting, his eyes half closed. He was tired.

"Doctor?" he spoke into the phone. "Not asleep, are you? Good. Sorry to bother you. Oh, still in your study. That's funny, so am I. We work too hard, you and I.

"Yes, I had a long talk with Gardner. Yes, left me about half an hour ago. I agree he's a good man. Too bad about what happened the other night. Yes, there wasn't much I could do. Oh, you told him that too?

I might run an editorial, but frankly I think it might do more harm than good. I'll have to think it over.

"What about Gardner's contract, Doctor? He's only on a year's tenure? I see. Has his appointment been renewed for next year yet? Oh, on your desk now to be initialed. I don't think it should be renewed."

He listened to Ezekiel's voice at the other end of the wire and waited until he was through.

"I know he's a good man, Doctor, and I'll take your word that he's a wonderful teacher. Sure, I know that. Yes. Well, you'll get somebody almost as good, maybe even better, for all I know."

He sighed and held the receiver off from his ear.

"Look, I don't want him back. It's too risky, in the light of what has already happened. No, it's not that he's radical, you're right there, but we can't take a chance. He's too outspoken and he just doesn't understand the South, he doesn't realize what you and I are up against, Doctor. Racial tensions are risky things, and we've had no trouble so far and I want to make sure that we keep it that way. Oh, he'll get a better job elsewhere. I can't help that, Doctor. Having him back would hurt the college more. Yeah, I'm dead set on that. Don't reappoint him."

Once more he held the receiver off from his ear. He was beginning to feel the hint of a migraine; at his left temple there was a faint but sharp stabbing pain.

"I said I don't want him reappointed," he said, and hung up.

For a few moments he sat at the desk waiting, in case Ezekiel might call back, but he was almost sure that he wouldn't. A nigger like that never would; he hadn't the spine of a jellyfish. He propped his head up with his palms, his elbows on the desk, then closed his ears with his hands to blot out the too loud music in the living room.

He could not seem to get Kay off his mind. Kay, he thought, Kay, and it was as though she were there in the room. He remembered the mornings that he had awakened in her apartment when it was hardly morning and, looking down at her, had run his finger along her bare flank and up her side until she had awakened. It seemed to him that she never awakened the way other women did, all puffy from sleep, and as Willie Mae did, a little more stupefied than usual. No, with Kay it was clear-eyed and sharp, then the slow smile and the wrinkled-up eyes as she pulled him down to her and kissed him gently.

Well, there was no more Kay. Gone were the clear-eyed look and the long clean flank and the high, proud breasts. Now there was only Willie

Mae and her father's money which had gotten the paper back on its feet. Kay had wanted him to be against everything that was shoddy and rotten. That was gone too, worn away like the plating on a dollar watch to show underneath the same sleazy metal. He felt like crying but he did not. Instead he whispered: Kay, I'm a no-good sonofabitch. And then went out to Willie Mae to make his peace.

34. It had all happened so fast that even now, packing the last of her things, Bessie found it hard to absorb. First Eric had been called into the president's office and told that his appointment for the following year was not going to be renewed. This did not surprise her, nor did it surprise Eric; but he had been disappointed, for he really had wanted to come back. He had tried to force the issue with Ezekiel but had been met by a stone wall, and something about the way that Ezekiel had acted had made him aware that the whole situation had somehow been taken out of the president's hands.

When he had come out he had taken her to lunch at the Co-op and, sitting at a table in the corner, had told her that he was going to leave as soon as possible. He did not even want to stay for commencement, and she had been filled with panic, for it seemed to her that this was to be the end, that he would go now and, though he was intending to send for her later, he never would. But she had said nothing.

When she had left him to return to her office he had merely said that he would, as usual, drive her home at five. As they had driven along at that time he had reached into his pocket and handed her a paper. Looking down, she saw that it was a wedding license.

"When?" she had asked.

"Right now, just as soon as you can change your clothes."

"Can I tell Mama?"

"No, you can't tell Mama. When we're married we'll both tell Mama. If we tell her now, she and Eulia are going to get their heads together and we'll end up by having a public wedding. I don't mind marrying you, baby, but I'm just not in the mood for that."

"Yes, sir," she said softly.

"We're leaving tomorrow, so you better be packed and ready to go by noon."

"Eric, I can't. Besides, I can't leave Prexy like this."

"You'll be ready at noon."

"Yes, sir."

She put the last of her things into the suitcase and looked around the room carefully to be certain there was nothing she had overlooked. They had been married by a colored justice of the peace in Eatonville and had gone on into Citrus City to dinner. This morning she had driven out to the college with Eric, and as soon as Ezekiel arrived she had gone into his office and told him that she and Eric were married and that he wanted to leave that noon.

"I'm glad," he had told her. "I always thought that you and Eric were a good pair. You leave right now. One of the other girls can see me through till after commencement. I'll miss you, Bessie. May I kiss the bride?"

She had come forward and, placing his hands on her shoulders, he had kissed her gently on the forehead.

"Good-by," he said. "Write me, Bessie. I guess I can always reach you through Eric's folks?"

She nodded. He took out his handkerchief and blew his nose loudly.

"Bessie, I tried to stick by Eric. I want you to know I tried. I did everything I could. I hope he knows it."

"He does, Prexy."

He sighed and walked to the window. For a moment he was silent and she started to leave him, but presently he turned back to her.

"Perhaps I could have done more," he said, "but I don't know how."

She started to interrupt him, but again he stopped her.

"It used to be," he said in a bitter voice, "that the white folks wanted preachers for college presidents. Now I see by the *Courier* that down in Texas they've chosen a veterinarian. Perhaps this denotes a new trend."

It was the nearest that she had ever known him to come to bitterness. Standing there, looking out across the campus, it seemed to her that overnight he had grown old and tired. Her sympathy went out to him, but she knew better than to let him see the way she felt.

"Good-by, Prexy," she said. "I hate to leave you in the lurch like this. It makes me feel guilty. Will you say good-by to Mrs. Rogers for me? I'd like to drop by but I haven't the time."

He turned again and came over to her and shook hands.

"I'll tell her, Bessie," he boomed. For a moment he seemed the way that he had always been, then his whole body seemed to sag. "Tell Eric good-by for me. I'd like to see him but I'm much too busy."

She nodded.

"Bless you both," he said. "The best of luck always."

He turned and went back to the window. His back was to her as she left the room, and it seemed to her that he had turned away because he had felt tears coming to his eyes.

She closed her bag firmly and sprung the two snaps. She almost tip-toed out of the room.

Mama came into the bedroom and stood watching as Bessie wormed herself into her going-away dress.

"Eric here," she said. "My, I cain believe my baby married. Now you going away. Don't seem but yestiday that you was nothin but a youngun."

Bessie put her arms around her mother and hugged her tight.

"Kind of beat you to it, didn't I, Mama?"

"Sho did, chile."

But something in the way her mother had spoken made Bessie hold her at arm's length and look deeply into her eyes.

"Mama."

"Hunh, baby?"

"Mama!"

Her mother giggled. "Shucks, chile, I might as well fess up. Sho, Jeff and me been married since right after Eulia had her baby. Doan yuh go tellin Eulia now!"

"Mama, you old rascal. But why keep it a secret?"

"There was so much goin on, chile. We didn want to have no fuss. Then, too, we figurin to sell the two houses. Jeff aimin to buy us a little place over on the St. John's. We kin have us a cow and some chickens and maybe a brood sow. We fixin to plant us some collards and black-eyed peas and the like, might even some pinders to fatten up them shoats. We can fish right there in the river."

"Mama, I can't see you farming."

Esther laughed. "Lots uh things you cain see til they happen, baby. I seen the place an hit right nice. Ain fer to the store and they's a bus runs right into Citrus City."

Bessie hugged her again and kissed her happily

"It makes it easier going knowing that you're all taken care of, Mama. But I better get out there. I can't keep my husband waiting."

She put her arm around Esther and the two of them walked out into the living room.

"It's about time," Eric said.

"The bags are ready," she told him. "Put them in the car and stop picking on me. Here we haven't even been married a whole day and you've started already."

Eric laughed and went into Bessie's room for the bags. In a moment he came back with them.

"Sorry to leave, baby?" Esther asked.

"Sorry to leave you and Luther, Mama."

Esther nodded. "Folks got to move on," she said. "I done my share an soon I be goin again. Got yo hat and coat, chile?"

Bessie nodded and, gathering them up from the chair, walked toward the door.

"Baby?"

"Yes, Mama."

"You likely to see Alberta?"

Bessie didn't answer at once. "I doubt it, Mama."

"You do, tell her bout me and Jeff, hear?"

"Sure, Mama."

Eric had everything in the car. Bessie kissed her mother, and just as she was about to get into the car Jeff walked up.

"Hoped I'd catch you," he said.

Bessie went up and kissed him on the cheek.

"You old rascal," she whispered in his ear.

"That woman blabbed already?" he asked good-naturedly. "I knowed she couldn keep no secret. No woman can, I reckon."

"What's all this?" Eric asked.

"They've been married for almost a month, Eric."

"What? Well, that does it. I resign from the race." He turned to Bessie. "I think they did it on purpose, just to spoil ours."

He went over to Esther and kissed her on both cheeks.

"May all your troubles be little ones," he said. "Good-by, both of you. I'll miss your chicken and your pecan pie."

Then he turned to Jeff and held out his hand. The older man grasped it firmly.

"Good-by, Jeff," Eric said. "The best of luck."

"The same, Eric. Sorry to see you go, boy, but you well shet of that place out there. That's a spineless nigger that the white folks done bought years ago. That's the trouble with them churchy niggers. I ain never seen a preacher yet with the guts of a chicken."

"Jeff."

"What, Miss Esther?" He looked over at Bessie and Eric and winked. "I had me three womans to wife," he said, "and they all tried to boss me. Looks like this one startin early."

They got into the car and Eric started the motor, then drove off. At the corner he turned back toward the college. Bessie looked at him questioningly and he grinned.

"I did something without consulting you, Bessie."

"What?"

"Well, George is going along with us to Washington."

"Oh, Eric! This was to be our wedding trip."

"I know, baby, but we'll have a real honeymoon at Oak Bluffs. Ethel says he can't fly, and I don't blame him for not wanting to go by train."

"It's all right, Eric."

Bessie knew the way that George felt about Eric not being reappointed and the violent argument that he had had with Ezekiel about it. The only thing was that she hated to go back to the college. It was behind them now and she wanted to keep it that way.

When they got over to Luther's the two of them were just finishing lunch and the baby was wide awake. They sat in the living room as Eulia brought him in and, laying a pad on the floor, put him down on the rug. He was fairer than Luther and his eyes seemed startlingly dark in his tan face.

"He's all right, Luther," Eric said. "You going to keep him?"

Luther grinned. "I reckon so, Eric."

Eulia was out in the kitchen warming the baby's formula, and Bessie had gone out to help her. The three who were left—George, Eric, and Luther—sat looking down at the baby, who was still on the floor.

"You going to bring him up to be a good union man, Luther?" George asked.

Luther nodded and grinned. "When he was born they found a union label on his left leg."

The room was quiet and it was peaceful there, so that Luther hated to leave to go back to his afternoon shift. He looked up at the clock by the window, then got up slowly.

"Well," he said, "I got to be gettin back. We goin tuh miss you, Eric. Sorry things turned out the way they did."

Eric shrugged. "Maybe it wouldn't have happened if the college had been unionized."

"Say, Eric, you got somethin there. You go into the national office there in Washington with George. Get a job organizing down here. This part of Florida woan seem the same without you and Bessie."

He held out his hand. "I got to run along, Eric. Been good knowin you; you too, George. Work hard up there; CIO got a job to do. I reckon the war about over now."

He went out into the kitchen to say good-by to Bessie, and shortly after they heard him go out the back door.

George turned to Eric.

"Eric, what'll happen when the war's over? Seems to me we started to sag already."

Eric shrugged. "It doesn't look too good, George. People have been all keyed up, and now the thing that kept them that way is starting to slip away from them."

"What about us, Eric, not you and me, but people like us?"

"We'll get along. Probably we'll get pushed back some, but not all the way back. Next time maybe we'll go past where we are now. But the important thing is that we've got to keep pushing."

He looked down at the baby and thought: That's what I want, that's what Bessie and I need. He laughed.

"Maybe he'll make it if we don't. That's good enough for me."

Eulia and Bessie came in from the kitchen, and Eulia took the baby in her arms and began to feed him from the bottle. Bessie came over and sat on the arm of Eulia's chair.

"You're calling him Hezekiah, then?"

"Yeah, Huzzie, after yo daddy."

Bessie looked over at Eric. "Hadn't we better get started?"

He nodded.

"Well, Eulia, I guess this is it. You and Luther be sure to come up and see us once we know where we'll be."

Eulia laughed. "I reckon I got a steady job for a year or so right here. We gonna miss you and Bessie, though."

Bessie went over and kissed her, then looked down at the baby.

"Anyway, you got a good boss, Eulia. He's sure a cute baby. I'll write you as soon as we get settled."

"Do that, Bessie. Luther an I will want to know how you gettin

264

along. Looks like Huzzie gone to sleep. Lemme put him in the crib an I walk you out to the car."

The three of them stood waiting until Eulia came back into the room, then they walked out the door and down toward the street.

"You know, I never been out the state of Florida," Eulia said and laughed. "Maybe I will come on up there an see you after all, once Huzzie gets travelin size. I reckon hit would do Luther an me good."

She said good-by to each of them and waited with her foot on the running board until Eric started the motor.

"Have uh good trip," she said, "an come back and see us soon."

She stood watching the car until it turned the corner out of sight.

They cut straight across to the ocean, then up the coast by the old road, which had run alongside of the beach before the new highway had been built on the other side of the river. It was slower, but Eric had wanted to stay by the ocean for as long as possible. Besides, it really did not matter too much; they were planning to spend the night in Jacksonville anyway.

Once they left Ormond behind, it was almost as though they had gone past the last of civilization. Save for the pitted gray macadam road, they went for miles without seeing any other trace of civilization, save for the rusted tin Burma Shave signs, now worn down to illegibility by the sun and the corrosive salt air.

To the right of them and slightly below lay the ocean, hidden by the dunes crowned with palmetto and an occasional clutch of sea oats. Then they would come upon an open spot suddenly as they rounded a curve, and there it lay, nearer than it had been behind them at Ormond, the beach dropping steeper to the pounding surf. Every now and then they would cross a bridge and see not only the ocean but inland a shallow lagoon stretching back and around almost out of sight. Once as they skirted a long stretch of beach Eric slowed the car almost to a stop.

Bessie nudged George. "Look at him. He's going to stop and go to fishing in a minute. Did you bring a good book?"

But Eric would only laugh and speed the car up again once the beach slid out of sight again. Soon they passed Flagler's Beach, a real-estate dream which had refused to jell into anything more inspiring than one dilapidated store, the crumbling pillars of an arch that had once, no doubt, led to paradise, and a few tired fishermen sitting far out on the high pier which jutted out into the water.

"You guys were good to take me along," George said suddenly. "I feel like I ought to ride in the back."

"So we could be alone?" Bessie asked. "Pooh. We need a chaperon; at least I do. I don't like the look in his eye. Didn't you know that all Negro men are sex maniacs?"

They passed over another bridge, the loose planking sounding like thunder under the wheels of the slow-moving car. The beach came into sight again, and offshore a fleet of two or three shrimpers moved slowly southward toward Mosquito Inlet.

"I'm going to miss this," Eric said.

"Mmm," Bessie answered, "that's a good old ocean." She looked up at Eric and grinned. "Can I compete against an ocean, Papa?"

"You can try, baby."

Suddenly her feeling for him washed over her like a wave. She reached up and kissed him suddenly.

"I love you," she said.

"And I you," Eric answered.

"I don't like to butt in," George said, "but after all, we do want to get to Jacksonville sometime tonight. Want me to drive?"

The three of them laughed.

"You know, I'm glad we brought him along, Eric."

"Sure, helps to relieve the monotony."

Off ahead of them they saw St. Augustine.

"Want to stop and see the historic slave mart?" George asked bitterly. "For all we know, we may never have another chance. Never miss the old historic landmarks, I always say."

"Not for me," Eric said. "I'd be afraid one of those crackers might try to sell Bessie. Comely wench, that Bessie."

They did not have to go into town, and soon they were back to nature again. Bessie closed her eyes. She was tired; it has been a day too full with everything.

"Eric," she said drowsily, "what if your mother and father don't like me? What if they won't let us in the house?"

"You're too black," he said.

"No, I'm brown."

Across her she could hear them talking.

"How does it feel to be leaving, George?"

"Like I was going ahead into something big and exciting. You?"

"That I muffed things a little, but that somehow I'll be back. I want to teach in the South again. I'll miss those kids, George. They were all right, and I hope nothing beats it out of them."

How did it feel? She wanted Eric's family to like her, and beyond that? Before she could make up her mind she was asleep.

35. The delegation of students had left Ezekiel's office but it no longer seemed to matter. He had not even tried to give them a full explanation, and he realized now that he had been brusque with them, hardly listening to what they had to say and all but shoving them out the door. Had he even listened at all? Probably not, he thought, but what was the use? They wanted Eric back the following year. Well, so did he, but there was nothing that could be done about that. It was over with, finished; he had told them that, what more did they want?

He sighed. Today was the day that he usually liked better than any other in the academic year. It had always seemed to him that there was something almost spiritual about Commencement Day, a feeling that appeared to him not unlike the Resurrection. In other years it had found him cheerful and in an expansive mood. Such a delegation as had just left him would have been greeted cordially when they came into his office and he would have listened to everything they had to say. If he could not oblige them he would have made certain that they realized that this was only because it was not possible, not because he did not wish to do so.

He would have sized up the delegation too, listened to them almost eagerly to try to find out if there was within any of them something that he had never before noted. This one would suddenly seem eloquent enough to become a successful lawyer, he would think, or that one enough of a realist to be a good businessman. Well, it was too late now; it was done and it could not be undone.

He sighed and, without bothering to get up from his desk, looked out across the campus. There was yet a good hour before the ceremonies were scheduled to begin, but already he could see people milling around. In former years he had always gone out there with them. There were old students come back and the parents of those who were leaving the college that day to go out into the world. He remembered how he used to feel when some old student would come up to him with his or her first-born and tell him proudly that along about fifteen years from now he would have this to contend with. Dropping down on one knee, he would look at the youngster and try to see in the infantile face a clue to the boy or girl at eighteen. He chuckled to himself when he remembered how often he was wrong.

But the thing that pleased him most, though it happened all too rarely, was when some old student would return who had really made good. Talking with him, walking across the campus, he would feel that somehow that success had been in some small measure due to his work, to the influences of the college.

Well, he was not going out there now, and if there had been any possible way to avoid it, he would not even have gone to the commencement exercises. He would have preferred to go home and, changing into his pajamas, go to bed, or to take the car and drive off someplace where he would never have to think of the college again.

George was gone and so was Eric. Even Bessie had left, Bessie whom he had come to depend on almost as much as his good right arm. They were all leaving him, deserting him, going away when he needed them most.

He looked at the clock again. It was almost time for him to be going over to the house to change into his cap and gown, but to do so would mean that he would have to see Ethel, and he had no desire to have her at him all over again. She had taken to her sickbed yesterday when George had left with Eric and Bessie, but she had been up at the breakfast table that morning. In her eyes he could see that somehow she still regarded him as responsible for the fact that George was gone.

Damn the woman, he thought. Then suddenly he remembered that there was a spare cap and gown here in the office in his closet. He would wear them instead of going home to change. Reaching out angrily, he punched the buzzer on his desk.

Presently the door opened and the girl who was filling in for Bessie stood looking in at him cautiously. She was young, a little too plump for the white dress she was wearing, and obviously frightened both at her new responsibility and of him.

"Come in," he boomed angrily, "don't stand there like a ninny."

She broke into a sickly smile and came halfway to his desk. As she stood there, holding her hands as though they were some strange newly sprouted appendages that she did not know quite what to do with, he felt his anger about to explode. How could he ever train a nincompoop like this to take the place of Bessie?

"Well?" he boomed.

"Yessah," she answered, then flushed and looked away.

He sighed. "Call Mrs. Rogers," he said, then added, "On the phone. Tell her I have a cap and gown here in the office, so I won't be home before the ceremonies. Tell her I'll see her after they are over."

He looked at her, and for a moment he thought she was going to cry.

"Yessah," she said, and slowly backed out.

Her rural accent grated on his nerves, but he forced himself to be civil. "Thank you," he said. "I'm not to be disturbed."

She closed the door behind her almost in terror.

Wearily he looked again at the clock on his desk. He had yet a little time before he must get into his hot cap and gown, stripping first, as he always did, to his undershirt above the waist. The day had been fairly cool earlier, but now it had settled down in earnest to becoming a real scorcher.

Suddenly he remembered something in the personal file of his desk and, reaching into the second drawer from the bottom on the left, he placed a folder on the desk before him. It had been written in heat after his phone conversation with Cal Thornton several nights ago, then put aside until his temper had cooled and his good judgment returned.

He read:

To: Calvin Thornton and/or the Board.
From: Ezekiel Rogers.

This is to announce my resignation, to take effect immediately. When a man finds it no longer possible to fulfill the duties he should perform, it is his duty to step aside and let another take his place. I have reached that point. I find it no longer possible to co-operate with suggestions that I feel are contrary to my ideals and to the best interests of the college.

He reached out his hand to take up the memorandum and, crumbling it into a ball, drop it into the bronze ash tray where he would carefully burn it. But he paused in mid-air and returned his hand to his lap. Well, why not? It was true, and there was really nothing left for which he need remain. George was gone, so were Eric and Bessie; now there was only himself and Ethel.

He had always wanted to go away and write, and here was his chance to do so. His mind ran ahead into plans of what he would do. He had a little money put aside, and the house in which he lived belonged to himself and not to the college. He would sell it, and then?

All at once it came to him. He would return to South Carolina and buy the little farmhouse where he was born and where his father had died. There would be enough money to do it over, to make it into a place where he and Ethel could live comfortably. When he was writing of his early years it would be good to be right on the spot where he had spent them.

It would be a place where he could have the privacy he so desperately needed and the time in which to utilize it. But he would do more than merely write; he would put down roots there and maybe in a different way complete the work that his father had attempted to do. He thought of his father, and this in a way seemed to him a partial repayment for the neglect of which he had been guilty. He felt his excitement quicken.

But Ethel would never go, she would never give up the position she had struggled so hard to attain and which she guarded now so jealously. All right, he thought, she'll come or else she can get along as best she can. It would be good to tell her that, then watch her buckle under for perhaps the first time in their married life.

But most of all it would give him back his self-respect. At the end of the ceremonies he would step to the front of the platform and make a simple announcement to the audience telling of his resignation and, in carefully guarded words, the reasons for it. The students would get it all right and they would tell the others.

He stripped off his coat and shirt and put on the cap and gown. Outside the door he stopped at the desk of the girl who had taken Bessie's place. He realized that he had forgotten her name, but it really did not matter.

"Close the office," he boomed. "Go on home. We're through for the year."

She did not answer him, but merely looked in wide-eyed amazement as he strode down the corridor to the front door of the administration building.

Even under the canopy that sheltered the raised platform from the late morning sun it was hot. Under his cap and gown Ezekiel could feel the perspiration gather at his neck and shoulders, then slide easily down through the matted hair of his chest to gather caught in a pool at his waist. Soon his glasses would fog up and he would have to clean them again and wipe them dry, only to have them shortly cloud up all over again.

Below him he was conscious of the partially upturned faces—the students in front, their parents and friends of the college behind them, and lastly, but separated by a discreet row of unoccupied seats, the few white people who seemed to come each year. Their faces were always the same, and he wondered why they came, whether it was because of any real interest or, as he suspected, because they unconsciously felt guilty and used this occasion as a sort of hair-shirt proof of their sincere desire to wash away their past sins. Before he had always felt their eyes upon him and it had made him uncomfortable; now they no longer upset him, for soon he would be free of them forever.

The singing started and he felt it swell from a whisper to almost a roar of defiance. It affected him deeply, for he was a profoundly religious man, and he realized that this was probably what he would miss most of all. Behind him he heard old man Daniels whisper loudly to Cal, and the interruption hit him almost like a physical blow.

"Godam, Cal, them niggers can sho sing. Lissen at em, boy, they're good enough to be on the radio."

He felt a blush spread over his whole body and then it turned to a feeling of bitter hatred. Without looking behind him, he knew that Cal had hushed his father-in-law and were he to turn around would give him a helpless but slightly amused look, as though to say: What can I do, he is a child or an old fool, even perhaps both, but I am not like that, no, I am a man of good will.

At that moment he hated one as much as the other, for both were white. That one was a fool, a slightly dirty old man with a hint of tobacco-juice stain at the corners of his mouth, and the other cleanly scrubbed and of intelligence, could not erase that one fact. They were one and the same, as was the scattering of others with white skins who sat alone in the rear of the audience. Even the white quality gentlemen his father so often spoke to him about, or his own benefactor who had put him where he was today, all were by this same common denominator lumped together as one. Their skins were white.

The singing died to a whisper, then seemed to disappear like a solvent in water. Slowly he got to his feet and read a prayer. He went through the familiar motions, and then it was time to introduce the principal speaker, who this year was Cal Thornton. This he did easily and quickly, without the flowery embellishments he was used to giving in the past. Then he took his seat and closed his eyes.

The words of the speaker were no more distinguishable to him than the hum of some distant car. Instead he thought back into his own life and nursed his hatred into full flower like some man of nature with a green thumb. It reached out even to include Ethel for her color snobbery, which he supposed he had even to a degree shared, because her acceptance of him had given to him a feeling of false security.

But he thought most of that good and true white man whom he had always looked upon as even more of a father than the black man from whose loins he had really sprung. And it seemed to him at that moment, in a revelation that was so crystal clear as to be almost as dazzling as a blinding light, that for the first time he saw him for what he was. He was only another white man.

It had been an unfair and one-sided bargain, he thought, but not in the same way that he imagined in the past. He had received money and clothes, railroad tickets, and even an influence that had helped open doors for him wherever he had gone, but what had this white man received in return? No one, surely, had ever bought another human being so cheaply—bought him wholly; not, as in slavery, his strong black back alone, but his all—his mind, his loyalty, but most of all his personal integrity, so that forever after he could be nothing but his owner's creature. He shuddered; this, then, was he.

His hatred tightened him in a grip so powerful that he could feel it in his bowels, in the bitter bilelike dry taste of his mouth.

At last it was over. Cal Thornton stopped talking and was turning, in his whitened superiority, to go back to his seat, followed by polite applause. Unconsciously Ezekiel gathered his feet under him; within he felt a sudden buoyant elation, as though that by what he was about to do he would be freed and made whole again.

In his mind it was clear what he would say and how he would slyly phrase it so that those in the rear who were white would take no offense but those in the front who were not could not mistake what lay behind his words. He thought of George suddenly, tenderly, and with almost a sexual emotion.

George, he thought, my son; flesh of my flesh, blood of my blood— the product of my male hardness, my son. And it seemed to him that now, by an almost mystical and symbolic action, he was going to repair the shattered bond between them. He thought too of his own father, and then he remembered that when his benefactor had died, this white man who had bought him as completely as the devil bought Faust, he had sent two dozen American-beauty roses, without a card, as though it were between only the two of them, and his father, in his white omniscience, would need no clue even in death, but actually because he, being black, was afraid to include one.

Those roses were really his own father's blood, which he had spilled as surely as by the deep cleavage of a knife. He waited a moment until the white speaker, who had also been his father, if only by proxy, sat down, and then he got easily to his feet and walked to the front of the platform.

"It is not my usual wont to say anything after the main speaker has finished," he started easily.

There was still a scattering of applause at the outer fringes of the crowd, and as he waited for it to die out he looked out over the audience.

He saw Ethel then, to one side but near the front. Her slightly bovine face looked up at him and he could not seem to look away. Suddenly he thought: She will never come with me, never, I must go alone. The thought shook him a little, but he knew, in spite of anything he might hope to the contrary, that it was true. And with this one doubt he felt himself weaken a little, almost imperceptibly, and also almost in wonder, as the small child seeing the pricked balloon disintegrating into nothingness asks: Why, how, it was here and now it is gone, I do not understand. It was in his legs where it had not been before; it seemed to him that it was spreading up and through his body, slowly but too relentlessly ever to be checked.

He tried not to look at the whites in the rear of the audience, but their faces seemed suddenly to have become larger, as a close-up in a motion picture shoots out from the projection screen. He could see them clearly, almost orgiastic, at last emancipated, excited and eager to run forward and claim this white man in shining armor who had freed them from their guilt. Peace, it's wonderful, and so easily attained!

He started again, faltered, then his voice grew strong.

"I do not usually provide an anticlimax like I am doing now, but Mr. Thornton's speech has affected me deeply. In all my years here at the college I have never had the honor of hearing a better one. But a word more. It is not the speech alone that concerns me. Most of us read the *Telegram*. It is good to know that we have not only a white friend in Mr. Thornton but so loud a voice, every day, and in every paper that is read in central Florida."

Although he had finished, he waited a moment for the applause. It came, from the rear first, where he could see white faces turning one to the other like marionettes, then, reassured, back to him as though saying: Yes, give him his due, for he's a good nigger, yes, a hand, give the Negro a hand. Then it spread politely toward the front until it reached the students, where it seemed to have died to a whisper.

He turned and walked back toward his seat, hardly knowing that he was doing so. Someone stopped him, his hand on his arm. Looking up, he saw Cal Thornton. They were surrounded by people and it was difficult to carry on a conversation.

"Thank me? No, thank you, Mr. Thornton. I meant every word of it. Yes. Coming to the reception? Good. Oh, your father-in-law can't make it? Meeting of the Citrus Board at two. I see. Sorry about your wife? Oh, the woman's club. Well, I know those club women!"

Together they walked down the steps and across the campus.

"By the way," Ezekiel said, now that they were away from the crowd, "we're a bit early. I think, though, that if you would like to see my study, I might find a bottle of bourbon in there."

Cal Thornton smiled and familiarly put his hand on Ezekiel's arm.

"Well," he answered, "I don't see why two old friends like us can't have a drink, Ezekiel. You won't report me for breaking the rules of the sovereign state of Florida?"

Ezekiel chuckled. "No, Thornton, we'll forget the laws. About that bourbon. It's a funny thing, but when I was over on the coast at the conference in Daytona I found a colored liquor store full of bonded bourbon. Ceiling prices, too. If you'd like me to, I could get you some next time I'm over that way. Yes, I think I could get you a case. Not at all, glad to do it. Believe me, I stocked up myself."

And together they walked up the path which led to the house of the president of the college.